TH

CA

DOG STORIES

The Exile Book of

CANADIAN DOG STORIES

edited by

Richard Teleky

Exile Editions

Publishers of singular

Fiction, Poetry, Translation, Nonfiction, Drama, and Graphic Books

2009

Library and Archives Canada Cataloguing in Publication

The Exile book of Canadian dog stories / edited by Richard Teleky.

ISBN 978-1-55096-126-3

1. Dogs--Fiction. 2. Human-animal relationships--Fiction. 3. Short stories, Canadian. I. Teleky, Richard, 1946- II. Title: Canadian dog stories.

PS8323.D64C36 2009   C813'.01083629772   C2009-905142-7

Design and Composition by Active Design Haus
Typeset in Garamond and Gill Sans at the Moons of Jupiter Studios
Cover painting by Diana Thorne
Printed in Canada by Gauvin Imprimerie

The publisher would like to acknowledge the financial assistance of the Canada Council for the Arts and the Ontario Arts Council, which is an agency of the Government of Ontario.

Conseil des Arts du Canada   Canada Council for the Arts

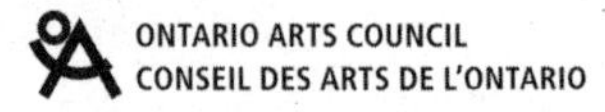

Published in Canada by Exile Editions Ltd.
144483 Southgate Road 14
General Delivery
Holstein, Ontario, N0G 2A0
info@exileeditions.com
www.ExileEditions.com

Canadian Sales Distribution:
McArthur & Company
c/o Harper Collins
1995 Markham Road
Toronto, ON M1B 5M8
toll free: 1 800 387 0117

U.S. Sales Distribution:
Independent Publishers Group
814 North Franklin Street
Chicago, IL 60610
www.ipgbook.com
toll free: 1 800 888 4741

For Richard Medhurst D.V.M.

CONTENTS

Introduction

What, you might reasonably ask, is a Canadian dog story? To begin, it's not a story about one of the breeds associated with Canada – the Newfoundland, for instance, or the Nova Scotia water spaniel. Nor is it a sentimental tale about a noble dog doing heroic deeds, something children might be urged to read. Simply put, it's any story by a Canadian about the rich and complex and mysterious bond between dogs and humans. Most national literatures include some notable dog stories – Russia, for example, has such classics as Anton Chekhov's "Kashtanka" and Ivan Turgenev's "Mumu," and more recently, Vassily Aksyonov's splendid "Around Dupont." Canada is not the exception. And it couldn't be otherwise, because the human/dog bond has been a serious subject since Homer told of a loyal dog, Argos, who was the only creature to recognize his master Ulysses when he returned home from twenty years of adventurous wandering. Argos set the pattern for loyal literary dogs.

From Canada's earliest days, European explorers and settlers wrote about their companion dogs. Pierre-Esprit Radisson, the Provençal adventurer whose expeditions along Lake Superior ultimately led to the founding of the Hudson's Bay Company in 1670, kept a journal of his exploits. During the brutal winter of 1659-60, when he and his men faced starvation, Radisson recorded that "The two first weeke we did eate our doggs," and described an encounter with "two men from a strange Country who had a dogg, the buissinesse was how to catch him cunningly, knowing well those people love their be[a]sts." The story ends badly for the dog ("very l[e]ane, and as hungry as we weare"), but Radisson at least didn't hesitate to use the word "love" for the human/dog bond – remember, this was written in 1660. More than a century and a half later, Susanna Moodie had this to say, in *Roughing it in the Bush*, about arriving in Grosse Isle [sic], Quebec, in 1832: "Even Oscar, the Captain's Scotch Terrier, who had formed a devoted attachment to me during the voyage, forgot his allegiance, became possessed of the land mania, and was away with the rest." After nine weeks at sea, no wonder. "Land mania" – that might be a fitting description of most national histories. And we know that dogs, like humans, are territorial.

Of course the Aboriginal population in North America had dogs, but that's a fascinating subject beyond the scope of this introduction. (Interested readers will want to seek out Marion Schwartz's *A History of Dogs in the Early Americas.*) In the centuries since those early days, as rural life gave way to industrial and post-industrial society, pet-keeping became common in North America. Dogs were at the heart of this social evolution, just as they had previously co-evolved alongside Homo sapiens (another vast subject). It should come as no surprise that dogs have finally caught the attention of scholars in the humanities – for a start, Katherine C. Grier in her *Pets in America: A History* – or that in recent decades social scientists have also produced exciting books about dogs and humans. Canadian psychologist Stanley Coren, along with Stephen Budiansky, Vilmos Csányi, Mark Derr, Jeffrey Moussaieff Masson and Elizabeth Marshall Thomas are only a few of the more insightful. Any dog-lover will enjoy their books, along with classics like J.R. Ackerley's *My Dog Tulip*, Konrad Lorenz's *Man Meets Dog* and Virginia Woolf's *Flush*. And if they can find them, readers can turn to some of the unique, old anthologies that have collected dog stories from writers around the world – *Famous Dogs in Fiction* (1921), edited by J. Walker McSpadden; *The Fireside Book of Dog Stories* (1943), edited by Jack Goodman; and more recently, *The Literary Dog: Great Contemporary Dog Stories* (1990), edited by Jeanne Schinto.

But what about Canadian fiction writers? Their contribution to our understanding of the human/dog bond – sometimes direct, sometimes off-hand – has its own truths to tell: the truths of fiction. This is the first anthology to gather together some of the best Canadian literary writing about dogs. But as I said earlier, this is not a collection of stories about heroic dogs like Lassie, nor is the book filled with heartwarming anecdotes in the manner of James Herriot's *All Creatures Great and Small.* First of all, the stories included here are short stories in themselves, not chapters extracted from novels or memoirs. The short-story form, in which Canadian writers have excelled, seems ideally suited to capturing the nature of the human/dog bond; this bond is generally wordless and, while perhaps limited in scope, not limited in intensity. However, my initial decision to choose only short stories meant that I could not represent some fine and popular books and writers, such as Farley Mowat's memoir of his childhood on the Saskatchewan prairie, *The Dog Who Wouldn't Be* (1957), or Sheila Burnford's haunting adventure novel, *The Incredible Journey* (1961), or even a passage from (Margaret) Marshall Saunders' *Beautiful Joe* (1894), a once-popular children's novel, with an evangelical message, thought to be the first Canadian-authored book to sell a million copies outside of Canada. (By the way, Burnford's own red-gold Labrador retriever, as well as an actual white bull terrier and Siamese cat, were the models for her animal characters, and I suspect that she was not alone in drawing stories from life and altering them for fiction.)

In order to take its place in this anthology, a story had to shed light on some aspect of the human/dog bond while being a good story in itself. Although there are many wonderful Canadian stories where dogs have a minor role or are mentioned in passing (Timothy Findley's "Dreams" and Alice Munro's "Miles City, Montana" come to mind), these weren't sufficiently doggy to be included. As well, some turgidly written stories by nineteenth-century poet Isabella Valancy Crawford ("Where the Laugh Came In" and "The Peculiar Marchesa") have been excluded because of their clumsy, even confusing, manner of telling. (Valancy Crawford does, however, offer up the old belief that dogs are a good judge of people and can see through human deception.) Issues of gender and regional balance, which often concern anthologists, have been a secondary matter for collecting dog stories – not every writer of every Canadian locale or ethnic tradition has chosen to write about dogs. But those who have are worth our attention.

The names of the earliest writers in this anthology may have a familiar ring even if their work is largely unread today outside of university courses. Don't let that discourage you. Arranged chronologically by the year of an author's birth, *The Exile Book of Canadian Dog Stories* suggests the care and serious regard our writers have felt for their canine subjects (it may also indicate for some readers the changing character of the short-story form itself). Charles G.D. Roberts' "The Stone Dog," which opens the collection, echoes the fabulist tradition of Edgar Allan Poe; if space had permitted I also would have liked to include his story "The Dog That Saved the Bridge," a more realistic example of World War I fiction (and propaganda) about life in the Belgian trenches. Ernest Thompson Seton, generally considered to be a writer of nature stories, admitted in a Note to the Reader that prefaced *Wild Animals I Have Known* – the source of "Bingo, the Story of My Dog" – that he often blurred the line between fiction and non-fiction, altering details and combining stories. ("Although I have left the strict line of historical truth in many places," he wrote, "the animals in this book were all real characters.") From E. Pauline Johnson's troubling tale of a Native boy's love for his dog and his community, to Duncan Campbell Scott's haunting yarn, to Stephen Leacock's satirical sketch of the house guest from hell, dogs serve as the measure of a protagonist's relation with his world as well as a mirror to his psychic life. L.M. Montgomery's bickering courtship, Mazo de la Roche's springtime fox hunt (along with her popular *Jalna* series, she also wrote a book about one of her own dogs, a Scottish terrier), and the ironic twist in Ethel Wilson's "I Just Love Dogs," show a more lighthearted, though no less serious, aspect of the human/dog bond. After all, we keep dogs beside us because they give us pleasure.

Canadian fiction writers following the modernist movement of the early twentieth century often turned from a tradition of strict realism to a looser, more experimental approach to fictional style, and truth. Realism, however, didn't vanish – fiction still remained grounded in sharply observed detail. Morley Callaghan's coming-of-age story, reminiscent of the popular collie stories of American novelist Albert Payson Terhune, and Eric Knight's famed *Lassie Come-Home*, is a distinctly Canadian turn on a popular genre. Sheila Watson's eloquent allegory, P.K. Page's experiment with speculative fiction (written decades before global warming was a common topic, and first published as part of a poetry collection), and Jacques Ferron's modern fable, each extend the role that dogs have played in fiction where dogs serve as metaphors for troubling human predicaments. Dogs can also be the background of our lives, voiceless witnesses to our triumphs and follies. In Mavis Gallant's "Luc and His Father," someone always has to walk the dog, and a weary middle-aged man advises his son, "Whatever happens, don't get your life mixed up with a dog's"; in Jane Rule's "Dulce," a dog named Rocket, adopted from an animal shelter one Christmas, has more to offer the protagonist than any of her human loves; in Leon Rooke's "Painting the Dog," human pretensions work themselves out in terms of a couple's pet. The canine characters here may not be the focus of the human stories – you might even wish they had a bigger role to play. But these dogs are an essential counterpoint to the human characters, embodying each author's meaning, and the stories would be incomplete without them. In a very basic way, we reveal ourselves in the regard we have for our dogs, and good writers know this and show it.

Canadian fiction of the last three decades or so has often been noted for its irony – a common feature of much postmodern writing – and this may help explain why the dogs in the stories by contemporary writers are as far removed from sentimental representation as anyone could imagine. The ambivalence humans feel about their animal nature also occasionally comes to the foreground of these dog stories. It's easy to forget that dogs and humans are mammals, subject to similar physical drives and needs, but good writers seldom overlook this link. When dogs as metaphors run through the stories by Stan Dragland, Claire Dé, Janice Kulyk Keefer and Lynn Coady, it's human behaviour that's the actual subject, though dogs allow us to look at it more closely, if abstractly. The metaphoric link between dogs and marriage, explored by Mark Strand and Matt Shaw, suggest how essential dogs are to our understanding of ourselves; we can turn to them when there is no better way to express our deepest sense of our failings and frailties, and even our alienation from ourselves. (Generally thought of as an American poet, Strand was born in Prince Edward Island. Since dogs don't concern themselves with national boundaries, his doggy protagonist belongs in this anthology.) Symbolic dogs, then, allow writers, and readers, to see human reflections from a safe distance. After all, dogs have evolved at our side, so why wouldn't we be reflections of each other? In the process, it's to be hoped that we've gained a deeper appreciation, and understanding, of the dogs in our lives.

It was Ernest Thompson Seton, once again, who wrote of his own work, "The fact that these stories are true is the reason why all are tragic. The life of a wild animal *always has a tragic end"* (Seton's italics). The same might be said of all animals, even domestic dogs. With their short lifespans, they always die too soon. Anyone acquiring a dog has to recognize that it is an invitation, sooner or later, to mortality. This may help explain, in part, why the flesh-and-blood dogs in the stories by Alistair MacLeod, Barry Callaghan, Douglas Glover and Katherine Govier – in fact, in all the stories gathered here – are so touching, and make us recognize the essential separateness of our dogs, while the human cruelty and casual carelessness presented by Kenneth J. Harvey and Timothy Taylor can make us cringe at ourselves. Yet, like our own pets, most of the dogs you'll meet in these pages have memorable personalities. There's Bingo's bravery and Rocket's jealousy, Dexter, who needs special protection from the sun, Sylvestre, who always seems in the way, Anselm and Argos, Monica and Mike, Fidele, Sophocles (yes) and a nameless old beagle... the list goes on and on. In her memory story "Homage to Scheila," Marie-Claire Blais' autobiographical meditation written especially for this anthology, Blais explores the mysterious relation of fact and fiction and time. Recollecting her beloved dog Scheila, a furry white mixed-breed of German shepherd-Samoyed lineage, long ago rescued as a puppy by Blais and her younger sister, she concludes: "Now that she's gone, her love is irreplaceable, for she was just that, love, gentleness, and nothing in this world seems like her." No one has said it better.

Richard Teleky
January 2009

Acknowledgements

Many thanks to Concetta Principe, my graduate assistant at York University, who turned out to be an exemplary canine sleuth. Appreciation, also, to friends and colleagues who pointed me in various literary directions: Barry Callaghan, Len Early, Ray Ellenwood, Anna Graham, Evan Jones, Mary Rubio, William Toye, and Priscila Uppal. Finally, while I read and researched the stories for this collection, my pug Rennie was curled up at my side, or snoring in my lap, and this acknowledgement would be incomplete without a nod to his gentle presence. – RT

CHARLES G.D. ROBERTS

The Stone Dog

It was drawing towards sunset, and I had reached the outskirts of the city, which here came to an abrupt end upon the very edge of the marshes. The marshes stretched before me bare and grey, with here and there a flush of evening colour, serving but to emphasize their utterness of desolation. Here and there, also, lay broad pools, their shore and water gradually intermerging through a sullen fringe of reeds. The river, which had been my day-long companion – a noisy stream flowing through breezy hills, and villages, and vineyards – having loitered to draw its circle about the city walls, had fallen under a spell. It met me here a featureless, brimming ditch, and wound away in torpid coils to the monotonous horizon. And now this shrunken city, its edges dead and fallen to decay, these naked levels, where not even a bittern's voice had courage to startle the stillness, filled me, in spite of myself, with a vague apprehensiveness. Just as one who is groping in profound darkness feels his eyes dilate in the effort to catch the least glimmer of light, I found my senses all on the strain, attentive to their very utmost. Though the atmosphere was heavy and deadening, my eyes were so watchful that not even the uprising of some weeds, trodden down, perhaps, hours before by a passing foot, escaped their notice. My nostrils were keenly conscious of the sick metallic odour from the marshes, of the pleasanter perfume of dry reed panicles, of the chill, damp smell of mouldering stone-work, and of a strangely disagreeable haunting essence from a certain dull-coloured weed, whose leaves, which shot up within tempting reach of my hand, I had idly bruised in passing. My ears, for all their painful expectancy, heard at first no sound save the rustle of a frightened mouse in the dead grass near; but at length they detected the gurgle of running water, made audible by a faint stray wind which breathed in my direction.

Instinctively I turned and followed the sound. On my right a huge fragment of the wall jutted into the marsh, and passing this I saw before me, brightened by the sunset, a narrow stretch of dry, baked soil, raised somewhat above the level of the pools, and strewn with shattered bricks and scraps of tiling and potsherds. The musical lapsing of the water now fell upon my ears distinctly, and I saw a little way off a quaint old fountain, standing half a stonecast clear of the wall. With the sunlight bathing it, the limpid water sparkling away from its base, it was the only cheerful object in the landscape; yet I felt an unaccountable reluctance to approach it. The evil enchantment which seemed to brood over the place, the weird fantasies chasing each other through my unconsenting brain, annoyed me greatly, for I profess to hold my imagination pretty well under control, and to have but small concern for ghostly horrors. Shaking aside my nervousness, I began to whistle softly as I strolled up to examine the old fountain. But on noticing how lugubrious, how appropriate to the neighbourhood and my feelings was the air that came to my lips, I laughed aloud. At the sudden sound of my voice I felt both startled and somewhat abased. Laughter here was clearly out of place; and besides, the echo that followed was obtrusively and unpleasantly distinct, appearing to come both from a deep-arched doorway in the wall near by, and from the vaulted hollow of the basin of the fount, which lay just beneath the dog's jaws. As I should have said before, the fountain was a great cube of darkish stone, along the top of which a stone dog crouched; and the water gushed from between its carved forepaws into a deep basin, the side of which was cleft two thirds of the way to its base. Through this break, which I saw to be an old one from the layers of green film lining it, the stream bubbled out and ran off among barren heaps of débris, to sink itself in the weeds of some stagnant pool. The head of the dog was thrust forward and rested upon the forepaws as if the brute were sleeping; but its half-open eyes seemed to watch the approaches to the doorway in the wall. As a piece of sculpture, the animal was simply marvellous. In its gathered limbs, though relaxed and perfectly at rest, a capacity for swift and terrible action seemed to hold itself in reserve, and a breath almost appeared to come from the half-opened jaws, momentarily dimming the crystal that smoothly gushed beneath. No scrap of vegetation could the rill persuade out of the inexorable sterility around, saving for some curdled greenish mosses that waved slowly from the sides of the basin, or pointed from roothold on brick and shard, where the small current loitered a little. I am not a taker of notes, nor, for all my vagrant and exploring tendencies, am I a very close observer. Nevertheless, though it is now a year and a half since what I am telling of took place, the minutest details of that strange fountain, and of the scene about it, are as definitely before me as if I had been there but yesterday. I am not going to inflict them all upon my reader, yet would do so without a spark of compunction, if by such means I could dim the all too vivid remembrance. The experiences that befell me by this fountain have shaken painfully the confidence I once enjoyed as to the fullness of my knowledge of the powers of things material. I cannot say that I have become credulous; but I have ceased to regard as necessarily absurd whatever I find it difficult to explain.

From the fountain it was not a score of paces to the doorway in the wall, which was sunk below the surface of the ground, so that the crumbling arch surmounting it was scarcely on a level with my feet. Steep narrow stairs of brick work, consisting, I think, of seven steps, led down to it. The doorway had once been elaborately ornamented with mouldings in yellow stucco, most of which had fallen, and all but choked the stairs. The crude pale colour of these fragments jarred harshly against the olive of the damp stone foundations and the stained brown of the mouldy brick. After my usual fashion, I set myself to explore this doorway, in my interest half forgetting my apprehensions. As I descended the steps the sound of the running water faded out, with a suddenness which caught my ear, though failing to fix my attention. But as I made to grasp the great rusty iron door-handle, which was curiously wrought of two dragons intertwisted neck and tail, again my every sense sprang on the alert, and a chill of terror crept tingling through my frame. My straining ears could detect not the slightest sound from the fountain, which was within plain view behind me. I felt as if some eye were fixed upon me. I faced sharply about and set foot on the steps to ascend. And I saw the water at that very moment burst forth afresh between the feet of the dog, from whose eye a dull white glow seemed just vanishing. It must be borne in mind that the beast's flank was toward the doorway, and, in consequence, only one of its half-closed eyes visible from where I stood. I ascended and went straight to the fountain. I grasped the great stone head and gave it a wrench, but found it just as immovable as it looked. Vexed at my idiotic fears, I vowed to take my fill of investigating that doorway, and to find out if there lay anything of interest beyond it. I knew this part of the city was quite deserted, and that no outraged householder in the flesh was likely to confront my trespassings. But the last of the daylight was now upon me, and I thought best to postpone my enterprise till the morrow. As I betook myself back toward humanity and lodgings, I felt that eye piercing me till I rounded the buttress of the wall; but I denied my folly permission to look back.

The following morning was spent among the curious old cafés, the unexpected squares, and the gorgeous but dilapidated churches of the inhabited city. All these things, however, failed to interest me. With more time on my hands than I quite knew what to do with, I yet felt as if my time were being wasted. The spell of the dead outskirts, of the shadowless dead marshes, of that mysterious and inscrutable dog, clung to me with unrelenting persistence. And the early afternoon found me standing again by the fountain.

Familiarly I scooped up the cool water and drank it from my palm. I scattered it over the parched bricks and clay, which instantly soaked it in. I dashed a few drops also, playfully, upon the image of the dog, which had taken, the evening before, such fantastic liberties with my overwrought fancy. But these drops gathered themselves up nimbly into little shining balls, and fell off to the ground like so much quicksilver. I looked out upon the wan pools and marshes, whence a greenish mist steamed up, and seemed to poison the sunlight streaming through it. It is possible that this semblance of an unwholesome mist was not so much the fault of the marshes as a condition of the atmosphere, premonitory of the fierce electric storms and the earthquake which visited the city that same night. The greenish light beat full on the sunken doorway, so that only the lowermost steps remained in shadow. However unattractive the temporary complexion of the sun, I was glad of his company as I descended the steps. The twisting dragons of the door-handle attracted me as I drew near. As for the dog, I had exorcised it from my imagination with those nimble drops of water; and for the old door, it looked as if a little persuasion would make it yield whatever secret it might chance to have in keeping. But certainly, if I might credit my ears, which had once more grown abnormally attentive, the sound of the water had ceased. My flesh began to creep a little, though I told myself the fading of the sound was entirely due to my position – that the walls of the stairway intercepted it. At the same time I felt that eye watching me, and a chilly sweat broke out upon my limbs; but I execrated my folly, and refused to turn my head. Meanwhile, so alert had become my hearing that the escape of some gases, bubbling up from the bottom of the pool far out in the marsh, resounded as if close beside me. I tried to force the bolt back, but in vain; and I had just come to the conclusion that a sharp wrench would break away bolt, socket, and all, when an uncontrollable instinct of fear turned me about to see what peril threatened. The head of the dog was facing directly toward me, and its eyes, now wide open, flamed upon me with strange and awful whiteness. I sprang up the steps and was at the beast's side in an instant; but I found the head, as before, resting upon the paws, the eyes half closed and dull, the water gushing down into the basin.

As I bathed my shaking hands and clammy forehead, I laughed with deep irritation. I said then to myself that the ignorant could hardly be blamed for even the wildest superstitions, when a cool-headed and enlightened modern like myself was so wrought upon by the fictions of his brain. I philosophized for some time, however, before I got the better of my repugnance to that doorway. I humorously assured myself that, at the worst, this incomprehensible beast was securely anchored to his fountain; and that if anything terrible were at the other side of the door which I was going to open, it surely could not be capable of much, good or ill, after its century or so of imprisonment. Then I walked firmly straight to the doorway and down the seven steps; and I knew that first one eye was turned upon me, then both; the water was silent before I had gone ten paces.

It was useless trying to conquer the creeping of my skin, the fear that pricked along my nerves; so, bidding my reason ignore these minor discomforts, I busied myself with the problem of loosening the bolt socket. It occurred to me at the time that there might be an easier entrance at the other side of the wall, as nothing in this neighbourhood was in good enough repair to boast of more than three walls standing; but no, that would have been a concession to my illusions. I chipped away at the soft stone with my knife. I jerked hard upon the bolt, which gave a little, with clatter of falling stucco; and on the instant I faced around like lightning, in an indescribable horror. There, at the very top of the steps, crouched the dog, its head thrust down close to my face. The stone jaws were grinning apart. A most appalling menace was in the wide, white eyes. I know I tugged once more upon the bolt, for a great piece of the door and arch crumbled and came away; and I thought, as the head closed down, that I made a wild spring to get past the crouching form. Then reason and consciousness forsook me.

When sense returned, I found myself lying on a pile of rags, in a darkish, garlicky hut, with the morning sunlight streaming in through the open door. I sat up, with the memory of my horror vivid upon me, and wondered, with a sigh of relief at the change, what sort of a place I had got to. I was in a very different quarter of the city from the neighbourhood of the fountain. Here were still the ruined outskirts, still the desolate marshes, but the highlands backing the city on the north began to rise just beyond the hut's door. I got up, but found my right shoulder almost disabled. I could not lift my arm without great pain. Yet my clothing was not torn, and bore no marks save of dust and travel. I was about to uncover and examine the damaged shoulder, when in came the owner of the hut, an honest-looking, heavy-set muleteer, who showed all his teeth in his gratification at observing my recovery.

As I gathered from my host, he had had occasion to pass what he called the "Fonte del Cano" near sunset of the afternoon preceding. He had found me lying in a stupor, face down, across the basin of the fount, and directly beneath the jaws of the dog, which he piously crossed himself on mentioning. Not stopping to look for explanations, though he saw the old door was partly broken away, he had put me on his mule and made haste homeward, in fear of the coming of twilight in that grim place. There had come up a great storm in the night, and then an earthquake, shaking down many old walls that had long been toppling to their fall. After sunrise, being a bold fellow, he had gone again to the place, in hope of finding some treasure revealed by the disturbance. Report said there was treasure of some kind hidden within the wall; but none had dared to look for it since the day, years before his birth, when two men undertaking the search had gone mad, with the great white eyes of the dog turned terribly upon them. There were other strange things said about the spot, he acknowledged reluctantly, which, however, he would not talk of even in daylight; and for himself, in truth, he knew but little of them. Now, he continued, in place of anything having been laid bare, the whole top of the wall had fallen down and buried steps and doorway in masses of ruin. But the fountain and the dog were untouched, and he had not cared to go nearer than was necessary.

Having reached my lodgings, I rewarded the honest fellow and sent him away in high feather, all-forgetful of the treasure which the earthquake had failed to unearth for him. Once alone in my room, I made haste to examine my shoulder. I found it green and livid. I found also, with a sick feeling which I shall not soon forget, that it was bruised on either side with deep prints of massive teeth.

ERNEST THOMPSON SETON

BINGO, THE STORY OF MY DOG

I

It was early in November, 1882, and the Manitoba winter had just set in. I was tilting back in my chair for a few lazy moments after breakfast idly alternating my gaze from the one window-pane of our shanty, through which was framed a bit of the prairie and the end of our cowshed, to the old rhyme of the "Francke-lyn's dogge" pinned on the logs near by. But the dreamy mixture of rhyme and view was quickly dispelled by the sight of a large grey animal dashing across the prairie into the cowshed, with a smaller black and white animal in hot pursuit.

"A wolf," I exclaimed, and seizing a rifle dashed out to help the dog. But before I could get there they had left the stable, and after a short run over the snow the wolf again turned at bay, and the dog, our neighbour's collie, circled about watching his chance to snap.

I fired a couple of long shots, which had the effect only of setting them off again over the prairie. After another run this matchless dog closed and seized the wolf by the haunch, but again retreated to avoid the fierce return chop. Then there was another stand at bay, and again a race over the snow. Every few hundred yards this scene was repeated. The dog managing so that each fresh rush should be toward the settlement, while the wolf vainly tried to break back toward the dark belt of trees in the east. At last after a mile of this fighting and running I overtook them, and the dog, seeing that he now had good backing, closed in for the finish.

After a few seconds the whirl of struggling animals resolved itself into a wolf, on his back, with a bleeding collie gripping his throat, and it was now easy for me to step up and end the fight by putting a ball through the wolf's head.

Then, when this dog of marvellous wind saw that his foe was dead, he gave him no second glance, but set out at a lope for a farm four miles across the snow where he had left his master when first the wolf was startled. He was a wonderful dog, and even if I had not come he undoubtedly would have killed the wolf alone, as I learned he had already done with others of the kind, in spite of the fact that the wolf, though of the smaller or prairie race, was much larger than himself.

I was filled with admiration for the dog's prowess and at once sought to buy him at any price. The scornful reply of his owner was, "Why don't you try to buy one of the children?"

Since Frank was not in the market I was obliged to content myself with the next best thing, one of his alleged progeny. That is, a son of his wife. This probable offspring of an illustrious sire was a roly-poly ball of black fur that looked more like a long-tailed bear-cub than a puppy. But he had some tan markings like those on Frank's coat, that were, I hoped, guarantees of future greatness, and also a very characteristic ring of white that he always wore on his muzzle.

Having got possession of his person, the next thing was to find him a name. Surely this puzzle was already solved. The rhyme of the "Franckelyn's dogge" was inbuilt with the foundation of our acquaintance, so with adequate pomp we "yclept him little Bingo."

II

The rest of that winter Bingo spent in our shanty, living the life of a lubberly, fat, well-meaning, ill-doing puppy; gorging himself with food and growing bigger and clumsier each day. Even sad experiences failed to teach him that he must keep his nose out of the rat-trap. His most friendly overtures to the cat were wholly misunderstood and resulted only in an armed neutrality that, varied by occasional reigns of terror, continued to the end; which came when Bingo, who early showed a mind of his own, got a notion for sleeping at the barn and avoiding the shanty altogether.

When the spring came I set about his serious education. After much pains on my behalf and many pains on his, he learned to go at the word in quest of our old yellow cow, that pastured at will on the unfenced prairie.

Once he had learned his business, he became very fond of it and nothing pleased him more than an order to go and fetch the cow. Away he would dash, barking with pleasure and leaping high in the air that he might better scan the plain for his victim. In a short time he would return driving her at full gallop before him, and gave her no peace until, puffing and blowing, she was safely driven into the farthest corner of her stable.

Less energy on his part would have been more satisfactory, but we bore with him until he grew so fond of this semi-daily hunt that he began to bring "old Dunne" without being told. And at length not once or twice but a dozen times a day this energetic cowherd would sally forth on his own responsibility and drive the cow home to the stable.

At last things came to such a pass that whenever he felt like taking a little exercise, or had a few minutes of spare time, or even happened to think of it, Bingo would sally forth at racing speed over the plain and a few minutes later return, driving the unhappy yellow cow at full gallop before him.

At first this did not seem very bad, as it kept the cow from straying too far; but soon it was seen that it hindered her feeding. She became thin and gave less milk; it seemed to weigh on her mind too, as she was always watching nervously for that hateful dog, and in the mornings would hang around the stable as though afraid to venture off and subject herself at once to an onset.

This was going too far. All attempts to make Bingo more moderate in his pleasure were failures, so he was compelled to give it up altogether. After this, though he dared not bring her home, he continued to show his interest by lying at her stable door while she was being milked.

As the summer came on the mosquitoes became a dreadful plague, and the consequent vicious switching of Dunne's tail at milking time even more annoying than the mosquitoes.

Fred, the brother who did the milking, was of an inventive as well as an impatient turn of mind, and he devised a simple plan to stop the switching. He fastened a brick to the cow's tail, then set blithely about his work assured of unusual comfort while the rest of us looked on in doubt.

Suddenly through the mist of mosquitoes came a dull whack and an outburst of "language." The cow went on placidly chewing till Fred got on his feet and furiously attacked her with the milking-stool. It was bad enough to be whacked on the ear with a brick by a stupid old cow, but the uproarious enjoyment and ridicule of the bystanders made it unendurable.

Bingo, hearing the uproar, and divining that he was needed, rushed in and attacked Dunne on the other side. Before the affair quieted down the milk was spilt, the pail and stool were broken, and the cow and the dog severely beaten.

Poor Bingo could not understand it at all. He had long ago learned to despise that cow, and now in utter disgust he decided to forsake even her stable door, and from that time he attached himself exclusively to the horses and their stable.

The cattle were mine, the horses were my brother's, and in transferring his allegiance from the cow-stable to the horse-stable Bingo seemed to give me up too, and anything like daily companionship ceased, and, yet, whenever any emergency arose Bingo turned to me and I to him, and both seemed to feel that the bond between man and dog is one that lasts as long as life.

The only other occasion on which Bingo acted as cowherd was in the autumn of the same year at the annual Carberry Fair. Among the dazzling inducements to enter one's stock there was, in addition to a prospect of glory, a cash prize of "two dollars," for the "best collie in training."

Misled by a false friend, I entered Bingo, and early on the day fixed, the cow was driven to the prairie just outside of the village. When the time came she was pointed out to Bingo and the word given – "Go fetch the cow." It was the intention, of course, that he should bring her to me at the judge's stand.

But the animals knew better. They hadn't rehearsed all summer for nothing. When Dunne saw Bingo's careering form she knew that her only hope for safety was to get into her stable, and Bingo was equally sure that his sole mission in life was to quicken her pace in that direction. So off they raced over the prairie, like a wolf after a deer, and heading straight toward their home two miles away, they disappeared from view.

That was the last that judge or jury ever saw of dog or cow. The prize was awarded to the only other entry.

III

Bingo's loyalty to the horses was quite remarkable; by day he trotted beside them, and by night he slept at the stable door. Where the team went Bingo went, and nothing kept him away from them. This interesting assumption of ownership lent the greater significance to the following circumstance.

I was not superstitious, and up to this time had had no faith in omens, but was now deeply impressed by a strange occurrence in which Bingo took a leading part. There were but two of us now living on the De Winton Farm. One morning my brother John set out for Boggy Creek for a load of hay. It was a long day's journey there and back, and he made an early start. Strange to tell, Bingo, for once in his life, did not follow the team. My brother called to him, but still he stood at a safe distance, and eyeing the team askance, refused to stir. Suddenly he raised his nose in the air and gave vent to a long, melancholy howl. He watched the wagon out of sight, and even followed for a hundred yards or so, raising his voice from time to time in the most doleful howlings. All that day he stayed about the barn, the only time that he was willingly separated from the horses, and at intervals howled a very death dirge. I was alone, and the dog's behaviour inspired me with an awful foreboding of calamity, that weighed upon me more and more as the hours passed away.

About six o'clock Bingo's howlings became unbearable, so that for lack of a better thought I threw something at him, and ordered him away. But oh, the feeling of horror that filled me! Why did I let my brother go away alone? Should I ever again see him alive? I might have known from the dog's actions that something dreadful was about to happen.

At length the hour for his return arrived, and there was John on his load. I took charge of the horses, vastly relieved, and with an air of assumed unconcern, asked, "All right?"

"Right," was the laconic answer.

Who now can say that there is nothing in omens?

And yet, when long afterward, I told this to one skilled in the occult, he looked grave, and said, "Bingo always turned to you in a crisis?"

"Yes."

"Then do not smile. It was you that were in danger that day; he stayed and saved your life, though you never knew from what."

IV

Early in the spring I had begun Bingo's education. Very shortly afterward he began mine.

Midway on the two-mile stretch of prairie that lay between our shanty and the village of Carberry was the corner-stake of the farm; it was a stout post in a low mound of earth, and was visible from afar.

I soon noticed that Bingo never passed without minutely examining this mysterious post. Next I learned that it was also visited by the prairie wolves as well as by all the dogs in the neighbourhood, and at length, with the aid of a telescope, I made a number of observations that helped me to an understanding of the matter and enabled me to enter more fully into Bingo's private life.

The post was by common agreement a registry of the canine tribes. Their exquisite sense of smell enabled each individual to tell at once by the track and trace what other had recently been at the post. When the snow came much more was revealed. I then discovered that this post was but one of a system that covered the country; that in short, the entire region was laid out in signal stations at convenient intervals. These were marked by any conspicuous post, stone, buffalo skull, or other object that chanced to be in the desired locality, and extensive observation showed that it was a very complete system for getting and giving the news.

Each dog or wolf makes a point of calling at those stations that are near his line of travel to learn who has recently been there, just as a man calls at his club on returning to town and looks up the register.

I have seen Bingo approach the post, sniff, examine the ground about, then growl, and with bristling mane and glowing eyes, scratch fiercely and contemptuously with his hind feet, finally walking off very stiffly, glancing back from time to time. All of which, being interpreted, said:

"Grrrh! woof! there's that dirty cur of McCarthy's. *Woof!* I'll 'tend to him tonight. *Woof! woof!"* On another occasion, after the preliminaries, he became keenly interested and studied a coyote's track that came and went, saying to himself, as I afterward learned:

"A coyote track coming from the north smelling of dead cow. Indeed? Pollworth's old Brindle must be dead at last. This is worth looking into."

At other times he would wag his tail, trot about the vicinity and come again and again to make his own visit more evident, perhaps for the benefit of his brother Bill just back from Brandon! So that it was not by chance that one night Bill turned up at Bingo's home and was taken to the hills where a delicious dead horse afforded a chance to suitably celebrate the reunion.

At other times he would be suddenly aroused by the news, take up the trail, and race to the next station for later information.

Sometimes his inspection produced only an air of grave attention, as though he said to himself, "Dear me, who the deuce is this?" or "It seems to me I met that fellow at the Portage last summer."

One morning on approaching the post Bingo's every hair stood on end, his tail dropped and quivered, and he gave proof that he was suddenly sick at the stomach, sure signs of terror. He showed no desire to follow up or know more of the matter, but returned to the house, and half an hour afterward his mane was still bristling and his expression one of hate or fear.

I studied the dreaded track and learned that in Bingo's language the half-terrified, deep-gurgled "*grrr-wff*" means "*timber wolf.*"

These were among the things that Bingo taught me. And in the after time when I might chance to see him arouse from his frosty nest by the stable door, and after stretching himself and shaking the snow from his shaggy coat, disappear into the gloom at a steady trot, trot, trot, I used to think:

"Aha! old dog, I know where you are off to, and why you eschew the shelter of the shanty. Now I know why your nightly trips over the country are so well timed, and how you know just where to go for what you want, and when and how to seek it."

V

In the autumn of 1884, the shanty at De Winton farm was closed and Bingo changed his home to the establishment, that is, to the stable, not the house, of Gordon Wright, our most intimate neighbour.

Since the winter of his puppyhood he had declined to enter a house at any time excepting during a thunderstorm. Of thunder and guns he had a deep dread – no doubt the fear of the first originated in the second, and that arose from some unpleasant shotgun experiences, the cause of which will be seen. His nightly couch was outside the stable, even during the coldest weather, and it was easy to see that he enjoyed to the full the complete nocturnal liberty entailed. Bingo's midnight wanderings extended across the plains for miles. There was plenty of proof of this. Some farmers at very remote points send word to old Gordon that if he did not keep his dog home nights, they would use the shotgun, and Bingo's terror of firearms would indicate that the threats were not idle. A man, living as far away as Petrel, said he saw a large black wolf kill a coyote on the snow one winter evening, but afterward he changed his opinion and "reckoned it must 'a' been Wright's dog." Whenever the body of a winter-killed ox or horse was exposed, Bingo was sure to repair to it nightly, and, driving away the prairie wolves, feast to repletion.

Sometimes the object of a night foray was merely to maul some distant neighbour's dog, and notwithstanding vengeful threats, there seemed no reason to fear that the Bingo breed would die out. One man even avowed that he had seen a prairie wolf accompanied by three young ones which resembled the mother, excepting that they were very large and black and had a ring of white around the muzzle.

True or not as that may be, I know that late in March, while we were out in the sleigh with Bingo trotting behind, a prairie wolf was started from a hollow. Away it went with Bingo in full chase, but the wolf did not greatly exert itself to escape, and within a short distance Bingo was close up, yet strange to tell, there was no grappling, no fight!

Bingo trotted amiably alongside and licked the wolf's nose.

We were astounded, and shouted to urge Bingo on. Our shouting and approach several times started the wolf off at speed and Bingo again pursued until he had overtaken it, but his gentleness was too obvious.

"It is a she-wolf, he won't harm her," I exclaimed as the truth dawned on me. And Gordon said: "Well, I be darned."

So we called our unwilling dog and drove on.

For weeks after this we were annoyed by the depredations of a prairie wolf who killed our chickens, stole pieces of pork from the end of the house, and several times terrified the children by looking into the window of the shanty while the men were away.

Against this animal Bingo seemed to be no safeguard. At length the wolf, a female, was killed, and then Bingo plainly showed his hand by his lasting enmity toward Oliver, the man who did the deed.

VI

It is wonderful and beautiful how a man and his dog will stick to one another, through thick and thin. Butler tells of an undivided Indian tribe, in the Far North which was all but exterminated by an internecine feud over a dog that belonged to one man and was killed by his neighbour; and among ourselves we have lawsuits, fights, and deadly feuds, all pointing the same old moral, "Love me, love my dog."

One of our neighbours had a very fine hound that he thought the best and dearest dog in the world. I loved him, so I loved his dog, and when one day poor Tan crawled home terribly mangled and died by the door, I joined my threats of vengeance with those of his master and thenceforth lost no opportunity of tracing the miscreant, both by offering rewards and by collecting scraps of evidence. At length it was clear that one of three men to the southward had had a hand in the cruel affair. The scent was warming up, and soon we should have been in a position to exact rigorous justice at least, from the wretch who had murdered poor old Tan.

Then something took place which at once changed my mind and led me to believe that the mangling of the old hound was not by any means an unpardonable crime, but indeed on second thoughts was rather commendable than otherwise.

Gordon Wright's farm lay to the south of us, and while there one day, Gordon Jr., knowing that I was tracking the murderer, took me aside and looking about furtively, he whispered, in tragic tones:

"It was Bing done it."

And the matter dropped right there. For I confess that from that moment I did all in my power to baffle the justice I had previously striven so hard to further.

I had given Bingo away long before, but the feeling of ownership did not die; and of this indissoluble fellowship of dog and man he was soon to take part in another important illustration.

Old Gordon and Oliver were close neighbours and friends; they joined in a contract to cut wood, and worked together harmoniously till late on in winter. Then Oliver's old horse died, and he, determining to profit as far as possible, dragged it out on the plain and laid poison baits for wolves around it. Alas, for poor Bingo! He would lead a wolfish life, though again and again it brought him into wolfish misfortunes.

He was as fond of dead horse as any of his wild kindred. That very night, with Wright's own dog Curley, he visited the carcass. It seemed as though Bing had busied himself chiefly keeping off the wolves, but Curley feasted immoderately. The tracks in the snow told the story of the banquet; the interruption as the poison began to work, and of the dreadful spasms of pain during the erratic course back home where Curley, falling in convulsions at Gordon's feet, died in the greatest agony.

"Love me, love my dog," no explanations or apology were acceptable; it was useless to urge that it was accidental, the long-standing feud between Bingo and Oliver was now remembered as an important side-light. The wood-contract was thrown up, all friendly relations ceased, and to this day there is no county big enough to hold the rival factions which were called at once into existence and to arms by Curley's dying yell.

It was months before Bingo really recovered from the poison. We believed indeed that he never again would be the sturdy old-time Bingo. But when the spring came he began to gain strength, and bettering as the grass grew, he was within a few weeks once more in full health and vigour to be a pride to his friends and a nuisance to his neighbours.

VII

Changes took me far away from Manitoba, and on my return in 1886 Bingo was still a member of Wright's household. I thought he would have forgotten me after two years' absence, but not so. One day early in the winter, after having been lost for forty-eight hours, he crawled home to Wright's with a wolf-trap and a heavy log fast to one foot, and the foot frozen to stony hardness. No one had been able to approach to help him, he was so savage, when I, the stranger now, stooped down and laid hold of the trap with one hand and his leg with the other. Instantly he seized my wrist in his teeth.

Without stirring I said, "Bing, don't you know me?"

He had not broken the skin and at once released his hold and offered no further resistance although he whined a good deal during the removal of the trap. He still acknowledged me his master in spite of his change of residence and my long absence, and notwithstanding my surrender of ownership I still felt that he was my dog.

Bing was carried into the house much against his will and his frozen foot thawed out. During the rest of the winter he went lame and two of his toes eventually dropped off. But before the return of warm weather his health and strength were fully restored, and to a casual glance he bore no mark of his dreadful experience in the steel trap.

VIII

During that same winter I caught many wolves and foxes who did not have Bingo's good luck in escaping the traps, which I kept out right into the spring, for bounties are good even when fur is not.

Kennedy's Plain was always a good trapping ground because it was unfrequented by man and yet lay between the heavy woods and the settlement. I had been fortunate with the fur here, and late in April rode in on one of my regular rounds.

The wolf-traps are made of heavy steel and have two springs, each of one hundred pounds power. They are set in fours around a buried bait, and after being strongly fastened to concealed logs are carefully covered in cotton and in fine sand so as to be quite invisible.

A prairie wolf was caught in one of these. I killed him with a club and throwing him aside proceeded to reset the trap as I had done so many hundred times before. All was quickly done. I threw the trap-wrench over toward the pony, and seeing some fine sand nearby, I reached out for a handful of it to add a good finish to the setting.

Oh, unlucky thought! Oh, mad heedlessness born of long immunity! That fine sand was *on the next wolf-trap* and in an instant I was a prisoner. Although not wounded, for the traps have no teeth, and my thick trapping gloves deadened the snap, I was firmly caught across the hand above the knuckles. Not greatly alarmed at this, I tried to reach the trap-wrench with my right foot. Stretching out at full length, face downward, I worked myself toward it, making my imprisoned arm as long and straight as possible. I could not see and reach at the same time, but counted on my toe telling me when I touched the little iron key to my fetters. My first effort was a failure; strain as I might at the chain my toe struck no metal. I swung slowly around my anchor, but still failed. Then a painfully taken observation showed I was much too far to the west. I set about working around, tapping blindly with my toe to discover the key. Thus wildly groping with my right foot I forgot about the other till there was a sharp clank and the iron jaws of trap No. 3 closed tight on my left foot.

The terrors of the situation did not, at first, impress me, but I soon found that all my struggles were in vain. I could not get free from either trap or move the traps together, and there I lay stretched out and firmly staked to the ground.

What would become of me now? There was not much danger of freezing for the cold weather was over, but Kennedy's Plain was never visited excepting by the winter wood-cutters. No one knew where I had gone, and unless I could manage to free myself there was no prospect ahead but to be devoured by wolves, or else die of cold and starvation.

As I lay there the red sun went down over the spruce swamp west of the plain, and a shorelark on a gopher mound a few yards off twittered his evening song, just as one had done the night before at our shanty door, and though the numb pains were creeping up my arm, and a deadly chill possessed me, I noticed how long his little ear tufts were. Then my thoughts went to the comfortable supper-table at Wright's shanty, and I thought, Now they are frying the pork for supper, or just sitting down. My pony still stood as I left him with his bridle on the ground, patiently waiting to take me home. He did not understand the long delay, and when I called, he ceased nibbling the grass and looked at me in dumb, helpless inquiry. If he would only go home the empty saddle might tell the tale and bring help. But his very faithfulness kept him waiting hour after hour while I was perishing of cold and hunger.

Then I remembered how old Girou the trapper had been lost, and in the following spring his comrades found his skeleton held by the leg in a bear-trap. I wondered which part of my clothing would show my identity. Then a new thought came to me. This is how a wolf feels when he is trapped. Oh! what misery have I been responsible for! Now I'm to pay for it.

Night came slowly on. A prairie wolf howled, the pony pricked up his ears and walking nearer to me, stood with his head down. Then another prairie wolf howled and another, and I could make out that they were gathering in the neighbourhood. There I lay prone and helpless, wondering if it would not be strictly just that they should come and tear me to pieces. I heard them calling for a long time before I realized that dim, shadowy forms were sneaking near. The horse saw them first, and his terrified snort drove them back at first, but they came nearer next time and sat around me on the prairie. Soon one bolder than the others crawled up and tugged at the body of his dead relative. I shouted and he retreated growling. The pony ran to a distance in terror. Presently the wolf returned, and after two or three of these retreats and returns, the body was dragged off and devoured by the rest in a few minutes.

After this they gathered nearer and sat on their haunches to look at me, and the boldest one smelt the rifle and scratched dirt on it. He retreated when I kicked at him with my free foot and shouted, but growing bolder as I grew weaker he came and snarled right in my face. At this several others snarled and came up closer, and I realized that I was to be devoured by the foe that I most despised, when suddenly out of the gloom with a guttural roar sprang a great black wolf. The prairie wolves scattered like chaff except the bold one, which seized by the black newcomer was in a few moments a draggled corpse, and then, oh horrors! this mighty brute bounded at me and – Bingo – noble Bingo, rubbed his shaggy, panting sides against me and licked my cold face.

"Bingo – Bing – old – boy – Fetch me the trap-wrench!"

Away he went and returned dragging the rifle, for he knew only that I wanted something.

"No – Bing – the trap-wrench." This time it was my sash, but at last he brought the wrench and wagged his tail in joy that it was right. Reaching out with my free hand, after much difficulty I unscrewed the pillar-nut. The trap fell apart and my hand was released, and a minute later I was free. Bing brought the pony up, and after slowly walking to restore the circulation I was able to mount. Then slowly at first but soon at a gallop, with Bingo as herald careering and barking ahead, we set out for home, there to learn that the night before, though never taken on the trapping rounds, the brave dog had acted strangely, whimpering and watching the timber-trail; and at last when night came on, in spite of attempts to detain him he had set out in the gloom and guided by a knowledge that is beyond us had reached the spot in time to avenge me as well as set me free.

Staunch old Bing – he was a strange dog. Though his heart was with me, he passed me next day with scarcely a look, but responded with alacrity when little Gordon called him to a gopher-hunt. And it was so to the end; and to the end also he lived the wolfish life that he loved, and never failed to seek the winter-killed horses and found one again with a poisoned bait, and wolfishly bolted that; then feeling the pang, set out, not for

Wright's but to find me, and reached the door of my shanty where I should have been. Next day on returning I found him dead in the snow with his head on the sill of the door – the door of his puppyhood's days; my dog to the last in his heart of hearts – it was my help he sought, and vainly sought, in the hour of his bitter extremity.

E. PAULINE JOHNSON

WE-HRO'S SACRIFICE

We-hro was a small Onondaga Indian boy, a good-looking, black-eyed little chap with as pagan a heart as ever beat under a copper-coloured skin. His father and grandfathers were pagans. His ancestors for a thousand years back, and yet a thousand years back of that, had been pagans, and We-hro, with the pride of his religion and his race, would not have turned from the faith of his fathers for all the world. But the world, as he knew it, consisted entirely of the Great Indian Reserve, that lay on the banks of the beautiful Grand River, sixty miles west of the great Canadian city of Toronto.

Now, the boys that read this tale must not confuse a pagan with a heathen. The heathen nations that worship idols are terribly pitied and despised by the pagan Indians, who are worshippers of "The Great Spirit," a kind and loving God, who, they say, will reward them by giving them happy hunting grounds to live in after they die, that is, if they live good, honest, upright lives in this world.

We-hro would have scowled blackly if anyone had dared to name him a heathen. He thoroughly ignored the little Delaware boys, whose fathers worshipped idols fifty years ago, and on all the feast days and dance days he would accompany his parents to the Longhouse (which was their church), and take his little part in the religious festivities. He could remember well as a tiny child being carried in his mother's blanket "pick-a-back," while she dropped into the soft swinging movement of the dance, for

We-hro's people did not worship their "Great Spirit" with hymns of praise and lowly prayers, the way the Christian Indians did. We-hro's people worshipped their God by dancing beautiful, soft, dignified steps, with no noisy clicking heels to annoy one, but only the velvety shuffle of the moccasined feet, the weird beat of the Indian drums, the mournful chanting of the old chiefs, keeping time with the throb of their devoted hearts.

Then, when he grew too big to be carried, he was allowed to clasp his mother's hand, and himself learn the pretty steps, following his father, who danced ahead, dressed in full costume of scarlet cloth and buckskin, with gay beads and bear claws about his neck, and wonderful carven silver ornaments, massive and solid, decorating his shirt and leggings. We-hro loved the tawny fringes and the hammered silver quite as much as a white lady loves diamonds and pearls; he loved to see his father's face painted in fierce reds, yellows, and blacks, but most of all he loved the unvarying *chuck-a, chuck-a, chuck-a* of the great mud-turtle rattles that the "musicians" skilfully beat upon the benches before them. Oh, he was a thorough little pagan, was We-hro! His loves and his hates were as decided as his comical but stately step in the dance of his ancestors' religion. Those were great days for the small Onondaga boy. His father taught him to shape axe-handles, to curve lacrosse sticks, to weave their deer-sinew netting, to tan skins, to plant corn, to model arrows, and – most difficult of all – to "feather" them, to "season" bows, to chop trees, to burn, hollow, fashion, and "man" a dugout canoe, to use the paddle, to gauge the wind and current of that treacherous Grand River, to learn wild cries to decoy bird and beast for food. Oh, little pagan We-hro had his life filled to overflowing with much that the civilized white-boy would give all his dimes and dollars to know.

And it was then that the great day came, the marvellous day when We-hro discovered his *second self*, his playmate, his loyal, unselfish, loving friend – his underbred, unwashed, hungry, vagabond dog, born white and spotless, but begrimed by contact with the world, the mud, and the white man's hovel.

It happened this way:

We-hro was cleaning his father's dugout canoe, after a night of fish spearing. The soot, the scales, the fire ashes, the mud – all had to be "swabbed" out at the river's brink by means of much water and an Indian "slat" broom. We-hro was up to his little ears in work, when suddenly, above him, on the river road, he heard the coarse voice and thundering whipfalls of a man urging and beating his horse – a white man, for no Indian used such language, no Indian beat an animal that served him. We-hro looked up. Stuck in the mud of the river road was a huge wagon, grain-filled. The driver, purple of face, was whaling the poor team, and shouting to a cringing little drab-white dog, of fox-terrier lineage, to "Get out of there or I'll—!"

The horses were dragging and tugging. The little dog, terrified, was sneaking off with tail between its hind legs. Then the brutal driver's whip came down, curling its lash about the dog's thin body, forcing from the little speechless brute a howl of agony. Then We-hro spoke – spoke in all the English he knew.

"Bad! Bad! You die some day – you! You hurt that dog. White man's God, he no like you. Indian's Great Spirit, he not let you shoot in happy hunting grounds. You die some day – you *bad!*"

"Well, if I *am* bad I'm no pagan Indian Hottentot like you!" yelled the angry driver. "Take the dog, and begone!"

"Me, no Hottentot," said We-hro, slowly. "Me Onondaga, all right. Me take dog," and from that hour the poor little white cur and the copper-coloured little boy were friends for all time.

The Superintendent of Indian Affairs was taking his periodical drive about the Reserve when he chanced to meet old Ten-Canoes, We-hro's father.

The superintendent was a very important person. He was a great white gentleman, who lived in the city of Brantford, fifteen miles away. He was a kindly, handsome man, who loved and honoured every Indian on the Grand River Reserve. He had a genial smile, a warm handshake, so when he stopped his horse and greeted the old pagan, Ten-Canoes smiled too.

"Ah, Ten-Canoes!" cried the superintendent, "a great man told me he was coming to see your people – a big man, none less than Great Black-Coat, the bishop of the Anglican Church. He thinks you are a bad lot, because you are pagans; he wonders why it is that you have never turned Christian. Some of the missionaries have told him you pagans are no good, so the great man wants to come and see for himself. He wants to see some of your religious dances – the "Dance of the White Dog," if you will have him; he wants to see if it is really *bad!*"

Ten-Canoes laughed. "I welcome him," he said, earnestly. "Welcome the 'Great Black-Coat.' I honour him, though I do not think as he does. He is a good man, a just man; I welcome him, bid him come."

Thus was his lordship, the Bishop, invited to see the great pagan Onondaga "Festival of the White Dog."

But what was *this* that happened?

Never yet had a February moon waned but that the powerful Onondaga tribe had offered the burnt "Sacrifice of the White Dog," that most devout of all native rites. But now, search as they might, not a single spotlessly white dog could be found. No other animal would do. It was the law of this great Indian tribe that no other burnt sacrifice could possibly be offered than the strangled body of a white dog.

We-hro heard all the great chiefs talking of it all. He listened to plans for searching the entire Reserve for a dog, and the following morning he arose at dawn, took his own pet dog down to the river and washed him as he had seen white men wash their sheep. Then out of the water dashed the gay little animal, yelping and barking in play, rolling in the snow, tearing madly about, and finally rushing off towards the log house which was We-hro's home, and scratching at the door to get in by the warm fire to dry his shaggy coat. Oh! what an ache that coat caused in We-hro's heart. From a dull drab grey, the dog's hair had washed pure white, not a spot or a blemish on it, and in an agony of grief the little pagan boy realized that through his own action he had endangered the life of his dog friend; that should his father and his father's friends see that small white terrier, they would take it away for the nation's sacrifice.

Stumbling and panting and breathless, We-hro hurried after his pet, and seizing the dog in his arms, he wrapped his own shabby coat about the trembling, half-dry creature, and carried him to where the cedars grew thick at the back of the house. Crouched in their shadows he hugged his treasured companion, thinking with horror of the hour when the blow would surely fall.

For days the boy kept his dog in the shelter of the cedars, tied up tightly with an old rope, and sleeping in a warm raccoon skin, which We-hro smuggled away from his own simple bed. The dog contented himself with what little food We-hro managed to carry to him, but the hiding could not keep up forever, and one dark, dreaded day We-hro's father came into the house and sat smoking in silence for many minutes. When at last he spoke, he said:

"We-hro, your dog is known to me. I have seen him, white as the snow that fell last night. It is the law that someone must always suffer for the good of the people. We-hro, would you have the great 'Black-Coat,' the great white preacher, come to see our beautiful ceremony, and would you have the great Onondaga tribe fail to show the white man how we worship our ancient Great Spirit? Would you have us fail to burn the sacrifice? Or will you give your white dog for the honour of our people?"

The world is full of heroes, but at that moment it held none greater than the little pagan boy, who crushed down his grief and battled back his tears as he answered:

"Father, you are old and honoured and wise. For you and for my people alone would I give the dog."

At last the wonderful Dance Day arrived. His lordship, the Bishop of the Anglican Church, drove down from the city of Brantford; with him the Superintendent of Indian Affairs, and a man who understood both the English and the Onondaga languages. Long before they reached the Longhouse they could hear the wild beat of the drum, could count the beats of the dance rattles, could distinguish the half-sad chant of the worshippers. The kind face of the great bishop was very grave. It pained his gentle old heart to know that this great tribe of Indians were pagans – savages, as he thought – but when he entered that plain log building that the Onondagas held as their church, he took off his hat with the beautiful reverence all great men pay to other great men's religion, and he stood bareheaded while old Ten-Canoes chanted forth this speech:

"Oh, brothers of mine! We welcome the white man's friend, the great 'Black-Coat,' to this, our solemn worship. We offer to the red man's God – the Great Spirit – a burnt offering. We do not think that anything save what is pure and faithful and without blemish can go into the sight of the Great Spirit. Therefore do we offer this dog, pure as we hope our spirits are, that the God of the red man may accept it with our devotion, knowing that we, too, would gladly be as spotless as this sacrifice."

Then was a dog carried in dead, and beautifully decorated with wampum, beads, and porcupine embroidery. Oh! so mercifully dead and out of pain, gently strangled by reverent fingers, for an Indian is never unkind to an animal. And far over in a corner of the room was a little brown figure, twisted with agony, choking back the sobs and tears – for was he not taught that tears were for babies alone, and not for boys that grew up into warriors?

"Oh, my dog! My dog!" he muttered. "They have taken you away from me, but it was for the honour of my father and of my own people."

The great Anglican bishop turned at that moment, and, catching the sight of suffering on little We-hro's face, said aloud to the man who spoke both languages:

"That little boy over there seems in torture. Can I do anything for him, do you think?"

"That little boy," replied the man who spoke both languages, "is the son of the great Onondaga chief. No white dog could be found for this ceremony but his. This dog was his pet, but for the honour of his father and of his tribe he has given up his pet as a sacrifice."

For a moment the great Anglican bishop was blinded by his own tears. Then he walked slowly across the wide long building and laid his white hand tenderly on the head of the little Onondaga boy. His kindly old eyes closed, and his lips moved – noiselessly, for a space, then he said aloud:

"Oh, that the white boys of my great city church knew and practised half as much of self-denial as has this little pagan Indian lad, who has given up his heart's dearest because his father and the honour of his people required it."

DUNCAN CAMPBELL SCOTT

The Tragedy of the Seigniory

There was a house on the outskirts of Viger called, by courtesy, the Seigniory. Passing down one of the side-streets you caught sight of it, set upon a rise, having nothing to do with the street, or seemingly with any part of the town. Built into the bank, as it was, the front had three storeys, while the back had but two. The lower flat, half cellar, half kitchen, was lighted from a broad door and two windows facing the south-east. Entrance to the second floor was had by a flight of steps to a wide gallery running completely across the front of the house. Then, above this second storey, there was a sharply peaked roof, with dormer windows. The walls of the kitchen storey were rough stone, while the upper part had been plastered and overlaid with a buff-coloured wash; but time had cracked off the plaster in many places, and showed the solid stones.

With all the ravages of time upon it, and with all its old surroundings gone, it yet had an air of some distinction. With its shoulder to the street, and its independent solidity, it made men remember days gone by, when it was only a farmhouse on the Estate of the Rioux family. Yet of that estate this old house, with its surrounding three acres of land, was all that remained; and of the retainers that once held allegiance to this proud name, Louis Bois was the last.

Living alone in the old house, growing old with it, guarding some secret and keeping at a proper distance the inquisitive and loquacious villagers, had given Louis also some distinction.

He was reported an old soldier, and bore about the witness of it in a wooden leg. He swore, when angry, in a cavalier fashion, using the heavier English oaths with some freedom. His bravery, having never been put to proof, rested securely upon these foundations. But he had a more definite charm for the villagers; he was supposed to have money of his own, and afforded the charming spectacle of a human being vegetating like a plant, without effort and without trouble. Louis Bois had grown large in his indolence, and towards the end of his career he moved with less frequency and greater difficulty. His face was round and fat; the hair had never grown on it, and the skin was fine and smooth as an orange, without wrinkles, but marked with very decided pores. The expression of amiability that his mouth promised was destroyed by an eye of suspicious restlessness. About fifteen years before the time of his release Louis had been sworn to his post by the last of the Rioux family – Hugo Armand Theophile.

This young man, of high spirit and passionate courage, found himself, at the age of twenty-five, after two years of intermittent study at a Jesuit College, fatherless, and without a sou to call his own. Of the family estate, the farmhouse, round which Viger had closed, was all that remained, and from its windows this fiery youth might look across the ten acres that were his, over miles of hill and wood to which his grandfather had been born. This vista tortured him for three days, when he sold seven of his acres, keeping the rest from pride. Then he shook off the dust of Viger, but not before swearing Louis Bois, who was old enough to be his father, and loved him as such, to stay and watch the forlorn hope of the Rioux Estate until he, the last of the line, should return and redeem his ancient heritage. He would be gone ten years, he said; and Louis reflected with pride that his own money would keep him that long, and longer.

At first he kept the whole house open, and entertained some of his friends; but he soon discovered that he lost money by that, and gradually he boarded up the windows and lived in the kitchen and one room of the upper flat.

He was a sensitive being, this, and his master's idea had taken hold upon him. His burly frame contained a faint heart; he had no physical courage; and he was as suspicious as a savage. Moreover, he was superstitious, as superstitious as an old wife, and odd occurrences made him uneasy. If he could have been allowed to doze on his gallery in the sun all his days, and sleep secure of dreams and visitations all his nights, his life might have been bearable. The first three years of his stewardship were comparatively uneventful. He traced his liege's progress through the civilized world by the postmark on his letters, which sometimes contained a bill of exchange, of which the great and safe bank of Bardé Brothers took charge. As yet his master had not captured a treasure ship; but seven years remained.

At the beginning of his fourth year something happened which disturbed Louis' existence to its centre. An emissary of the devil, in the guise of a surveyor, planned his theodolite, and ran a roadway which took off a corner of his three acres, and for this he received only an arbitrator's allowance. In vain he stumped up and down his gallery, and in vain his English oaths – the roadway went though. To add to his trouble, the letters from the wanderer ceased. Was he dead? Had he forgotten? No more money was coming in, and Louis had the perpetual sight of the alienated lands before his eyes.

One day, when he was coming home from the bank, his eye caught a poster that made him think; it was an announcement of a famous lottery. Do what he would he could not get it out of his head; and that evening, when he was cooking his supper, he resolved to make money after a fashion of his own. He saw himself a suddenly rich man, the winner of the seventy-five-thousand-dollar prize. He felt his knee burn under him, and felt also what a dead thing his wooden leg was.

He began to venture small sums in the lottery, hoarding half his monthly allowance until he should have sufficient funds to purchase a ticket. Waiting for the moment when he could buy, and then waiting for the moment when he could receive news of the drawing, lent a feverish interest to his life. But he failed to win. With his failure grew a sort of exasperation – he would win, he said, if he spent every cent he owned. He had moments when he suspected that he was being duped, but he was always reassured upon spelling out the lottery circular, where the drawing by the two orphan children was so touchingly described.

At last, after repeated failures, he drew every cent of his own that he could muster, and bought a whole ticket. He never rested a moment until the returns came. He had days of high spirits, when he touched his gains and saw them heaped before him, and other days of depression when he cursed his ill luck, and saw blanks written everywhere. When he learned the result his last disappointment was his greatest. He had drawn a blank.

He was in a perfect fury of rage, and went off to bed cursing like a sea-pirate. When he took off his wooden leg, he took it by the foot and beat the floor with the knee-end until he got some relief. Could he have captured, he would have murdered the innocent orphan children. He swore never to be tempted again, but the morning when he took that oath, April was bleak on the hills, and a tardy spring circled in cold sunshine, leaving the buds suspended.

When May came, his hope again blossomed. Slowly and certainly his mind approached that money he had in trust for his master, until, one sultry day in June, he saw his way to success, and felt his conscience lulled. That afternoon he dozed on the gallery and dreamed. He felt he was in Heaven, and the heaven of his dreams was a large cathedral whose nave he had walked somewhere in his journeyings. He saw the solemn passages, the penetrating shafts of light, the obscure altar rising dimly in the star-hung alcove; and from the glamour round the altar floated down a magnificent angel, and with a look of perfect knowledge in his eyes shamed him for his base resolve. Slowly, as Louis quailed before him, he dwindled, shimmering in the glory shaken from his vesture, until he grew very faint and indistinct, and dissolved slowly into light. Then his vision swayed aside, and he saw his own gallery, and a little cream-coloured dog, that sat with his back half-turned towards him, eyeing him over his shoulder. Superstitious Louis shuddered when he saw this dog. He thought there was something uncanny about him; but to a casual observer he was an ordinary dog of mixed blood. He had a sharp nose and ears, piercing eyes, straight, cream-coloured hair rather white upon the breast, and a tail curled down upon his back. He was a small dog; an intense nervousness animated his every movement.

Louis was afraid to drive him away, and so long as he saw him he could not forget his dream and the reproof he had had from heaven; gradually he came to believe the animal was a spirit in canine form. His reasons for this were that the dog never slept, or at least never seemed to sleep. All day long he followed Louis about. If he dozed in his chair the dog laid his nose between his paws and watched him. If he woke at night his eyes burned in the darkness. Again, he never seemed to eat anything, and he was never heard to utter a sound.

Louis, half-afraid of him, gave him a name; he called him Fidele. He also tried to coax him, but to no purpose. The dog never approached him except when he went to sleep; then he would move nearer to him. At last he got greater confidence;

and Louis awoke from a doze one day to find him gnawing on his wooden leg. He tried to frighten him off; but Fidele had acquired the habit and stuck to it. Whenever Louis would fall asleep, Fidele would approach him softly and chew his leg. Perhaps it was the soft tremor that was imparted to his fleshy leg from the gnawing of the wooden one; but Louis never slept more soundly than when this was progressing. He saw, however, with dismay, his hickory support vanishing, and to avoid wasting his money on wooden legs he covered the one he had with brass-headed tacks. In the end the dog came to be a sort of conscience for him. He could never look at his piercing eyes without thinking of the way he had been warned.

To pay for his recklessness Louis had to live on a pittance for years; just enough to keep himself alive. He might have lost his taste for gambling, through this rigour, and his temptation to use his master's money might never have returned; but in his lottery business he had made a confidant of one of the messengers of the Bardé Bank. The fellow's name was Jacques Potvin. He was full of dissimulation; he loved a lie for its own sake; he devoured the simple character of Louis Bois. Whenever they met, Louis was treated to a flushed account of all sorts of escapades – thousands made in a night – tens of thousands by a pen-stroke.

At last, as a crowning success, Jacques Potvin himself had won a thousand dollars in a drawing that Louis could not participate in. This was galling. To have that money lying idle; never to hear from his master Rioux, who was probably dead, and to see chance after chance slip by him. He gave his trouble to Potvin! Potvin took the weight lightly and threw it over his shoulder:

"Bah!" he said. "If I had that money under my fingers, I would be a rich man before the year was out."

The fever was in Louis' blood again. He tossed a sleepless night, and then resolved desperately. He shut Fidele up in the attic, and went off and bought a ticket with his master's money. When he came back from the bank, the first thing he saw was Fidele seated in one of the dormer windows, watching him. It would be six months before he could get any news of his venture; six months of Fidele and an accusing conscience.

Half the time was scarcely over when, to his horror and joy, came a letter from his master. It was dated at Rio. He was on his way home; he would arrive in about six months. The probable failure of his scheme gave Louis agony now. He would have to face his master, who would arrive at Christmas if his plans were discharged, with a rifled bank account. On the other hand, if he should be successful! – Oh! that gold, how it haunted him!

One night, on the eve of his expectation, Louis fell asleep as he was cooking his supper. He slept long, and when he awoke his stove was red-hot. He started up, staring at something figured on the red stove door.

It was only the number of the stove, but it was also the number of his ticket. He waited, after that, in perfect serenity, and when his notice came he opened it with calmness. He had won the seventy-five-thousand-dollar prize.

He went off hot foot to Potvin.

"Of course," he said, "I'll have them send it to the Bardé Bank."

"Just keep cool," said Potvin. "Of course you'll do nothing of the sort."

"But why?"

"Why? Wait and see. The Imperial Bank is safe enough for you."

Louis had the money sent to the Imperial Bank.

A short time after this, when Louis passed the Bardé Bank, a crowd of people were besieging the doors and reading the placards; the bank had suspended payment. The shrewdness of Potvin had saved his seventy-five thousand.

When he next met Jacques, he hugged him to his heart. Jacques laid his finger on his nose:

"Deeper still," he said. "I know, I *know* that the Imperial itself is totterish. This affair of the Bardés has made things shaky; see? Everything is on three legs. If I were you, now; if *I* were you, I'd just draw that seventy-five thousand dollars and lay it away in a strongbox till this blows over."

"But," said Louis, in a panic, "I have no strongbox."

"But *I* have," said Jacques.

Louis laid his hands on his shoulders, and could have wept.

Christmas passed, but no sign of Hugo Armand Theophile. But the second week in January brought a letter, two days old, from New York. Rioux would be in Viger in a week at the latest. Louis was in great spirits. He planned a surprise for his master. He went off to find Jacques Potvin, but Jacques was not to be found.

Louis arranged that Jacques was to meet him at a tavern called "The Blue Bells" the next day.

"But," said Jacques, when they met, "this is absurd. What do you want the money for?"

"Never mind, I want it, that's all."

"But think; seventy-five thousand dollars!"

"I want it for a few days. Just the money – myself – I – is it not mine?"

Someone in the next compartment rose, and put his ear to the partition. The voices were low, but he could hear them well. Listening intently, his eyes seemed to sink into his head, and burn there darkly.

"Well, so it is," concluded Jacques. "I will get it for you. But we'll have to do the thing quietly, very quietly. I'll drive out to Viger tomorrow night, say. I'll meet you at that vacant field next the church, at eleven, and the money will be there."

The listener in the next compartment withdrew hastily, and mingled with the crowd at the bar. That night he wandered out to Viger. He observed the church and the vacant lot, and saw that there were here and there hollows under the sidewalk, where a man might crouch.

He afterward wandered about for a while, and found himself in front of the old farmhouse. A side window of the second storey was filled with the flicker of a fire. A ladder leaned against the wall and ran up past the window. He hesitated whether to ascend the gallery-steps or the ladder. He chose the ladder. With his foot on the lowest rung, he said:

"If I hadn't this little scheme on hand I would go in, but..."

He went up the ladder and looked in at the window. Louis Bois was asleep before the fire. Fidele lay by his side. The man caught the dog's eye.

Louis woke nervously, and saw a figure at the window. The only thing he discerned distinctly was a white sort of cap. In his sudden fear, seeking something to throw, he touched Fidele, and without thinking, he hurled him full at the man.

The dog's body broke the old sash and crashed through the glass. The fellow vanished. When Louis had regained his courage, he let Fidele in. There was not a scratch on him. He lay down about ten yards from Louis, and looked at him fixedly.

The old soldier had no sleep that night, and no peace the next day.

The next night was wild. Louis looked from his window. The moon was shining brightly on the icy fields that glared with as white a radiance; over the polished surface drifted loose masses of snow, and clouds rushed across the moon.

He took his cloak, his stick, and a dirk-knife, and locking Fidele in, started forth. A few moments after he reached the rendezvous, Jacques drove up in a berlin.

"Here it is," Jacques said, pressing a box into his hands. "The key that hangs there will open it. I must be off. Be careful!"

Jacques whirled away in the wind. There was not a soul to be seen. Louis clutched his knife, and turned toward home. He had not left the church very far behind, when he thought he heard something moving. A cloud obscured the moon. A figure leaned out from under the sidewalk and observed him. A moment later it sprang upon the pathway and leaped forward.

Louis was sure someone was there; half looking round, he made a swipe in the air with his knife. It encountered something. Looking round fairly he saw a man with a whitish cap stagger off the sidewalk and fall in the snow.

Hurrying on, he looked back a moment later, and saw the figure of the man, receding, making with incredible swiftness across the vacant space.

Louis once out of sight, the man doubled with the rapidity of a wounded beast, and after plunging through side streets was again in front of the farmhouse. He ascended the ladder with some difficulty, and entered the room by the window. Where he expected to find his faithful steward, there was only a white dog that neither moved nor barked, and that watched him fixedly as he fell, huddled and fainting, on the bunk.

A few minutes later Louis reached home. The sickness of fear possessed him. He staggered into the room and sat before the fire, trying to control himself. When he was calmer, he found himself clutching the box. He threw off his cloak and took the key to fit it into the lock. The key was too large. In vain he fussed and turned – it would not go in. He shook the box; nothing rattled or moved. A horrid suspicion crossed his mind. What if Jacques had stolen the money! What if there was nothing in the box!

He seized the poker in a frenzy and beat the box open. It was empty – empty – empty!

His hand went round in it mechanically, while he gazed, wild with conjecture. Then, with an oath he flung the box on the fire and turned away. The disturbed brands shot a glow into every part of the room, and Louis saw by one flash a grey Persian-lamb cap, which he recognized, lying on the floor. By the next, he saw the head, from which it had rolled, pillowed on his bunk.

He tried to utter a cry, but sank into his chair stricken dumb, for death had not yet softened the lines of desperate cunning on the face, which, in spite of the scars of a wild life, he recognized as that of Hugo Armand Theophile Rioux.

The look of that cap as he had seen it through the window; the glimpse he had of it a few minutes ago, when he swept his knife back through the air; the face of his master – dead; the thought of himself, duped and robbed, fixed him in his chair, where he hung half-lifeless.

Everything reeled before him, but in a dull glare he saw Fidele, his nose between his extended paws, and his eyes fixed keenly upon him. They seemed to pierce him to the soul, until their gleam, which had followed him for so many years, faded out with all the familiar lines and corners of his room, engulfed in one intense, palpitating light.

The people who broke open the house saw the unexplained tragedy of the Seigniory, but they did not find Fidele, nor was he ever seen again.

STEPHEN LEACOCK

Weejee, the Pet Dog. An Idyll of Summer

We were sitting on the veranda of Sopley's summer cottage.

"How lovely it is here," I said to my host and hostess, "and how still."

It was at this moment that Weejee, the pet dog, took a sharp nip at the end of my tennis trousers.

"Weejee!" exclaimed his mistress with great emphasis, "*bad* dog! how dare you, sir! *bad* dog!"

"I hope he hasn't hurt you," said my host.

"Oh, it's nothing," I answered cheerfully. "He hardly scratched me."

"You know I don't think he means anything by it," said Mrs. Sopley.

"Oh, I'm *sure* he doesn't," I answered.

Weejee was coming nearer to me again as I spoke.

"*Weejee!!*" cried my hostess, "naughty dog, bad!"

"Funny thing about that dog," said Sopley, "the way he knows people. It's a sort of instinct. He knew right away that you were a stranger. Now, yesterday, when the butcher came – there was a new driver on the cart and Weejee knew it right away – he grabbed the man by the leg at once, wouldn't let go. I called out to the man that it was all right or he might have done Weejee some harm."

At this moment Weejee took the second nip at my other trouser leg. There was a short *gur-r-r* and a slight mix-up.

"Weejee! Weejee!" called Mrs. Sopley. "How dare you, sir! You're just a *bad* dog!! Go and lie down, sir. I'm so sorry. I think, you know, it's your white trousers. For some reason Weejee simply *hates* white trousers. I do hope he hasn't torn them."

"Oh, no," I said, "it's nothing – only a slight tear."

"Here, Weejee, Weejee," said Sopley, anxious to make a diversion and picking up a little chip of wood "chase it, fetch it out!" and he made the motions of throwing it into the lake.

"Don't throw it too far, Charles," said his wife. "He doesn't swim awfully well," she continued, turning to me, "and I'm always afraid he might get out of his depth. Last week he was ever so nearly drowned. Mr. Van Toy was in swimming, and he had on a dark blue suit – dark blue seems simply to infuriate Weejee – and Weejee just dashed in after him. He don't *mean* anything, you know, it was only the *suit* made him angry – he really likes Mr. Van Toy – but just for a minute we were quite alarmed. If Mr. Van Toy hadn't carried Weejee in I think he might have been drowned."

"By Jove!" I said in a tone to indicate how appalled I was.

"Let me throw the stick, Charles," continued Mrs. Sopley.

"Now, Weejee, look. Weejee; here, good dog, look! look now. Sometimes Weejee simply won't do what one wants. Here, Weejee; now, good dog!"

Weejee had his tail sideways between his legs and was moving towards me again.

"Hold on," said Sopley in a stern tone, "let me throw him in."

"Do be careful, Charles," said his wife.

Sopley picked Weejee up by the collar and carried him to the edge of the water – it was about six inches deep – and threw him in, with much the same force as, let us say, a pen is thrown into ink or a brush dipped into a pot of varnish.

"That's enough; that's quite enough, Charles," exclaimed Mrs. Sopley. "I think he'd better not swim. The water in the evening is always a little cold. Good dog, good doggie, good Weejee!"

Meantime "good Weejee" had come out of the water and was moving again towards me.

"He goes straight to you," said my hostess. "I think he must have taken a fancy to you."

He had.

To prove it, Weejee gave himself a rotary whirl like a twirled mop.

"Oh, I'm so sorry," said Mrs. Sopley. "I am. He's wetted you. Weejee, lie down, down, sir, good dog, bad dog, lie down!"

"It's all right," I said. "I've another white suit in my valise."

"But you must be wet through," said Mrs. Sopley. "Perhaps we'd better go in. It's getting late, anyway, isn't it?" And then she added to her husband, "I don't think Weejee ought to sit out here now that he's wet."

So he went in.

"I think you'll find everything you need," said Sopley, as he showed me to my room, "and, by the way, don't mind if Weejee comes into your room at night. We like to let him run all over the house and he often sleeps on this bed."

"All right," I said cheerfully, "I'll look after him."

That night Weejee came.

And when it was far on in the dead of night, so that even the lake and the trees were hushed in sleep, I took Weejee out and – but there is no need to give the details of it.

And the Sopleys are still wondering where Weejee has gone to, and waiting for him to come back, because he is so clever at finding his way.

But from where Weejee is, no one finds his way back.

L.M. MONTGOMERY

The Quarantine at Alexander Abraham's

I refused to take that class in Sunday School the first time I was asked. It was not that I objected to teaching in the Sunday School. On the contrary, I rather liked the idea; but it was the Rev. Mr. Allan who asked me, and it had always been a matter of principle with me never to do anything a man asked me to do if I could help it. I was noted for that. It saves a great deal of trouble and it simplifies everything beautifully. I had always disliked men. It must have been born in me, because, as far back as I can remember, an antipathy to men and dogs was one of my strongest characteristics. I was noted for that. My experiences through life only served to deepen it. The more I saw of men, the more I liked cats.

So, of course, when the Rev. Allan asked me if I would consent to take a class in Sunday School I said no in a fashion calculated to chasten him wholesomely. If he had sent his wife the first time, as he did the second, it would have been wiser. People generally do what Mrs. Allan asks them to do because they know it saves time.

Mrs. Allan talked smoothly for half an hour before she mentioned the Sunday School, and paid me several compliments. Mrs. Allan is famous for her tact. Tact is a faculty for meandering around to a given point instead of making a beeline. I have no tact. I am noted for that. As soon as Mrs. Allan's conversation came in sight of the Sunday School, I, who knew all along whither it was tending, said, straight out, "What class do you want me to teach?"

Mrs. Allan was so surprised that she forgot to be tactful, and answered plainly for once in her life, "There are two classes – one of boys and one of girls – needing a teacher. I have been teaching the girls' class, but I shall have to give it up for a little time on account of the baby's health. You may have your choice, Miss MacPherson."

"Then I shall take the boys," I said decidedly. I am noted for my decision. "Since they have to grow up to be men it's well to train them properly betimes. Nuisances they are bound to become under any circumstances; but if they are taken in hand young enough they may not grow up to be such nuisances as they otherwise would and that will be some unfortunate woman's gain."

Mrs. Allan looked dubious. I knew she had expected me to choose the girls.

"They are a very wild set of boys," she said.

"I never knew boys who weren't," I retorted.

"I – I – think perhaps you would like the girls best," said Mrs. Allan hesitatingly. If it had not been for one thing – which I would never in this world have admitted to Mrs. Allan – I might have liked the girls' class best myself. But the truth was, Anne Shirley was in that class; and Anne Shirley was the one living human being that I was afraid of. Not that I disliked her. But she had such a habit of asking weird, unexpected questions, which a Philadelphia lawyer couldn't answer. Miss Rogerson had that class once and Anne routed her, horse, foot and artillery. *I* wasn't going to undertake a class with a walking interrogation point in it like that. Besides, I thought Mrs. Allan required a slight snub. Ministers' wives are rather apt to think they can run everything and everybody, if they are not wholesomely corrected now and again.

"It is not what *I* like best that must be considered, Mrs. Allan," I said rebukingly. "It is what is best for those boys. I feel that *I* shall be best for *them*."

"Oh, I've no doubt of that, Miss MacPherson," said Mrs. Allan amiably. It was a fib for her, minister's wife though she was. She *had* doubt. She thought I would be a dismal failure as teacher of a boys' class.

But I was not. I am not often a dismal failure when I make up my mind to do a thing. I am noted for that.

"It is wonderful what a reformation you have worked in that class, Miss MacPherson – wonderful," said the Rev. Mr. Allan some weeks later. He didn't mean to show how amazing a thing he thought it that an old maid noted for being a man hater should have managed it, but his face betrayed him.

"Where does Jimmy Spencer live?" I asked him crisply. "He came one Sunday three weeks ago and hasn't been back since. I mean to find out why."

Mr. Allan coughed.

"I believe he is hired as a handy boy with Alexander Abraham Bennett, out on the White Sands road," he said.

"Then I am going out to Alexander Abraham Bennett's on the White Sands road to see why Jimmy Spencer doesn't come to Sunday School," I said firmly.

Mr. Allan's eye twinkled ever so slightly. I have always insisted that if that man were not a minister he would have a sense of humour.

"Possibly Mr. Bennett will not appreciate your kind interest! He has – ah – a singular aversion to your sex, I understand. No woman has ever been known to get inside of Mr. Bennett's house since his sister died twenty years ago."

"Oh, he is the one, is he?" I said, remembering. "He is the woman hater who threatens that if a woman comes into his yard he'll chase her out with a pitchfork. Well, he will not chase *me* out!"

Mr. Allan gave a chuckle – a ministerial chuckle, but still a chuckle. It irritated me slightly, because it seemed to imply that he thought Alexander Abraham Bennett would be one too many for me. But I did not show Mr. Allan that he annoyed me. It is always a great mistake to let a man see that he can vex you.

The next afternoon I harnessed my sorrel pony to the buggy and drove down to Alexander Abraham Bennett's. As usual, I took William Adolphus with me for company. William Adolphus is my favourite among my six cats. He is black, with a white dicky and beautiful white paws. He sat up on the seat beside me and looked far more like a gentleman than many a man I've seen in a similar position.

Alexander Abraham's place was about three miles along the White Sands road. I knew the house as soon as I came to it by its neglected appearance. It needed paint badly; the blinds were crooked and torn; weeds grew up to the very door. Plainly, there was no woman about *that* place. Still, it was a nice house, and the barns were splendid. My father always said that when a man's barns were bigger than his house it was a sign that his income exceeded his expenditure. So it was all right that they should be bigger; but it was all wrong that they should be trimmer and better painted. Still, thought I, what else could you expect of a woman hater?

"But Alexander Abraham evidently knows how to run a farm, even if he is a woman hater," I remarked to William Adolphus as I got out and tied the pony to the railing.

I had driven up to the house from the back way and now I was opposite a side door opening on the veranda. I thought I might as well go to it, so I tucked William Adolphus under my arm and marched up the path. Just as I was halfway up a dog swooped around the front corner and made straight for me. He was the ugliest dog I had ever seen; and he didn't even bark – just came silently and speedily on, with a business-like eye.

I never stop to argue matters with a dog that doesn't bark. I know when discretion is the better part of valour. Firmly clasping William Adolphus, I ran – not to the door, because the dog was between me and it, but to a big, low-branching cherry tree at the back corner of the house. I reached it in time and no more. First thrusting William Adolphus on to a limb above my head, I scrambled up into that blessed tree without stopping to think how it might look to Alexander Abraham if he happened to be watching.

My time for reflection came when I found myself perched halfway up the tree with William Adolphus beside me. William Adolphus was quite calm and unruffled. I can hardly say with truthfulness that I was. On the contrary, I admit that I felt considerably upset.

The dog was sitting on his haunches on the ground below, watching us, and it was quite plain to be seen, from his leisurely manner, that it was not his busy day. He bared his teeth and growled when he caught my eye.

"You *look* like a woman hater's dog," I told him. I meant it for an insult; but the beast took it for a compliment.

Then I set myself to solving the question, "How am I to get out of this predicament?"

It did not seem easy to solve it.

"Shall I scream, William Adolphus?" I demanded of that intelligent animal. William Adolphus shook his head. This is a fact. And I agreed with him.

"No, I shall not scream, William Adolphus," I said. "There is probably no one to hear me except Alexander Abraham, and I have my painful doubts about his tender mercies. Now, it is impossible to go down. Is it, then, William Adolphus, possible to go up?"

I looked up. Just above my head was an open window with a tolerably stout branch extending right across it.

"Shall we try that way, William Adolphus?" I asked.

William Adolphus, wasting no words, began to climb the tree. I followed his example. The dog ran in circles about the tree and looked things not lawful to be uttered. It probably would have been a relief to him to bark if it hadn't been so against his principles.

I got in by the window easily enough, and found myself in a bedroom the like of which for disorder and dust and general awfulness I had never seen in all my life. But I did not pause to take in details. With William Adolphus under my arm I marched downstairs, fervently hoping I should meet no one on the way.

I did not. The hall below was empty and dusty. I opened the first door I came to and walked boldly in. A man was sitting by the window, looking moodily out. I should have known him for Alexander Abraham anywhere. He had just the same uncared-for, ragged appearance that the house had; and yet, like the house, it seemed that he would not be bad looking if he were trimmed up a little. His hair looked as if it had never been combed, and his whiskers were wild in the extreme.

He looked at me with blank amazement in his countenance.

"Where is Jimmy Spencer?" I demanded. "I have come to see him."

"How did he ever let you in?" asked the man, staring at me.

"He didn't let me in," I retorted. "He chased me all over the lawn, and I only saved myself from being torn piecemeal by scrambling up a tree. You ought to be prosecuted for keeping such a dog! Where is Jimmy?"

Instead of answering Alexander Abraham began to laugh in a most unpleasant fashion.

"Trust a woman for getting into a man's house if she had made up her mind to," he said disagreeably.

Seeing that it was his intention to vex me I remained cool and collected.

"Oh, I wasn't particular about getting into your house, Mr. Bennett," I said calmly. "I had but little choice in the matter. It was get in lest a worse fate befall me. It was not you or your house I wanted to see – although I admit that it is worth seeing if a person is anxious to find out how dirty a place *can* be. It was Jimmy. For the third and last time – where is Jimmy?"

"Jimmy is not here," said Mr. Bennett gruffly – but not quite so assuredly. "He left last week and hired with a man over at Newbridge."

"In that case," I said, picking up William Adolphus, who had been exploring the room with a disdainful air, "I won't disturb you any longer. I shall go."

"Yes, I think it would be the wisest thing," said Alexander Abraham – not disagreeably this time, but reflectively, as if there was some doubt about the matter. "I'll let you out by the back door. Then the – ahem! – the dog will not interfere with you. Please go away quietly and quickly."

I wondered if Alexander Abraham thought I would go away with a whoop. But I said nothing, thinking this the most dignified course of conduct, and I followed him out to the kitchen as quickly and quietly as he could have wished. Such a kitchen!

Alexander Abraham opened the door – which was locked – just as a buggy containing two men drove into the yard.

"Too late!" he exclaimed in a tragic tone. I understood that something dreadful must have happened, but I did not care, since, as I fondly supposed, it did not concern me. I pushed out past Alexander Abraham – who was looking as guilty as if he had been caught burglarizing – and came face to face with the man who had sprung from the buggy. It was old Dr. Blair, from

Carmody, and he was looking at me as if he had found me shoplifting.

"My dear Peter," he said gravely, "I am *very* sorry to see you here – very sorry indeed."

I admit that this exasperated me. Besides, no man on earth, not even my old family doctor, has any right to "My dear Peter" me!

"There is no loud call for sorrow, doctor," I said loftily. "If a woman, forty-eight years of age, a member of the Presbyterian Church in good and regular standing, cannot call upon one of her Sunday School scholars without wrecking all the proprieties, how old must she be before she can?"

The doctor did not answer my question. Instead, he looked reproachfully at Alexander Abraham.

"Is this how you keep your word, Mr. Bennett?" he said. "I thought that you promised me that you would not let anyone into the house."

"I didn't let her in," growled Mr. Bennett. "Good heavens, man, she climbed in at an upstairs window, despite the presence on my grounds of a policeman and a dog! What is to be done with a woman like that?"

"I do not understand what all this means," I said, addressing myself to the doctor and ignoring Alexander Abraham entirely, "but if my presence here is so extremely inconvenient to all concerned you can soon be relieved of it. I am going at once."

"I am very sorry, my dear Peter," said the doctor impressively, "but that is just what I cannot allow you to do. This house is under quarantine for smallpox. You will have to stay here."

Smallpox! For the first and last time in my life I openly lost my temper with a man. I wheeled furiously upon Alexander Abraham.

"Why didn't you tell me?" I cried.

"Tell you!" he said, glaring at me. "When I first saw you it was too late to tell you. I thought the kindest thing I could do was to hold my tongue and let you get away in happy ignorance. This will teach you to take a man's house by storm, madam!"

"Now, now, don't quarrel, my good people." Interposed the doctor seriously – but I saw a twinkle in his eye. "You'll have to spend some time together under the same roof and you won't improve the situation by disagreeing. You see, Peter, it was this way. Mr. Bennett was in town yesterday – where, as you are aware, there is a bad outbreak of smallpox – and took dinner in a boarding-house where one of the maids was ill. Last night she developed unmistakable symptoms of smallpox. The Board of Health at once got after all the people who were in the house yesterday, so far as they could locate them, and put them under quarantine. I came down here this morning and explained the matter to Mr. Bennett. I brought Jeremiah Jeffries to guard the front of the house and Mr. Bennett gave me his word of honour that he would not let anyone in by the back way while I went to get another policeman and make all the necessary arrangements. I have brought Thomas Wright and have secured the services of another man to attend to Mr. Bennett's barn work and bring provisions to the house. Jacob Green and Cleophas Lee will watch at night. I don't think there is much danger of Mr. Bennett's taking the smallpox, but until we are sure you must remain here, Peter."

While listening to the doctor I had been thinking. It was the most distressing predicament I had ever got into in my life, but there was no sense in making it worse.

"Very well, Doctor," I said calmly. "Yes, I was vaccinated a month ago, when the news of the smallpox first came. When you go back through Avonlea kindly go to Sarah Pye and ask her to live in my house during my absence and look after things, especially the cats. Tell her to give them new milk twice a day and a square inch of butter apiece once a week. Get her to put my two dark print wrappers, some aprons, and some changes of underclothing in my third best valise and have it sent down to me. My pony is tied out there to the fence. Please take him home. That is all, I think."

"No, it isn't all," said Alexander Abraham grumpily. "Send that cat home, too. I won't have a cat around the place – I'd rather have the smallpox."

I looked Alexander Abraham over gradually, in a way I have, beginning at his feet and travelling up to his head. I took my time over it; and then I said, very quietly, "You may have both. Anyway, you'll have to have William Adolphus. He is under quarantine as well as you and I. Do you suppose I am going to have my cat ranging at large through Avonlea, scattering smallpox germs among innocent people? I'll have to put up with that dog of yours. You will have to endure William Adolphus."

Alexander Abraham groaned, but I could see that the way I had looked him over had chastened him considerably.

The doctor drove away, and I went into the house, not choosing to linger outside and be grinned at by Thomas Wright. I hung my coat up in the hall and laid my bonnet carefully on the sitting-room table, having first dusted a clean place for it with my handkerchief. I longed to fall upon that house at once and clean it up, but I had to wait until the doctor came back with my wrapper. I could not clean house in my new suit and a silk shirtwaist.

Alexander Abraham was sitting on a chair looking at me. Presently he said,

"I am *not* curious – but will you kindly tell me why the doctor called you Peter?"

"Because that is my name, I suppose," I answered, shaking up a cushion for William Adolphus and thereby disturbing the dust of years.

Alexander Abraham coughed gently.

"Isn't that – ahem! – rather a peculiar name for a woman?"

"It is," I said, wondering how much soap, if any, there was in the house.

"I am *not* curious," said Alexander Abraham, "but would you mind telling me how you came to be called Peter?"

"If I had been a boy my parents intended to call me Peter in honour of a rich uncle. When I – fortunately – turned out to be a girl my mother insisted that I should be called Angelina. They gave me both names and called me Angelina, but as soon as I grew old enough I decided to be called Peter. It was bad enough, but not so bad as Angelina."

"I should say it was more appropriate," said Alexander Abraham, intending, as I perceived, to be disagreeable.

"Precisely," I agreed calmly. "My last name is MacPherson, and I live in Avonlea. As you are *not* curious, that will be all the information you will need about me."

"Oh!" Alexander Abraham looked as if a light had broken in on him. "I've heard of you. You – ah – pretend to dislike men."

Pretend! Goodness only knows what would have happened to Alexander Abraham just then if a diversion had not taken place. But the door opened and a dog came in – *the* dog. I suppose he had got tired waiting under the cherry tree for William Adolphus and me to come down. He was even uglier indoors than out.

"Oh, Mr. Riley, Mr. Riley, see what you have let me in for," said Alexander Abraham reproachfully.

But Mr. Riley – since that was the brute's name – paid no attention to Alexander Abraham. He had caught sight of William Adolphus curled up on the cushion, and he started across the room to investigate him. William Adolphus sat up and began to take notice.

"Call off that dog," I said warningly to Alexander Abraham.

"Call him off yourself," he retorted. "Since you've brought that cat here you can protect him."

"Oh, it wasn't for William Adolphus' sake I spoke," I said pleasantly. "William Adolphus can protect himself."

William Adolphus could and did. He humped his back, flattened his ears, swore once, and then made a flying leap for Mr. Riley. William Adolphus landed squarely on Mr. Riley's brindled back and promptly took fast hold, spitting and clawing and caterwauling.

You never saw a more astonished dog than Mr. Riley. With a yell of terror he bolted out to the kitchen, out of the kitchen into the hall, through the hall into the room, and so into the kitchen and round again. With each circuit he went faster and faster, until he looked like a brindled streak with a dash of black and white on top. Such a racket and commotion I never heard, and I laughed until the tears came into my eyes. Mr. Riley flew around and around, and William Adolphus held on grimly and clawed. Alexander Abraham turned purple with rage.

"Woman, call off that infernal cat before he kills my dog," he shouted above the din of yelps and yowls.

"Oh, he won't kill him," I said reassuringly, "and he's going too fast to hear me if I did call him. If you can stop the dog, Mr. Bennett, I'll guarantee to make William Adolphus listen to reason, but there's no use trying to argue with a lightning flash."

Alexander Abraham made a frantic lunge at the brindled streak as it whirled past him, with the result that he overbalanced himself and went sprawling on the floor with a crash. I ran to help him up, which only seemed to enrage him further.

"Woman," he spluttered viciously, "I wish you and your fiend of a cat were in – in – "

"In Avonlea," I finished quickly, to save Alexander Abraham from committing profanity. "So do I, Mr. Bennett, with all my heart. But since we are not, let us make the best of it like sensible people. And in future you will kindly remember that my name is Miss MacPherson, *not* Woman!"

With this the end came and I was thankful, for the noise those two animals made was so terrific that I expected the policeman would be rushing in, smallpox or no smallpox, to see if Alexander Abraham and I were trying to murder each other. Mr. Riley suddenly veered in his mad career and bolted into a dark corner between the stove and the wood-box. William Adolphus let go just in time.

There never was any more trouble with Mr. Riley after that. A meeker, more thoroughly chastened dog you could not find. William Adolphus had the best of it and he kept it.

Seeing that things had calmed down and that it was five o'clock I decided to get tea. I told Alexander Abraham that I would prepare it, if he would show me where the eatables were.

"You needn't mind," said Alexander Abraham. "I've been in the habit of getting my own tea for twenty years."

"I daresay. But you haven't been in the habit of getting mine," I said firmly. "I wouldn't eat anything you cooked if I starved to death. If you want some occupation you'd better get some salve and anoint the scratches on that poor dog's back."

Alexander Abraham said something that I prudently did not hear. Seeing that he had no information to hand out I went on an exploring expedition into the pantry. The place was awful beyond description, and for the first time a vague sentiment of pity for Alexander Abraham glimmered in my breast. When a man had to live in such surroundings the wonder was, not that he hated women, but that he didn't hate the whole human race.

But I got up a supper somehow. I am noted for getting up suppers. The bread was from the Carmody bakery and I made good tea and excellent toast; besides, I found a can of peaches in the pantry which, as they were bought, I wasn't afraid to eat.

That tea and toast mellowed Alexander Abraham in spite of himself. He ate the last crust, and didn't growl when I gave William Adolphus all the cream that was left. Mr. Riley did not seem to want anything. He had no appetite.

By this time the doctor's boy had arrived with my valise. Alexander Abraham gave me quite civilly to understand that there was a spare room across the hall and that I might take possession of it. I went to it and put on a wrapper. There was a set of fine furniture in the room, and a comfortable bed. But the dust! William Adolphus had followed me in and his paws left marks everywhere he walked.

"Now," I said briskly, returning to the kitchen, "I'm going to clean up and I shall begin with this kitchen. You'd better betake yourself to the sitting-room, Mr. Bennett, so as to be out of the way."

Alexander Abraham glared at me.

"I'm not going to have my house meddled with," he snapped. "It suits me. If you don't like it you can leave it."

"No, I can't. That is just the trouble," I said pleasantly. "If I could leave it I shouldn't be here for a minute. Since I can't, it simply has to be cleaned. I can tolerate men and dogs when I am compelled to, but I cannot and will not tolerate dirt and disorder. Go into the sitting-room."

Alexander Abraham went. As he closed the door, I heard him say, in capitals, "WHAT AN AWFUL WOMAN!"

I cleaned that kitchen and the pantry adjoining. It was ten o'clock when I got through, and Alexander Abraham had gone to bed without deigning further speech. I locked Mr. Riley in one room and William Adolphus in another and went to bed, too. I had never felt so dead tired in my life before. It had been a hard day.

But I got up bright and early the next morning and got a tiptop breakfast, which Alexander Abraham condescended to eat. When the provision man came into the yard I called to him from the window to bring me a box of soap in the afternoon, and then I tackled the sitting-room.

It took me the best part of a week to get that house in order, but I did it thoroughly. I am noted for doing things thoroughly. At the end of the time it was clean from garret to cellar. Alexander Abraham made no comments on my operations, though he groaned loud and often, and said caustic things to poor Mr. Riley, who hadn't the spirit to answer back after his drubbing by William Adolphus. I made allowances for Alexander Abraham because his vaccination had taken and his arm was real sore; and I cooked elegant meals, not having much else to do, once I had got things scoured up. The house was full of provisions – Alexander Abraham wasn't mean about such things, I will say that for him. Altogether, I was more comfortable than I had expected to be. When Alexander Abraham wouldn't talk I let him alone; and when he would I just said as sarcastic things as he did, only I said them smiling and pleasant. I could see he had a wholesome awe of me. But now and then he seemed to forget his disposition and talked like a human being. We had one or two real interesting conversations. Alexander Abraham was an intelligent man, though he had got terribly warped. I told him once I thought he must have been nice when he was a boy.

One day he astonished me by appearing at the dinner table with his hair brushed and a white collar on. We had a tiptop dinner that day, and I had made a pudding that was far too good for a woman hater. When Alexander Abraham had disposed of two large platefuls of it, he sighed and said, "You can certainly cook. It's a pity you are such a detestable crank in other respects."

"It's kind of convenient being a crank," I said. "People are careful how they meddle with you. Haven't you found that out in your own experience?"

"I am *not* a crank," growled Alexander Abraham resentfully. "All I ask is to be let alone."

"That's the very crankiest kind of a crank," I said. "A person who wants to be let alone flies in the face of Providence, who decreed that folks for their own good were not to be let alone. But cheer up, Mr. Bennett. The quarantine will be up on Tuesday and then you'll certainly be let alone for the rest of your natural life, as far as William Adolphus and I are concerned. You may then return to your wallowing in the mire and be as dirty and comfortable as of yore."

Alexander Abraham growled again. The prospect didn't seem to cheer him up as much as I should have expected. Then he did an amazing thing. He poured some cream into a saucer and set it down before William Adolphus. William Adolphus lapped it up, keeping one eye on Alexander Abraham lest the latter should change his mind. Not to be outdone, I handed Mr. Riley a bone.

Neither Alexander Abraham nor I had worried much about the smallpox. We didn't believe he would take it, for he hadn't even seen the girl who was sick. But the very next morning I heard him calling me from the upstairs landing.

"Miss MacPherson," he said in a voice so uncommonly mild that it gave me an uncanny feeling, "what are the symptoms of smallpox?"

"Chills and flushes, pain in the limbs and back, nausea and vomiting." I answered promptly, for I had been reading them up in a patent medicine almanac.

"I've got them all," said Alexander Abraham hollowly.

I didn't feel as much scared as I should have expected. After enduring a woman hater and a brindled dog and the early disorder of that house – and coming off best with all three – small pox seemed rather insignificant. I went to the window and called to Thomas Wright to send for the doctor.

The doctor came down from Alexander Abraham's room looking grave.

"It's impossible to pronounce on the disease yet," he said. "There is no certainty until the eruption appears. But, of course, there is every likelihood that it is the smallpox. It is very unfortunate. I am afraid that it will be difficult to get a nurse. All the nurses in town who will take smallpox cases are overbusy now, for the epidemic is still raging there. However, I'll go into town tonight and do my best. Meanwhile, as Mr. Bennett does not require any attendance at present, you must not go near him, Peter."

I wasn't going to take orders from any man, and as soon as the doctor had gone I marched straight up to Alexander Abraham's room with some dinner for him on a tray. There was a lemon cream I thought he could eat even if he had the smallpox.

"You shouldn't come near me," he growled. "You are risking your life."

"I am not going to see a fellow creature starve to death, even if he is a man," I retorted.

"The worst of it all," groaned Alexander Abraham, between mouthfuls of lemon cream, "is that the doctor says I've got to have a nurse. I've got so kind of used to you being in the house that I don't mind you, but the thought of another woman coming here is too much. Did you give my poor dog anything to eat?"

"He has had a better dinner than many a Christian," I said severely.

Alexander Abraham need not have worried about another woman coming in. The doctor came back that night with care on his brow.

"I don't know what is to be done," he said. "I can't get a soul to come here."

"*I* shall nurse Mr. Bennett," I said with dignity. "It is my duty and I never shirk my duty. I am noted for that. He is a man, and he has smallpox, and he keeps a vile dog; but I am not going to see him die for lack of care for all that."

"You're a good soul, Peter," said the doctor, looking relieved, manlike, as soon as he found a woman to shoulder the responsibility.

I nursed Alexander Abraham through the smallpox, and I didn't mind it much. He was much more amiable sick than well, and he had the disease in a very mild form. Below stairs I reigned supreme and Mr. Riley and William Adolphus lay down together like the lion and the lamb. I fed Mr. Riley regularly, and once, seeing him looking lonesome, I patted him gingerly. It was nicer than I thought it would be. Mr. Riley lifted his head and looked at me with an expression in his eyes which cured me of wondering why on earth Alexander Abraham was so fond of the beast.

When Alexander Abraham was able to sit up he began to make up for the time he'd lost being pleasant. Anything more sarcastic than that man in his convalescence you couldn't imagine. I just laughed at him, having found out that that could be depended on to irritate him. To irritate him still further I cleaned the house all over again. But what vexed him most of all was that Mr. Riley took to following me about and wagging what he had of a tail at me.

"It wasn't enough that you should come into my peaceful home and turn it upside down, but you have to alienate the affections of my dog," complained Alexander Abraham.

"He'll get fond of you again when I go home," I said comfortingly. "Dogs aren't very particular that way. What they want is bones. Cats now, they love disinterestedly. William Adolphus has never swerved in his allegiance to me, although you do give him cream in the pantry on the sly."

Alexander Abraham looked foolish. He hadn't thought I knew that.

I didn't take the smallpox and in another week the doctor came out and sent the policeman home. I was disinfected and William Adophus was fumigated, and then we were free to go.

"Good-bye, Mr. Bennett," I said, offering to shake hands in a forgiving spirit. "I've no doubt that you are glad to be rid of me, but you are no gladder than I am to go. I suppose this house will be dirtier than ever in a month's time, and Mr. Riley will have discarded the little polish his manners have taken on. Reformation with men and dogs never goes very deep."

With this Parthian shaft I walked out of the house, supposing that I had seen the last of it and Alexander Abraham.

I was glad to get back home, of course; but it did seem queer and lonesome. The cats hardly knew me, and William Adolphus roamed about forlornly and appeared to feel like an exile. I didn't take as much pleasure in cooking as usual, for it seemed kind of foolish to be fussing over oneself. The sight of a bone made me think of poor Mr. Riley. The neighbours avoided me pointedly, for they couldn't get rid of the fear that I might erupt into smallpox at any moment. My Sunday School class had been given to another woman, and altogether I felt as if I didn't belong anywhere.

I had existed like this for a fortnight when Alexander Abraham suddenly appeared. He walked in one evening at dusk, but at first sight I didn't know him he was so spruced and barbered up. But William Adolphus knew him. Will you believe it, William Adolphus, my own William Adolphus, rubbed up against that man's trouser leg with an undisguised purr of satisfaction.

"I had to come, Angelina," said Alexander Abraham. "I couldn't stand it any longer."

"My name is Peter," I said coldly, although I was feeling ridiculously glad about something.

"It isn't," said Alexander Abraham stubbornly. "It is Angelina for me, and always will be. I shall never call you Peter. Angelina just suits you exactly; and Angelina Bennett would suit you still better. You must come back, Angelina. Mr. Riley is moping for you, and I can't get along without somebody to appreciate my sarcasms, now that you have accustomed me to the luxury."

"What about the other five cats?" I demanded.

Alexander Abraham sighed.

"I suppose they'll have to come too," he sighed, "though no doubt they'll chase poor Mr. Riley clean off the premises. But I can live without him, and I can't without you. How soon can you be ready to marry me?"

"I haven't said that I was going to marry you at all, have I?" I said tartly, just to be consistent. For I wasn't feeling tart.

"No, but you will, won't you?" said Alexander Abraham anxiously. "Because if you won't I wish you'd let me die of the smallpox. Do, dear Angelina."

To think that a man should dare to call me his "dear Angelina!" And to think that I shouldn't mind!

"Where I go, William Adophus goes," I said, "but I shall give away the other five cats for – for the sake of Mr. Riley."

MAZO DE LA ROCHE

OLD REYNARD IN SPRINGTIME

It was a pity to leave the garden on this March day, for it was springing with a new, a varied life. All the little spring flowers were singing together, some with their faces just visible above the spears of grass, others swaying on such delicate stems that they seemed at any moment ready to fly skyward.

Their song must surely have been audible to the goldfish in the pond, for they showed a new vivacity in their movements and the largest leapt clear of the water, with a flourish of his spear-shaped tail. There are seven goldfish, and my children have named them for the days of the week. The one which had just leapt is called "Sunday," and so they are graduated down to little "Saturday Pence," for Saturday cannot be separated from the thought of the weekly allowance of tuppence apiece.

It needed no sensitive ear of a goldfish to hear the song of the birds. The missel thrush, perched among the glistening buds of the magnolia tree, poured out his heavenly chatter, and the blackbird whistled richly. In the deep shadow of the trees the ringdove gave forth the sulky sweetness of his call.

How beautiful the trees were in their fine new leafage! Even the pines had a new shine on their needles. The weeping beech trees, which send long trailers drooping to the ground, were forming their thin, satiny leaves. "Like the leaves of my new prayer book," said my little girl, and she could pay them no higher compliment.

Ours is rather a grim-looking house, despite the ivy that enfolds it, but it stands on a lovely slope which rises to the mystery of a wood. Up this slope the daffodils were uncovering their golden heads in a brave procession, and in the wood the stalks of the bluebells swelled as they drew up moisture from the deep, rich earth.

Halfway up the slope there is a thatched summerhouse, and an old sundial bearing the words: "Make the passing shadow work thy will." They seemed stern words to me on this blowy soft March morning. How could I make a shadow work my will? And I but another shadow! The motto was better suited to that noted engineer who once lived here. He built Jubilee Drive that climbs the hills to the Herefordshire Beacon, in commemoration of Queen Victoria's Golden Jubilee. Just beside the sundial a large, thrice-circling hoop of iron hangs from the spreading branch of an oak. In those days the engineer's servants used to beat on this to summon him from across the valley to his forgotten meals.

I had a fancy to hear its voice speak again. I picked up a stone and struck the hoops sharply. I made them sound their heavy note again and again. Then silence came, and regret. I had frightened the birds. Silence lay thick among the trees. A bloom like the bloom on grapes lay there – silence made palpable.

Then a new sound, as though an echo of the gong, rose from a neighbouring wood. Our two puppies came running along the mossy path and looked eagerly up into my face. The Scottie's tail was a tense question mark above his muscular haunches, the Cairn's eyes were luminous under a fringe of mouse-coloured hair. "The hounds!" tail and eyes said to me, as plain as words could speak. "The hounds are baying and we want to go to the Hunt!"

I had their leads looped over my arm, and before they could run off again I fastened the Scottie's plaid collar round his neck and slipped on the Cairn's green harness. The Scottie lay prostrate, grinning up at me. Little shivers ran over the Cairn. When we set off they trotted so close together that their sides touched – the one jogging like a pony, the other moving with smooth slinky grace.

A rabbit darted across the path and there were two simultaneous tugs at the leads. The rabbit disappeared into the rhododendrons and again that sad sweet music of the hounds came on the breeze. We trotted along the path to the iron gate that stands at the back of the grounds. We followed another path to the public road and climbed the steep hill toward the Wyche, with far ahead the Worchestershire Beacon hunched against the blue sky.

We were not the only ones who had heard the baying of the hounds. When we neared the top of the hill, where there is a scattering of small houses, I saw that out of each women and children had come and were standing fascinated, their eyes fixed on a copse on the steep above. Two youths on bicycles had dismounted; two more had clambered down from the seat of a lorry; a farmer had drawn up his pony and sat looking on from the seat of his gig. A man raking in a garden, a labourer digging a drain, threw down their tools and joined us others who had gathered by a low stone wall on which we could rest our arms. I lifted the Scottie and the Cairn on to it and all stared at the copse from where the sound of a horn now rose.

Yet, while we fixed our eyes on this small space, a spacious panorama was spread before us, hill upon hill, fold upon fold, embracing the lovely valleys, encircling the fields where flocks of black-faced sheep grazed. And in the distance the sunlight silvered the black mountains of Wales.

"There he is!" cried one of the youths, and "Yon's the fox!" called a woman, holding up her child to see.

Across a pale-green field he flashed – a bronze arrow of fear. The hounds came tumbling out of the copse after him, in a stream of liver and white, their bellies close to the ground, their throats swelling with the bell-like notes. And after the hounds the horses with flying manes and streaming tails, their riders in pink or brown or grey, stretched their powerful legs across the tender grass.

"This is the last day of the huntin'," observed an old man at my side. "If he gets away today he's safe till autumn." The man's voice expressed neither hope that the fox would escape nor desire that he should be caught. It expressed, in its rich Herefordshire accent, only complete satisfaction in the spectacle before him and complete acquiescence in its finish – whatever that might be.

Suddenly the hounds showed bewilderment; they became silent and scattered themselves across the field. The horses slackened to a trot. The fox had disappeared into some undergrowth that fringed a little stream. A bird began to sing timidly. The Scottie and the Cairn became restive; they looked questioningly into my face. The old man gave it as his opinion that the fox had gone to earth. A gentle spring sweetness rose from the land over which the ancestors of this same fox and these hounds had raced for many generations.

Then a hound raised up his voice and all the pack joined in the clamour. The horn sounded. The Whip shouted. The scent was again strong.

"Look! Look! There he is! By gum, he's coming straight this way!" Excited voices rose all about me. Then I saw the fox.

He came down the hillside toward us, clearly seen by us but still invisible to the Hunt. He came at an easy trot, not spending himself, his head turning warily from left to right as he sought for escape. He showed no fear at the sight of all these people, but drew nearer in his soft, loping trot, his pointed muzzle turning this way and that.

For a moment he disappeared, but again we saw him, now posed on the top of the wall surrounding a cottage garden. A woman stood in the doorway, staring at him open-mouthed. She had been feeding her fowls, which were pecking at the corn, oblivious of the nearness of their enemy.

He hesitated, turning his bright gaze on them, as though he had a mind to pick one up on his way, but the baying of the hounds rose from the other side of the wall and he moved delicately across the vegetable garden. The gate stood open and he trotted through it, like an accustomed visitor, on to the road where we stood.

I have seen foxes in captivity, foxes stuffed, and many skins of foxes, but he was the handsomest I have ever seen. He was large, in beautiful condition, sleek and graceful. His fur was a lovely red russet, and strength and experienced maturity were in every movement.

He gave us a glance, half sneering, wholly self-contained, and crossed the road. I felt the bodies of the terriers rigid against my side. Their hackles rose. The Scottie gave a loud yell of fury as the fox clambered over the wall near us, and struggled to be after him. The Cairn lifted his lip and turned his pretty little face into a mask of hate.

Now through a farm gate the Hunt poured, in a confusion of hounds, horses, and pink coats, into the road. The sides of the horses were heaving; foam flecked their bright coats. I knew some of the riders, but they passed, seeing nothing outside the chase, excepting one, an elderly man who came last and shut the gate after them. He recognized me and touched his cap with his crop. "He's a tough old rascal," he exclaimed. "He's been hunted a dozen times this season." He himself looked tough-sinewed and wiry. The skin of his thin aquiline face was weatherbeaten and red. The sleeves of his coat were too short – his red wrists protruded; and he had evidently had a fall, for his back was plastered with mud.

Now old Reynard stretched his supple length in desperate need. He flew down the green slope with the hounds baying closer to the red plume of his tail. Their voices had become hysterical, half mad with the lust to tear him to pieces. The horses thundered after the hounds, rising to jump a thorn hedge under which he had slipped. The hounds pressed, whimpering at the delay, through a thorny gap. A young boy was thrown from his pony, but he captured it, remounted, and went boldly after the others.

We, at the top, looked down on the scene, not with godlike impartiality, but heart and soul for the escape of the fox. There had been something in the way he had looked at us. He had taken us into his confidence. "See me!" he had seemed to say. "Watch how I will diddle them!"

We could see his russet body flying across a smooth meadow – too smooth, for it meant that the hounds gained on him. But ahead was a wood, and if he could win that he might have a chance.

"Ah, I do hope he gets away!" cried the woman whose garden he had passed through. "He came that near me I could have touched him and he'd such bright eyes!"

Now the fox did a strange thing. He turned aside and glided into the sparse undergrowth by the edge of the stream. He seemed to be throwing away his one chance of escape. The hounds ran here and there, muzzles snuffling, tails waving. Then one raised his voice, the others jostled him, and again they were off. They disappeared into the wood.

"'Twas a master stroke," said the man at my side. "He came on the scent of another fox and crossed it to save his own skin! He's thrown the hounds off the scent. I warrant they'll never get him now."

It was true. Up the hill side to the right we saw the old fox gliding. There was no mistaking his unusual colour, his size, the almost studied grace of his movements. But he moved slowly now. He was very tired.

In the valley the tumult went on. It came mysteriously out of the wood, invisible to us except for the occasional gleam of a polished flank, the flash of a pink coat. The silent hills unrolled themselves, fold upon fold, dark green upon pale green, blue upon purple, purple on the azure horizon.

At last beyond the wood we saw the Hunt flash out and stream across the fields. We saw the hounds slither across the stepping stones of a stream, the horses arched above it for a spectacular moment. The horn sounded faintly, the bright colours dissolved into the colours of hedge and mead.

"My goodness!" exclaimed the cottage woman. "I thought he was for snatching one of my hens! But just the same I'm glad he got away!"

"Him's a noble-looking feller," said the old man. "'Tis to be hoped he breeds more of his kind this year."

More of his kind to be hunted! More of his kind to strain with breaking hearts to reach the haven of their burrows or be torn to pieces! Little cubs, playing at their mother's side through the summer days – reared for this tragic culmination of their strength and speed!

Was it better, I wondered, to be born for this than never to be born at all? For certainly it is the Hunt which preserves the fox. If it were not for the Hunt the farmers would soon demand his extermination, as he increased in boldness and numbers. I thought of old Reynard, now stretched at ease, his breathing gradually becoming tranquil, the baying of the hounds no more than the faint ringing of a distant bell; his woods, his meadows, safe for the summer. Yes, it was better to be born to suffer in the beauty of this world than not to be born at all.

I had lifted the puppies from the wall. The Scottie was already engaged in digging a hole. The Cairn was submitting coyly to the advances of a woman in a Burberry coat. The little group of people was already dispersed. Bicycle, lorry, and cart were continuing their way.

As we went toward home my mind turned to the first meet of the season on a day last November. The meet had been at Barton Court and we had gone, packed in our car. The children's kindergarten class had been given a holiday; so had the boys of the nearby preparatory school. It was a chill morning, but there was rich colour on the countryside. The beech mast lay thick beneath the great smooth-boled trees, the russet oak leaves clung sparsely to the wide branches. Sheep grazed close together on the rimy green pastures. A roan pony drew wisps of hay from a shapely new rick.

When we had arrived most of the Hunt was already gathered at the Court. Plates of sandwiches and plum cake, glasses of cherry brandy, were being passed to those who rode and those who came as onlookers. The children ran to join their little friends. Indoors our host was talking to villagers who were enjoying the unusual treat of plum cake and coffee in mid-morning.

The cobbles of the yard were wet and slippery; the horses sidled on them impatiently, while their riders cajoled or shouted at them. The dappled hounds stood shoulder to shoulder, gently surging, like a gathering wave. A deep undertone of excitement stirred through all.

Now the hunting season was over. There was peace for the hunted.

ETHEL WILSON

I Just Love Dogs

Well, said my friend from Vancouver, one Saturday I had lunch at the Club, you know, the Ladies' Club. I was leaving, and had just turned the corner of Dunsmuir Street, going down to Granville Street (that's our principal business street), and there, right out on the sidewalk beside the bank building, on the corner of Granville and Dunsmuir, but up a bit, lay the body of an enormous yellow-haired collie, apparently very old, and it was all stiff-looking. A beautiful dead dog.

There was no one near but an old lady with a string bag and little parcels, and she was poking the dog with her walking-stick, and saying, Poor dog, poor dog, what a shame to leave it here. And I felt just the same, and I said, Oh, dear, the poor dog, what can we do? And she said, I don't know, dearie, but someone ought to get the Society for the Prevention of Cruelty to Animals. Oh, yes, I said, someone ought to telephone Inspector Snape at once. (I wanted her to know that I knew about the S.P.C.A., too, and who was the head of it, and everything.) The old lady said quite simply, Inspector Snape is dead, he has been dead for over six months. I felt rather taken aback, because I'd been so pleased about knowing about Inspector Snape, but I said, Oh, well, it's no good telephoning Inspector Snape. All this time the old lady kept on poking the dog in different parts, but he never stirred. We felt just terrible, he was such a lovely dog.

Then the old lady said, Inspector Perkins, he's the new man. And I said, Oh, yes, someone ought to telephone Inspector

Perkins then, and the old lady said, Well, dearie, I'd go and telephone Inspector Perkins in a minute, only my husband is sick in bed, has been for three days. He gets these attacks, so I don't think I'd better telephone Inspector Perkins. Couldn't you do that, dearie? I was just trying to work that out in my head when a lady came up in a purple velvet hat. Oh, she said, look at the poor dog! Isn't that dreadful, and such a lovely dog, too. My, she said. I just love dogs. I'm crazy about dogs. I like dogs a whole lot better than I like people. The old lady with the string bag and I said, yes, indeed, we did too, and I think we all felt a bit better after that. But, there lay the dog, all stiff.

This is terrible, said the lady in the purple hat, this beautiful dog lying here dead, and nobody doing one thing. And she looked round at me and at the old lady with the string bag, who kept on prodding the dog's ear with her walking-stick. I don't know why she kept on doing that.

So I said, yes, indeed, it was terrible, and someone ought to telephone the S.P.C.A. So the lady in the purple hat looked very stern and very practical and said yes, that someone ought to telephone Inspector Snape at once. So the old lady and I said, both speaking together, But Inspector Snape is dead, he has been dead for over six months. The lady in the purple hat seemed a little taken aback by this. But, we said, there is Inspector Perkins, and she said, Oh, well then, we must telephone Inspector Perkins at once.

Well, dearie, said the old lady, who was still prodding the body of the dog, and he certainly was a lovely dog, I'd go, only I don't feel that I can. I'd go in a minute, she said, only my husband is sick in bed. He has been for three days, and I think if you and this young lady (she meant me) went, it would be nice.

Just then some young men came up, and they said, Gosh, look at the dead dog, but they didn't seem to mean to do anything about it. They just stood and looked at the body of the dog. That seemed to make the lady in the purple hat very very angry, and she said, Well, anyway I am going to telephone Inspector Perkins, and I said, I will go, too. Let us go together, I said, let us go across to the Supreme Drug Store and telephone Inspector Perkins on the pay phone. And the old lady said, Yes, do, dearie, and I will stay here with the dog.

So the lady in the purple hat and I went across the road to the Supreme Drug Store, and left the old lady and the young men standing beside the dog. The old lady was still poking it here and there with her stick, and she seemed by this time to be sort of owning the dog, and in a way, I suppose, it was her dog, as she'd found it first. And the crowd was growing round the dog, and people were saying oh, what a pity, what a beautiful dog, why doesn't someone do something.

But the lady in the purple hat and I felt, I think, that we were the kind of people who really do things, though I'm sure I wouldn't have known what to do if it hadn't been for her. Well, we hurried across the street to the Supreme Drug Store, and all the way she kept saying how fond she was of dogs, and I said I was, too. And she said she loved her dog far better than she loved most human beings. In fact, she loved her dog far, far better than she loved her older brother, and I tried to think of something equally strong to say, only we haven't got a dog, and by the time we reached the pay phone in the Supreme Drug Store, you'd think we both hated the whole human race, and thought dogs should be in parliament.

I am shy anyway about speaking to strangers, very shy, even on the telephone, so I said, Please do let me give you this nickel, and then you can speak to Inspector Snape – no – Perkins. And she said, Oh no, I wouldn't think of it, and I said, No, really, you must. So by the time we had talked about the nickel quite a bit, she put my nickel in the pay phone, and got Inspector Perkins's office. He wasn't at his office, this being

Saturday. So I found another nickel, and she got his house, and he was away for the week-end, and so was Mrs. Perkins, the maid said.

She was very very angry at this. I felt quite angry too, and the lady in the purple hat said it was an outrage, and what was to prevent a valuable dog from dying on a Saturday afternoon, and there was the head of the S.P.C.A. away for the week-end. So I said it was an outrage too, and whatever should we do?

So she said, I'm going straight up Granville Street, two blocks, till I come to the traffic policeman, and I'm going to bring him right down here, whether he wants to or not, and see that something is done about this, and right away too. She was very very angry. Yes do, I said, because I knew I would never sound angry enough to make any traffic policeman leave his place, I should just make it sound silly, so I said, Yes, do, and I will go back to the dog.

By this time the lady in the purple hat and I were feeling very important only she was feeling more important than I was, because I can never manage to feel as important as other people, although I do try, and she set off, her eyes flashing, and round the corner and up Granville Street, which was very very crowded, and I went back across to the dog.

When I arrived back at the dog a large crowd had gathered, and the old lady with the string bag was giving a kind of lecture to all the people, and poking with her stick, and when she saw me coming, she pointed at me with her stick, and all the people turned and looked at me, and I still tried to feel important. But when all the people looked at me, I stopped feeling important at once and blushed and explained about the lady in the purple hat going for the policeman, and all the people said, oh, what a good thing, and what a valuable dog, and wasn't it too bad!

Just at that moment I heard the queerest whistle, you know, the kind of whistle that families have, and boys, like a signal it was. Well, it was a special kind of whistle, like that, and done twice. We all turned and looked, and there, driving up Dunsmuir Street from Granville Street was a large car, driven by a young man, and the back door was open. The young man drove slower and slower, as he reached the crowd, and at the same moment as the young man whistled the second time, the dog sprang to its feet and wagged its tail – my, he had a marvellous tail – and shot through the crowd and into the car. And the boy slammed the door and drove quickly away. The car had an Oklahoma licence. Everyone was too astonished to speak. It was the queerest feeling. A minute ago there had been the dog dead, as you might say, and us all bound together, feeling very important, and very sorry about the dog, and the next minute there was the dog alive and gone, and us all feeling pretty silly.

Well, I hadn't time but to think how funny it all was, and I turned to speak to the old lady with the string bag. But she was away up Dunsmuir Street, walking very fast with her stick. And all the crowd just wasn't there, and where the dog had been was nothing, and there was just me. And I looked quickly towards Granville Street to see if the lady with the purple hat was coming, very angry, with the policeman, and no doubt the policeman very angry, too, and I couldn't see her in the crowds of people walking up and down Granville Street. So I went very quickly to where my car was parked and drove home.

And when I told my husband that evening, all he said was for me to cultivate that dog's disposition. He said that dog had fine qualities. But I didn't get over feeling silly for days, and I was so mad at myself that I hadn't even gone into a store and watched for the lady in the purple hat and the policeman exploding at each other down Granville Street to where there was no dog.

MORLEY CALLAGHAN

THE LITTLE BUSINESSMAN

That summer when twelve-year-old Luke Baldwin came to live with his Uncle Henry in the house on the stream by the sawmill, he did not forget that he had promised his dying father he would try to learn things from his uncle; so he used to watch him very carefully.

Uncle Henry, who was the manager of the sawmill, was a big, burly man weighing more than two hundred and thirty pounds, and he had a rough-skinned, brick-coloured face. He looked like a powerful man, but his health was not good. He had aches and pains in his back and shoulders, which puzzled the doctor. The first thing Luke learned about Uncle Henry was that everybody had great respect for him. The four men he employed in the sawmill were always polite and attentive when he spoke to them. His wife, Luke's Aunt Helen, a kindly, plump, straightforward woman, never argued with him. "You should try and be like your Uncle Henry," she would say to Luke. "He's so wonderfully practical. He takes care of everything in a sensible, easy way."

Luke used to trail around the sawmill after Uncle Henry not only because he liked the fresh clean smell of the newly cut wood and the big piles of sawdust, but because he was impressed by his uncle's precise, firm tone when he spoke to the men.

Sometimes Uncle Henry would stop and explain to Luke something about a piece of timber. "Always try and learn the essential facts, son," he would say. "If you've got the facts, you know what's useful and what isn't useful, and no one can fool you."

He showed Luke that nothing of value was ever wasted around the mill. Luke used to listen, and wonder if there was another man in the world who knew so well what was needed and what ought to be thrown away. Uncle Henry had known at once that Luke needed a bicycle to ride to his school, which was two miles away in town, and he bought him a good one. He knew that Luke needed good, serviceable clothes. He also knew exactly how much Aunt Helen needed to run the house, the price of everything, and how much a woman should be paid for doing the family washing. In the evenings Luke used to sit in the living room watching his uncle making notations in a black notebook which he always carried in his vest pocket, and he knew that he was assessing the value of the smallest transaction that had taken place during the day.

Luke promised himself that when he grew up he, too, would be admired for his good, sound judgement. But, of course, he couldn't always be watching and learning from his Uncle Henry, for too often when he watched him he thought of his own father; then he was lonely. So he began to build up another secret life for himself around the sawmill, and his companion was the eleven-year-old collie, Dan, a dog blind in one eye and with a slight limp in his left hind leg. Dan was a fat slow-moving old dog. He was very affectionate and his eye was the colour of amber. His fur was amber, too. When Luke left for school in the morning, the old dog followed him for half a mile down the road, and when he returned in the afternoon, there was Dan waiting at the gate.

Sometimes they would play around the millpond or by the dam, or go down the stream to the lake. Luke was never lonely when the dog was with him. There was an old rowboat that they used as a pirate ship in the stream, and they would be pirates together, with Luke shouting instructions to Captain Dan and with the dog seeming to understand and wagging his tail enthusiastically. His amber eye was alert, intelligent, and approving. Then they would plunge into the brush on the other side of the stream, pretending they were hunting tigers. Of course, the old dog was no longer much good for hunting; he was too slow and too lazy. Uncle Henry no longer used him for hunting rabbits or anything else.

When they came out of the brush, they would lie together on the cool, grassy bank being affectionate with each other, with Luke talking earnestly, while the collie, as Luke believed, smiled with the good eye. Lying in the grass, Luke would say things to Dan he could not say to his uncle or his aunt. Not that what he said was important; it was just stuff about himself that he might have told to his own father or mother if they had been alive. Then they would go back to the house for dinner, and after dinner Dan would follow him down the road to Mr. Kemp's house, where they would ask old Mr. Kemp if they could go with him to round up his four cows. The old man was always glad to see them. He seemed to like watching Luke and the collie running around the cows, pretending they were riding on a vast range in the foothills of the Rockies.

Uncle Henry no longer paid much attention to the collie, though once when he tripped over him on the veranda, he shook his head and said thoughtfully, "Poor fellow, he's through. Can't use him for anything. He just eats and sleeps and gets in the way."

One Sunday during Luke's summer holidays, when they had returned from church and had had their lunch, they all moved out to the veranda where the collie was sleeping. Luke sat down on the steps, his back against the veranda post, Uncle Henry took the rocking chair, and Aunt Helen stretched herself out in the hammock, sighing contentedly. Then Luke, eyeing the collie, tapped the step with the palm of his hand, giving three little taps like a signal, and the collie, lifting his head, got up stiffly with a slow wagging of the tail as an acknowledgement that the signal had been heard, and began to cross the veranda to Luke. But the dog was sleepy; his bad eye was turned to the rocking chair; in passing, his left front paw went under the rocker. With a frantic yelp, the dog went bounding down the steps and hobbled around the corner of the house, where he stopped, hearing Luke coming after him. All he needed was the touch of Luke's hand. Then he began to lick the hand methodically, as if apologizing.

"Luke," Uncle Henry called sharply, "bring that dog here."

When Luke led the collie back to the veranda, Uncle Henry nodded and said, "Thanks, Luke." Then he took out a cigar, lit it, put his big hands on his knees, and began to rock in the chair, while he frowned and eyed the dog steadily. Obviously he was making some kind of an important decision about the collie.

"What's the matter, Uncle Henry?" Luke asked nervously.

"That dog can't see any more," Uncle Henry said.

"Oh, yes, he can," Luke said quickly. "His bad eye got turned to the chair, that's all, Uncle Henry."

"And his teeth are gone, too," Uncle Henry went on, paying no attention to what Luke had said. Turning to the hammock, he called, "Helen, sit up a minute, will you?"

When she got up and stood beside him, he went on, "I was thinking about this old dog the other day, Helen. It's not only that he's just about blind, but did you notice that when we drove up after church he didn't even bark?"

"It's a fact he didn't, Henry."

"No, not much good even as a watchdog now."

"Poor old fellow. It's a pity, isn't it?"

"And no good for hunting either. And he eats a lot, I suppose."

"About as much as he ever did, Henry."

"The plain fact is the old dog isn't worth his keep any more. It's time we got rid of him."

"It's always so hard to know how to get rid of a dog, Henry."

"I was thinking about it the other day. Some people think it's best to shoot a dog. I haven't had any shells for that shotgun for over a year. Poisoning is a hard death for a dog. Maybe drowning is the easiest and quickest way. Well, I'll speak to one of the mill hands and have him look after it."

Crouching on the ground, his arms around the old collie's neck, Luke cried out, "Uncle Henry, Dan's a wonderful dog! You don't know how wonderful he is!"

"He's just a very old dog, son," Uncle Henry said calmly. "The time comes when you have to get rid of any old dog. We've got to be practical about it. I'll get you a pup, son. A smart little dog that'll be worth its keep. A pup that will grow up with you."

"I don't want a pup!" Luke cried, turning his face away. Circling around him, the dog began to bark, then flick his long pink tongue at the back of Luke's neck.

Aunt Helen, catching her husband's eye, put her finger on her lips, warning him not to go on talking in front of the boy. "An old dog like that often wanders into the brush and sort of picks a place to die when the time comes. Isn't that so, Henry?"

"Oh, sure," he agreed quickly. "In fact, when Dan didn't show up yesterday, I was sure that was what had happened." Then he yawned and seemed to forget about the dog.

But Luke was frightened, for he knew what his uncle was like. He knew that if his uncle had decided that the dog was useless and that it was sane and sensible to get rid of it, he would be ashamed of himself if he were diverted by any sentimental considerations. Luke knew in his heart that he could not move his uncle. All he could do, he thought, was keep the dog away from his uncle, keep him out of the house, feed him when Uncle Henry wasn't around.

Next day at noontime Luke saw his uncle walking from the mill toward the house with old Sam Carter, a mill hand. Sam Carter was a dull, stooped, slow-witted man of sixty with an iron-grey beard, who was wearing blue overalls and a blue shirt. Watching from the veranda, Luke noticed that his uncle suddenly gave Sam Carter a cigar, which Sam put in his pocket. Luke had never seen his uncle give Sam a cigar or pay much attention to him.

Then, after lunch, Uncle Henry said lazily that he would like Luke to take his bicycle and go into town and get him some cigars.

"I'll take Dan," Luke said.

"Better not, son," Uncle Henry said. "It'll take you all afternoon. I want those cigars. Get going, Luke."

His uncle's tone was so casual that Luke tried to believe they were not merely getting rid of him. Of course he had to do what he was told. He had never dared to refuse to obey an order from his uncle. But when he had taken his bicycle and had ridden down the path that followed the stream to the town road and had got about a quarter of a mile along the road, he found that all he could think of was his uncle handing old Sam Carter the cigar.

Slowing down, sick with worry now, he got off the bike and stood uncertainly on the sunlit road. Sam Carter was a gruff, aloof old man who would have no feeling for a dog. Then suddenly Luke could go no farther without getting some assurance that the collie would not be harmed while he was away. Across the fields he could see the house.

Leaving the bike in the ditch, he started to cross the field, intending to get close enough to the house so Dan could hear him if he whistled softly. He got about fifty yards away from the house and whistled and waited, but there was no sign of the dog, which might be asleep at the front of the house, he knew, or over at the sawmill. With the saws whining, the dog couldn't hear the soft whistle. For a few minutes Luke couldn't make up his mind what to do, then he decided to go back to the road, get on his bike, and go back the way he had come until he got to the place where the river path joined the road. There he could leave his bike, go up the path, then into the tall grass and get close to the front of the house and the sawmill without being seen.

He had followed the river path for about a hundred yards, and when he came to the place where the river began to bend sharply toward the house his heart fluttered and his legs felt paralyzed, for he saw the old rowboat in the one place where the river was deep, and in the rowboat was Sam Carter with the collie.

The bearded man in the blue overalls was smoking his cigar; the dog, with a rope around its neck, sat contentedly beside him, its tongue going out in a friendly lick at the hand holding the rope. It was all like a crazy dream picture to Luke; all wrong because it looked so lazy and friendly, even the curling smoke from Sam Carter's cigar. But as Luke cried out, "Dan, Dan! Come on, boy!" and the dog jumped at the water, he saw that Carter's left hand was hanging deep in the water, holding a foot of rope with a heavy stone at the end. As Luke cried out wildly, "Don't! Please don't!" Carter dropped the stone, for the cry came too late; it was blurred by the screech of the big saws at the mill. But Carter was startled, and he stared stupidly at the riverbank, then he ducked his head and began to row quickly to the bank.

But Luke was watching the collie take what looked like a long, shallow dive, except that the hind legs suddenly kicked up above the surface, then shot down, and while he watched, Luke sobbed and trembled, for it was as if the happy secret part of his life around the sawmill was being torn away from him. But even while he watched, he seemed to be following a plan without knowing it, for he was already fumbling in his pocket for his jackknife, jerking the blade open, pulling off his pants, kicking his shoes off, while he muttered fiercely and prayed that Sam Carter would get out of sight.

It hardly took the mill hand a minute to reach the bank and go slinking furtively around the bend as if he felt that the boy was following him. But Luke hadn't taken his eyes off the exact spot in the water where Dan had disappeared. As soon as the mill hand was out of sight, Luke slid down the bank and took a leap at the water, the sun glistening on his slender body, his eyes wild with eagerness as he ran out to the deep place, then arched his back and dived, swimming under water, his open eyes getting used to the greenish-grey haze of the water, the sandy bottom, and the imbedded rocks.

His lungs began to ache, then he saw the shadow of the collie, floating at the end of the taut rope, rock-held in the sand. He slashed at the rope with his knife. He couldn't get much strength in his arm because of the resistance of the water. He grabbed the rope with his left hand, hacking with his knife. The collie suddenly drifted up slowly, like a water-soaked log. Then his own head shot above the surface, and, while he was sucking in the air, he was drawing in the rope, pulling the collie toward him and treading water. In a few strokes he was away from the deep place and his feet touched the bottom.

Hoisting the collie out of the water, he scrambled toward the bank, lurching and stumbling in fright because the collie felt like a dead weight.

He went on up the bank and across the path to the tall grass, where he fell flat, hugging the dog and trying to warm him with his own body. But the collie didn't stir, the good amber eye remained closed. Then suddenly Luke wanted to act like a resourceful, competent man. Getting up on his knees, he stretched the dog out on his belly, drew him between his knees, felt with trembling hands for the soft places on the flanks just above the hip-bones, and rocked back and forth, pressing with all his weight, then relaxing the pressure as he straightened up. He hoped that he was working the dog's lungs like a bellows. He had read that men who had been thought drowned had been saved in this way.

"Come on, Dan. Come on, old boy," he pleaded softly. As a little water came from the collie's mouth, Luke's heart jumped, and he muttered over and over, "You can't be dead, Dan! You can't, you can't! I won't let you die, Dan!" He rocked back and forth tirelessly, applying the pressure to the flanks. More water dribbled from the mouth. In the collie's body he felt a faint tremor. "Oh, gee, Dan, you're alive," he whispered. "Come on, boy. Keep it up."

With a cough the collie suddenly jerked his head back, the amber eye opened, and there they were looking at each other. Then the collie, thrusting his legs out stiffly, tried to hoist himself up, staggered, tried again, then stood there in a stupor. He shook himself like any other wet dog, turned his head, eyed Luke, and the red tongue came out in a weak flick at Luke's cheek.

"Lie down, Dan," Luke said. As the dog lay down beside him, Luke closed his eyes, buried his head in the wet fur, and wondered why the muscles of his arms and legs began to jerk in a nervous reaction, now that it was all over. "Stay there, Dan," he said softly, and he went back to the path, got his clothes, and came back beside Dan and put them on. "I think we'd better get away from this spot, Dan," he said. "Keep down, boy. Come on." He crawled on through the tall grass till they were about seventy-five yards from the place where he had undressed. There they lay down together.

In a little while he heard his aunt's voice calling, "Luke. Oh, Luke! Come here, Luke!"

"Quiet, Dan," Luke whispered. A few minutes passed, and then Uncle Henry called, "Luke, Luke!" and he began to come down the path. They could see him standing there, massive and imposing, his hands on his hips as he looked down the path, then he turned and went back to the house.

As he watched the sunlight shine on the back of his uncle's neck, the exultation Luke had felt at knowing the collie was safe beside him turned to bewildered despair, for he knew that even if he should be forgiven for saving the dog when he saw it drowning, the fact was that his uncle had been thwarted. His mind was made up to get rid of Dan, and in a few days' time in another way, he would get rid of him, as he got rid of anything around the mill that he believed to be useless or a waste of money.

As he lay back and looked up at the hardly moving clouds, he began to grow frightened. He couldn't go back to the house, nor could he take the collie into the woods and hide him and feed him there unless he tied him up. If he didn't tie him up, Dan would wander back to the house.

"I guess there's just no place to go, Dan," he whispered sadly. "Even if we start off along the road, somebody is sure to see us."

But Dan was watching a butterfly that was circling above them. Raising himself a little, Luke looked through the grass at the corner of the house, then he turned and looked the other way to the wide blue lake. With a sigh he lay down again, and for hours they lay together, until there was no sound from the saws in the mill and the sun moved low in the western sky.

"Well, we can't stay here any longer, Dan," he said at last. "We'll just have to get as far away as we can. Keep down, old boy," and he began to crawl through the grass, going farther away from the house. When he could no longer be seen he got up and began to trot across the field toward the gravel road leading to town.

On the road, the collie would turn from time to time as if wondering why Luke shuffled along, dragging his feet wearily, head down. "I'm stumped, that's all, Dan," Luke explained. "I can't seem to think of a place to take you."

When they were passing the Kemp place, they saw the old man sitting on the veranda, and Luke stopped. All he could think of was that Mr. Kemp had liked them both and it had been a pleasure to help him get the cows in the evening. Dan had always been with them. Staring at the figure of the old man on the veranda, he said in a worried tone, "I wish I could be sure of him, Dan. I wish he was a dumb, stupid man who wouldn't know or care whether you were worth anything... Well, come on." He opened the gate bravely, but he felt shy and unimportant.

"Hello, son. What's on your mind?" Mr. Kemp called from the veranda. He was a thin, wiry man in a tan-coloured shirt. He had a grey untidy moustache, his skin was wrinkled and leathery, but his eyes were always friendly and amused.

"Could I speak to you, Mr. Kemp?" Luke asked when they were close to the veranda.

"Sure. Go ahead."

"It's about Dan. He's a great dog, but I guess you know that as well as I do. I was wondering if you could keep him here for me."

"Why should I keep Dan here, son?"

"Well, it's like this," Luke said, fumbling the words awkwardly: "My uncle won't let me keep him any more... says he's too old." His mouth began to tremble, then he blurted out the story.

"I see, I see," Mr. Kemp said slowly, and he got up and came over to the steps and sat down and began to stroke the collie's head. "Of course, Dan's an old dog, son," he said quietly. "And sooner or later you've got to get rid of an old dog. Your uncle knows that. Maybe it's true that Dan isn't worth his keep."

"He doesn't eat much, Mr. Kemp. Just one meal a day."

"I wouldn't want you to think your uncle was cruel and unfeeling, Luke," Mr. Kemp went on. "He's a fine man... maybe just a little bit too practical and straightforward."

"I guess that's right," Luke agreed, but he was really waiting and trusting the expression in the old man's eyes.

"Maybe you should make him a special proposition."

"I – I don't know what you mean."

"Well, I sort of like the way you get the cows for me in the evenings," Mr. Kemp said, smiling to himself. "In fact, I don't think you need me to go along with you at all. Now, supposing I gave you seventy-five cents a week. Would you get the cows for me every night?"

"Sure, I would, Mr. Kemp. I like doing it, anyway."

"All right, son. It's a deal. Now I'll tell you what to do. You go back to your uncle, and before he has a chance to open up on you, you say right out that you've come to him with a business proposition. Say it like a man, just like that. Offer to pay him the seventy-five cents a week for the dog's keep."

"But my uncle doesn't need seventy-five cents, Mr. Kemp," Luke said uneasily.

"Of course not," Mr. Kemp agreed. "It's the principle of the thing. Be confident. Remember that he's got nothing against the dog. Go to it, son. Let me know how you do," he added, with an amused smile. "If I know your uncle at all, I think it'll work."

"I'll try it, Mr. Kemp," Luke said. "Thanks very much." But he didn't have any confidence, for even though he knew that Mr. Kemp was a wise old man who would not deceive him, he couldn't believe that seventy-five cents a week would stop his uncle, who was an important man. "Come on, Dan," he called, and he went slowly and apprehensively back to the house.

When they were going up the path, his aunt cried from the open window, "Henry, in heaven's name, it's Luke with the dog!"

Ten paces from the veranda, Luke stopped and waited nervously for his uncle to come out. Uncle Henry came out in a rush, but when he saw the collie and Luke standing there, he stopped stiffly, turned pale, and his mouth hung open.

"Luke," he whispered, "that dog had a stone around his neck."

"I fished him out of the stream," Luke said uneasily.

"Oh. Oh, I see," Uncle Henry said, and gradually the colour came back to his face. "You fished him out, eh?" he asked, still looking at the dog. "Well, you shouldn't have done that. I told Sam Carter to get rid of the dog, you know."

"Just a minute, Uncle Henry," Luke said, trying not to falter. He gained confidence as Aunt Helen came out and stood beside her husband, for her eyes seemed to be gentle, and he went on bravely, "I want to make you a practical proposition."

"A what?" Uncle Henry asked, still feeling insecure, and wishing the boy and the dog weren't confronting him.

"A practical proposition," Luke blurted out quickly. "I know Dan isn't worth his keep to you. I guess he isn't anything to anybody but me. So I'll pay you seventy-five cents a week for his keep."

"What's this?" Uncle Henry asked, looking bewildered. "Where would you get seventy-five cents a week, Luke?"

"I'm going to get the cows every night for Mr. Kemp."

"Oh, for heaven's sake, Henry," Aunt Helen pleaded, looking distressed, "let him keep the dog!" and she fled into the house.

"None of that kind of talk!" Uncle Henry called after her. "We've got to be sensible about this!" But he was shaken himself, and overwhelmed with a distress that destroyed his confidence. As he sat down slowly in the rocking chair and stroked the side of his big face, he wanted to say, "All right, keep the dog," but he was ashamed of being so weak and sentimental. He stubbornly refused to yield to this emotion; he was trying desperately to turn his emotion into a bit of good, useful common sense, so he could justify his distress. So he rocked and pondered. At last he smiled, "You're a smart little shaver, Luke," he said slowly. "Imagine you working it out like this. I'm tempted to accept your proposition."

"Thanks, Uncle Henry."

"I'm accepting it because I think you'll learn something out of this," he went on ponderously.

"Yes, Uncle Henry."

"You'll learn that useless luxuries cost the smartest of men hard-earned money."

"I don't mind."

"Well, it's a thing you'll have to learn sometime. I think you'll learn, too, because you certainly seem to have a practical streak in you. It's a streak I like to see in a boy. O.K., son," he said, and he smiled with relief and went into the house.

Turning to Dan, Luke whispered softly, "Well, what do you know about that?"

As he sat down on the step with the collie beside him and listened to Uncle Henry talking to his wife, he began to glow with exultation. Then gradually his exultation began to change to a vast wonder that Mr. Kemp should have had such a perfect understanding of Uncle Henry. He began to dream of some day being as wise as old Mr. Kemp and knowing exactly how to handle people. It was possible, too, that he had already learned some of the things about his uncle that his father had wanted him to learn.

Putting his head down on the dog's neck, he vowed to himself fervently that he would always have some money on hand, no matter what became of him, so that he would be able to protect all that was truly valuable from the practical people of the world.

SHEILA WATSON

AND THE FOUR ANIMALS

The foothills slept. Over their yellow limbs the blue sky crouched. Only a fugitive green suggested life which claimed kinship with both and acknowledged kinship with neither.

Around the curve of the hill, or out of the hill itself, came three black dogs. The watching eye could not record with precision anything but the fact of their presence. Against the faded contour of the earth the things were. The watcher could not have said whether they had come or whether the eye had focused them into being. In the place of the hills before and after have no more meaning than the land gives. Now there were the dogs where before were only the hills and the transparent stir of the dragonfly.

Had the dogs worn the colour of the hills, had they swung tail round leg, ears oblique and muzzles quivering to scent carrion, or mischief, or the astringency of grouse mingled with the acrid smell of low-clinging sage, the eye might have recognized a congruence between them and the land. Here Coyote, the primitive one, the god-baiter and troublemaker, the thirster after power, the vainglorious, might have walked since the dawn of creation – for Coyote had walked early on the first day.

The dogs, however, were elegant and lithe. They paced with rhythmic dignity. In the downshafts of light their coats shone ebony. The eye observed the fineness of bone, the accuracy of adjustment. As the dogs advanced they gained altitude, circling, until they stood as if freed from the land against the flat blue of the sky.

The eye closed and the dogs sank back into their proper darkness. The eye opened and the dogs stood black against the blue of the iris for the sky was in the eye yet severed from it.

In the light of the eye the dogs could be observed clearly – three Labrador retrievers, gentle, courteous, and playful with the sedate bearing of dogs well-schooled to know their worth, to know their place, and to bend willingly to their master's will. One stretched out, face flattened. Its eyes, darker than the grass on which it lay, looked over the rolling hills to the distant saw-tooth pattern of volcanic stone. Behind it the other two sat, tongues dripping red over the saw-tooth pattern of volcanic lip.

The dogs were against the eye and in the eye. They were in the land but not of it. They were of Coyote's house, but become aristocrats in time which had now yielded them up to the time-less hills. They, too, were gods, but civil gods made tractable by use and useless by custom. Here in the hills they would starve or lose themselves in wandering. They were aliens in this spot or exiles returned as if they had never been.

The eye closed. It opened and closed again. Each time the eye opened the dogs circled the hill to the top and trained their gaze on the distant rock. Each time they reached the height of land with more difficulty. At last all three lay pressing thin bellies and jaws against the unyielding earth.

Now when the eye opened there were four dogs and a man and the eye belonged to the man and stared from the hill of his head along the slope of his arm on which the four dogs lay. And the fourth which he had whistled up from his own depths was glossy and fat as the others had been. But this, too, he knew in the end would climb lacklustre as the rest.

So he opened the volcanic ridge of his jaws and bit the tail from each dog and stood with the four tails in his hand and the dogs fawned graciously before him begging decorously for food. And he fed the tail of the first dog to the fourth and the tail of the fourth to the first. In the same way he disposed of the tails of the second and the third. And the dogs sat with their eyes on his mouth.

Then he bit the off-hind leg from each and offered it to the other; then the near-hind leg, and the dogs grew plump and shone in the downlight of his glance. Then the jaw opened and closed on the two forelegs and on the left haunch and the right and each dog bowed and slavered and ate what was offered.

Soon four fanged jaws lay on the hill and before them the man stood rolling the amber eyes in his hands and these he tossed impartially to the waiting jaws. Then he fed the bone of the first jaw to the fourth and that of the second to the third. And taking the two jaws that lay before him he fed tooth to tooth until one tooth remained and this he hid in his own belly.

P.K. PAGE

UNLESS THE EYE CATCH FIRE

Unless the eye catch fire
The God will not be seen...

– THEODORE ROSZAK
Where the Wasteland Ends

Wednesday, September 17.

The day began normally enough. The quails, cockaded as antique foot soldiers, arrived while I was having breakfast. The males black-faced, white-necklaced, cinnamon-crowned, with short, sharp, dark plumes. Square bibs, Payne's grey; belly and sides with a pattern of small stitches. Reassuring, the flock of them. They tell me the macadamization of the world is not complete.

A sudden alarm, and as if they had one brain among them, they were gone in a rush – a sideways ascending Niagara – shutting out the light, obscuring the sky and exposing a rectangle of lawn, unexpectedly emerald. How bright the berries on the cotoneaster. Random leaves on the cherry twirled like gold spinners. The garden was high-keyed, vivid, locked in aspic.

Without warning, and as if I were looking down the tube of a kaleidoscope, the merest shake occurred – moiréed the garden – rectified itself. Or, more precisely, as if a rangefinder through which I had been sighting, found of itself a more accurate focus. Sharpened, in fact, to an excoriating exactness.

And then the colours changed. Shifted to a higher octave – a *bright spectrum*. Each colour with its own *light*, its own shape. The leaves of the trees, the berries, the grasses – as if shedding successive films – disclosed layer after layer of hidden perfections. And upon these rapidly changing surfaces the "rangefinder" – to really play hob with metaphor! – sharpened its small invisible blades.

I don't know how to describe the intensity and speed of focus of this gratuitous zoom lens through which I stared, or the swift and dizzying adjustments within me. I became a "sleeping top," perfectly centred, perfectly – sighted. The colours vibrated beyond the visible range of the spectrum. Yet I saw them. With some matching eye. Whole galaxies of them, blazing and glowing, flowing in rivulets, gushing in fountains – volatile, mercurial, and making lack-lustre and off-key the colours of the rainbow.

I had no time or inclination to wonder, intellectualize. My mind seemed astonishingly clear and quite still. Like a crystal. A burning glass.

And then the rangefinder sharpened once again. To alter space.

The lawn, the bushes, the trees – still super-brilliant – were no longer *there. There,* in fact, had ceased to exist. They were now, of all places in the world, *here*. Right in the centre of my being. Occupying an immense inner space. Part of me. Mine. Except the whole idea of ownership was beside the point. As true to say I was theirs as they mine. I and they were here, they and I, there. (*There, here*... odd... but for an irrelevant, inconsequential 't' which comes and goes, the words are the same.)

As suddenly as the world had altered, it returned to normal. I looked at my watch. A ridiculous mechanical habit. As I had no idea when the experience began it was impossible to know how long it had lasted. What had seemed eternity couldn't have been more than a minute or so. My coffee was still steaming in its mug.

The garden, through the window, was as it had always been. Yet not as it had always been. Less. Like listening to mono after hearing stereo. But with a far greater loss of dimension. A grievous loss.

I rubbed my eyes. Wondered, not without alarm, if this was the onset of some disease of the retina – glaucoma or some cellular change in the eye itself – superlatively packaged, fatally sweet as the marzipan cherry I ate as a child and *knew* was poison.

If it *is* a disease, the symptoms will recur. It will happen again.

Tuesday, September 23.

It *has* happened again.

Tonight, taking Dexter for his late walk, I looked up at the crocheted tangle of boughs against the sky. Dark silhouettes against the lesser dark, but beating now with an extraordinary black brilliance. The golden glints in obsidian or the lurking embers in black opals are the nearest I can come to describing them. But it's a false description, emphasizing as it does, the wrong end of the scale. This was a *dark spectrum*. As if the starry heavens were translated into densities of black – black Mars, black Saturn, black Jupiter; or a master jeweller had crossed his jewels with jet and set them to burn and wink in the branches and twigs of oaks whose leaves shone luminous – a leafy Milky Way – fired by black chlorophyll.

Dexter stopped as dead as I. Transfixed. His thick honey-coloured coat and amber eyes glowing with their own intense brightness, suggested yet another spectrum. A *spectrum of light*. He was a constellated dog, shining, supra-real, against the foothills and mountain ranges of midnight.

I am reminded now, as I write, of a collection of Lepidoptera in Brazil – one entire wall covered with butterflies, creatures of daylight – enormous or tiny – blue, orange, black. Strong-coloured. And on the opposite wall their anti-selves – pale night flyers spanning such a range of silver and white and lightest snuff-colour that once one entered their spectral scale there was no end to the subtleties and delicate nuances. But I didn't think like this then. All thought, all comparisons were prevented by the startling infinities of darkness and light.

Then, as before, the additional shake occurred and the two spectrums moved swiftly from without to within. As if two equal and complementary circles centred inside me – or I in them. How explain that I not only *saw* but actually *was* the two spectrums? (I underline a simple, but in this case, exactly appropriate anagram.)

Then the rangefinder lost its focus and the world, once again, was back to normal. Dexter, a pale, blurred blob, bounded about within the field of my peripheral vision, going on with his doggy interests just as if a moment before he had not been frozen in his tracks, a dog entranced.

I am no longer concerned about my eyesight. Wonder only if we are both mad, Dexter and I? Angelically mad, sharing hallucinations of epiphany. *Folie à deux?*

Friday, October 3.

It's hard to account for my secrecy, for I *have* been secretive. As if the cat had my tongue. It's not that I don't long to talk about the colours but I can't risk the wrong response – (as Gaby once said of a companion after a faultless performance of *Giselle*: "If she had criticized the least detail of it, I'd have hit her!").

Once or twice I've gone so far as to say, "I had the most extraordinary experience the other day…" hoping to find some look or phrase, some answering, "So did I." None has been forthcoming.

I can't forget the beauty. Can't get it out of my head. Startling, unearthly, indescribable. Infuriatingly indescribable. A glimpse of – somewhere else. Somewhere alive, miraculous, newly made yet timeless. And more important still – significant, luminous, with a meaning of which I was part. Except that I – the I who is writing this – did not exist; was flooded out, dissolved in that immensity where subject and object are one.

I have to make a deliberate effort now not to live my life in terms of it; not to sit, immobilized, awaiting the shake that heralds a new world. Awaiting the transfiguration.

Luckily the necessities of life keep me busy. But upstream of my actions, behind a kind of plate glass, some part of me waits, listens, maintains a total attention.

Tuesday, October 7.

Things are moving very fast.

Some nights ago my eye was caught by a news item. "Trucker Blames Colours," said the headline. Reading on: "R.T. Ballantyne, driver for Island Trucks, failed to stop on a red light at the intersection of Fernhill and Spender. Questioned by traffic police, Ballantyne replied: 'I didn't see it, that's all. There was this shake, then all these colours suddenly in the trees. Real bright ones I'd never seen before. I guess they must have blinded me.' A breathalyser test proved negative." Full stop.

I had an overpowering desire to talk to R.T. Ballantyne. Even looked him up in the telephone book. Not listed. I debated reaching him through Island Trucks in the morning.

Hoping for some mention of the story, I switched on the local radio station, caught the announcer mid-sentence:

"…to come to the studio and talk to us. So far no one has been able to describe just what the 'new' colours are, but perhaps Ruby Howard can. Ruby, you say you actually *saw* 'new' colours?"

What might have been a flat, rather ordinary female voice was sharpened by wonder. "I was out in the garden, putting it to bed, you might say, getting it ready for winter. The hydrangeas are dried out – you know the way they go. Soft beiges and greys. And I was thinking maybe I should cut them back, when there was this – shake, like – and there they were shining. Pink. And blue. But not like they are in life. Different. Brighter. With little lights, like…"

The announcer's voice cut in, "You say 'not like they are in life.' D'you think this wasn't life? I mean, do you think maybe you were dreaming?"

"Oh, no," answered my good Mrs. Howard, positive, clear, totally unrattled. "Oh, no, I wasn't *dreaming*. Not *dreaming* — … Why – *this* is more like dreaming." She was quiet a moment and then, in a matter-of-fact voice, "I can't expect you to believe it," she said. "Why should you? I wouldn't believe it myself if I hadn't seen it." Her voice expressed a kind of compassion as if she was really sorry for the announcer.

I picked up the telephone book for the second time, looked up the number of the station. I had decided to tell Mrs. Howard what I had seen. I dialled, got a busy signal, depressed the bar and waited, cradle in hand. I dialled again. And again.

Later.

J. just phoned. Curious how she and I play the same game over and over.

J: Were you watching Channel 8?

Me: No, I…

J: An interview. With a lunatic. One who sees colours and flashing lights.

Me: Tell me about it.

J: He was a logger – a high-rigger – not that that has anything to do with it. He's retired now and lives in an apartment and has a window-box with geraniums. This morning the flowers were like neon, he said, flashing and shining... *Hon*estly!

Me: Perhaps he saw something you can't...

J: *(Amused)* I might have known you'd take his side. Seriously, what *could* he have seen?

Me: Flashing and shining – as he said.

J: But they couldn't. Not geraniums. And you know it as well as I do.

*Hon*estly, Babe... (She is the only person left who calls me the name my mother called me.) Why are you always so perverse?

I felt faithless. I put down the receiver, as if I had not borne witness to my God.

October 22.

Floods of letters to the papers. Endless interviews on radio and TV. Pros, cons, inevitable spoofs.

One develops an eye for authenticity. It's as easy to spot as sunlight. However they may vary in detail, true accounts of the colours have an unmistakable common factor – a common factor as difficult to convey as sweetness to those who know only salt. True accounts are inarticulate, diffuse, unlikely – impossible.

It's recently crossed my mind that there may be some relationship between having seen the colours and their actual manifestation – something as improbable as *the more one sees them the more they are able to be seen.* Perhaps they are always there in some normally invisible part of the electro-magnetic spectrum and only become visible to certain people at certain times. A combination of circumstances or some subtle refinement in the organ of sight. And then – from quantity to quality perhaps, like water to ice – a whole community changes, is able to see, catches fire.

For example, it was seven days between the first time I saw the colours and the second. During that time there were no reports to the media. But once the reports began, the time between lessened appreciably *for me.* Not proof, of course, but worth noting. And I can't help wondering why some people see the colours and others don't. Do some of us have extra vision? Are some so conditioned that they're virtually blind to what's there before their very noses? Is it a question of more, or less?

Reports come in from farther and farther afield; from all walks of life. I think now there is no portion of the inhabited globe without "shake freaks" and no acceptable reason for the sightings. Often, only one member of a family will testify to the heightened vision. In my own small circle, I am the only witness – or so I think. I feel curiously hypocritical as I listen to my friends denouncing the "shakers." Drugs, they say. Irrational – possibly dangerous. Although no sinister incidents have occurred yet – just some mild shake-baiting here and there – one is uneasily reminded of Salem.

Scientists pronounce us hallucinated or mistaken, pointing out that so far there is no hard evidence, no objective proof. That means, I suppose, no photographs, no spectroscopic measurement – if such is possible. Interestingly, seismographs show very minor earthquake tremors – showers of them, like shooting stars in August. Pundits claim "shake fever" – as it has come to be called – is a variant on flying saucer fever and that it will subside in its own time. Beneficent physiologists suggest we are suffering (why is it *always* suffering, never enjoying?) a distorted form of *ocular spectrum* or after-image. (An after-image of what?) Psychologists disagree among themselves. All in all, it is not surprising that some of us prefer to keep our experiences to ourselves.

January 9.

Something new has occurred. Something impossible. Disturbing. So disturbing, in fact, that according to rumour it is already being taken with the utmost seriousness at the highest levels. TV, press and radio – with good reason – talk of little else.

What seemingly began as a mild winter has assumed sinister overtones. Farmers in southern Alberta are claiming the earth is unnaturally hot to the touch. Golfers at Harrison complain that the soles of their feet burn. Here on the coast, we notice it less. Benign winters are our specialty.

Already we don't lack for explanations as to the why the earth could not be hotter than usual, nor why it is naturally "unnaturally" hot. Vague notes of reassurance creep into the speeches of public men. They may be unable to explain the issue, but they can no longer ignore it.

To confuse matters further, reports on temperatures seem curiously inconsistent. What information we get comes mainly from self-appointed "earth touchers." And now that the least thing can fire an argument, their conflicting readings lead often enough to inflammatory debate.

For myself, I can detect no change at all in my own garden.

Thursday...?

There is no longer any doubt. The temperature of the earth's surface *is* increasing.

It is unnerving, horrible, to go out and feel the ground like some great beast, warm, beneath one's feet. As if another presence – vast, invisible – attends one. Dexter, too, is perplexed. He barks at the earth with the same indignation and, I suppose, fear, with which he barks at the first rumblings of earth-quake.

Air temperatures, curiously, don't increase proportionately – or so we're told. It doesn't make sense, but at the moment nothing makes sense. Countless explanations have been offered. Elaborate explanations. None adequate. The fact that the air temperature remains temperate despite the higher ground heat must, I think, be helping to keep panic down. Even so, these are times of great tension.

Hard to understand these two unexplained – unrelated? – phenomena: the first capable of dividing families; the second menacing us all. We are like animals trapped in a burning building.

Later.

J. just phone. Terrified. Why don't I move in with her, she urges. After all she has the space and we have known each other forty years. (Hard to believe when I don't feel even forty!) She can't bear it – the loneliness.

Poor J. Always so protected, insulated by her money. And her charm. What one didn't provide, the other did… diversions, services, attention.

What do I think is responsible for the heat, she asks. But it turns out she means who. Her personal theory is that the "shake-freaks" are causing it – involuntarily, perhaps, but the two are surely linked.

"How could they possibly cause it?" I enquire. "By what reach of the imagination…?"

"Search *me!*" she protests. "How on earth should *I* know?" And the sound of the dated slang makes me really laugh.

But suddenly she is close to tears. "How can you *laugh?*" she calls. "This is nightmare. Nightmare!"

Dear J. I wish I could help but the only comfort I could offer would terrify her still more.

September.

Summer calmed us down. If the earth was hot, well, summers *are* hot. And we were simply having an abnormally hot one.

Now that it is fall – the season of cool nights, light frosts – and the earth like a feverish child remains worryingly hot, won't cool down, apprehension mounts.

At last we are given official readings. For months the authorities have assured us with irrefutable logic that the temperature of the earth could not be increasing. Now, without any apparent period of indecision or confusion, they are warning us with equal conviction and accurate statistical documentation that it has, in fact, increased. Something anyone with a pocket-handkerchief of lawn has known for some time.

Weather stations, science faculties, astronomical observatories all over the world, are measuring and reporting. Intricate computerized tables are quoted. Special departments of government have been set up. We speak now of a new Triassic Age – the Neo-Triassic – and of the accelerated melting of the ice caps. But we are elaborately assured that this could not, repeat not, occur in our lifetime.

Interpreters and analysts flourish. The media are filled with theories and explanations. The increased temperature has been attributed to impersonal agencies such as bacteria from outer space; a thinning of the earth's atmosphere; a build-up of carbon-dioxide in the air; some axial irregularity; a change in the earth's core (geologists are reported to have begun test borings). No theory is too far-fetched to have its supporters. And because man likes a scapegoat, blame has been laid upon NASA, atomic physicists, politicians, the occupants of flying saucers and finally upon mankind at large – improvident, greedy mankind – whose polluted, strike-ridden world is endangered now by the fabled flames of hell.

We are also informed that Nostradamus, the Bible, and Jeane Dixon have all foreseen our plight. A new paperback, *Let Edgar Cayce Tell You Why,* sold out in a matter of days. Attendance at churches has doubled. Cults proliferate. Yet even in this atmosphere, we, the "shake freaks," are considered lunatic fringe. Odd-men out. In certain quarters I believe we are seriously held responsible for the escalating heat, so J. is not alone. There have now been one or two nasty incidents. It is not surprising that even the most vocal among us have grown less willing to talk. I am glad to have kept silent. As a woman living alone, the less I draw attention to myself the better.

Our lives are greatly altered by this overhanging sense of doom. It is already hard to buy certain commodities. Dairy products are in very short supply. On the other hand, the market is flooded with citrus fruits. We are threatened with severe shortages for the future. The authorities are resisting rationing but it will have to come if only to prevent artificial shortages resulting from hoarding.

Luckily the colours are an almost daily event. I see them now, as it were, with my entire being. It is as if all my cells respond to their brilliance and become light too. At such times I feel I might shine in the dark.

No idea of the date.

It is evening and I am tired but I am so far behind in my notes I want to get something down. Events have moved too fast for me.

Gardens, parks, every tillable inch of soil have been appropriated for food crops. As an able, if aging body, with an acre of land and some knowledge of gardening, I have been made responsible for soy-beans – small trifoliate plants rich with the promise of protein. Neat rows of them cover what were once my vegetable garden, flower beds, lawn.

Young men from the Department of Agriculture came last month, bulldozed, cultivated, planted. Efficient, noisy desecrators of my twenty years of landscaping. Dexter barked at them from the moment they appeared and I admit I would have shared his indignation had the water shortage not already created its own desolation.

As a government gardener I'm a member of a new privileged class. I have watering and driving permits and coupons for gasoline and boots – an indication of what is to come. So far there has been no clothes rationing.

Daily instructions – when to water and how much, details of mulching, spraying – reach me from the government radio station to which I tune first thing in the morning. It also provides temperature readings, weather forecasts and the latest news releases on emergency measures, curfews, rationing, insulation. From the way things are going I think it will soon be our only station. I doubt that newspapers will be able to print much longer. In any event, I have already given them up. At first it was interesting to see how quickly drugs, pollution, education, Women's Lib., all became bygone issues; and, initially, I was fascinated to see how we rationalized. Then I became bored. Then disheartened. Now I am too busy.

Evening.

A call came from J. Will I come for Christmas?

Christmas! Extraordinary thought. Like a word from another language learned in my youth, now forgotten.

"I've still got some Heidsieck. We can get tight."

The word takes me back to my teens. "Like old times..."

"Yes." She is eager. I hate to let her down. "J., I can't. How could I get to you?"

"In your *car*, silly. *You* still have gas. You're the only one of us who has." Do I detect a slight hint of accusation, as if I had acquired it illegally?

"But J., it's only for emergencies."

"My God, Babe, d'you think *this* isn't an emergency?"

"J., dear..."

"*Please*, Babe," she pleads. "I'm so afraid. Of the looters. The eeriness. You must be afraid too. *Please!*"

I should have said, yes, that of course I was afraid. It's only natural to be afraid. Or, unable to say that, I should have made the soothing noises a mother makes to her child. Instead, "There's no reason to be afraid, J.," I said. It must have sounded insufferably pompous.

"No reason!" She was exasperated with me. "I'd have thought there was every reason."

She will phone again. In the night perhaps when she can't sleep. Poor J. She feels so alone. She *is* so alone. And so idle. I don't suppose it's occurred to her yet that telephones will soon go. That a whole way of life is vanishing completely.

It's different for me. I have the soy-beans which keep me busy all the daylight hours. And Dexter. And above all I have the colours and with them the knowledge that there are others, other people, whose sensibilities I share. We are invisibly, inviolably related to one another as the components of a molecule. I say "we." Perhaps I should speak only for myself, yet I feel as sure of these others as if they had spoken. Like the quails, we share one brain – no, I think it is one heart – between us. How do I know this? How *do* I know? I know by knowing. We are less alarmed by the increasing heat than those who have not seen the colours. I can't explain why. But seeing the colours seems to change one

– just as certain diagnostic procedures cure the complaint they are attempting to diagnose.

In all honesty I admit to having had moments when this sense of community was not enough, when I have had a great longing for my own kind – for so have I come to think of these others – in the way one has a great longing for someone one loves. Their presence in the world is not enough. One must see them. Touch them. Speak with them.

But lately that longing has lessened. All longing, in fact. And fear. Even my once great dread that I might cease to see the colours has vanished. It is as if through seeing them I have learned to see them. Have learned to be ready to see – passive; not striving to see – active. It keeps me very wide awake. Transparent even. Still.

The colours come daily now. Dizzying. Transforming. Life-giving. My sometimes back-breaking toil in the garden is lightened, made full of wonder, by the incredible colours shooting in the manner of children's sparklers from the plants themselves and from my own work-worn hands. I hadn't realized that I too am part of this vibrating luminescence.

Later.

I have no idea how long it is since I abandoned these notes. Without seasons to measure its passing, without normal activities – preparations for festivals, occasional outings – time feels longer, shorter or – more curious still – simultaneous, undifferentiated. Future and past fused in the present. Linearity broken.

I had intended to write regularly, but the soy-beans keep me busy pretty well all day and by evening I'm usually ready for bed. I'm sorry however to have missed recording the day-to-day changes. They were more or less minor at first. But once the heat began its deadly escalation, the world as we have known it

– "our world" – had you been able to put it alongside "this world" – would have seemed almost entirely different.

No one, I think, could have foreseen the speed with which everything has broken down. For instance, the elaborate plans made to maintain transportation became useless in a matter of months. Private traffic was first curtailed, then forbidden. If a man from another planet had looked in on us, he would have been astonished to see us trapped who were apparently free.

The big changes only really began after the first panic evacuations from the cities. Insulated by concrete, sewer pipes and underground parkades, high density areas responded slowly to the increasing temperatures. But once the heat penetrated their insulations, Gehennas were created overnight and whole populations fled in hysterical exodus, jamming highways in their futile attempts to escape.

Prior to this the government had not publicly acknowledged a crisis situation. They had taken certain precautions, brought in temporary measures to ease shortages and dealt with new developments on an *ad hoc* basis. Endeavoured to play it cool. Or so it seemed. Now they levelled with us. It was obvious that they must have been planning for months, only awaiting the right psychological moment to take everything over. That moment had clearly come. What we had previously thought of as a free world ended. We could no longer eat, drink, move without permits or coupons. This was full-scale emergency.

Yet nothing proceeds logically. Plans are made only to be remade to accommodate new and totally unexpected developments. The heat, unpatterned as disseminated sclerosis, attacks first here, then there. Areas of high temperature suddenly and inexplicably cool off – or vice versa. Agronomists are doing everything possible to keep crops coming – taking advantage of hot-house conditions to force two crops where one had grown before – frantically playing a kind of agricultural roulette, gambling on the length of time a specific region might continue to grow temperate-zone produce.

Mails have long since stopped. And newspapers. And telephones. As a member of a new privileged class, I have been equipped with a two-way radio and a permit to drive on government business. Schools have of course closed. An attempt was made for a time to provide lessons over TV. Thankfully the looting and rioting seem over. Those desperate gangs of angry citizens who for some time made life additionally difficult, have now disappeared. We seem at last to understand that we are all in this together.

Life is very simple without electricity. I get up with the light and go to bed as darkness falls. My food supply is still substantial and because of the soy-bean crop I am all right for water. Dexter has adapted well to his new life. He is outdoors less than he used to be and has switched to a mainly vegetable diet without too much difficulty.

Evening.

This morning a new order over the radio. All of us with special driving privileges were asked to report to our zone garage to have our tires treated with heat resistant plastic.

I had not been into town for months. I felt rather as one does on returning home from hospital – that the world is unexpectedly large, with voluminous airy spaces. This was exaggerated perhaps by the fact that our whole zone had been given over to soy-beans. Everywhere the same rows of green plants – small pods already formed – march across gardens and boulevards. I was glad to see the climate prove so favourable. But there was little else to make me rejoice as I drove through ominously deserted streets, paint blistering and peeling on fences and houses, while overhead a haze of dust, now always with us, created a green sun.

The prolonged heat has made bleak the little park opposite the garage. A rocky little park, once all mosses and rhododendrons, it is bare now, and brown. I was seeing the day as everyone saw it. Untransmuted.

As I stepped out of my car to speak to the attendant I cursed that I had not brought my insulators. The burning tarmac made me shift rapidly from foot to foot. Anyone from another planet would have wondered at this extraordinary quirk of earthlings. But my feet were forgotten as my eyes alighted a second time on the park across the way. I had never before seen so dazzling and variegated a display of colours. How could there be such prismed brilliance in the range of greys and browns? It was as if the perceiving organ – wherever it is – sensitized by earlier experience, was now correctly tuned for this further perception.

The process was as before: the merest shake and the whole park was "rainbow, rainbow, rainbow." A further shake brought the park from *there* to *here*. Interior. But this time the interior space had increased. Doubled. By a kind of instant knowledge that rid me of all doubt, I knew that the garage attendant was seeing it too. We *saw the colours*.

Then, with that slight shift of focus, as if a gelatinous film had moved briefly across my sight, everything slipped back.

I really looked at the attendant for the first time. He was a skinny young man standing up naked inside a pair of loose striped overalls cut off at the knee, *Sidney* embroidered in red over his left breast pocket. He was blond, small-boned, with nothing about him to stick in the memory except his clear eyes which at that moment bore an expression of total comprehension.

"You..." we began together and laughed.

"Have you seen them before?" I asked. But it was rather as one would say "How do you do" – not so much a question as a salutation.

We looked at each other for a long time, as if committing each other to memory.

"Do you know anyone else?" I said.

"One or two. Three, actually. Do you?"

I shook my head. "You are the first. Is it… is it… always like that?"

"You mean…?" he gestured towards his heart.

I nodded.

"Yes," he said. "Yes, it is."

There didn't seem anything more to talk about. Your right hand hasn't much to say to your left, or one eye to the other. There was comfort in the experience, if comfort is the word, which it isn't. More as if an old faculty had been extended. Or a new one activated.

Sidney put my car on the hoist and sprayed its tires.

Some time later.

I have not seen Sidney again. Two weeks ago when I went back he was not there and as of yesterday, cars have become obsolete. Not that we will use that word publicly. The official word is *suspended.*

Strange to be idle after months of hard labour. A lull only before the boys from the Department of Agriculture come back to prepare the land again. I am pleased that the soy-beans are harvested, that I was able to nurse them along to maturity despite the scorching sun, the intermittent plagues and the problems with water. Often the pressure was too low to turn on the sprinklers and I would stand, hour after hour, hose in hand, trying to get the most use from the tiny trickle spilling from the nozzle.

Sometimes my heart turns over as I look through the kitchen window and see the plants shrivelled and grotesque, the baked earth scored by a web of fine cracks like the glaze on a plate subjected to too high an oven. Then it comes to me in a flash that of course, the beans are gone, the harvest is over.

The world is uncannily quiet. I don't think anyone had any idea of how much noise even distant traffic made until we were without it. It is rare indeed for vehicles other than Government mini-cars to be seen on the streets. And there are fewer and fewer pedestrians. Those who do venture out, move on their thick insulators with the slow gait of rocking horses. Surreal and alien, they heighten rather than lessen one's sense of isolation. For one *is* isolated. We have grown used to the sight of helicopters like large dragonflies hovering overhead – addressing us through their P.A. systems, dropping supplies – welcome but impersonal.

Dexter is my only physical contact. He is delighted to have me inside again. The heat is too great for him in the garden and as, officially, he no longer exists, we only go out under cover of dark.

The order to destroy pets, when it came, indicated more clearly than anything that had gone before, that the government had abandoned hope. In an animal-loving culture, only direct necessity could validate such an order. It fell upon us like a heavy pall.

When the Government truck stopped by for Dexter, I reported him dead. Now that the welfare of so many depends upon our cooperation with authority, law-breaking is a serious offence. But I am not uneasy about breaking this law. As long as he remains healthy and happy, Dexter and I will share our dwindling provisions.

No need to be an ecologist or dependent on non-existent media to know all life is dying and the very atmosphere of our planet is changing radically. Already no birds sing in the hideous hot dawns as the sun, rising through a haze of dust, sheds its curious bronze-green light on a brown world. The trees that once gave us shade stand leafless now in an infernal winter. Yet, as if in the masts and riggings of ships, St. Elmo's fire flickers and shines in their high branches, and bioplasmic pyrotechnics light the dying soy-beans. I am reminded of how the ghostly form of a limb remains attached to the body from which it has been amputated. And I can't help thinking of all the people who don't see the colours, the practical earth-touchers with only their blunt senses to inform them. I wonder about J. and if, since we last talked, she had perhaps been able to see the colours too. But I think not. After so many years of friendship, surely I would be able to sense her, had she broken through.

Evening...?

The heat has increased greatly in the last few weeks – in a quantum leap. This has resulted immediately in two things: a steady rising of the sea level throughout the world – with panic reactions and mild flooding in coastal areas; and, at last, a noticeably higher air temperature. It is causing great physical discomfort.

It was against this probability that the authorities provided us with insulator spray. Like giant cans of pressurized shaving cream. I have shut all rooms but the kitchen and by concentrating my insulating zeal on this one small area, we have managed to keep fairly cool. The world is relative, of course. The radio has stopped giving temperature readings and I have no thermometer. I have filled all cracks and crannies with the foaming plastic, even applied a layer to the exterior wall. There are no baths, of course, and no cold drinks. On the other hand I've abandoned clothes and given Dexter a shave and a haircut. Myself as well. We are a fine pair. Hairless and naked.

When the world state of emergency was declared we didn't need to be told that science had given up. The official line had been that the process would reverse itself as inexplicably as it had begun. The official policy – to hold out as long as possible. With this in mind, task forces worked day and night on survival strategy. On the municipal level, which is all I really knew about, everything that could be centralized was. Telephone exchanges, hydro plants, radio stations became centres around which vital activities took place. Research teams investigated the effects of heat on water mains, sewer pipes, electrical wiring; work crews were employed to prevent, protect or even destroy incipient causes of fire, flood and asphyxiation.

For some time now the city has been zoned. In each zone a large building has been selected, stocked with food, medical supplies and insulating materials. We have been provided with zone maps and an instruction sheet telling us to stay where we are until ordered to move to what is euphemistically called our "home." When ordered, we are to load our cars with whatever we still have of provisions and medicines and drive off *at once*. Helicopters have already dropped kits with enough gasoline for the trip and a small packet, somewhat surprisingly labelled "emergency rations" which contains one cyanide capsule – grim reminder that all may not go as the planners plan. We have been asked to mark our maps, in advance, with the shortest route from our house to our "home," so that in a crisis we will know what we are doing. These instructions are repeated *ad nauseam* over the radio, along with hearty assurances that everything is under control and that there is no cause for alarm. The Government station is now all that remains of our multimedia. When it is not broadcasting instructions, its mainly prerecorded tapes sound inanely complacent and repetitive. Evacuation Day, as we have been told again and again, will be announced by whistle blast. Anyone who runs out of food before that or who is in need of medical aid is to use the special gas ration and go "home" at once.

As a long-time preserver of fruits and vegetables, I hope to hold out until E. Day. When that time comes it will be a sign that broadcasts are no longer possible, that contact can no longer be maintained between the various areas of the community, that the process will not reverse itself in time and that, in fact, our world is well on the way to becoming – oh, wonder of the modern kitchen – a self-cleaning oven.

Spring, Summer, Winter, Fall.
What season is it after all?

I sense the hours by some inner clock. I have applied so many layers of insulating spray that almost no heat comes through from outside. But we have to have air and the small window I have left exposed acts like a furnace. Yet through it I see the dazzling colours; sense my fellow-men.

Noon.

The sun is hidden directly overhead. The world is topaz. I see it through the minute eye of my window. I, the perceiving organ that peers through the house's only aperture. We are one, the house and I – parts of some vibrating sensitive organism in which Dexter plays his differentiated but integral role. The light enters us, dissolves us. We are the golden motes in the jewel.

Midnight.

The sun is directly below. Beneath the burning soles of my arching feet it shines, a globe on fire. Its rays penetrate the earth. Upward beaming, they support and sustain us. We are held aloft, a perfectly balanced ball in the jet of a golden fountain. Light, dancing, infinitely upheld.

Who knows how much later.

I have just "buried" Dexter.

This morning I realized this hot little cell was no longer a possible place for a dog.

I had saved one can of dog food against this day. As I opened it Dexter's eyes swivelled in the direction of so unexpected and delicious a smell. He struggled to his feet, joyous, animated. The old Dexter. I was almost persuaded to delay, to wait and see if the heat subsided. What if tomorrow we awakened to rain? But something in me, stronger than this wavering self, carried on with its purpose.

He sat up, begging, expectant.

I slipped the meat out of the can.

"You're going to have a really good dinner," I said, but as my voice was unsteady, I stopped.

I scooped a generous portion of the meat into his dish and placed it on the floor. He was excited, and as always when excited about food, he was curiously ceremonial, unhurried – approaching his dish and backing away from it, only to approach it again at a slightly different angle. As if the exact position was of the greatest importance. It was one of his most amusing and endearing characteristics. I let him eat his meal in his own leisurely and appreciative manner and then, as I have done so many times before, I fed him his final *bon bouche* by hand. The cyanide pill, provided by a beneficent government for me, went down in a gulp.

I hadn't expected it to be so sudden. Life and death so close. His small frame convulsed violently, then collapsed. Simultaneously, as if synchronized, the familiar "shake" occurred in my vision. Dexter glowed brightly, whitely, like phosphorus. In that dazzling, light-filled moment he was no longer a small dead dog lying there. I could have thought him a lion, my sense of scale had so altered. His beautiful body blinded me with its fires.

With the second "shake" his consciousness must have entered mine for I felt a surge in my heart as if his loyalty and love had flooded it. And like a kind of ground bass, I was aware of scents and sounds I had not known before. Then a great peace filled me – an immense space, light and sweet – and I realized that this was death. Dexter's death.

But how describe what is beyond description?

As the fires emanating from his slight frame died down, glowed weakly, residually, I put on my insulators and carried his body into the now fever-hot garden. I laid him on what had been at one time an azalea bed. I was unable to dig a grave in the baked earth or to cover him with leaves. But there are no predators now to pick the flesh from his bones. Only the heat which will, in time, desiccate it.

I returned to the house, opening the door as little as possible to prevent the barbs and briars of burning air from entering with me. I sealed the door from inside with foam sealer.

The smell of the canned dog food permeated the kitchen. It rang in my nostrils. Olfactory chimes, lingering, delicious. I was intensely aware of Dexter. Dexter immanent. I contained him as simply as a dish contains water. But the simile is not exact. For I missed his physical presence. One relies on the physical more than I had known. My hands sought palpable contact. The flesh forgets slowly.

Idly, abstractedly, I turned on the radio. I seldom do now as the batteries are low and they are my last. Also, there is little incentive. Broadcasts are intermittent and I've heard the old tapes over and over.

But the government station was on the air. I tuned with extreme care and placed my ear close to the speaker. A voice, faint, broken by static, sounded like that of the Prime Minister.

"...all human beings can do, your government has done for you." (Surely not a political speech *now?*) "But we have failed. Failed to hold back the heat. Failed to protect ourselves against it; to protect you against it. It is with profound grief that I send this farewell message to you all." I realized that this, too, had been pre-recorded, reserved for the final broadcast. "Even now, let us not give up hope..."

And then, blasting through the speech, monstrously loud in the stone-silent world, the screech of the whistle summoning us "home." I could no longer hear the P.M.'s words.

I began automatically, obediently, to collect my few remaining foodstuffs, reaching for a can of raspberries, the last of the crop to have grown in my garden when the dawns were dewy and cool and noon sun fell upon us like golden pollen. My hand stopped in mid-air.

I would not go "home."

The whistle shrilled for a very long time. A curious great steam-driven cry – man's last. Weird that our final utterance should be this anguished inhuman wail.

The end.

Now that it is virtually too late, I regret not having kept a daily record. Now that the part of me that writes has become nearly absorbed, I feel obliged to do the best I can.

I am down to the last of my food and water. Have lived on little for some days – weeks, perhaps. How can one measure passing time? Eternal time grows like a tree, its roots in my heart. If I lie on my back I see winds moving in its high branches and a chorus of birds is singing in its leaves. The song is sweeter than any music I have ever heard.

My kitchen is as strange as I am myself. Its walls bulge with many layers of spray. It is without geometry. Like the inside of an eccentric Styrofoam coconut. Yet, with some inner eye, I see its intricate mathematical structure. It is as ordered and no more random than an atom.

My face is unrecognizable in the mirror. Wisps of short damp hair. Enormous eyes. I swim in their irises. Could I drown in the pits of their pupils?

Through my tiny window when I raise the blind, a dead world shines. Sometimes dust storms fill the air with myriad particles burning bright and white as the lion body of Dexter. Sometimes great clouds swirl, like those from which saints receive revelations.

The colours are almost constant now. There are times when, light-headed, I dance a dizzying dance, feel part of that whirling incandescent matter – what I might once have called inorganic matter!

On still days the blameless air, bright as a glistening wing, hangs over us, hangs its extraordinary beneficence over us.

We are together now, united, indissoluble. Bonded.

Because there is no expectation, there is no frustration.

Because there is nothing we can have, there is nothing we can want.

We are hungry of course. Have cramps and weakness. But they are as if in *another body. Our* body is inviolate. Inviolable.

We share one heart.

We are one with the starry heavens and our bodies are stars.

Inner and outer are the same. A continuum. The water in the locks is level. We move to a higher water. A high sea.

A ship could pass through.

JACQUES FERRON

The Grey Dog

Translated by Betty Bednarski

Peter Bezeau, Seigneur of Grand-Etang, had become a widower soon after his marriage, and had replaced his wife with the bottle of rum he drank each night. As the years went by he drained his bottle faster and got to bed earlier, and in this way, little by little, went into his decline. But each morning he was always up again at the very same time, tough and fearless as before. Four big black dogs went with him everywhere, and it was over their heads that he spoke to his men. As the beasts had the reputation of being vicious, his words intimidated. The fishermen and farm workers he employed all feared him. A few respected him. No one thought of loving him.

When evening came Peter Bezeau would suddenly age. His face grew lined, his eyes glassy and wild. The approach of night filled him with alarm. It was then that he drank his bottle. When he had finished it he would call to this daughter, Nelly, to fetch in the dogs. Then he would hurl himself flat on the bed and sink into a deep sleep. Nelly would let in the dogs and go to bed herself.

One morning the Seigneur woke to find among his animals a mysterious grey dog, whose red eyes and furtive manner disconcerted him. He opened the door, and the intruder slipped out, supple as a shadow. One month later it was there again. This time the Seigneur picked up a gun and pushed open the door. The animal fled. But just as he was taking aim it stopped and looked back at him, and from its eyes darted such flames that the Seigneur was forced to lower his weapon. The dog ran on and disappeared. "Next month, flames or no, I'll shoot," said Seigneur Peter Bezeau. And shoot he did. But when the shot rang out the grey dog was no longer there to receive it.

"It must be a werewolf," he thought.

That night, after he'd finished his rum, he called to Nelly to fetch in the dogs, adding: "The dogs, mind! Not the werewolf!" Nelly thought her father was drunk. Now in the old days she would never have thought such a thing. But lately she had not been herself. The next day, when she brought him his bottle, he made a point of telling her so. She shrugged her shoulders. He did the same and turned his attention to his bottle.

One more month passed. The fateful day arrived. Peter Bezeau rose with a feeling of apprehension. He went down to the kitchen. His four big black dogs were there, but of the grey dog there was not a sign. He could breathe again. The nightmare was over. It was then that Nelly appeared on the scene. She was not usually about so early. Surprised, Peter Bezeau studied her closely. Her delicate features seemed smaller than before, her shoulders were thrust back, and her stomach...

"Nelly?"

Nelly didn't move.

"Do you know what's the matter with you, then?"

She did not. Peter Bezeau waited to hear no more. He rushed outside, followed by his four big black dogs. To Madame Marie's house he headed. He left his dogs outside her door and went in.

"Peter Bezeau," says the old woman, "you look worried. Are you ill?"

Without his dogs the Seigneur is a pathetic figure, just an old man of sixty years or more.

"I'm not ill," says he. "I'm worried about my daughter. Come back to the house and tell me what's the matter with her."

Madame Marie had a look at Nelly.

"Your daughter, Peter Bezeau, is in the family way. And it's pretty far along she is too."

"Now listen to me, Madame Marie!" says the Seigneur, and this time he's talking to her over the heads of his four big black dogs. "Just you listen to me. If any harm comes to Nelly I'll have you dried and salted like an old cod-fish."

"Will you, indeed, Peter Bezeau? Well, I'm not good for much more than that as it is. But come back and see me tomorrow and I'll give you an answer then."

The next day the Seigneur was at her house at the crack of dawn. He left his dogs outside. He was just a pathetic figure again, an old man of sixty years or more.

"Who got Nelly in this state, Peter Bezeau?"

"I don't know."

The old woman looked hard at him.

"Are you sure?"

Peter Bezeau became uneasy. He admitted what he knew.

"A grey dog with red eyes? A werewolf, then?"

"I was thinking the same myself."

"Peter Bezeau, are you serious? You expect me to deliver your daughter when we don't even know what she's got in her belly! I don't intend to get myself dried and salted like an old cod-fish."

The Seigneur didn't have his dogs. He was just a pathetic figure, an old man of sixty years or more, in despair over his daughter's misfortune. He begged the old woman to have pity on him.

"I'll have pity on you, Peter Bezeau. But you must do as I say. Fetch me Madame Rose, Thomette Tardif, Pope Jane from Gros-Morne and Madame Germaine. With their help I'll deliver Nelly, I swear, even if she's pregnant with a unicorn."

No sooner had she spoken than the Seigneur was running toward the shore, his four big black dogs bounding ahead of him and barking in the wind. Seagulls burst from their mouths and flew out to the wharf, where they merged with the foam of the waves. Presently four boats weighed anchor and put out to sea.

The first boat would sail back from Cloridorme with Madame Rose, who was thin and cunning and knew the art of deceiving young women as to the nature of their pains, making them believe they were only stomach cramps that would soon pass, while the labour pains would not start for another nine days. She denied labour in its early stages, the better to affirm it later on, when it was nearly over. She was a very useful old lady. The second boat would come in from Gros-Morne with Jane Andicotte, known as Pope Jane, because she owned a huge English Bible. From this Bible she drew strange magical incantations that had the power to seize the soul and raise it a full two feet above the bed, leaving the belly free to get on and do its work, without any fuss or bother. The third boat would have on board Madame Germaine from Echourie who handled a babe like a piece of fine satin. And, last of all, Thomette Tardif would arrive in the fourth boat from Mont-Louis, bringing hooks he'd made himself, to be used in the event the child (or monster) got stuck in Nelly's loins.

When the boats were all in, the three midwives, Pope Jane, and the man with the hooks shut themselves up with the Seigneur's daughter. The Seigneur himself was banished from the house and stayed outside. From time to time a young man came out to bring him news. And in this way he learned that Madame Rose had finished her little deceits and that Pope Jane had replaced her and was reading from her big book. The hours seemed long. At last, as day drew to a close, the young man came out, beaming.

"The women have sent Thomette away," he announced.

The Seigneur looked at him over the heads of his four big black dogs.

"Who are you, young man?" he asked. "And how do you know so much?"

"I am your manager. Don't you recognize me?"

"I don't like my managers. They're too ambitious. They all want to steal my estate."

The young man didn't answer. Night was falling.

"Monsieur Bezeau," he said, "come to the store. We'll be more comfortable waiting there."

The Seigneur followed him. They sat down inside the store. The four big black dogs began at once to sniff at the cellar door.

"What do they smell?"

"I've no idea."

"Open the door and we'll soon see."

The manager opened the door and the Seigneur saw a grey dog with red eyes that he knew well.

"Whose animal is this?" he asked.

"Mine," replied the manager.

At that moment someone came to inform them that a son had been born to Nelly in the most felicitous manner possible. The two men went back to the house, which was all lit up. When the lamps had been blown out, the Seigneur asked, "Who will bring me my rum?" It was the able young manager who brought it. Peter Bezeau emptied the bottle, hurled himself flat on his bed and fell asleep as usual. In the days that followed, however, he seemed changed. Now everyone saw that he was a pathetic figure, just an old man of sixty years or more. He died soon after.

His four big black dogs searched for a time around his grave, then, finding nothing, they too disappeared from Grand-Etang. The grey dog took their place.

MAVIS GALLANT

LUC AND HIS FATHER

To the astonishment of no one except his father and mother, Luc Clairevoie failed the examination that should have propelled him straight into one of the finest schools of engineering in Paris; failed it so disastrously, in fact, that an examiner, who knew someone in the same ministry as Luc's father, confided it was the sort of labour in vain that should be written up. Luc's was a prime case of universal education gone crazy. He was a victim of the current belief that any student, by dint of application, could answer what he was asked.

Luc's father blamed the late President de Gaulle. If de Gaulle had not opened the schools and universities to hordes of qualified but otherwise uninteresting young people, teachers would have had more time to spare for Luc. De Gaulle had been dead for years, but Roger Clairevoie still suspected him of cosmic mischief and double-dealing. (Like his wife, Roger had never got over the loss of Algeria. When the price of fresh fruit went high, as it did every winter, the Clairevoies told each other it was because of the loss of all those Algerian orchards.)

Where Luc was concerned, they took a practical course, lowered their sights to a lesser but still elegant engineering school, and sent Luc to a crammer for a year to get ready for a new trial. His mother took Luc to the dentist, had his glasses changed, and bought him a Honda 125 to make up for his recent loss of self-esteem. Roger's contribution took the form of long talks. Cornering Luc in the kitchen after breakfast, or in his own study, now used as a family television room, Roger told Luc how he had been graduated with honours from the noblest engineering institute in France; how he could address other alumni using the second person singular, even by Christian name, regardless of whether they spoke across a ministerial desk or a lunch table. Many of Roger's fellow graduates had chosen civil-service careers. They bumped into one another in marble halls, under oil portraits of public servants who wore the steadfast look of advisers to gods; and these distinguished graduates, Roger among them, had a charming, particular way of seeming like brothers – or so it appeared to those who could only envy them, who had to keep to "Have I the honour of" and "If Mr. Assistant Under-Secretary would be good enough to" and "Should it suit the convenience." To this fraternity Luc could no longer aspire, but there was still some hope for future rank and dignity: he could become an engineer in the building trades. Luc did not reply; he did not even ask, "Do you mean houses, or garages, or what?" Roger supposed he was turning things over in his mind.

The crammer he went to was a brisk, costly examination factory in Rennes, run by Jesuits, with the reputation for being able to jostle any student, even the dreamiest, into a respectable institute for higher learning. The last six words were from the school's brochure. They ran through Roger Clairevoie's head like an election promise.

Starting in September, Luc spent Monday to Friday in Rennes. Weekends, he came home by train, laden with books, and shut himself up to study. Sometimes Roger would hear him trying chords on his guitar: pale sound without rhythm or sequence. When Luc had studied enough, he buckled on his white helmet and roared around Paris on the Honda. (The promise of a BMW R/80 was in the air, as reward or consolation, depending on next year's results.) On the helmet Luc had lettered IN CASE OF ACCIDENT DO NOT REMOVE. "You see, he does think of things," his mother said. "Luc thinks of good, useful things."

Like many Parisian students, Luc was without close friends, and in Rennes he knew nobody. His parents were somewhat relieved when, in the autumn, he became caught like a strand of seaweed on the edge of a political discussion group. The group met every Sunday afternoon in some member's house. Once, the group assembled at the Clairevoies'; Simone Clairevoie, pleased to see that Luc was showing interest in adult problems, served fruit juice, pâté sandwiches, and two kinds of ice cream. Luc's friends did not paint slogans on the sidewalk, or throw petrol bombs at police stations, or carry weapons (at least, Roger hoped not), or wear ragtag uniforms bought at the flea market. A few old men talked, and the younger men, those Luc's age, sat on a windowsill or on the floor, and seemed to listen. Among the speakers the day they came to the Clairevoies' was a retired journalist, once thought ironic and alarming, and the former secretary of a minor visionary, now in decrepit exile in Spain. Extremist movements were banned, but, as Roger pointed out to his wife, one could not really call this a movement. There was no law against meeting on a winter afternoon to consider the false starts of history. Luc never said much, but his parents supposed he must be taking to heart the message of the failed old men; and it was curious to see how Luc could grasp a slippery, allusive message so easily when he could not keep in mind his own private destiny as an engineer. Luc could vote, get married without permission, have his own bank account, run up bills. He could leave home, though a course so eccentric had probably not yet occurred to him. He was of age; adult; a grown man.

The Clairevoies had spent their married life in an apartment on the second floor of a house of venturesome design, built just after the First World War, in a quiet street near the Bois de Boulogne. The designer of the house, whose name they could never recall, had been German or Austrian. Roger, when questioned by colleagues surprised to find him in surroundings so bizarre, would say, "The architect was Swiss," which made him sound safer. Students of architecture rang the bell to ask if they might visit the rooms and take photographs. Often they seemed taken aback by the sight of the furniture, a wedding gift from Roger's side of the family, decorated with swans and sphinxes; the armchairs were as hard and uncompromising as the Judgment Seat. To Roger, the furniture served as counterpoise to the house, which belonged to the alien Paris of the 1920s, described by Roger's father as full of artists and immigrants of a shiftless kind – the flotsam of Europe.

The apartment, a wedding present from Simone's parents, was her personal choice. Roger's people, needing the choice explained away, went on saying for years that Simone had up-to-date ideas; but Roger was not sure this was true. After all, the house was some forty years old by the time the Clairevoies moved in. The street, at least, barely changed from year to year, unless one counted the increasing number of prostitutes that drifted in from the Bois. Directly across from the house, a café, the only place of business in sight, served as headquarters for the prostitutes' rest periods, conversations, and quarrels. Sometimes Roger went there when he ran out of cigarettes. He knew some of the older women by sight, and he addressed them courteously; and they, of course, were polite to him. Once, pausing under the awning to light a cigarette, he glanced up and saw Luc standing at a window, the curtain held aside with an elbow. He seemed to be staring at nothing in particular, merely waiting for something that might fix his attention. Roger had a middle-aged, paternal reflex: is that what he calls studying? If Luc noticed his father, he gave no sign.

Simone Clairevoie called it the year of shocks. There had been Luc's failure, then Roger had suffered a second heart attack, infinitely more frightening than the first. He was home all day on convalescent leave from his ministry, restless and bored, smoking on the sly, grudgingly walking the family dog by way of moderate exercise. Finally, even though all three Clairevoies had voted against it, a Socialist government came to power. Simone foresaw nothing but further decline. If Luc failed again, it would mean a humble career, preceded by a tour of Army duty – plain military service, backpack and drill, with the sons of peasants and Algerian delinquents. Roger would never be able to get him out of it: He knew absolutely no one in the new system of favours. Those friends whose careers had not been lopped sat hard on their jobs, almost afraid to pick up the telephone. Every call was bad news. The worst news would be the voice of an old acquaintance, harking back to a foundered regime and expecting a good turn. Although the Clairevoies seldom went to church now – the new Mass was the enemy – Simone prayed hard on Christmas Eve, singling out in particular St. Odile, who had been useful in the past, around a time when Roger had seemed to regret his engagement to Simone and may have wanted to break it off.

Soon after the New Year, however, there came a message from the guidance counsellor of the Jesuit school, summoning the Clairevoies for "a frank and open discussion."

"About being immortal?" said Roger to Simone, recalling an alarming talk with another Jesuit teacher long ago.

"About your son," she replied.

A card on his door identified the counsellor as "F.-X. Rousseau, Orientation." Orientation wore a track suit and did not look to Roger like a Jesuit, or even much like a priest. Leaning forward (the Clairevoies instinctively drew back), he offered American cigarettes before lighting his own. It was not Luc's chances of passing that seemed to worry him but Luc's fragmented image of women. On the Rorschach test, for instance, he had seen a ballet skirt and a pair of legs, and a female head in a fishing net.

"You brought me here to tell me what?" said Roger. "My son has poor eyesight?"

Simone placed her hand on Father Rousseau's desk as she might have touched his sleeve. She was saying, Be careful. My husband is irritable, old-fashioned, ill. "I think that Father Rousseau is trying to tell us that Luc has no complete view of women because Luc has no complete view of himself as a man. Is that it?"

Father Rousseau added, "And he cannot see his future because he can't see himself."

It was Roger's turn to remonstrate with Luc. Simone suggested masculine, virile surroundings for their talk, and so he took Luc to the café across the street. There, over beer for Luc and mineral water for Roger, he told Luc about satisfaction. It was the duty of children to satisfy their parents. Roger, by doing extremely well at his studies, had given Luc's grandparents this mysterious pleasure. They had been able to tell their friends, "Roger has given us great satisfaction." He took Luc on a fresh tour of things to come, showing him the slow-grinding machinery of state competitive examinations against which fathers measured their sons. He said, "Your future. If you fail. A poor degree is worse than none. Thousands of embittered young men, all voting Socialist. If you fail, you will sink into the swamp from which there is no rising. Do you want to sell brooms? Sweep the streets? Sell tickets in the Métro? Do you want to spend your life in a bank?

"Not that there is anything wrong with working in a bank," he corrected. Entrusted in his wife's family was a small rural bank with a staff of seventeen. Simone did not often see her provincial cousins, but the bank was always mentioned with respect. To say "a small bank" was no worse than saying "a small crown jewel." Simone, in a sense, personified a reliable and almost magical trade; she had brought to Roger the goods and the dream. What had Roger brought? Hideous Empire furniture and a dubious nineteenth-century title Simone scarcely dared used because of the Communists.

Only the word "Socialist" seemed to stir Luc. "We need a good little civil war," he declared, as someone who has never been near the ocean might announce, "We need a good little tidal wave" – so Roger thought.

He said, "There are no good little civil wars." But he knew what was said of him: that his heart attacks had altered his personality, made him afraid. On a November day, Roger and his father had followed the coffin of Charles Maurras, the nationalist leader, jailed after the war for collaboration. "My son," said Roger's father, introducing Roger to thin-faced men, some wearing the Action Française emblem. Roger's father had stood for office on a Royalist platform, and had come out of the election the last of five candidates, one an impertinent youngster with an alien name, full of "z"s and "k"s. He was not bitter; he was scornful and dry, and he wanted Roger to be dry and proud. Roger had only lately started to think, My father always said, and, My father believed. As he spoke, now, to Luc about satisfaction and failure, he remembered how he had shuffled behind the hearse of a dead old man, perhaps mistaken, certainly dispossessed. They got up to leave, and Roger bowed to an elderly woman he recognized. His son had already turned away.

In order to give Luc a fully virile image, Simone redecorated his room. The desk lamp was a galleon in full sail with a bright red shade – the colour of decision and activity. She took down the photograph of Roger's graduating class and hung a framed poster of Che Guevara. Stepping back to see the effect, she realized Guevara would never do. The face was feminine, soft. She wondered if the whole legend was not a hoax and if Guevara had been a woman in disguise. Guevara had no political significance, of course; he had become manly, decorative kitsch. (The salesman had assured her of this; otherwise, she would never have run the risk of offending Roger.) As she removed the poster she noticed for the first time a hole drilled in the wall. She put her eye to it and had a partial view of the maid's bathroom, used in the past by a succession of *au pair* visitors, in Paris to improve their French and to keep an eye on a younger Luc.

She called Roger and made him look: "Who says Luc has no view of women?"

Roger glanced round at the new curtains and bedspread, with their pattern of Formula 1 racing cars. Near the bed someone – Luc, probably – had tacked a photo of Hitler. Roger, without saying anything, took it down. He did not want Luc quite that manly.

"You can't actually see the shower," said Simone, trying the perspective again. "But I suppose that when she stands drying on the mat… We'd better tell him."

"Tell Luc?"

"Rousseau. Orientation."

Not "Father Rousseau," he noticed. It was not true that women were devoted guardians of tradition. They rode every new wave like so much plankton. My father was right, he decided. He always said it was a mistake to give them the vote. He said they had no ideas – just notions. My father was proud to stand up for the past. He was proud to be called a Maurrassien, even when Charles Maurras was in defeat, in disgrace. But who has ever heard of a Maurrassienne? The very idea made Roger smile. Simone, catching the smile, took it to mean a sudden feeling of tolerance, and so she chose the moment to remind him they would have an *au pair* guest at Easter – oh, not to keep an eye on Luc; Luc was too old. (She sounded sorry.) But Luc had been three times to England, to a family named Brunt, and now, in all fairness, it was the Clairevoies' obligation to have Cassandra.

"Another learner?" Roger was remembering the tall, glum girls from northern capitals and their strides in colloquial French: That is my friend. He did not sleep in my bed – he spent the night on the doormat. I am homesick. I am ill. A bee has stung me. I am allergic and may die.

"You won't have to worry about Cassandra," Simone said. "She is a mature young woman of fifteen, a whole head taller than Luc."

Simone clipped a leash to the dog's collar and grasped Roger firmly by the arm. She was taking two of her charges for a walk, along streets she used to follow when Luc was still in his pram. On Boulevard Lannes a taxi stopped and two men wearing white furs, high-heeled white boots, and Marilyn Monroe wigs got out and made for the Bois. Roger knew that transvestites worked the fringe of the Bois now, congregating mostly toward the Porte Maillot, where there were hotels. He had heard the women in the café across the street complaining that the police were not vigilant enough, much the way an established artisan might grumble about black-market labour. Roger had imagined them vaguely as night creatures, glittering and sequined, caught like dragonflies in the headlights of roving automobiles. This pair was altogether real, and the man who had just paid the taxi driver shut his gold-mesh handbag with the firm snap of a housewife settling the butcher's bill. The dog at once began to strain and bark.

"Brazilians," said Simone, who watched educational television in the afternoon. "They send all their money home."

"But in broad daylight," said Roger.

"They don't earn as much as you think."

"There could be little children playing in the Bois."

"We can't help our children by living in the past," said Simone. Roger wondered if she was having secret talks with Father Rousseau. "Stop that," she told the barking dog.

"He's not deliberately trying to hurt their feelings," Roger said. Because he disliked animals – in particular, dogs – he tended to make excuses for the one they owned. Actually, the dog was an accident in their lives, purchased only after the staff psychologist in Luc's old school had said the boy's grades were poor because he had no siblings to love and hate, no rivals for his parents' attention, no responsibility to any living creature.

"A dog will teach my son to add and subtract?" said Roger. Simone had wondered if a dog would make Luc affectionate and polite, more grateful for his parents' devotion, aware of the many sacrifices they had made on his behalf.

Yes, yes, they had been assured. A dog could do all that.

Luc was twelve years old, the puppy ten weeks. Encouraged to find a name for him, Luc came up with "Mongrel." Simone chose "Sylvestre." Sylvestre spent his first night in Luc's room – part of the night, that is. When he began to whine, Luc put him out. After that, Sylvestre was fed, trained, and walked by Luc's parents, while Luc continued to find school a mystery and to show indifference and ingratitude. Want of thanks is a parent's lot, but blindness to simple arithmetic was like an early warning of catastrophe. Luc's parents had already told him he was to train as an engineer.

"Do you know how stiff the competition is?" his mother asked.

"Yes."

"Do you want to be turned down by the best schools?"

"I don't know."

"Do you want to be sent to a third-rate school, miles from home? Have you thought about that?"

Roger leaned on Simone, though he did not need to, and became querulous: "Sylvestre and I are two old men."

This was not what Simone liked to talk about. She said, "Your family never took you into consideration. You slept in your father's study. You took second best."

"It didn't feel that way."

"Look at our miserable country house. Look at your Cousin Henri's estate."

"His godmother gave it to him," said Roger, as though she needed reminding.

"He should have given you compensation."

"People don't do that," said Roger. "All I needed was a richer godmother."

"The apartment is mine," said Simone, as they walked arm in arm. "The furniture is yours. The house in the country is yours, but most of the furniture belongs to me. You paid for the pool and the tennis court." It was not unpleasant conversation.

Roger stopped in front of a pastry shop and showed Simone a chocolate cake. "Why can't we have that?"

"Because it would kill you. The specialist said so."

"We could have oysters," Roger said. "I'm allowed oysters."

"Luc will be home," said Simone. "He doesn't like them."

Father Rousseau sent for the Clairevoies again. This time he wore a tweed jacket over a white sweater, with a small crucifix on one lapel and a Solidarność badge on the other. After lighting his cigarette he sat drumming his fingers, as if wondering how to put his grim news into focus. At last he said, "No one can concentrate on an exam and on a woman. Not at the same time."

"Women?" cried Simone. "What women?"

"Woman," Roger corrected, unheard.

There was a woman in Luc's life. It seemed unbelievable, but it was so.

"French?" said Roger instantly.

Father Rousseau was unable to swear to it. Her name was Katia, her surname Martin, but if Martin was the most common family name in France it might be because so many foreigners adopted it.

"I can find out," Simone interrupted. "What's her age?"

Katia was eighteen. Her parents were divorced.

"That's bad," said Simone. "Who's her father?"

She lived in Biarritz with her mother, but came often to Paris to stay with her father and brother. Her brother belonged to a political debating society.

"I've seen him," said Simone. "I know the one. She's a terrorist. Am I right?"

Father Rousseau doubted it. "She is a spoiled, rich, undereducated young woman, used to having her own way. She is also very much in love."

"With Luc?" said Roger.

"Luc is a Capricorn," said Simone. "The most level-headed of all the signs."

So was Katia, Father Rousseau said. She and Luc wrote "Capricorn loves Capricorn" in the dust on parked cars.

"Does Luc want to marry her?" said Simone, getting over the worst.

"He wants something." But Father Rousseau hoped it would not be Katia. She seemed to have left school early, after a number of misadventures. She was hardly the person to inspire Luc, who needed a model he could copy. When Katia was around, Luc did not even pretend to study. When she was in Biarritz, he waited for letters. The two collected lump sugar from cafés but seemed to have no other cultural interest.

"She's from a rich family?" Simone said. "And she has just the one brother?"

"Luc has got to pass his entrance examination," said Roger. "After he gets his degree he can marry anyone he likes."

"'Rich' is a relative term," said Simone, implying that Father Rousseau was too unworldly to define such a thing.

Roger said, "How do you know about the sugar and 'Capricorn loves Capricorn' and how Luc and Katia got to know each other?"

"Why, from Katia's letters, of course," said Father Rousseau, sounding surprised.

"Did you keep copies?" said Simone.

"Do you know that Luc is of age, and that he could take you to court for reading his mail?" said Roger.

Father Rousseau turned to Simone, the rational parent. "Not a word of reproach," he warned her. "Just keep an eye on the situation. We feel that Luc should spend the next few weeks at home, close to his parents." He would come back to Rennes just before the examination, for last-minute heavy cramming. Roger understood this to be a smooth Jesuitical manner of getting rid of Luc.

Luc came home, and no one reproached him. He promised to work hard and proposed going alone to the country house, which was near Auxerre. Simone objected that the place had been unheated all winter. Luc replied that he would live in one room and take his meals in the village. Roger guessed that Luc intended to spend a good amount of time with Cousin Henri, who lived nearby, and whom Luc – no one knew why – professed to admire. Cousin Henri and Roger enjoyed property litigation of long standing, but as there was a dim, far chance of Henri's leaving something to Luc, Roger said nothing. And as Simone pointed out, meaning by this nothing unkind or offensive, any male model for Luc was better than none.

In the meantime, letters from Katia, forwarded from Rennes, arrived at the Paris apartment. Roger watched in pure amazement the way Simone managed to open them, rolling a kitchen match under the flap. Having read the letter, she resealed it without a trace. The better quality of the paper, the easier the match trick, she explained. She held a page up to the light, approving the watermark.

"We'll need a huge apartment, because we will have so many children," Katia wrote. "And we'll need space for the sugar collection."

The only huge apartment Simone could think of was her own. "They wish we were dead," she told Roger. "My son wishes I were out of the way." She read aloud, "'What would you be without me? One more little Frenchman, eternally studying for exams.'"

"What does she mean by 'little Frenchman'?" said Roger. He decided that Katia must be foreign – a descendant of White Russians, perhaps. There had been a colony in Biarritz in his father's day, the men gambling away their wives' tiaras before settling down as headwaiters and croupiers. Luc was entangled in a foreign love affair; he was already alien, estranged. Roger had seen him standing at the window, like an idle landowner in a Russian novel. What did Roger know about Russians? There were the modern ones, dressed in grey, with bulldog faces; there were the slothful, mournful people in books, the impulsive and slender women, the indecisive men. But it had been years since Roger had opened a novel; what he saw were overlapping images, like stills from old films.

"'Where are you, where are you?'" read Simone. "'There is a light in your parents' room, but your windows are dark. I'm standing under the awning across the street. My shoes are soaked. I am too miserable to care.'

"She can't be moping in the rain and writing all at the same time," said Simone. "And the postmark is Biarritz. She comes to Paris to stir up trouble. How does she know which room is ours? Luc is probably sick of her. He must have been at a meeting."

Yes, he had probably been at a meeting, sitting on the floor of a pale room, with a soft-voiced old man telling him about an older, truer Europe. Luc was learning a Europe caught in amber, unchanging, with trees for gods. There was no law against paganism and politics, or soft-voiced old men.

At least there are no guns, Roger told himself. And where had Simone learned the way to open other people's letters? He marvelled at Katia's doing for his son what no woman had ever done for him; she had stood in the rain, crying probably, watching for a light.

Ten days before Easter, Cassandra Brunt arrived. Her father was a civil servant, like Roger. He was also an author: two books had been published, one about Napoleon's retreat from Moscow, the other about the failure of the Maginot Line and the disgraceful conduct of the French officer class. Both had been sent to the Clairevoies, with courteous inscriptions. When Simone had gone over to England alone, to see if the Brunts would do for Luc, Mrs. Brunt confided that her husband was more interested in the philosophy of combat than in success and defeat. He was a dreamer, and that was why he had never got ahead. Simone replied that Roger, too, had been hampered by guiding principles. As a youth, he had read for his own pleasure. His life was a dream. Mrs. Brunt suggested a major difference: Mr. Brunt was no full-time dreamer. He had written five books, two of which had been printed, one in 1952 and one in

1966. The two women had then considered each other's child, decided it was sexless and safe and that Luc and Cassandra could spend time under the same roof. After that, Luc crossed the Channel for three visits, while Simone managed not to have Cassandra even once. Her excuse was the extreme youth of Cassandra and the dangers of Paris. Now that Cassandra was fifteen Mrs. Brunt, suddenly exercising her sense of things owed, had written to say that Cassandra was ready for perils and the French.

Roger and Simone met Cassandra at the Gare du Nord. The moment he saw her, Roger understood she had been forced by her parents to make the trip, and that they were ruining her Easter holiday. He marvelled that a fifteen-year-old of her size and apparent strength could be bullied into anything.

"I'll be seeing Luc, what fun," said Cassandra, jackknifed into the car, her knees all but touching her chin. "It will be nice to see Luc," she said sadly. Her fair hair almost covered her face.

"Luc is at our country residence, studying with all the strength of his soul," said Simone. "He is in the Yonne," she added. Cassandra looked puzzled. Roger supposed that to a foreigner it must sound as though Luc had fallen into a river.

There had been no coaxing Luc, no pleading; no threat was strong enough to frighten him. They could keep the BMW, they could stop his allowance; they could put him in jail. He would not come to Paris to welcome Cassandra. He was through with England, through with the Brunts – through, for that matter, with his mother and father. Katia had taken their place.

"We'll have her in Paris for a week, alone," Simone had wailed. Luc's argument was unassailable; alone, he could study. Once they were all there, he would have to be kind to Cassandra, making conversation and showing her the village church. Simone put the blame on Mrs. Brunt, who had insisted in a wholly obtuse way on having her rights.

"How are your delicious parents?" she asked, turning as well as the seat belt allowed, seeming to let the car drive itself in Paris traffic.

"Daddy's at home now. He's retired from the minstrel."

"The ministry," said Simone deeply. Cassandra's was the only English she had ever completely understood. "My husband has also retired from public service. It was too much for his heart. He is much younger than Mr. Brunt, I believe."

"Daddy was a late starter," said Cassandra. "But he'll last a long time. At least, I hope so."

Like the dog bought to improve Luc's arithmetic; like the tropical fish Simone had tended for Luc, and eventually mourned; like the tennis court in which Luc had at once lost interest and on which Roger had had his first heart attack, so Cassandra fell to Luc's parents. With Simone, she watched television; with Roger, she walked uphill and down, to parks and museums.

"What was your minstrel?" she asked Roger, as they marched toward the Bois.

"Years ago, when there was a grave shortage of telephones, thanks to President de Gaulle – " Roger began. "Do you recall that unhappy time?"

"I'm afraid I'm dreffly ignorant."

"I was good at getting friends off the waiting list. That was what I did best."

He clutched her arm, dragging her out of the way of buses and taxis that rushed from the left while Cassandra looked hopelessly right.

"You like the nature?" he said, letting Sylvestre run free in the Bois. "The trees?"

"My mother does. Though this is hardly nature, is it?"

Sylvestre loped, snuffling, into a clump of dusty shrubbery. He gave a yelp and came waddling out. All Roger saw of the person who had kicked him was a flash of white boot.

"You have them in England?" said Roger.

"Have what?"

"That. Male, female. Prostitutes."

"Yes, of course. But they aren't vile to animals."

"You like the modern art?" Roger asked, breathless, as they plodded up the stalled escalators of the Beaubourg museum.

"I'm horribly old-fashioned, I'm afraid."

Halfway, he paused to let his heart rest. His heart was an old pump, clogged and filthy. Cassandra's heart was of bright new metal; it beat more quietly and regularly than any clock.

Above the city stretched a haze of pollution, unstirring, all of an even colour. The sun suffused the haze with amber dye, which by some grim alchemy was turned into dun. Roger saw through the haze to a forgotten city, unchanging, and it was enough to wrench the heart. A hand, reaching inside the rib cage, seemed to grasp the glutted machine. He knew that some part of the machine was intact, faithful to him; when his heart disowned him entirely he might as well die.

Cassandra, murmuring that looking down made her feel giddy, turned her back. Roger watched a couple, below, walking hand in hand. He was too far away to see their faces. They were eating out of a shared paper bag. The young man looked around, perhaps for a bin. Finding none, he handed the bag to the girl, who flung it down. The two were dressed nearly alike, in blue jackets and jeans. Simone had assured Roger that Katia was French, but he still saw her Russian. He saw Katia in winter furs, with a fur hat, and long fair hair over a snowy collar. She removed a glove and gave the hand, warm, to Luc to hold.

"I'm afraid I must be getting lazy," Cassandra remarked. "I found that quite a climb."

The couple in blue had turned a corner. Of Luc and Katia there remained footsteps on lightly fallen snow.

"This place reminds me of a giant food processor," said Cassandra. "What does it make you think of?"

"Young lovers," Roger said.

Cassandra had a good point in Simone's eyes: she kept a diary, which Simone used to improve her English.

"'The Baron has sex on the brain,'" Simone read. "'Even a museum reminds him of sex. In the Bois de Boulogne he tried to twist the conversation around to sex and bestiality. You have to be careful every minute. Each time we have to cross the road he tries to squeeze my arm.'"

When Cassandra had been shown enough of Paris, Simone packed the car with food that Luc liked to eat and drove south and east with the dog, Roger, and Cassandra. They stopped often during the journey so that Cassandra, who sat in the back of the car, could get out and be sick. They found Luc living like an elderly squatter in a ground-floor room full of toast crumbs. It was three in the afternoon, and he was still wearing pyjamas. Inevitably, Cassandra asked if he was ill.

"Katia's been here," said Simone, going round the house and opening shutters. "I can tell. It's in the air."

Luc was occupying the room meant for Cassandra. He showed no willingness to give it up. He took slight notice of his parents, and none whatever of their guest. It seemed to Roger that he had grown taller, but this was surely an illusion, a psychological image in Roger's mind. His affair, if Roger could call it that, had certainly made him bolder. He mentioned Katia by name, saying that one advantage of living alone was that he could read his mail before anyone else got to it. Roger foresaw a holiday of bursting quarrels. He supposed Cassandra would go home and tell her father, the historian, that the French were always like that.

On the day they arrived, Simone intercepted and read a letter. Katia, apparently in answer to some questioning from Luc, explained that she had almost, but not entirely, submitted to the advances of a cousin. (Luc, to forestall his mother, met the postman at the gate. Simone, to short-circuit Luc, had already picked up the letters that interested her at the village post office.) Katia's near seduction had taken place in a field of barley, while her cousin was on leave from military service. A lyrical account of clouds, birds, and crickets took up most of a page.

Roger would not touch the letter, but he listened as Simone read aloud. It seemed to him that some coarse appreciation of the cousin was concealed behind all those crickets and birds. Katia's blithe candour was insolent, a slur on his son. At the same time, he took heart: If a cousin was liable for Army duty, some part of the family must be French. On the other hand, who would rape his cousin in a barley field, if not a Russian?

"You swore Katia was French," he said, greatly troubled.

He knew nothing of Katia, but he did know something about fields. Roger decided he did not believe a word of the story. Katia was trying to turn Luc into a harmless and impotent bachelor friend. The two belonged in a novel of the early nineteen-fifties. (Simone, as Roger said this, began to frown.) "Luc is the good, kind man she can tell stories to," he said. "Her stories will be more and more about other men." As Simone drew breath, he said quickly, "Not that I see Luc in a novel."

"No, but I can see you in the diary of a hysterical English girl," said Simone, and she told him about Cassandra.

Roger, scarcely listening, went on, "In a novel, Katia's visit would be a real-estate tour. She would drive up from Biarritz with her mother and take pictures from the road. Katia's mother would find the house squat and suburban, and so Luc would show them Cousin Henri's. They would take pictures of that, too. Luc would now be going round with chalk and a tape measure, marking the furniture he wants to sell once we're buried, planning the rooms he will build for Katia when the place is his."

All at once he felt the thrust of the next generation, and for the first time he shared some of Simone's fear of the unknown girl.

"The house is yours," said Simone, mistaking his meaning. "The furniture is mine. They can't change that by going round with a piece of chalk. There's always the bank. She can't find *that* suburban." The bank had recently acquired a new and unexpected advantage: it was too small to be nationalized. "Your son is a dreamer," said Simone. "He dreams he is studying, and he fails his exams. He dreams about sex and revolutions, and he waits around for letters and listens to old men telling silly tales."

Roger remembered the hole drilled in the wall. An *au pair* girl in the shower was Luc's symbol of sexual mystery. From the great courtesans of his grandfather's time to the prettiest children of the poor in bordellos to a girl glimpsed as she stood drying herself – what a decline! Here was the true comedown, the real debasement of the middle class. Perhaps he would write a book about it; it would at least rival Mr. Brunt's opus about the decline of French officers.

"She can't spell," said Simone, examining the letter again. "If Luc marries her, he will have to write all her invitations and her postcards." What else did women write? She paused, wondering.

"Her journal?" Roger said.

In Cassandra's journal Simone read, "'They expect such a lot from that poor clod of a Luc.'" That night at dinner Simone remarked, "My father once said he could die happy. He had never entertained a foreigner or shaken hands with an English man."

Cassandra stared at Roger as if to say: Is she joking? Roger, married twenty-three years, thought she was not. Cassandra's pale hair swung down as she drooped over her plate. She began to pick at something that, according to her diary, made her sick: underdone lamb, cooked the French way, stinking of garlic and spilling blood.

At dawn there was a spring thunderstorm, like the start of civil war. The gunfire died, and a hard, steady rain soaked the tennis court and lawn. Roger got up, first in the household, and let the dog out of the garage, where it slept among piles of paperbacks and rusting cans of weed killer. Roger was forty-eight that day; he hoped no one would notice. He thought he saw yellow roses running along the hedge, but it was a shaft of sunlight. In the kitchen, he found a pot with the remains of last night's coffee and heated some in a saucepan. While he drank, standing, looking out the window, the sky cleared entirely and became soft and blue.

"Happy birthday."

He turned his head, and there was Cassandra in the doorway, wearing a long gypsy skirt and an embroidered nightshirt, with toy rings on every finger. "I thought I'd dress because of Sunday," she explained. "I thought we might be going to church."

"I could offer you better coffee in the village," said Roger. "If you do not mind the walk." He imagined her diary entry: "The Baron tried to get me alone on a country road, miles from any sign of habitation."

"The dog will come, too," he assured her.

They walked on the rim of wet fields, in which the freed dog leaped. The hem of Cassandra's skirt showed dark where it brushed against drenched grasses. Roger told her that the fields and woods, almost all they could see, had belonged to his grandparents. Cousin Henri owned the land now.

Cassandra knew; when Simone was not talking about Luc and Katia and the government, she talked about Cousin Henri.

"My father wants to write another book, about Torquemada and Stalin and I think, Cromwell," Cassandra said. "The theme would be single-mindedness. But he can't get down to it. My mother doesn't see why he can't write for an hour, then talk to her for an hour. She asks him to help look for things she's lost, like the keys to the car. Before he retired, she was never bored. Now that he's home all day, she wants company and she loses everything."

"How did he write his other books?" said Roger.

"In the minstrel he had a private office and secretary. Two, in fact. He expected to write even more, once he was free, but he obviously won't. If he were alone, I could look after him." That was unexpected. Perhaps Luc knew just how unexpected Cassandra could be, and that was why he stayed away from her. "I don't mean I imagine my mother not there," she said. "I only meant that I could look after him, if I had to."

Half a mile before the village stood Cousin Henri's house. Roger told Cassandra why he and Henri were not speaking, except through lawyers. Henri had been grossly favoured by their mutual grandparents, thanks to the trickery of an aunt by marriage, who was Henri's godmother. The aunt, who was very rich as well as mad and childless, had acquired the grandparents' domain, in their lifetime, by offering more money than it was worth. She had done this wicked thing in order to hand it over, intact, unshared, undivided, to Henri, whom she worshipped. The transaction had been brought off on the wrong side of the law, thanks to a clan of Protestants and Freemasons.

Cassandra looked puzzled and pained.

"You see, the government of that time..." said Roger, but he fell silent, seeing that Cassandra had stopped understanding. When he was over-wrought he sounded like his wife. It was hardly surprising: he was simply repeating, word for word, everything Simone had been saying since they were married. In his own voice, which was ironic and diffident, he told Cassandra why Cousin Henri had never married. At the age of twenty Henry had been made trustee of a family secret. Henri's mother was illegitimate – at any rate, hatched from a cuckoo's egg. Henri's father was not his mother's husband but a country neighbour. Henri had been warned never to marry any of the such-and-such girls, because he might be marrying his own half-sister. Henri might not have wanted to: the such-and-suches were ugly and poor. He had used the secret as good reason not to marry anyone, had settled down in the handsomest house in the Yonne (half of which should have been Roger's), and had peopled the neighbourhood with his random children.

They slowed walking, and Cassandra looked at a brick-and-stucco box, and some dirty-faced children playing on the steps.

"There, behind the farmhouse," said Roger, showing a dark, severe manor house at the top of a straight drive.

"It looks more like a monastery, don't you think?" said Cassandra. Although Roger seemed to be waiting, she could think of nothing more to say. They walked on, toward Cassan-dra's breakfast.

On the road back, Roger neither looked at Cousin Henri's house nor mentioned it. They were still at some distance from home when they began to hear Simone: "Marry her! Marry Katia! Live with Katia! I don't care what you do. Anything, anything, so long as you pass your exam." Roger pushed open the gate and there was Simone, still in her dressing gown, standing on a lawn strewn with Luc's clothes, and Luc at the window, still in pyjamas. Luc heaved a chair over the sill, then a couple of pillows and a whole armful of books. Having yelled something vile about the family (they were in disagreement later about what it was), he jumped out, too, and landed easily in a flower bed. He paused to pick up shoes he had flung out earlier, ran awkwardly across the lawn; pushed through a gap in the hedge, and vanished.

"He'll be back," said Simone, gathering books. "He'll want his breakfast. He really is a remarkable athlete. With proper guidance, Luc could have done anything. But Roger never took much interest."

"What was the last thing he said?" said Cassandra.

"Fools," said Simone. "But a common word for it. Never repeat that word, if you want people to think well of you."

"Spies," Roger had heard. In Luc's room he found a pair of sunglasses on the floor. He had noticed Luc limping as he made for the hedge; perhaps he had sprained an ankle. He remembered how Luc had been too tired to walk a dog, too worn out to feed a goldfish. Roger imagined him, now, wandering in muddy farmyards, in shoes and pyjamas, children giggling at him – the Clairevoies' mooncalf son. Perhaps he had gone to tell his troubles to that other eccentric, Cousin Henri.

Tears came easily since Roger's last attack. He had been told they were caused by the depressant effect of the pills he had to take. He leaned on the window frame, in the hope of seeing Luc, and wept quietly in the shelter of Luc's glasses.

"It's awfully curious of me," said Cassandra, helping Simone, "but what's got into Luc? When he stayed with us, in England, he was angelic. Your husband seems upset, too."

"The *Baron*," said Simone, letting it be known she had read the diary and was ready for combat, "the *Baron* is too sensible. Today is his birthday. He is forty-eight – nearly fifty."

Roger supposed she meant "sensitive." To correct Simone might create a diversion, but he could not be sure of what kind. To let it stand might bewilder the English girl; but, then, Cassandra was born bewildered.

Luc came home in time for dinner, dressed in a shirt and corduroys belonging to Cousin Henri. His silence, Roger thought, challenged them for questions; none came. He accepted a portion of Roger's birthday cake, which, of course, Roger could not touch, and left half on his plate. "Even as a small child, Luc never cared for chocolate," Simone explained to Cassandra.

The next day, only food favoured by Luc was served. Simone turned over a letter from Katia. It was brief and cool in tone: Katia had been exercising horses in a riding school, helping a friend.

The Clairevoies, preceded by Luc on the Honda, packed up and drove back to Paris. This time Cassandra was allowed to sit in front, next to Simone. Roger and the dog shared the back seat with Luc's books and a number of parcels.

They saw Cassandra off at the Gare du Nord. Roger was careful not to take her arm, brush against her, or otherwise inspire a mention in her diary. She wore a T-shirt decorated with a grinning mouth. "It's been really lovely," she said. Roger bowed.

Her letter of thanks arrived promptly. She was planning to help her father with his book on Stalin, Cromwell, and Torquemada. He wanted to include a woman on the list, to bring the work in line with trends of the day. Cassandra had suggested Boadicea, Queen of the Iceni. Boadicea stood for feminine rectitude, firmness, and true love of one's native culture. So Cassandra felt.

"Cassandra has written a most learned and affectionate letter," said Simone, who would never have to see Cassandra again. "I only hope Luc was as polite to the Brunts." Her voice held a new tone of maternal grievance and maternal threat.

Luc, who no longer found threats alarming, packed his books and took the train for Rennes. Katia's letters seemed to have stopped. Searching Luc's room, Simone found nothing to read except a paperback on private ownership. "I believe he is taking an interest in things," she told Roger.

It was late in May when the Clairevoies made their final trip to Rennes. Suspecting what awaited them, Simone wore mourning – a dark linen suit, black sandals, sunglasses. Father Rousseau had on a dark suit and black tie. After some hesitation he said what Roger was waiting to hear: it was useless to make Luc sit for an examination he had not even a remote chance of passing. Luc was unprepared, now and forever. He had, in fact, disappeared, though he had promised to come back once the talk with his parents was over. Luc had confided that he would be content to live like Cousin Henri, without a degree to his name, and with a reliable tenant farmer to keep things running.

My son is a fool, said Roger to himself. Katia, who was certainly beautiful, perhaps even clever, loved him. She stood crying in the street, trying to see a light in his room.

"Luc's cousin is rich," said Simone. "Luc is too pure to understand the difference. He will have to learn something. What about computer training?"

"Luc has a mind too fluid to be restrained," said Father Rousseau.

"Literature?" said Simone, bringing up the last resort.

Roger came to life. "Sorting letters in the post office?"

"Machines do that," said Father Rousseau. "Luc would have to pass a test to show he understands the machine. I have been wondering if there might be in Luc's close environment a family affair." The Clairevoies fell silent. "A family business," Father Rousseau repeated. "Families are open, airy structures. They take in the dreamy as well as the alert. There is always an extra corner somewhere.

Like most of her women friends, Simone had given up wearing jewellery: the streets were full of anarchists and muggers. One of her friends knew of someone who had had a string of pearls ripped off her neck by a bearded intellectual of the Mediterranean type – that is, quite dark. Simone still kept, for luck, a pair of gold earrings, so large and heavy they looked fake. She touched her talisman earrings and said, “We have in our family a bank too small to be nationalized.”

“Congratulations,” said Father Rousseau, sincerely. When he got up to see them to the door, Roger saw he wore running shoes.

It fell to Roger to tell Luc what was to become of him. After military service of the most humdrum and unprotected kind, he would move to a provincial town and learn about banks. The conversation took place late one night in Luc's room. Simone had persuaded Roger that Luc needed to be among his own things – the galleon lamp, the Foreign Legion recruiting poster that had replaced Che Guevara, the photograph of Simone that replaced Roger's graduating class. Roger said, somewhat shyly, “You will be that much closer to Biarritz.”

“Katia is getting married,” said Luc. “His father has a riding school.” He said this looking away, rolling a pencil between thumb and finger, something like the way his mother had rolled a kitchen match. Reflected in the dark window, Luc's cheeks were hollowed, his eyes blazing and black. He looked almost like a hero and, like most heroes, lonely.

“What happened to your friends?” said Roger. “The friends you used to see every Sunday.”

“Oh, that... that fell apart. All the people they ever talked about were already dead. And some of the parents were worried. You were the only parents who never interfered.”

“We wanted you to live your own life,” said Roger. “It must have been that. Could you get her back?”

"You can do anything with a woman if you give her enough money."

"Who told you a thing like that?" In the window Roger examined the reflected lamp, the very sight of which was supposed to have made a man of Luc.

"Everyone. Cousin Henri. I told her we owned a bank, because Cousin Henri said it would be a good thing to tell her. She asked me how to go about getting a bank loan. That was all."

Does he really believe he owns a bank, Roger wondered. "About money," he said. "Nothing of Cousin Henri's is likely to be ours. Illegitimate children are allowed to inherit now, and my cousin," said Roger with some wonder, "has acknowledged everyone. I pity the schoolteacher. All she ever sees is the same face." This was not what Luc was waiting to hear. "You will inherit everything your mother owns. I have to share with my cousin, because that is how our grandparents arranged it." He did not go on about the Freemasons and Protestants, because Luc already knew.

"It isn't fair," said Luc.

"Then you and your mother share my share."

"How much of yours is mine?" said Luc politely.

"Oh, something at least the size of the tennis court," said Roger.

On Luc's desk stood, silver-framed, another picture of Simone, a charming one taken at the time of her engagement. She wore, already, the gold earrings. Her hair was in the upswept balloon style of the time. Her expression was smiling, confident but untried. Both Luc and Roger suddenly looked at it in silence.

It was Simone's belief that, after Katia, Luc had started sleeping with one of her own friends. She thought she knew the one: the Hungarian wife of an architect, fond of saying she wished she had a daughter the right age for Luc. This was a direct sexual compliment, based on experience, Simone thought. Roger thought it meant nothing at all. It was the kind of empty declaration mothers mistook for appreciation. Simone had asked Roger to find out what he could, for this was the last chance either of them would ever have to talk to Luc. From now on, he would undoubtedly get along better with his parents, but where there had been a fence there would be a wall. Luc was on his own.

Roger said, "It was often thought, in my day, mainly by foreigners who had never been to France, that young men began their lives with their mother's best friend. Absurd, when you consider it. Why pick an old woman when you can have a young one?" *Buy* a young one, he had been about to say, by mistake. "Your mother's friends often seem young to me. I suppose it has to do with their clothes – so loose, unbuttoned. The disorder is already there. My mother's best friends wore armour. It was called the New Look, invented by Christian Dior, a great defender of matronly virtue." A direct glance from Luc – the first. "There really was a Mr. Dior, just as I suppose there was a Mr. Mercedes and a Mr. Benz. My mother and her friends were put into boned corsets, stiff petticoats, wide-brimmed, murderous hats. Their nails were pointed, and a red as your lampshade. They carried furled parasols with silver handles and metal-edged handbags. Even the heels of their shoes were contrived for braining people. No young man would have gone anywhere near." Luc's eyes met Roger's in the window. "I have often wondered," said Roger, "though I'm not trying to make it my business, what you and Katia could have done. Where could you have taken her? Well, unless she had some private place of her own. There's more and more of that. Daughters of nice couples, people we know. Their own apartment, car, money. Holidays no one knows where. Credit cards, bank accounts, abortions. In my day, we had a miserable amount of spending money, but we had the girls in the Rue Spontini. Long after the bordellos were closed, there was the Rue Spontini place. Do you know who first took me there? Cousin Henri. Not surprising, considering the life he has led since. Henri called it 'the annex,' because he ran into so many friends from his school. On Thursday afternoons, that was." A slight question in Luc's eyes. "Thursday was our weekly holiday, like Wednesdays for you. I don't suppose every Wednesday – no, I'm sure you don't. Besides, even the last of those places vanished years ago. There were Belgian girls, Spanish girls from Algeria. Some were so young – oh, very young. One told me I was like a brother. I asked Cousin Henri what she meant. He said he didn't know."

Luc said, "Katia could cry whenever she wanted to." Her face never altered, but two great tears would suddenly brim over and course along her cheeks.

The curtains and shutters were open. Anyone could look in. There was no one in the street – not even a ghost. How real Katia and Luc had seemed; how they had touched what was left of Roger's heart; how he had loved them. Giving them up forever, he said, "I always admired that picture of your mother."

Simone and Roger had become engaged while Roger was still a lieutenant in Algeria. On the night before their wedding, which was to take place at ten o'clock in the morning in the church of Saint-Pierre de Chaillot, Roger paid a wholly unwelcome call. Simone received him alone, in her dressing gown, wearing a fine net over her carefully ballooned hair. Her parents, listening at the door, took it for granted Roger had caught a venereal disease in a North African brothel and wanted the wedding postponed; Simone supposed he had met a richer and prettier girl. All Roger had to say was that he had seen an Algerian prisoner being tortured to death. Simone had often asked Roger, since then, why he had tried to frighten her with something that had so little bearing on their future. Roger could not remember what his reason had been.

He tried, now, to think of something important to say to Luc, as if the essence of his own life could be bottled in words and handed over. Sylvestre, wakened by a familiar voice, came snuffling at the door, expecting at this unsuitable hour to be taken out. Roger remarked, "Whatever happens, don't get your life all mixed up with a dog's."

JANE RULE

DULCE

I was not perfectly born, as Samuel Butler prescribed, wrapped in banknotes, but I was orphaned at twenty-one without other relatives to turn to and with no material need of them. I was, in a way everyone else envied, free of emotional and financial obligations. I did not have to do anything, not even choose a place to live since I had the small and lovely house in Vancouver where I had grown up to shelter me from as much as developing my own taste in furniture. I did not, of course, feel fortunate. Ingratitude is the besetting sin of the young.

If I had been rich rather than simply comfortable, I might have learned to give my money away intelligently. What I tried to do instead was to give myself away, having no use of my own for it. It was not so reprehensible an aim for a young woman in the fifties as it is today. I was, again with a good fortune I was far from recognizing, unsuccessful.

My first and greatest insight as a child was being aware that I was innocent of my own motives. I did not know why I so often contrived to interrupt my father at his practising. Now I understand that he, otherwise a quiet and pensive man, frightened me when he played his violin. Or the instrument itself frightened me, seeming to contain an electrical charge that flung my father's body around helplessly the moment he laid hands on it. Though he died in a plane crash on tour for the troops in the Second World War when I was fifteen, I never quite believed it wasn't his violin that had killed him.

Wilson C. Wilson, a boy several years older than I, lived down the block with his aunt and uncle who gave him dutiful but reluctant room among their own children because he had been orphaned as a baby. That fact, accompanied by his dark good looks, had made him a romantic figure for me, but I had never expected him to climb up into our steep north slope of a garden where I made a habit of brooding on a favourite rock and often spying on him through the fringe of laurel, dogwood, mountain ash and alder that grew, and still does grow, down at the street. No handsome boy of my own age had ever paid the slightest attention to me.

If he had not come with such quick agility, I would have hidden from him and let him pay his respects to my grieving mother to whom I suspect he might have been more romantically drawn than he was to me. I was too terrified of him even to be self-conscious. I sat very still, hardly at first hearing what he had to say, waiting for him to leave, but he was so gentle with me and at the same time so eager that gradually I began to listen to him.

"Some day," he said, "you'll be glad you were old enough to remember his face."

He offered his own grief as a way of sharing mine, but I had not had time to let my raw loss mellow into something speakable. He did not expect me to be adequate then or, I suppose, ever.

After that, once or twice a week he would come to find me. Sometimes he talked about his weekend job as an apprentice to a printer, but more often he talked about the books he was reading. He did not expect me to be older or more intelligent than I was, but he did begin to bring me books to read. When I asked him a question that pleased him, he would say. "Dulce, you have an old soul," but he was normally content to have a good listener.

Sometimes he suggested a walk on the beach just several blocks below the house, even in winter weather. We both liked the mists that obscured the far views across Burrard Inlet to the north mountains and focused our attention on the salty debris at our feet. We liked finding puzzling objects and making up histories for them as we walked among gulls and crows, past ghostly trees emerging only a few feet from us.

Neither of us liked wearing a hat or hood, and we would come back as wet-headed as swimmers to a hearth fire and tea, to the personal questions my mother asked, which always began: "If you don't have to go..." or "If you're not called up..." or "If the war's over..." I never asked Wilson questions like that though I could see my mother's concern for his peaceful future gave him more confidence in it. He wanted to go back to Toronto where he had been born. He wanted to study literature and philosophy.

"And after that?" Mother asked.

"I'll be a philosopher... and a printer to feed myself."

I watched him, his strong, dark hair glistening rather than flattened, as I knew mine was, by the damp, his dark eyes glistening, too, and wished he were my brother or at least in some way related to me.

Wilson was called up two weeks before the war was over. Then his orders were cancelled, and he packed instead to go to Toronto. Before he left, he asked for my picture in exchange for his, taken for his high-school graduation, on which he had written, "For a good listener, Wilson C. Wilson."

"I so dislike my name," he once told me, "that I'll simply have to make it famous."

"How?"

He shrugged, but I wasn't really surprised when he sent me the first of his poems to be published in an eastern magazine. Some few of the images in them were ones we had found together, which made it easier for me to comment on them. Now that we were exchanging letters, I discovered that being a good listener by mail was learning to ask interesting rather than personal questions.

When Wilson came back the following summer to take up work with the printer, his aunt and uncle asked him to pay room and board. I was shocked by their lack of generosity, particularly since it would mean Wilson could not afford to go east again.

"My uncle points out that my cousins are perfectly satisfied to go to UBC."

"He doesn't charge them room and board, does he?"

"They're his own children," Wilson explained reasonably.

"You could pitch a tent in our garden," I suggested, "and you could pay Mother just the bit it cost to feed you."

"Don't make offers for your mother," he said.

"Are you in love with Wilson?" my mother asked me.

"I don't think so," I answered, both surprised and embarrassed by the question. "I just want us to help him."

"Is he in love with you?"

That I knew was preposterous. "I'm just a good listener," I answered.

The tent did go up on the flat square of lawn by the roses on the understanding that I would not visit Wilson in it. I would not have dreamed of invading his privacy.

More like a grown man, he assigned himself chores about the place without being asked. Mother and I had been used to a man who protected his hands and anyway had no eye or ear for the complaints of a house. By the end of the summer, nothing squeaked or dripped, and I had decided to go away to college myself and major in English.

I liked the idea of a women's college, for boys, except for Wilson, began to alarm me, taking on sudden height all around me, their noses and fingers thickening, their chins growing mossy, their voices cracking to new depths. I walked as defensively among them as I would through thickets of gorse or blackberry.

I chose Mills College in California partly because it was in the Bay Area, and I liked San Francisco, the city of my mother's girlhood. Though my mother had been sent to the Conservatory of Music and attended concerts with her handsome and handsomely dressed parents, they hadn't approved of her marriage to a fellow student who wanted to sit on the stage instead of in the prosperous audience.

"They said, 'He'll never buy you diamonds,'" my mother told me.

"Did you mind?"

"About the diamonds?"

"About their not approving."

"Yes, but it gave me the courage to do it."

I found it hard to associate courage with love.

Wilson did not come back to Vancouver the summer I graduated from high school. He had found a printing job in Toronto, a less expensive solution than living in a tent in our garden. I sent him my high-school graduation picture without signing it because I didn't know what to say. I signed my letters "As ever." He signed his "Yours," which I understood to be a formality.

Two of the poems he had published that year were love poems, dark and constrained, which made me unhappy for him and a little bewildered, too, for I could not imagine anyone incapable of returning his love. Since he wasn't in the habit of confiding in me about his personal affairs, I could hardly answer or question a poem. He wrote to me that his first collection of poems was about to be published, sent me the picture to be used on the cover and asked permission to dedicate the book to me.

"Does it mean anything, Mother? I mean, anything in particular?"

"It's not a proposal, if that's what you mean," Mother said. "But it certainly does mean you are important to him. It's all right to accept if he's important to you."

I accepted, feeling a new self-conscious place in his life, which I did not really understand. Surely, if he'd been in love with me, I would know. I studied the picture and saw simply his familiar intent and handsome face. Experimentally I kissed it, a kiss as chaste as any I gave my mother. Then quite crossly I thought, "If I'm so important to him, he could at least have come to my graduation and taken me to the dance."

Yet who of my school friends could boast of having a book dedicated to her? Wilson would never have taken me to a dance. Nor would I have asked him to. He did not belong to my silly social world. Even I had outgrown it and longed to begin my own serious education in a part of the world nearly as beautiful and far more sophisticated than my own.

To the relief of some of my disgruntled, liberal professors, I shunned the child development and dietary courses newly introduced to make servantless wives out of my post-war generation and to redomesticate those few female veterans who had returned. Instead I chose traditional art history, religious history and philosophy courses as electives around my requirements in literature. If there had been a history of science, I would have chosen that over biology, the least mathematical of the sciences available. In that lab, cutting up flat worms, crayfish and cats, I came as close to domestic experience as I would get in college. I sent my laundry out every week to a war widow, left not as well off as my mother.

Thanks to Wilson, I was better read than many of the other incoming freshmen, and, though I rarely offered an opinion in class, I asked very good questions. My written assignments were not immediately successful, but again Wilson had trained me to listen and comprehend not only the material but the mood and bias of the instructor before me. Once I got the hang of being a logical positivist in philosophy, a new critic in contemporary literature, a propounder of the history of ideas in Milton, my grades bounded upwards.

There were students at the college who actually engaged in the arts, notably in music, but I avoided the rich offering of concerts. In fact, any performing art was difficult for me to deal with; for, like my father, the performers all seemed in the grip of an energy that made spastic victims of them, leaping inexplicably around the stage, shouting in unrecognizable voices, faces either entirely expressionless or distorted in unimaginable pain. Poetry was for me a superior art. I had never had to watch Wilson write a poem. It was a relief to me to study Shakespeare on the page, a prejudice I shared with my professor who considered any available production a defiler of the poetry of the bard.

At a performance of *Macbeth*, put on by St. Mary's, a men's college in the neighbourhood, the wife of a faculty member played Lady Macbeth in the same red housecoat even after she'd become queen; the wind for the witches' scene was her vacuum cleaner. Macbeth himself was a speech major with a lisp, who murdered more than sleep. His severed head was presented at the end of the play in a paper bag that looked like someone's forgotten lunch and perhaps was.

Granting the limitations of amateurs, I could not imagine even great actors tastefully gouging out eyes on stage on the way to a climax of corpses. The blood and gore were a convention of a barbarous time, which the poetry transcended.

In my letters to Wilson, both of whose pictures sat framed on my desk, I sometimes confided academic puzzlement. Though styles of poetry changed through the ages, particular poems were recognizably great in each period. Prose, on the other hand, seemed to improve, become more economical, lucid and beautiful. "Are you going to make an idol out of Hemingway," Wilson demanded, "at the expense of Donne and Milton?" I'd had F. Scott Fitzgerald in mind. I went back to Donne's sermons, and, when I imaged them, as instructed by Wilson, recited by the Dean of St. Paul's with tears streaming down his face, their excesses seemed more appropriate; yet I also had to admit that a man in tears would embarrass more than move me.

I found few fellow students with whom I could raise such questions. Only a small band of rather aggressive scholarship students discussed their studies. The more acceptable topics of conversation were menstrual cramps, other people's sexual habits, the foibles of parents and professors, and God. Nor were academic subjects acceptable topics on dates. Any conversation was impossible over the noise at fraternity parties, football games and bars. The only virtue of the gross abuse of alcohol at such gatherings was that, more often than not, my young man of the evening was incapable of a sexual ending in the back seat of a dangerously driven car.

At first I was uneasy at the status my pictures of Wilson gave me. When I confessed that he had also dedicated a book of poems to me, it was simply assumed that I was unofficially engaged to the handsome young man with the unhandsome name. He wrote me letters, which was more than could be said for some who had even presented diamond rings.

"Are you going to see Wilson at Christmas?"

"Oh, he probably can't afford the trip. He's putting himself through…"

Explanations true enough, but I did not think of myself as the object of Wilson's romantic interest. There were more love poems, flickering with unredeeming fire that certainly had nothing to do with me, but they gave rise to shocked and admiring speculations among my friends who read them.

Gradually I used Wilson as the protection I wanted from a social life too barbarous to bear, even if it meant remaining among the humiliated on Saturday nights. If I was not writing love letters to Wilson, I was writing loving ones, for he was the one human being, aside from my mother, with whom I could really talk.

To Wilson's great disappointment, the only fellowship open to him for graduate studies was at UBC. He frankly confessed that it would be all right with him if he never laid eyes on Vancouver again. The university was inferior, the city really not a city at all, for it was without cultural reality, and he had been personally unhappy there. He did kindly add, "Except for that summer in your garden." But he was competing with too many men older than himself, more mature in their judgments, with Americans and Englishmen as well as his own countrymen, and he had to take what he could get.

Wilson met me at the airport when I came home to bury my mother. It was the first time we had seen each other in four years, and we embraced in the way we signed our letters because we had to do something. Wilson seemed to me more substantial and attentive in those few days, but my need was also extraordinary. It was Wilson who would not hear of my simply staying there, moving into the house to begin a grief-dazed life. He put me back on the plane to finish my education.

In the next year and a half, Wilson became my unofficial guardian. He rented the house for me, effectively preventing me from coming home in the summer, which he said I should spend in Europe where he had not yet been himself.

He outlined a trip he would like to have taken, but I was far too timid to travel alone, and, since he didn't offer to come with me, I elected instead to take the Shakespeare summer session at Stratford.

Younger than most of the other international students and not as well prepared for the work, I was at first intimidated, but my listening, question-asking habits soon provided me with a couple of unofficial tutors, also willing to indulge my uncertain sensibilities about the theatre.

"Why, it's meant to be vulgar!" I exclaimed after a performance of *Measure for Measure.* "All that bawdy fooling around."

If it hadn't been for Wilson, I might have fallen in love with either of the two young men, one English, one American, who also took me punting on the Avon, day tripping to Oxford, to Wales, pub crawling and simply walking country lanes in the late summer light. While both of them talked nearly as well as Wilson about matters literary and historical, they were also flirtatious and entertaining. Instead I fell in love with England and wrote to tell Wilson that we had both been born on the wrong continent. We were not after all freaks, simply freaks in the new world.

"This bloke of yours back in Canada, are you going to marry him then?" the Englishman asked.

"Oh, eventually," I answered, and I found that I believed what I said.

I spent my final year at college in a postponing aura of serene industry, my essays enlivened by new insights that were my own, for I had been in that green and pleasant land and knew that birds do sing.

But at last I did have to go home to discover that my mother really was dead, that I was alone. If the house had been on an ordinary street in an ordinary city, I might have been persuaded to sell it and live the more vagabond life of my contemporaries, brash and brave among the new ruins of Europe, before returning to mow lawns and pay taxes. But it was built sturdily on a high piece of ground overlooking the inlet, the mountains and the growing city of Vancouver, and it contained my childhood, which was prematurely precious to me as my parents were.

Wilson had not met my plane, nor did he come to see me until I'd had several days of blank passivity. I did not think it odd at the time. When he did arrive, I greeted him less shyly than before and felt him pull back. His Dulce was still not a woman but a docile, intelligent child in need of his guidance.

I could not ask him, as I very much wanted to, "What are we going to do with the rest of our lives?" He considered his to be publicly disposed, as a poet and teacher. He would give up printing, though he might one day use that practical knowledge if he founded a literary press.

"Vancouver is changing," Wilson admitted as we looked together at the view, the skyline altered by the first of so many high-rises that would eventually make it look more like New York than itself.

Then he asked, as if an uninvolved spectator, "What are you going to do now?"

"I don't know."

"You haven't thought about it?"

"I wondered if I'd get a dog… no, I haven't."

"Why?"

"Do I have to do anything?"

"Well, eventually," Wilson said. "You haven't got enough capital to live on, not the way you'd like to live."

I was furious with him for speaking as if I might never marry him or anyone else: yet I knew he would think it beneath me to leave my life to such an eventuality. I must be held accountable for my future.

All the girls I had known at school were either locked in combat with their parents or already married. Only two had jobs, chosen for their proximity to marriageable men, which, of course, Wilson was not and would not be for some time until he could translate his years of learning into a modest academic salary. If I had to mark time until then, I might as well do it with him. I could get a teaching assistantship and take my MA.

At first, witness to all the fawning young women who surrounded Wilson, I was both daunted and repelled, but, as I watched him treat them like bodies on a crowded bus, I was reassured. He was a little aloof from me, too, at first, as if he did not want any display of our friendship, but gradually we formed the habit of having lunch together several times a week. For his birthday, I gave him season tickets next to my own for the theatre and the foreign film series. We became in public, rather than in private, a pair.

Wilson had rooms in a widow's house on the second floor with only a hotplate to cook on and a glimpse of view through a small, stained-glass window in his bathroom, which I saw only in the lines of one of his poems. He never invited me there, in deference to the widow's sensibilities perhaps but in keeping with his appetite for privacy.

He visited me comfortably enough, and he did the same things for me as he had done for Mother as well as advising me about my responsibilities as an owner. But we almost always went out after the simple meals I was learning to prepare under his direction and with his help.

To my relief, Wilson did not want to go to poetry readings. He said he had nothing in common with the other students who claimed to be poets and brought out a magazine called *Tish*. "It's not really necessary to spell it backwards," Wilson said. To focus on the human breath and the heartbeat for a theory of aesthetics was simply an excuse to ignore the great traditions of poetry. For Wilson the roots of poetry were in knowledge, discipline and concentration. He admired Auden,

Eliot, the best of Dylan Thomas, a good reason for avoiding the drunken bellowings of that undersized bull on the stage. About giving readings of his own, Wilson was non-committal. "I'm not ready."

We went instead to the Art Gallery for every visiting show. Wilson was fascinated by the question of great subjects. I was more interested in paint and stone and metal; therefore I didn't have the trouble with modern art that often daunted Wilson, fearful of being tricked by fads and impostors. How could he judge technique without subject matter, he wanted to know. "Think of it as more like music," I suggested.

When he went with me to openings at local galleries, Wilson stood back from the conversations I got into, I suppose because he was more comfortable with answers than with questions, but he did listen, and occasionally he would go with me to parties held after the shows for the artist and his friends.

Wilson would have preferred me to invest in something like first editions, about which he was relatively well informed, but the only first editions I've ever bought are new books. I have no taste for books as objects. What I wanted were paintings. For me they were as pure as poems.

In asserting that aesthetic independence, I did not feel so much Wilson's equal as a better, more independent companion, one he would some day come to see as a woman rather than a fifteen-year-old with an old soul. He dedicated his second book of poems to me with the words, "For Dulce, my muse."

Just the other day I came upon a metaphorical distinction between the romantic and classical poets in Northrop Frye: "Warm mammalians who tenderly suckle their living creations and the cold reptilian intellectuals who lay abstract eggs." There were no love poems at all in this second collection. Like the canvases Wilson was drawn to, they were about great subjects. The title came from the longest and most difficult poem in the book, *Exercises in War.* Trained as I had been, it didn't occur to me to wonder whether or not I liked Wilson's poetry. I admired it as intellectually requiring and courageously cruel about the nature of man.

Three months before Wilson received his PhD, he accepted a graduate fellowship in England.

"You'll never come back," I said.

"I hope not."

"Wilson, what about me?"

The eyes he turned to me were brilliant with unshed tears. "I'm sorry, Dulce."

Now that Wilson C. Wilson has made his name attractive with international honours, occasionally a graduate student comes to me to ask what Wilson was like as a young man. I can only say what he tried to be like as a young man in order to become what he now actually is, a very good poet whose poems I can't bear to read.

If Wilson was a coward, he wasn't coward enough to marry me. I was coward enough to have married him to seal myself away forever from learning either to live alone or truly with another. Instead, he left me when I was twenty-four in the cocoon of my independence, which exposed rather than hid my humiliation, for very soon after Wilson left, Oscar Kaufman, a sculptor at whose studio we had often been, said to me, "I thought at least he'd marry you for the view you've got here."

Perhaps because Oscar was as unlike Wilson as it is possible for a man to be, I was not so much attracted to him as resigned to him for the medicine I needed for a kill or cure remedy for the last ten years of my life.

He was, as most of our friends were in those days, older. Wilson felt safer among people settled in marriage and the raising of children than among other teaching assistants like ourselves who were marrying in nervous numbers and moving into the ugly and cramped married quarters on campus. Perhaps Wilson thought I might be as put off as he obviously was by family life if I could witness first-hand the emotional and physical squalor of it.

Oscar and Anita had three children under five years old. "Catching up after the war," Oscar explained. He was both efficient and tender with them, and he gave Anita a day off every Saturday in exchange for a Saturday night for himself, no questions asked.

When he first stopped by, he had the children with him, and I discovered very quickly how inappropriate my house was for any child neither tied up nor caged. The baby was putting an ant trap in his mouth before anyone had taken a coat off, and Mother's favourite lamp was smashed on the hearth in the next five minutes. After that, Oscar got ahead of them, kid-proofing the room while I got out cookies.

While the children climbed all over him, covering him with enough crumbs to feed every bird in the garden, he said to me, "You know, Dulce, what you've needed for a long time is a real man."

"What's unreal about Wilson?"

"He's a faggot." When I looked blank, Oscar explained, "A queer, a homosexual."

"How do you know such a thing?"

"Don't get mad at *me*," Oscar said. "Do you have any better explanation? Did he ever take you to bed?"

If it hadn't been for the presence of the children, I would have ordered Oscar out of the house. Instead, we both used them as a distraction, and Oscar didn't speak of Wilson again, then or ever.

When he had gone, I took down Wilson's first volume of poems and turned to the love poems that had always bewildered me. What I thought had been about unrequited love was instead forbidden, I could quite clearly see, but nothing prevented the reader from supposing the object to be a female, married or otherwise lost to him. It was not, however, a better explanation. Had they been, in a perverse way, poems also for me, the only way Wilson knew how to tell me that he was incapable of loving me?

I had ignored his absolute lack of expressions of physical affection, rationalizing it as part of his extreme sensitivity or a peculiarity of his being raised without tenderness or his sense of honour or some lack in myself because I had loathed those aggressive and drunken young men when I was in college. And I had been relieved that I didn't have to compete with other women for his attention, but there had been no man in his life, of that I was sure. Was Oscar suggesting that Wilson was the kind of man who sought sex in parks and public washrooms? Such an accusation made Oscar rather than Wilson disgusting. If Oscar thought Wilson was queer, why did he also suppose Wilson might have married me?

I try to explain what happened in terms not only of my own ignorance but of the ignorant intolerance of that time. Oh, I had heard rumours of homosexuality in some of Shakespeare's sonnets, but I had dismissed them as I did suggestions that Bacon had really written the plays. I had heard a couple of very masculine girls at college referred to as lesbians, but I associated that with the inappropriateness of their style and manner, rather than with their sexual tastes. The only homosexual male I had ever been aware of was a very effeminate brother of a high-school friend of mine who cried because someone had called him a fairy.

Wilson was entirely masculine. Even in his good looks there was nothing pretty about him. His body was hard and competent, his voice deep. If there was an error in his manner it was an occasional hint of arrogance. There was nothing of the passive or sycophantic about him. He wasn't exactly a man's man either, without interest in either sports or dirty jokes. He was a loner, learning to command respect rather than affection. Yet who could call a man of such intense feelings cold?

I had never pretended to understand Wilson, but he was more real to me than anyone else, both gentler and stronger. My first wish about him, that he could have been my brother, probably most accurately described what we had been for each other and might have gone on being if I had not tried to break the taboo with one question, which created the irrevocable separation and silence between us.

Compared to Wilson, Oscar was transparent, his work hugely, joyously sexual, his needs blatant, his morality patriarchal. He worshipped his wife as the mother of his children; he loved his children, and as a man and an artist he deserved me, but I was also his good deed, part of a sexual altruism he had worked out for himself that drew him to unhappy women. Often in his life he has been bewildered to leave them even unhappier. For some years I let him come to me to be comforted when he was suffering their unreasonable demands and accusations. I can explain that only by my horror at ever again shutting a final door between me and someone I have cared about.

Oscar was from the first completely open with me. Anita didn't mind this sort of thing as long as she didn't have to know about it. His relationship with me was restricted to Saturday nights and would be as entirely private as mine with Wilson had been entirely public. It would end with summer when he was free of his university teaching responsibilities to concentrate on his work. By then I should have become a competent sexual being ready for the open market. No, he didn't put it that way. He was never again blunt as he had been about Wilson. Oscar knew how to be kind and funny about not quite savoury arrangements so that raising any objection seemed a regression to grammar-school morality.

Used to Wilson's Spartan taste in food, I was unprepared for Oscar's appetite, and he did not expect to help me in the kitchen or with any other domestic problem. He wanted to leave all husbandly and fatherly responsibilities behind him. He left whatever personal problems he might have had behind him, too. I've never known anyone as resolutely and often maddeningly cheerful as Oscar.

"I made a bargain," he told me once. "If I made it through the war, I'd spend the rest of my life celebrating it."

As he pointed out to me, I could have done worse than to offer my overdue virginity to Oscar. He did not rush me, and he was patient with my timidity and squeamishness. I felt rather like a child being taught to ride a bicycle, that is until *he* mounted *me*, and then I became my father's violin, a thing seemingly of wood and strings, that charged Oscar with crazed energy. I did not know whether I was terrified of him or myself for the power I apparently had to call up such a rutting.

He did not neglect my "pleasure," as he called it, so much as never clearly locate it. From his caresses, I thought I should gradually learn to purr like a cat, but I was too tense in my ignorance to feel the heat he called up as anything more than flashes of ambiguous feeling somewhere between pleasure and pain.

After he left, I often cried hysterically, a response that misled me to think I was in love with Oscar in a way I didn't consciously comprehend, for I also came to dread his arrival on Saturday night, and I was giddy with freedom the few times he was unable to get away.

I did have the sense to refuse Anita's invitation to spend Christmas Day with the family. Wilson and I had always planned something to circumvent rather than celebrate that holiday, he not wishing to be politely tolerated in the house where he had grown up, I not wanting to be reminded of the central delight I had been to my parents on such occasions. I have never even explored the cupboard where I supposed the Christmas decorations were stored.

I did what I had wanted to do when I first came home. I went to the Animal Shelter and picked out an already housebroken and spayed young dog, short-haired and black but not as large as a Lab. Then on a whim I picked up a black kitten as well. The major part of my Christmas buying, after I'd chosen extravagant presents for Oscar's children (nothing for Oscar at his request), was done in a pet shop.

The dog already had a name, "Rocket," suggesting a male child's brief infatuation with a puppy. I didn't like it, but she was old enough to be used to it. The kitten I named Maud, as all vain, bright and beguiling females should be. From the first night they slept together in the laundry-room by the back door.

Rocket's occasional growl and brief, sharp bark woke me several times during the night. Only someone who has lived years alone can know the absolute pleasure of those animal sounds in the no longer empty house.

"What's this, Dulce?" Oscar exclaimed, when Rocket raised her hackles and growled at him and Maud clawed to her highest perch on the bookcase. "A zoo?"

Oscar didn't seem able to like an animal he didn't own. Either Rocket had been abused by a male or she was jealous because, even when I insisted on her good manners, she was sullen about them. She tried to keep herself warm between me and Oscar, and his slightest affectionate gesture started up a hostile singing in her throat. I finally had to tie her up on the back porch, but just as Oscar went into his fit of passion, Rocket began to howl. I had to disengage myself and go speak to her in my firmest tones.

When Oscar left that night, I had hysterical giggles.

"You're turning yourself into a witch," Oscar decided. "Next it will be a black mynah bird."

Neither the image nor the idea of the bird was distasteful to me. But Rocket's continued hostility was becoming a real problem.

"Look, Dulce, you have to get rid of her before you become too attached to her. You can't have a dog around that doesn't like people."

I did not tell him that Rocket was not only polite but quite friendly with the friends I occasionally had in for drinks or dinner, but I did not take Oscar's advice.

Finally he laid down his ultimatum: "Me or that dog."

When I chose the dog, he thought I was joking.

"I know it's shameful to admit it, Oscar, but what I need are pets, not a lover."

"But that's crazy."

I did not argue with him though I knew Rocket and Maud were my first investments in sanity, creatures with whom I could exchange affection and loyalty, about whom I could be ordinarily responsible. How many bad whims and potential disasters can be more simply avoided than with the words, "I have to go home to feed the animals?"

Later I understood that Oscar didn't have the time or energy for more than one woman a winter, and he had to sulk through the rest of that one until he could return to sculpting and to being my friend.

That summer he introduced into his group of huge phallic and pregnant shapes some less voluptuous figures, empty at the centre. I bought one and placed it in the garden by the roses where Wilson had once pitched his impregnable tent.

I would have liked to declare my independence of Wilson's influence by dropping out of the PhD program since there was no longer any point in winning his approval. I was, I think, worried that having such a degree might intimidate another more ordinary sort of man who might make friends with my animals, like my view and marry me. I began research for my thesis simply because I didn't know what else to do.

Conception and development of character fascinated me in Shakespeare where in the early plays crude models of later great characters could be found. Left to myself, I would not have spent months locating other scholars who had noted and explored that subject to see if there were any observations left to be made. But it was a more humane topic than many with teasing application to life.

I wondered if Wilson and Oscar were early, crude models of extremes of male influence in my life or the great characters before whom others would pale. I waffled between a sense that my life was already over and that it had not really begun. I was so much more settled than most of the other people I knew, yet my commitments seemed to have dwindled rather than increased.

My fellow students worried about money and pregnancy and the constant irritation of intimacy in ugly surroundings. My artist friends were old enough not to have outgrown those concerns but to simplify the last of them to the constant irritation of intimacy anywhere.

I didn't have to keep late hours to get my work done, and Rocket encouraged me to take long walks on the beach, which have always been one of my greatest pleasures. With her protective company I was also free to explore the university grant-land bush, trails intersecting for miles through scrub forest edged with berries and wild flowers. At home Maud's antics often made me laugh aloud, and her warmth in my lap as I sat reading was a simple comfort.

After Oscar, I didn't encourage already attached men to come to call without their wives or girlfriends. I deflected any domestic complaints offered over public coffee at the university or a glass of wine at an opening. I did sometimes listen to their wives as an antidote to my envy. Very few of them seemed content with their lives. In those old days I thought, though never said, that they should be. I was surprised at how many of them envied me.

"You're the only one of us the men ever listen to," one wife observed, a woman both brighter and more committed to her own mind than I was, but she was delayed in her studies by two small children and her husband's academic needs.

The men did listen to me for the simple reason that I asked good questions. Their wives wanted equal time for giving answers. Even quiet men can't tolerate that; they stop listening.

Men married to artistic rather than academic women fared little better. To the complaint that time at home was eaten up with everyone else's needs, husbands were apt to shout, "God, if I had some time at home, I'd have a poem to show for it!" This was before the time that men did stay home, even the best of them, more than once a week. Though some did laundromat duty and food shopping, they thought of these tasks as interim measures until they could make enough money not to feel humble in their expectations of service. Yet their wives also looked forward to a time when life would be made more tolerable by money.

Only one out of all those graduate-school marriages survives into the eighties. Among male artists and their wives, the odds are better (or worse, of course, depending on one's point of view). I speculate that wives of artists don't expect life to get better, early on resign themselves to or embrace a role of cherishing genius without rationalization. My mother lived that way with my father, not expecting diamonds or a plumber either.

"If only men *were* superior," wailed one young wife, "it would make life so much easier."

For all their difficulties, for their envy of my freedom and serenity, I knew those women also pitied me, particularly on those occasions when I needed an escort, the more for their remembering the years of Wilson. I tried not to feel sorry for myself. I knew the Oscars of this world are worse than nothing. About the Wilsons of this world I wasn't entirely sure.

As a young woman of the eighties I might not have waited until I was thirty to consider what my own sexual tastes actually were. Perhaps I was backwards even for my own generation. I didn't give friends the opportunity to tell me so. Lee Fair was the first person, aside from my mother, in whom I ever confided. The impulse took me by surprise, for she was not only younger than I but one of my students.

Like Wilson, Lee had published a book of poems in her early twenties. Unlike him, she had then married and had a child, a choice no wiser for her than it would have been for him. Yet she defended what she had done on the grounds that motherhood is central to the female vision. No woman without that experience could have very much to say. She was too fiercely vulnerable for me to point out how few of our well-known women writers had children. The Brontës, Jane Austen, George Eliot, Emily Dickinson, Willa Cather, Gertrude Stein were all childless.

I had assumed rather than thought about children myself. I was not particularly interested in those belonging to my friends, but I did not read that as a dislike of children. Mine would be well brought up as I had been.

Lee's child, Carol, was both remarkably quiet and watchful compared to other five-year-olds I had known. I did not actively dislike her, but I was quite unnerved by the critical appraisal in her gaze. Any time she was due to arrive with her mother, I took as much care about my appearance as I would for a lover.

She asked odd questions, too, like, "Were you a sad little girl?" She was attracted to sorrow, as Wilson had been. She told me, "My daddy didn't die. He just went away."

Some of my childhood books were still on the shelves, and I found some of my old dolls, stuffed animals, and forgotten games in the cupboard with the neglected Christmas ornaments. As Carol became accustomed to the place, she spent less time suspiciously staring, though she went on asking questions.

"Did you always play by yourself?"

"A lot of the time," I said. "I liked to. I liked to play in the garden."

Sometimes I stood by the window watching her climb among the rocks as I had done, and I supposed my mother often watched me when I was unaware of it. Then Carol would turn, look up and wave. I waved back and turned away, not wanting to seem to spy.

"You should have a child," Lee said. "Why don't you have one?"

"I manage better with animals," I replied, wondering for how many years I'd used self-deprecation as a way to defend myself against personal questions.

"You mother your students."

"Do I mother you? You don't seem to me that much younger than I am."

"I'm not," Lee said. "And at the rate I'm going, I'll be twenty years older than you are by the time I finish my MA."

Lee's face was dark and strained, and there was already a lot of grey in her mane of black hair. She was always exhausted, working as a cocktail waitress on weekends, studying late into week nights, finding time for Carol.

"I don't have your stamina," I said.

"I don't have it either. I just don't have any choice... now."

Like so many other women I knew, Lee made me feel guilty, but the others all had men to stand between them and any altruism I felt. Lee was alone, and I did want to do things for her to make her life easier.

"Don't offer to do things for me," she warned, "because I'll let you."

"Is there anything immoral about doing your laundry here while you have a meal rather than down at the laundromat?"

"Not yet," Lee said.

Her guardedness, her fear of dependence, made me at first more careful of her feelings than I would otherwise have been and perhaps less aware of my own.

One afternoon, when I offered to pick Carol up at kindergarten to give Lee an extra hour at the library, she said, "Don't get indispensable."

"Oh, sometimes you seem to me as impossible as a man," I said in sudden irritation.

"Sometimes you seem as insensitive as one," she retorted.

That exchange, as I though about it, seemed to me basically funny.

"Does neither of us like men very much?" I asked her over coffee, after Carol had been settled in my study with some books.

"I don't have anything against them as long as they leave me alone," Lee said.

"You don't want to remarry ever?"

"No," she said. "Why do I seem to you impossible?"

"You don't. It's only that I don't expect to have to be as careful with you as…"

"With a man?"

"The men I've cared about anyway."

Then for the first time I tried to describe my years with Wilson to the final distress of having destroyed whatever it was between us by one fatal question. I talked about Oscar, too, the rigid, the controlling structures men made in which there was never simply room to be.

"Why did you choose men who didn't want you?" Lee asked.

"I wasn't aware... with Wilson anyway... that I had," I answered, but, as I saw the doubt in her expression, I supposed I wasn't telling the truth. "I don't know."

"Do you really not know now either that you're choosing a woman who does want you?" Lee asked quietly, and, when I did not respond, she said, "Is that to be my fatal question?"

"It mustn't be," I finally managed to say.

"You may not be able to help that," Lee said, and then she called Carol to her and went home.

Again I was faced with my peculiar blindness to my own motives. For months I had been courting Lee in the ways traditional to a lover, rerouting myself on campus on the off chance of meeting her, stupidly disappointed when a similar head of hair revealed a much older and less appealing face. I had brought her small presents, even flowers, and taken her to restaurants and the theatre. I had taken advantage of a convention of physical affection between women to take her arm as we walked along together, to hug and even sometimes kiss her.

When Lee warned me off, there was always also an invitation in it as there had never been with Wilson, and my impatience with her caution was my desire to set no limits on my love, to let it open and flower as it would, at last.

I had never been able to tolerate Oscar's charge that Wilson was a homosexual. It was with perverse relief that I could now exonerate him with my own sexuality, at least the possibility of it.

If I were, in fact, a lesbian, there did not have to be any limits set with Lee, who by now was no longer my student. I might even propose that she move in with me. Who could criticize such an arrangement, one woman helping another? Carol. Well, Carol could be my child, too. I had already begun to give her my childhood. Lee could give up her hideous job, even finally have time to write again. She could have my study. I did most of my work at the university anyway. And Carol could have my old room, which I now used as a guest-room.

So I sat happily rearranging the uses of the furniture without a single moral or emotional apprehension.

When I saw Lee the next day, I embraced her joyfully. Then I looked into her uncertain face and said, "Don't you see? It makes everything so much easier."

Lee laughed in disbelief.

"Tonight you won't have to wake Carol and take her home."

I felt neither shy nor frightened. Lee and I had been casually naked together in the changing-room at the pool. I already knew a delight in the shape of her breasts, the curve of her back, the length of her thighs. And I knew how tender and sure her hands were, tending her child. I also knew she wanted me and had wanted me for a long time.

When we finally lay together in absolute intimacy, all my sexual bewilderment and constraint left me. I understood my power because I could feel it in a singeing heat to be fed to a roaring. I was hardly aware of Rocket's one howl which soon faded into resignation.

"Rocket, you beast," Lee said to the dog in the morning, fondling her ears. "Did you have to make a public announcement?"

Carol said, "I had a funny dream, that I could float… in the air."

I was having the same sensation awake, a combination of euphoria and lack of sleep.

For Lee our love-making did not clear away all the obstacles. When I proposed that she give her landlord notice and move in with me, she wanted to know if I'd really thought about living not only with her but with Carol.

"She's not always an easy child."

"It isn't as if I didn't know her. Carol and I like each other."

"But you'll have to love her," Lee said.

"I do," I protested. "Why don't we ask her if she'd like it?"

"And if she says no?"

I realized I was not prepared to put my fate quite so simply at the whim of a five-year-old child.

Lee was embarrassed when I talked about money.

"You don't create a problem," I tried to explain. "You solve one."

With Lee and Carol to support there was a practical reason for me to take my academic career seriously, accept a full-time appointment the following term and have a real use for my salary. Lee could go on with her MA or not. Maybe it would be better for her to stay home, write and have more time for Carol.

"Even men resent dependents. Wouldn't you?" Lee asked.

"Why should I? You're the point of my life."

For a month Lee and Carol spent three or four nights a week with me, and we all grew increasingly tired and strained. Carol began to have unsympathetic dreams, woke needing her mother's attention.

One night I heard her say to Lee, "You smell funny."

After that Lee left a basin of water on my dresser and washed her face and hands quickly before going to Carol. I did not quote, "Will these hands ne'er be clean?"

One morning after a particularly unsettled night, Lee said, "It isn't going to work. Carol just can't handle it."

"She simply can't handle living in two different places. Half the time she doesn't know where she is when she wakes up. If you moved in, she'd be able to settle down."

"Why don't you ever go in to her?" Lee asked.

"Well, I will from now on. It didn't occur to me," I admitted.

Of course, when I did, Carol bellowed, "I want my mother."

We decided that I should keep Carol on my own over the weekend when she saw very little of her mother anyway. It would also give Lee a chance to get the rest she badly needed. It worked because I devoted myself to Carol. I took her to the zoo. We went to a toy shop and bought new books and some doll furniture, which we set up together in her room. I fixed her her favourite macaroni and cheese, and then read to her.

The effect of such attention backfired when Lee came home. Carol simply became as demanding of me as she was of her mother, behaving very like Rocket in her attempts to keep between us, making herself the centre of attention even at the price of our irritation. Again Lee's solution was to move out, mine for them to move in, and Carol was now on my side.

Lee did not so much change her mind as give in. All in one day, she gave her notice, quit her job and dropped out of university. Then all the nervous energy that had kept her going through her impossible schedule drained from her, and she slept like a patient after major surgery.

For several weeks, I got up if Carol called in the night, got up in the morning to get her off to kindergarten and myself to UBC, collected her and brought her home to Lee who increasingly often had not bothered to dress. I did the shopping, the cooking, the laundry, the cleaning, exercised the dog, mowed the lawn, electric with energy to be all things for Lee, provider, mother, lover, for Lee was filled with sleepy gratitude and sexual sweetness.

"Are you sick, Mommy?" Carol finally asked her.

"I suppose so," I heard Lee reply.

"Are you going to get well?"

"I suppose so," she said again, but the listlessness in her voice suddenly alarmed me.

"Are you all right?" I asked her later that night. "Are you getting rested?"

She only murmured and kissed me.

Early in the morning she was restless, got up, went to the bathroom, came back into the bedroom and stood by the window.

"Are you all right?" I asked again.

For an answer she came back to bed and held me in her arms.

When I woke again, her breathing was unnaturally heavy. I tried to wake her and couldn't. The empty bottle of pills was in the bathroom for me to find. I phoned the doctor who phoned an ambulance.

When Lee had recovered enough to talk, she said, "I should have told you. I was trying to find someone to love Carol…"

"But how could you not want to live?" I asked. "We've been so happy."

She turned her face away from me and closed her eyes.

Hysterical crying or giggling are the luxuries of a woman who lives alone. I had Carol to take care of, comfort, reassure. When she had gone to sleep, I hardly had time to note my own exhaustion before I was asleep myself.

When I woke to the new, requiring day and tried to think about Lee, I could not. I moved automatically through my appointments until lunch-time when I could spend a few minutes with her at the hospital.

"No Visitors" was posted on her shut door.

I went to find a nurse.

The nurse took me to a waiting-room. "Her mother's here. She's been trying to reach you."

"Her mother?"

I did know Lee had a mother and a father. She spoke of them very little, as little as she spoke of her ex-husband or anything else about her past. She came from Winnipeg and said that even the name of the city made her teeth hurt.

A woman with pure white hair and eyes even more exhausted than Lee's came into the room.

"Dulce?"

"Yes," I said.

"I must thank you for being so kind to Lee and Carol through this distressing time."

Kind? I could not imagine what Lee had told her mother.

"I'm making arrangements to take them back to Winnipeg with me tomorrow. Would it be convenient if I came and packed their things tonight?"

"Is that what Lee wants to do?"

"I'm afraid she doesn't have much choice. She can't simply be a burden to strangers."

"She's been no burden," I protested. "She was simply terribly tired..."

"Perhaps she hasn't told you," her mother said. "She has a history of... this."

"But Carol has just really settled in and started to feel at home."

"She hasn't had an easy life," Lee's mother said.

It wasn't exactly lack of sympathy for her own daughter that she expressed in concern for Carol; she seemed simply saddened and resigned.

"If Lee wanted to come home to me, I'd..." I began.

"I'm so sorry. She doesn't want to see you. I'm sure she's... well... ashamed of all the trouble she's caused."

When I picked up Carol that afternoon, I looked at her soft dark cap of hair, her watchful dark eyes and could no more bear the thought of losing her than of losing Lee. What craziness was it in Lee to have thought I would be allowed Carol?

"Your grandmother's here," I said. "She's going to take you and your mother home to Winnipeg until she's better."

"Then do we get to come back here to be with you?"

"I honestly don't know. I hope so."

Carol was quiet then until we got home. She came with me, as was now her habit, to walk Rocket, who did not take her customary long circlings in the bush but stayed with us, bumping clumsily and persistently against us on the narrow path.

Over dinner Carol said, "Mommy said you'd take care of me if anything happened to her."

"She's going to be fine."

"You should make her go to school. Even kids have to go to school."

"She was only having a rest."

"That's when she always gets sick."

First her mother and now her child were tattling on Lee, for whom I felt a pointless, painful loyalty.

"Can I take my doll furniture?"

The next day there was no trace left of either Lee or Carol. I did not even think to ask for their Winnipeg address. Lee had taken my life, if not her own, in a way that I had never meant to give her.

Though it has often seemed obvious to me that troubled friends are in need of psychiatric attention, I have never known what I would say to one about myself, except perhaps that I have too often been mistaken and don't seem able to learn from life as I believe I sometimes do from paintings and poems, even occasionally from a novel.

Lee Fair wrote a novel, part of which is based on or takes off from those brief passionate months we spent together. It is always difficult to know, even when one is not personally involved, how much feeling and judgment really reflect on the raw material of life. Perhaps I would more easily and resignedly accept the portrait of me in it as Lee's real view of me if she hadn't also dedicated the book to me. Am I a muse or a villain? For the artist there may be no clear distinction. My name as a character is Swete, and I am very like the other preying lesbians about whom I compulsively read for several years after Lee left me. Swete seduces the main character and robs her of her child's affection, then of her financial independence and finally of her will to study and write until finally her only way to regain her own life is to take it. The main character recovers to marry her psychiatrist, as Lee also did, though she divorced him not long after the book was published.

Lee is now one of Canada's best known lesbians, that first novel something of an embarrassment to her. To her credit, she uses it as an example of how we have been raised to trash each other and seek our salvation in men. Carol's two sons keep Lee from the extremes of separatism. Lee and I exchange Christmas cards, and we have dinner together occasionally when she is in Vancouver to give a reading or lecture. I don't ever attend them, and she has never asked for an explanation. Perhaps she remembers that I don't go to Wilson's either.

I have long since given up fantasies of nursing either one of them in old age. In any case, I will sooner need that attention than either of them will whose bones are not so well acquainted with sea mists as mine are.

What I have come to understand about myself is that I am interested in art rather than artists. Those who blundered into my life under the mistaken impression that I had either something to give or be given have only threatened my pleasure in their very real accomplishments.

So many people seem to draw their nourishment directly from passion as plants take nourishment directly from the sun.

I have been only badly burned by such heat. Yet the art that has been made from it has sustained me all my solitary life.

I still prefer those arts that don't require the presence of human beings: literature, painting, sculpture. Films are less threatening to me than live theatre, and I prefer my music canned.

After Lee, I encouraged neither men nor women in any sort of intimacy; yet I have gone on being for one artist or another a symbol until I've become something of a legend myself. It is not really respectable, in western Canada, anyway, for a poet to pass thirty without having written a poem to me. I have been muse, witch, preying lesbian. I have also been devouring mother, whore, Diana, spirit of Vancouver, daughter of the tides.

In a sense my life has been lived for me in the imaginations of other people, and there is nothing dangerous about that if I don't try to participate, for in that way disaster lies. My real companions, in my imagination, are my counterparts throughout history and the world who, whatever names they are given, are women very like myself, who holds the shell of a poem to her ear and hears the mighty sea at a safe and sorrowing distance.

LEON ROOKE

PAINTING THE DOG

Jacques Teak did all the moneyed people's pooches. This and that party swore to his excellence, you can't go wrong with terrible Jacques Teak, they said. "Why is he terrible?" Charmaine had asked. No manners, they said, first word out of his mouth you'll want to shoot him.

Charmaine's husband, Donald, told her, "Sure, go ahead, call the guy, he can't be that bad, you can handle him. When I get home next week, I'll expect to see one pink pooch. Jesus Christ, I've stumbled over that dog a thousand times."

Donald spoke the truth. Charmaine's white pooch, Monica, was getting lost against the white marble, she was getting stepped on, kicked for a loop. You're strolling along, sipping the Moët et Chandon, and suddenly you're sprawling, oops!

Unmentioned by tactful Donald was, one, his opinion, there was too much marble, forty thousand square feet of marble, a guy could go blind in this house; two, but for her yapping, the pooch Monica would be a pancake by now. "She yaps," he said to her this very morning, "at least you saw that red tongue, otherwise it's a fucking nightmare."

This pooch Monica, bunny-white like the marble, white like the walls, the flooring, carpets, the ceiling, like the sofas and chairs, lampshades, every room, even the whatnots white, this pooch blending in with forty thousand square feet of snowy field, come winter you can't even see the house. Donald was dead on, for those who couldn't hack white this ten-mill

Rockcliffe Park palace was a nightmare. How many broken arms, sprained ankles, how many noggins hitting the floor, all on account of that pooch?

Charmaine pouted, she said, "Permission to redirect, Your Honour." She wasn't without wit, our Charmaine, she wasn't without brains. You had the idea she was just a long-limbed bimbo from Chicoutimi with dyed blond hair who, but for plucky Donald, might still be fitting spectacles in the Sparks Street optical shop. I'd advise you to abandon that image right now.

"I wish you wouldn't use that F word," Charmaine said, and Donald only rolled his eyes at this reproof, he buzzed her lips nicely, gave a nice stroke to her fanny, then out the door, the limo waiting, he's got a plane to catch, for Chrissake. Charmaine had a foul mouth, too, you just had to crank her up with Moët et Chandon.

They got along, Charmaine and Donald. To put it another way, they had respect for each other, they were lovers, pals. You want the truth, they didn't see that much of each other except at special put-aside times, it was a happy marriage, exactly what both desired.

Charmaine sopped up her hurt feelings re the pooch, re their little squabble, she merely yelled out the white window, "Calm down, Donald, I said I would take care of it."

Meaning the dye job.

"Good," Donald shouted back. "He misbehaves, shoot the son of a bitch."

Meaning Jacques Teak.

This was at breakfast, six o'clock, after their usual sweat hour in the Nautilus gym off the bedroom, off and up a few landings, thirty-seven machines of customized chrome, no flab around here, any little jiggle of flesh we are hitting the machines, forgoing the stir-fry, letting only ginseng-and-spirulina shakes power our bones. Lean Charmaine checking in at five-eight, 116 on the scales, a bobsledder, a snowboarder, skydiver, dynamite on the squash court, great instincts on the slopes, powerful feet, trim ankles, a knockout, ask anyone.

Charmaine's in the pink, no question, but doesn't Donald have a point? There's the pooch's feelings to consider, the mutt getting slammed every which way, we don't want her personality undermined, we don't want her developing an attitude. We can take Donald's word for it, the mutt is getting whiny, she's safe only in the slumber hours, her up there on Charmaine and Donald's wraparound bed, the epoch cute as can be as she snoozes away in her very own thousand-buck Prada handbag, that being how she came, a gift from the prince fellow over in St. Moritz, thank you, Prince.

Here that same day came Jacques Teak, driving up in a red Porsche, for Chrissake, not even thinking about going around to the servants' entrance.

"Sure thing," Charmaine could hear him telling Ella the maid, that's me, the dye man." Then a quick scream, what, has he pinched her fanny? – a flurry of feet, a hard smack, nobody fools with Ella.

But the guy's coming right on in, like he's been accustomed to a swanky, high-tone manor like this from the moment of conception, like he lived this minute in one every bit as swell, such grandeur did not discompose Jacques Teak, didn't inhibit him, the guy only saying, in a lilt that expressed his amazement, "What a lot of white marble! Jeez, I needed my binocs just to find the house."

Charmaine hating him from that first minute.

"Carrara marble," she said. "Take the sofa, yes, that's the dog I want painted, Monica, darling, say hello to" – this asshole, she almost said – only correcting herself in the last second – "to Mr. Teak."

"Whoa," said Jacques Teak, "she blends right in, doesn't she? I nearly tripped over the mutt – how many lawsuits you had?"

Charmaine feeling a shiver go through her in that second, a premonition: this day isn't going to be an ordinary day, dire events are to transpire this day. Right that second, intuition told her to march upstairs, get the pistol, load this sucker, strap it to her waist.

But she subdued these rash thoughts, what on earth was the matter with her? "Would you like something to drink, Mr. Teak?" she asked, she will entertain the bastard a minute before getting down to business, she's no snob, just a simple girl from Chicoutimi who got lucky, who knew what she wanted and came equipped with the assets – "Champagne, a glass of Moët et Chandon?"

Charmaine lowers herself onto the down cushions, crosses those amazing legs, she's going informal today, the white leather catsuit, white gold adorning neck and wrists, bare feet because she loves that cool marble next to her flesh, she drinks nothing herself but Moët et Chandon.

"Whatever you're having," said Jacques Teak, looking about, measuring the property value, every newcomer did. Charmaine hated that, not the measuring so much as the very words issuing from his mouth. If a person can't abide the bubbly, if they prefer something else, let them speak right up, such is her view.

"Nifty layout," Jacques Teak said.

Charmaine wanted to sock him.

She'd done this house herself. Well, mostly, well, in concert with the supremo master Gunnar Birkerts. Charmaine was proud of this house, a showplace, you could find it on the pages of a dozen magazines, so it was a tad white, that was the whole idea, Gunnar had agreed with her. We've got to cut, snap, funnel and shape light into the most inaccessible space, Gunnar had said, think "snowy field, Charmaine."

Out there was the sculpture garden, sixteen alabaster nude women in acrobatic flight sixteen feet high around the gushing curved-earth fountain, columns imported from Italy, the pool house there in white marble, a white marble pool the size of a city park, place a value on that, Mr. Teak, Charmaine thought, and I'll bet you won't even be in the ballpark.

"Nifty sculpturi," the man said.

Charmaine dragged a hand through her hair, stifling a groan, wincing at something, maybe at Jacques Teak's voice, which was certainly on the fey side. She didn't cotton to this guy, he was too full of himself, a cockroach, and look at those ringed fingers, those cowboy boots, that blue ascot around his neck, woo, forgive me if I shudder, Mr. Teak.

But there was poor, bedraggled Monica, bunny-white with her pink eyes, her red tongue, hopping into the dye guy's lap, circling to sit, now doing so, and Jacques Teak lifting the pooch's ears, peering about as if he suspected ticks were in there.

"Monica," the man said. "Now, that's not a name I would ever give a dog. What, she's a typist, a porno star? Nice collar, though, a Gucci, I'll bet."

Impossible, who were these friends that had recommended this bug?

But Charmaine got control of herself, she wasn't about to let herself be undone by a lowly pet consultant, a pet stylist, whatever he called himself.

"I got a one-eyed Maltese the near twin," he said, "female just like Monica here, I call her Tessie."

Charmaine barked out a good laugh, you could say it was involuntary, the guy not knowing a Gucci neck collar from a Chanel and saddling a Maltese with such an insipid name, Tessie, my God, practically Victorian. She should have let Donald handle this, Donald would have put this guy in his place, Donald would have taken one look at that ascot, those boots, and kicked this Teak out the door. But Donald liked her to assert herself, Donald would have said she was every bit his equal on any front you could name, and better than him in many respects, his company had even named a tech system in her honour, Charmaine Catalyst 2000, that was the kind of marriage theirs was. No fooling around either, Charmaine had not the least interest in embarking on such as that. So she would just have to take care of this dye thingy, as well as any other domestic issue arising. Just because a woman had a demanding career, meaning the upcoming TV hostessy duty, and had for pride's sake to spend endless hours looking to her own upkeep and to set aside several months annually for a lock-in at the Ashram, that wonderful California boot camp spa, didn't mean you let home issues slide.

Charmaine pressed the button on the white side table, and there instantly was Ella popping through the open French doors, she must have been in the hallway waiting, good girl, Ella. Here Ella came, the face composed, black hair in a Cleopatra cut, white cap on top of her head, skin shaded with whitening a near match of the marble but for those sultry eyes, the buttercup lips, her imprisoned bosom, hipless, the poor thing, but attractive nevertheless in a very striking tight white uniform, quite a maid's ticket, in other words, that uniform being a design of Donald's own genius, with help from a celebrated designer in Paris, France, not that we want to drop names.

Jacques Teak was checking out Ella, legs slung over a carpet yanked from Arabic sands, bleached bone-white by five hundred years of Bedouin sun, six hundred knots per square inch – one boot propped above the other, leering, but that leer a bit phoney, a bogus copy, in Charmaine's judgment.

Ella pouring the fizz into two exceptionally tall glasses, finest cut crystal, at one time Charmaine had twenty-four of these beauties, now down to a mere trio, Donald with his big hands couldn't seem to get the hang of holding good crystal, he, after all, being a trucker's boy.

Then, can you imagine, not a pin dropping, Jacques Teak's hand coming up between Ella's legs, stroking over the white stockings, him there smirking at Charmaine for what seems like endless minutes, Ella shock-still in the instant but that Moët et Chandon still pouring, not a drop spilled, Charmaine filled with admiration for the woman even as she thinks, It's time I went upstairs and got that pistol.

"Thank you, Ella, that will be all," Charmaine said, her voice shaky, the girl in the instant retreating, Jacques Teak raising a brow, smiling, disdainful, as he observes Ella's slim-line hips, the streamlined legs, the high breasts, that uniform tight on her, tasteless, you could say, but Donald wasn't any too fond of loose rags on a female, that layered look women had gone in for over the past decade, well, that was just insane unless you were a fatso and had reason to hide it.

Charmaine rising, saying to Jacques Teak, "Excuse me one minute, sir," leaving the room hurriedly, but where has Ella got to, she's nowhere to be seen, just a great expanse of white space, a snowy field, the pooch's little paws going click-click behind her, but suddenly there's the black Cleopatra hair, a silver tray about chest high, Ella's figure emerging from the white wall. "Ella," Charmaine asks, "did I just see what I thought I saw in there, that creep's hands on you?" The girl has tears in her eyes, she says, "No, Miss Charmaine, you did not imagine it," and for a second Charmaine feels witless, she is without volition, as though stranded in a white wilderness, in mountainous snow, but this passes, dear Monica is gnawing at one of her toes.

"Then we shall just have to teach him a lesson," Charmaine tells Ella, and an instant later she is climbing the stairs, here she is in her bedroom, here she is hefting the pistol, she's had lessons, she's the proud owner of a sharpshooter badge made of sapphires and diamonds set in platinum, clip chalcedony, gift of the prince, she can drill that son of a bitch Jacques Teak between the eyes at fifty paces, if she must.

When she re-enters, he's there on the sofa, drinking from the bottle, looking her over, licking his lips, Moët et Chandon dripping from his chin. He's saying, "I use an aloe vera dye, best in the business, your mutt will have to be redyed every three weeks, purple, pink, green, blue, whatever you like, you want I should show you paint chips? Say your pooch lives ten years, the net to you will be approximately fifty thou, Jacques Teak don't come cheap. You understand, though, I got a waiting list a mile long, three months minimum before I can touch the mutt, and if you're thinking I might let you jump the queue because of that sexy catsuit you're wearing, because of who you are, you can forget it, Jacques Teak don't do no one no favours."

Charmaine drains her glass, she licks her lips, fans her hair, stares at Jacques Teak the longest time, her eyes squinting, cold, a test to see who will flinch first. But caught up short the next instant because she finds herself suddenly thinking of her mother, missing her childhood in Chicoutimi, even missing those carefree days in the Sparks Street optician's shop. The past is floating in front of her eyes, how amazing, there's no denying we are the custodian of our own lost selves.

The truth is, let's admit it, Charmaine doesn't want to dye her pooch, Monica, bless her, is just fine as she is, she blends into the white marble, you don't see Monica, you trip over the pooch, that's your own trouble, fix your own self up, get your own self dyed, that's what Charmaine is thinking.

"Of course," Jacques Teak is saying, "I'd have to have a hefty advance, and other than colour, it's me who calls the shots."

"Shots? You're calling the shots?"

"Yeah."

"Did you call this one?"

So Charmaine, that instant, shot him.

Afterward, she called Donald's office, she left a message with the secretary, "Tell him we've got a problem." She called the producer of her upcoming TV show, *Celebrity Pooch*, she told him there might be troubled waters ahead, hold the phone. Then she called the police. She and Ella sat on the sofa drinking a new Moët et Chandon, the pooch between them, all three watching Jacques Teak crawling tragically across the white marble, pretty soon he might reach the hallway, the front door, if he doesn't bleed to death he might even make it outside. If the son of a bitch had been wearing white, if those feet were not painting a crimson trail, in the fullness of the snowy landscape here at Rockcliffe Park they would hardly even have seen him.

All in all, it was kind of beautiful.

"Now," said Ella, another Chicoutimi girl, "to concoct a tale."

MARK STRAND

DOG LIFE

Glover Barlett and his wife, Tracy, lay in their king-size bed under a light blue cambric comforter stuffed with down. They stared into the velvety, perfumed dark. Then Glover turned on his side to look at his wife. Her golden hair surrounded her face, making it seem smaller. Her lips were slightly parted. He wanted to tell her something. But what he had to say was so charged that he hesitated. He had mulled it over in private; now he felt he must bring it into the open, regardless of the risks. "Darling," he said, "there's something I've been meaning to tell you."

Tracy eyes widened with apprehension. "Glover, please, if it's going to upset me, I'd rather not hear..."

"It's just that I was different before I met you."

"What do you mean 'different'?" Tracy asked, looking at him.

"I mean, darling, that I used to be a dog."

"You're putting me on," said Tracy.

"No, I'm not," said Glover.

Tracy stared at her husband with mute astonishment. A silence weighted with solitude filled the room. The time was ripe for intimacy; Tracy's gaze softened into a look of concern.

"A dog?"

"Yes, a collie," said Glover reassuringly. "The people who owned me lived in Connecticut in a big house with lots of lawn, and there were woods out back. All the neighbours had dogs, too. It was a happy time."

Tracy's eyes narrowed. "What do you mean 'a happy time'? How could it have been a 'a happy time'?"

"It was. Especially in autumn. We bounded about in the yellow twilight, excited by the clicking of branches and the parade of odours making each circuit of air an occasion for reverie. Burning leaves, chestnuts roasting, pies baking, the last exhalations of earth before freezing, drove us practically mad. But the autumn nights were even better: the blue lustre of stones under the moon, the spectral bushes, the gleaming grass. Our eyes shone with a new depth. We barked, bayed, and babbled, trying again and again to find the right note, a note that would reach back thousands of years into our origins. It was a note that if properly sustained would be the distilled wail of our species and would carry within it the triumph of our collective destiny. With our tails poised in the stunned atmosphere, we sang for our lost ancestors, our wild selves. Darling, there was something about those nights that I miss."

"Are you telling me that something is wrong with our marriage?"

"Not at all. I'm only saying that there was a tragic dimension to my life in those days. You have to imagine me with a friend or two on the top of a windswept knoll, crying for the buried fragments of our cunning, for the pride we lost during the period of our captivity, our exile in civilization, our fateful domestication. There were times when I could detect within the coarsest bark a futility I have not known since. I think of my friend Spot; her head high, her neck extended. Her voice was operatic and filled with a sadness that was thrilling as she released, howl by howl, the darkness of her being into the night."

"Did you love her?" Tracy asked.

"No, not really. I admired her more than anything."

"But there were dogs you did love?"

"It's hard to say that dogs actually love," said Glover.

"You know what I mean," said Tracy.

Glover turned on his back and stared at the ceiling. "Well, there was Flora, who had a lovely puff of hair on her head, inherited from her Dandie Dinmont mother. She was teeny, of course, and I felt foolish, but still… And there was Muriel, a melancholic Irish setter. And Cheryl, whose mother was a long-coated chihuahua and whose father was a cross between a fox terrier and a shelty. She was intelligent, but her owners made her wear a little tartan jacket which humiliated her. She ran off with a clever mutt – part puli, part dachshund. After that I saw her with a black-and-white papillon. Then she moved, and I never saw her again."

"Were there others?" said Tracy.

"There was Peggy Sue, a German short-haired pointer whose owners would play Buddy Holly on their stereo. The excitement we experienced when we heard her name is indescribable. We would immediately go to the door and whimper to be let out. How proudly we trotted under the gaudy scattering of stars! How immodest we were under the moon's opalescence! We pranced and pranced in the exuberant light."

"You make it sound so hunky-dory. There must've been bad times."

"The worst times were when my owners laughed. Suddenly they became strangers. The soft cadences of their conversation, the sharpness of their commands, gave way to howls, gurgles, and yelps. It was as if something were released in them, something absolute and demonic. Once they started it was hard for them to stop. You can't imagine how frightening and confusing it was to see my protectors out of control. The sounds they made seemed neither expressive or communicative, nor did they indicate pleasure or pain, but rather a weird mixture of both. It was a limbo of utterance from which I felt completely excluded. But why go on, those days are past."

"How do you know?"

"I just do. I feel it."

"But if you were a dog once, why not a dog twice?"

"Because there are no signs of that happening again. When I was a dog, there were indications that I would end up as I am now. I never liked exposing myself and was pained by having to perform private acts in public. I was embarrassed by the pomp of bitches in heat – their preening and wagging, by the panting lust of my brothers. I became withdrawn; I brooded; I actually suffered a kind of canine *terribilità*. It all pointed to one thing."

When Glover had finished, he waited for Tracy to speak. He was sorry he had told her so much. He felt ashamed. He hoped she would understand his having been a dog was not his choice, that such aberrations are born of necessity and are not lamentable. At times, the fury of a man's humanity will find its finest manifestation in amazing alterations of expectedness. For people are only marginally themselves. Glover, who earlier in the night had begun to slide into an agony of contrition, now felt righteous pride. He saw that Tracy's eyes were closed. She had fallen asleep. The truth had been endurable, had been overshadowed by a need that led her safely into the doom of another night. They would wake in the early morning and look at each other as always. What he had told her would be something they would never mention again, not out of politeness, or sensitivity for the other, but because such achievements of frailty, such lyrical lapses, are unavoidable in every life.

ALISTAIR MACLEOD

As Birds Bring Forth the Sun

Once there was a family with a Highland name who lived beside the sea. And the man had a dog of which he was very fond. She was large and grey, a sort of staghound from another time. And if she jumped up to lick his face, which she loved to do, her paws would jolt against his shoulders with such force that she would come close to knocking him down and he would be forced to take two or three backward steps before he could regain his balance. And he himself was not a small man, being slightly over six feet and perhaps one hundred and eighty pounds.

She had been left, when a pup, at the family's gate in a small handmade box and no one knew where she had come from or that she would eventually grow to such a size. Once, while still a small pup, she had been run over by the steel wheel of a horse-drawn cart which was hauling kelp from the shore to be used as fertilizer. It was in October and the rain had been falling for some weeks and the ground was soft. When the wheel of the cart passed over her, it sunk her body into the wet earth as well as crushing some of her ribs; and apparently the silhouette of her small crushed body was visible in the earth after the man lifted her to his chest while she yelped and screamed. He ran his fingers along her broken bones, ignoring the blood and urine which fell upon his shirt, trying to soothe her bulging eyes and her scrabbling front paws and her desperately licking tongue.

The more practical members of his family, who had seen run-over dogs before, suggested that her neck be broken by his strong hands or that he grasp her by the hind legs and swing her head against a rock, thus putting an end to her misery. But he would not do it.

Instead, he fashioned a small box and lined it with woollen remnants from a sheep's fleece and one of his old frayed shirts. He placed her within the box and placed the box behind the stove and then warmed some milk in a small saucepan and sweetened it with sugar. And he held open her small and trembling jaws with his left hand while spooning in the sweetened milk with his right, ignoring the needle-like sharpness of her small teeth. She lay in the box most of the remaining fall and into the early winter, watching everything with her large brown eyes.

Although some members of the family complained about her presence and the odour from the box and the waste of time she involved, they gradually adjusted to her; and as the weeks passed by, it became evident that her ribs were knitting together in some form or other and that she was recovering with the resilience of the young. It also became evident that she would grow to a tremendous size, as she outgrew one box and then another and the grey hair began to feather from her huge front paws. In the spring she was outside almost all of the time and followed the man everywhere; and when she came inside during the following months, she had grown so large that she would no longer fit into her accustomed place behind the stove and was forced to lie beside it. She was never given a name but was referred to in Gaelic as *cù mòr glas*, the big grey dog.

By the time she came into her first heat, she had grown to a tremendous height, and although her signs and her odour attracted many panting and highly aroused suitors, none was big enough to mount her and the frenzy of their disappointment and the longing of her unfulfillment were more than the man could stand. He went, so the story goes, to a place where he knew there was a big dog. A dog not as big as she was, but still a big dog, and brought him home with him. And at the proper time he took the *cù môr glas* and the big dog down to the sea where he knew there was a hollow in the rock which appeared only at low tide. He took some sacking to provide footing for the male dog and he placed the *cù môr glas* in the hollow of the rock and knelt beside her and steadied her with his left arm under her throat and helped position the male dog above her and guided his blood-engorged penis. He was a man used to working with the breeding of animals, with the guiding of rams and bulls and stallions and often with the funky smell of animal semen heavy on his large and gentle hands.

The winter that followed was a cold one and ice formed on the sea and frequent squalls and blizzards obliterated the offshore islands and caused people to stay near their fires much of the time, mending clothes and nets and harness and waiting for the change of season. The *cù môr glas* grew heavier and even more large until there was hardly room for her around the stove or even under the table. And then one morning, when it seemed that spring was about to break, she was gone.

The man and even the family, who had become more involved than they cared to admit, waited for her but she did not come. And as the frenzy of spring wore on, they busied themselves with readying their land and their fishing gear and all of the things that so desperately required their attention. And then they were into summer and fall and winter and another spring which saw the birth of the man and his wife's twelfth child. And then it was summer again.

That summer the man and two of his teenaged sons were pulling their herring nets about two miles offshore when the wind began to blow off the land and the water began to roughen. They became afraid that they could not make it safely back to shore, so they pulled in behind one of the offshore islands, knowing that they would be sheltered there and planning to outwait the storm. As the prow of their boat approached the gravelly shore, they heard a sound above them, and looking up they saw the *cù môr glas* silhouetted on the brow of the hill which was the small island's highest point.

"M'eudal cù môr glas," shouted the man in his happiness – M'eudal meaning something like dear or darling; and as he shouted, he jumped over the side of his boat into the waist-deep water, struggling for footing on the rolling gravel as he waded eagerly and awkwardly towards her and the shore. At the same time, the *cù môr glas* came hurtling down towards him in a shower of small rocks dislodged by her feet; and just as he was emerging from the water, she met him as she used to, rearing up on her hind legs and placing her huge front paws on his shoulders while extending her eager tongue.

The weight and the speed of her momentum met him as he tried to hold his balance on the sloping angle and the water rolling gravel beneath his feet, and he staggered backwards and lost his footing and fell beneath her force. And in that instant again, as the story goes, there appeared over the brow of the hill six more huge grey dogs hurtling down towards the gravelled strand. They had never seen him before; and seeing him stretched prone beneath their mother, they misunderstood, like so many armies, the intention of their leader.

They fell upon him in a fury, slashing his face and tearing aside his lower jaw and ripping out his throat, crazed with blood-lust or duty or perhaps starvation. The *cù môr glas* turned on them in her own savagery, slashing and snarling and, it seemed, crazed by their mistake; driving them bloodied and yelping before her, back over the brow of the hill where they vanished from sight but could still be heard screaming in the distance. It all took perhaps little more than a minute.

The man's two sons, who were still in the boat and had witnessed it all, ran sobbing through the salt water to where their mauled and mangled father lay; but there was little they could do other than hold his warm and bloodied hands for a few brief moments. Although his eyes "lived" for a small fraction of time, he could not speak to them because his face and throat had been torn away, and of course there was nothing they could do except to hold and be held tightly until that too slipped away and his eyes glazed over and they could no longer feel his hands holding theirs. The storm increased and they could not get home and so they were forced to spend the night huddled beside their father's body. They were afraid to try to carry the body to the rocking boat because he was so heavy and they were afraid also, huddled on the rocks, that the dogs might return. But they did not return at all and there was no sound from them, no sound at all, only the moaning of the wind and the washing of the water on the rocks.

In the morning they debated whether they should try to take his body with them or whether they should leave it and return in the company of older and wiser men. But they were afraid to leave it unattended and felt that the time needed to cover it with protective rocks would be better spent in trying to get across to their home shore. For a while they debated as to whether one should go in the boat and the other remain on the island, but each was afraid to be alone and so in the end they managed to drag and carry and almost float him towards the bobbing boat. They lay him face-down and covered him with what clothes there were and set off across the still-rolling sea. Those who waited on the shore missed the large presence of the man within the boat and some of them waded into the water and others rowed out in skiffs, attempting to hear the tearful messages called out across the rolling waves.

The *cù mòr glas* and her six young dogs were never seen again, or perhaps I should say they were never seen again in the same way. After some weeks, a group of men circled the island tentatively in their boats but they saw no sign. They went again and then again but found nothing. A year later, and grown much braver, they beached their boats and walked the island carefully, looking into the small sea caves and the hollows at the base of the wind-ripped trees, thinking perhaps that if they did not find the dogs, they might at least find their whitened bones; but again they discovered nothing.

The *cù môr glas*, though, was supposed to be sighted here and there for a number of years. Seen on a hill in one region or silhouetted on a ridge in another or loping across the valleys or glens in the early morning or the shadowy evening. Always in the area of the half perceived. For a while she became rather like the Loch Ness Monster or the Sasquatch on a smaller scale. Seen but not recorded. Seen when there were no cameras. Seen but never taken.

The mystery of where she went became entangled with the mystery of whence she came. There was an increased speculation about the handmade box in which she had been found and much theorizing as to the individual or individuals who might have left it. People went to look for the box but could not find it. It was felt she might have been part of a *buidseachd* or evil spell cast on the man by some mysterious enemy. But no one could go much farther than that. All of his caring for her was recounted over and over again and nobody missed any of the ironies.

What seemed literally known was that she had crossed the winter ice to have her pups and had been unable to get back. No one could remember ever seeing her swim; and in the early months at least, she could not have taken her young pups with her.

The large and gentle man with the smell of animal semen often heavy on his hands was my great-great-great-grandfather, and it may be argued that he died because he was too good at breeding animals or that he cared too much about their fulfillment and well-being. He was no longer there for his own child of the spring who, in turn, became my great-great-grandfather, and he was perhaps too much there in the memory of his older sons who saw him fall beneath the ambiguous force of the *cù môr glas*. The youngest boy in the boat was haunted and tormented by the awfulness of what he had seen. He would wake at night screaming that he had seen the *cù môr glas a' bhàis*, the big grey dog of death, and his screams filled the house and the ears and minds of the listeners, bringing home again and again the consequences of their loss. One morning, after a night in which he saw the *cù môr glas a' bhàis* so vividly that his sheets were drenched with sweat, he walked to the high cliff which faced the island and there he cut his throat with a fish knife and fell into the sea.

The other brother lived to be forty, but, again so the story goes, he found himself in a Glasgow pub one night, perhaps looking for answers, deep and sodden with the whisky which had become his anaesthetic. In the half darkness he saw a large, grey-haired man sitting by himself against the wall and mumbled something to him. Some say he saw the *cù môr glas a' bhàis* or uttered the name. And perhaps the man heard the phrase through ears equally affected by drink and felt he was being called a dog or a son of a bitch or something of that nature. They rose to meet one another and struggled outside into the cobblestoned passageway behind the pub where, most improbably, there was supposed to be six other large, grey-haired men who beat him to death on the cobblestones, smashing his bloodied head into the stone again and again before vanishing and leaving him to die with his face turned to the sky. The *cù môr glas a' bhàis* had come again, said his family, as they tried to piece the tale together.

This is how the *cù môr glas a' bhàis* came into our lives, and it is obvious that all of this happened a long, long time ago. Yet with succeeding generations it seemed the spectre had somehow come to stay and that it had become *ours* – not in the manner of an unwanted skeleton in the closet from a family's ancient past but more in the manner of something close to a genetic possibility. In the deaths of each generation, the grey dog was seen by some – by women who were to die in childbirth; by soldiers who went forth to the many wars but did not return; by those who went forth to feuds or dangerous love affairs; by those who answered mysterious midnight messages; by those who swerved on the highway to avoid the real or imagined grey dog and ended in masses of crumpled steel. And by one professional athlete who, in addition to his ritualized athletic superstitions, carried another fear or belief as well. Many of the man's descendants moved like careful haemophiliacs, fearing that they carried unwanted possibilities deep within them. And others, while they laughed, were like members of families in which there is a recurrence over the generations of repeated cancer or the diabetes which comes to those beyond middle age. The feeling of those who may say little to others but who may say often and quietly to themselves, "It has not happened to me," while adding always the cautionary *"yet."*

I am thinking all of this now as the October rain falls on the city of Toronto and the pleasant, white-clad nurses pad confidently in and out of my father's room. He lies quietly amidst the whiteness, his head and shoulders elevated so that he is in the hospital position of being neither quite prone nor yet sitting. His hair is white upon his pillow and he breathes softly and sometimes unevenly, although it is difficult ever to be sure.

My five grey-haired brothers and I take turns beside his bedside, holding his heavy hands in ours and feeling their response, hoping ambiguously that he will speak to us, although we know that it may tire him. And trying to read his life and ours into his eyes when they are open. He has been with us for a long time, well into our middle age. Unlike those boys in that boat of so long ago, we did not see him taken from us in our youth. And unlike their youngest brother who, in turn, became our great-great-grandfather, we did not grow into a world in which there was no father's touch. We have been lucky to have this large and gentle man so deep into our lives.

No one in this hospital has mentioned the *cù môr glas a' bhàis*. Yet as my mother said ten years ago, before slipping into her own death as quietly as a grownup child who leaves or enters her parents' house in the early hours, "It is hard to *not* know what you do know."

Even those who are most sceptical, like my oldest brother who had driven here from Montreal, betray themselves by their nervous actions. "I avoided the Greyhound bus stations in both Montreal and Toronto," he smiled upon his arrival, and then added, "Just in case."

He did not realize how ill our father was and has smiled little since then. I watch him turning the diamond ring upon his finger, knowing that he hopes he will not hear the Gaelic phrase he knows too well. Not having the luxury, as he once said, of some who live in Montreal and are able to pretend they do not understand the "other" language. You cannot *not* know what you do know.

Sitting here, taking turns holding the hands of the man who gave us life, we are afraid for him and for ourselves. We are afraid of what he may see and we are afraid to hear the phrase born of the vision. We are aware that it may become confused with what the doctors call "the will to live" and we are aware that some beliefs are what others would dismiss as "garbage." We are aware that there are men who believe the earth is flat and that the birds bring forth the sun.

Bound here in our peculiar mortality, we do not wish to see or see others see that which signifies life's demise. We do not want to hear the voice of our father, as did those other sons, calling down his own particular death upon him.

We would shut our eyes and plug our ears, even as we know such actions to be of no avail. Open still and fearful to the grey hair rising on our necks if and when we hear the scrabble of the paws and the scratching at the door.

BARRY CALLAGHAN

Dog Days of Love

Father Vernon Wilson was an old priest who led a quiet life. He said Mass every morning at the side altar of his church, read a short detective novel, had a light lunch, and went out walking with his dog. He was retired but he always made a few house calls to talk to old friends who weren't bothered by the dog, and though he had a special devotion to the Blessed Virgin and the Holy Shroud of Turin, he didn't talk much about faith.

Though he was still spry for a man in his early eighties, he gladly let the dog, a three-year-old golden retriever, set a leisurely pace on a loosely held leash, sniffing at curbs and shrub roots and fence posts. He'd had the dog for a year, a local veterinarian having come around to the parish house of an afternoon to leave the dog as a gift, telling the housekeeper, "I've always wanted to give Father Wilson a little dog. I always felt so at ease with myself and the world whenever I'd gone to him to confession."

In all his years as a parish priest, Father Wilson had never imagined that he might want a dog, and he certainly did not know if he could, in accordance with diocesan rules, keep a dog in the parish home. The new young pastor, Father Kukic, had at first said, No, no, he wasn't sure that it was a good idea at all, even if it was possible, but then the diocesan doctor had come by to give the priests their autumn flu shots and to check their blood pressure, and he had said, "No, no, it's a wonderful idea, I urge you, Father Kukic, if it's not usually done, to do it. It's a proven fact, older people who have the constant company of a dog live longer, maybe five years longer, maybe because all a dog asks is that you let him love you, and we all want Father Wilson to live longer, don't we?"

"I'm sure we do," Father Wilson said.

"Well," Father Kukic said, trying to be amiably amusing, "there could be two sides to that argument."

"Father Kukic," the old priest said, feigning surprise, "I've never known you to see two sides to an argument." He clapped the young priest on the shoulder. "Good for you, good for you."

"I'm sure, too, that the dog will be good for you," Father Kukic said.

"I'm sure he will," Father Wilson said, but he was not sure of the situation at all.

On their first night walk together he kept the dog on a short leash, calling him simply, "You, dog..." Then, after ten or eleven days, Father Wilson not only let the dog sleep on the floor at the end of the bed in his room, but sometimes up on the end of his bed, and then one morning he announced over breakfast that he had decided to call the dog, Anselm. "After the great old saint," he told Father Kukic, "Saint Anselm, who said the flesh is a dung hill, and this dog, I can tell you, has yet to meet doggy dung on a lawn he doesn't like."

"Oh, really now," Father Kukic said, and before he could add anything more, the old priest continued, "But then, look at it this way, nothing is ever what it seems. Most people get Saint Anselm all wrong. He was like the great hermit saints who went out into the desert, they renounced everything that gave off the smell of punishment and revenge, and so they renounced the flesh, but only so they could insist on the primacy of love over everything else in their spiritual lives... over knowledge, solitude, over prayer... love, in which all authoritarian brutality and condescension is absent, love in which nothing is hidden in the flesh..."

Father Kukic sat staring at him, breathing through his open mouth.

"You should be keeping up on your spiritual reading, Father, that's Thomas Merton I was giving you there, you should try him."

"Wasn't he something of a mystic?"

"My goodness," the old priest said, "I think Anselm and I should go for a walk, get our morning feet on the ground."

They walked together every morning just before lunch, sometimes in the afternoon if it wasn't too hot or too cold, and always at night, just before *Larry King*. "If you're going to be in touch, if you're going to keep up with your parishioners," he told Father Kukic, "you've got to know what the trash talk is, too."

When he visited homes in the parish, leaving the dog leashed on a porch or sitting in a vestibule, he talked candidly about anything and everything, pleasing the parishioners, but more and more as he and Anselm walked together, and particularly when they stopped to rest for a moment in front of a building like the Robarts Research Library, he leaned down and patted Anselm's neck and said quietly to him, "Good dog, now you look at that, there's real brutalism for you, that's the bunker mentality of a bully." He scowled at the massive slab-grey concrete windowless wall, the cramped doorway under a huge periscope projection of concrete into the sky. "This is the triumph of the architecture of condescension," he said, pleased that he'd found so apt a phrase for his thought, and amused and touched, too, by how Anselm, looking up at him, listened attentively, and how the dog, at the moment he had finished his thought, came up off his haunches and broke into a cantering walk, striding, the old priest thought, like a small blond horse.

"Beautiful," he said, "beautiful."

Parishioners and shopkeepers soon took for granted seeing them together.

The only times that Anselm was not with him, the only time he left the dog alone in his bedroom, was when he said Mass at the side altar early in the morning or when he went to visit a parishioner sick at home.

Once, while he was away on a sick call, Anselm had chewed the instep of a shoe he had left under the bed, and a week later he had swallowed a single black sock.

That had caused an awkward moment, because the dog had not been able to entirely pass the sock and Father Wilson had had to stand out on the parish-house lawn behind a tree and slowly drag the slime and shit-laden sock out of the dog.

"Anselm, my Anselm," he had said, "you sure are a creature of the flesh."

But it was while he was at prayer that he felt closest to Anselm.

It was while he knelt at prayer before going to bed, kneeling under the length of linen cloth that hung on the wall, a replica of the Holy Shroud of Turin, that Anselm had sat down beside him and had nestled his body in under his elbow so that the old priest had embraced Anselm with his right arm as he had said the Apostles Creed, feeling deeply, through the image of the dead face on the Shroud, the Presence of the Living Christ in his life. And now, every night, they knelt and sat together for ten minutes, after which Father Wilson would cross himself, get into bed, and Anselm would leap up on to the bed and curl at his feet so that as he went to sleep, the old priest was comforted not just by the heat and weight of the animal in his bed, but the sound of his breathing.

His devotion to the Shroud, however, had not been a comfort to his young pastor, Father Kukic, who had snorted dismissively, saying that when a seminarian in Paris he had travelled through the countryside one summer, and as a believer, about to be ordained, he had been embarrassed to come upon a church near Poitiers that had claimed to house "one of the two known heads of John the Baptist," and another that had said they possessed "a vial of the unsoured milk of the Virgin."

"The unsoured milk... I like that," the old priest had said, laughing.

"Well, I don't, and no one else does either," Father Kukic said. "It's embarrassing."

"Only a little."

"And as for your cloth, no one had ever heard of your Shroud til somewhere back in the 1500s."

"Not mine, Father. Our Lord's."

"Oh, please."

"The thing is this, Father, there are certain facts," and Father Wilson had patiently tried to describe the two images on the Shroud – the front and back of a man's wounded body and his bearded face, his staring eyes and skeletal crossed hands – and how all this, after experts had completed a microscopic examination of the linen, had revealed no paint or pigment that anyone knew of, nor did the image relate to any known style... and furthermore, "Somehow, the Shroud is a kind of photographic negative which becomes positive when reversed by a camera, the body of a man somehow embedded in the linen as only a camera can see him, a way of observing what no one could have known how to possibly paint."

"These all may be facts, Father, but they prove nothing."

"Exactly, my dear Father. But you see, I prefer that facts add up to a mystery that is true rather than facts that add up to an explanation that is true."

"Like what?"

"Like the Virgin Birth."

"Nonsense. That's a matter of faith."

"No, it's a matter of temperament, Father."

They had never spoken of the Shroud again.

There were nights through the winter when the old priest, before going to sleep, had felt, as he had told Anselm, "nicely confused." Kneeling under the Shroud, knowing how dark and freezing cold it was outside and staring up into the hollowed dead yet terrorized eyes of the Christ, he had felt only warmth and unconditional love from the dog under his arm, and after saying his prayers he had taken to nestling his face into Anselm's neck fur, laughing quietly and boyishly, as he hadn't heard himself laugh in years, before falling into a very sound sleep.

At the first smell of spring, he opened his bedroom window and aired out his dresser drawers and his closet, breathing in deeply and deeply pleased to be alive. He gave Anselm's head a brisk rubbing and then, having borrowed the housekeeper's feather duster, he took down the linen shroud that had been brought to him as a gift by a friend all the way from Turin, and he dusted it off at the window and then laid it out for airing over the sill, as his mother had done years ago with the family bedsheets.

In the early afternoon, leaving Anselm asleep, he went out alone to visit an elderly couple whose age and infirmness over the long winter had made them cranky and curt and finally cruel to each other, though they still loved each other very much, and he hoped that they would let him, as an old friend, go around their flat and open their windows, too, and bring the feel of the promise of spring air into their lives again.

When he returned to the parish house, to his room, he was exuberant, enormously pleased with himself, because his visit had ended with the elderly couple embracing him, saying, "We're just three old codgers waiting to die," laughing happily.

When he opened his door, he let out a roar of disbelief, "Nooooo, God." Anselm was on his belly on the bed and under him – gathered between his big web-toed paws – was the Shroud. He was thumping his tail as he snuffled and shoved his snout into the torn cloth. The old priest lunged, grabbing for the Shroud, yanking at it, the weight of the startled dog tearing it more, and when he saw, in disbelief, that the face, the Holy face and the Holy eyes of the Presence were all gone, shredded and swallowed by the dog, he raised his fist – hurt and enraged – and Anselm, seeing that rage and that fist, leaped off the bed, hitting the floor, tail between his legs, skidding into a corner wall where, cowering and trembling, trying to tuck his head into his shoulder, he looked up, waiting to be beaten.

"Oh my God, oh my God," the old priest moaned, sitting on the edge of the bed, drawing the ruined Shroud across his knees.

He could not believe the look of terror, and at the same time, the look of complete love in the dog's eyes, and for a moment he thought that that must have been the real look in Christ's eyes as He hung on the cross, His terror felt as a man, and His complete unconditional love as God, but before he could wonder if such a thought was blasphemous, he was struck by a fear that, having seen his rage and his fist, Anselm would always be afraid of him, would always cower and tremble at his coming. As a boy, he had seen dogs like that, dogs who had been beaten.

He fell on to his knees beside the dog in the corner where, night after night, he had prayed – saying the Apostles Creed, affirming his faith – and Anselm had sat there, too, waiting to go on to the bed to sleep. He took Anselm's head in his arms, feeling as he did his trouser leg become warm with an oily wetness, the dog, in the confusion of his fear and relief at being held, having peed. The old priest hugged him closer and laughed and Anselm came out of his cower and then stopped trembling. Rocking Anselm in his arms, he was about to tell him he was a good dog and he shouldn't worry, that he loved him, but then he thought how ludicrous it would be for a grown man to talk out loud to a dog about something so serious as love, and so he just sat in their wetness holding Anselm even tighter so that Anselm would understand and never doubt.

MARIE-CLAIRE BLAIS

HOMAGE TO SCHEILA

Translated by Richard Teleky

The memory of our lost animals plunges us into a deep sorrow, since we're powerless before their loss. What have we done to make them leave us? How did we happen to lose them so quickly, they lived fifteen years, sixteen years, but suddenly the lives of those who were so familiar to us cease while ours go on, those who seemed so strong in their fidelity, in a love without flaws when sometimes we love them so badly, treat them with so little respect, take brutal leave, and we feel how all this time they were short-lived, so fragile that a cold, a slight accident, could take them away, and that their presence at our sides for fifteen or sixteen years was a true miracle, but it's too late, we're forever at a loss, with the regret of having had them near us for such a short time. My younger sister Hélène and I had adopted Scheila when she was just a sickly pup, condemned if we were unable to cure her lung ailment. Daughter of a German shepherd mother and a Samoyed father – or is that not what we imagined looking at our white dog? – would her fur not fill out soon, would she not be a sled dog, for we had had high hopes of curing her, and she was cured slowly, with the help of bottle-feeding and caresses, and suddenly the metamorphosis took place, we had, before our eyes, a Scheila coughing a little but round beneath her white fur, a fur as white as snow, we observed our sled dog with joy, with admiration that she was so courageous, we took her into our arms, a bear cub all white with great black eyes, eyes whose liquid, warm gaze I feel all around me to this day, that seem to guide me as I raise my Siamese kittens who are still in a stage of playfulness and absolutely disobedient. Each of these orphaned animals that we've welcomed into our lives has a story that becomes our own, and often it's a tragic story, for we know that without us the little animal would not survive, and this wasn't only Scheila's story but also Sammy's, and all the animals that survived in their house at Ripon, like a farm at the summit of a mountain, if not for my friends Francine and Marie, who saved both of them, Sammy would have frozen to death at the edge of a Laurentian highway, snuggled against his sister on that day of glacial wind. How many dogs, cats, birds, ducks did they take in, providing a refuge to those who would have succumbed to the brutality of nature, or to that of men, newborns, these delicate, defenceless creatures, were they not doomed to a world that had forever been hostile to them, that had always mistreated them? Wouldn't Scheila and Sammy have been exterminated, like those animals that we kill every day with our indifference, our unconscious cruelty? Whether they're abandoned on the road, or euthanized, some human always hides behind these unlimited crimes, so vast and daily, someone who feels neither a sense of shame nor repentance, since an animal's life is nothing to us, and without the immense generosity of my friends Francine or Marie, and others who have this same respect for animals and for their survival, and who prove it by saving them, by caring for them, we would be constant witnesses to these sacrifices, which we think about so little, so utterly does this criminal attitude toward animals rule mankind, making us forget that the end of any animal's life is also the end of our own. Thus surrounded by care, by love, from my sister Hélène, Scheila decided to live, the white bear blossomed, became taller and longer, on solid paws, a greyhound or a doe in her burst of joy, running, bounding in the fields in summer, rolling about in the snow in winter – the outline of her almond-shaped eyes sharpening, the muzzle, the eyes so black, and the rosy interior of always raised ears – was everything about her not touched with beauty, didn't we know what frailty she'd had to surmount to attain this beauty, this grace, she had only one flaw, she didn't listen to us when we scolded her for her dangerous car chases, it was always the same happy burst overflowing, which she couldn't control, teeth sparkling, ears quivering, she seemed to scoff at reprimands with her smile, for this was the most amazing thing about her, the smile I still find in all the photographs, whether resting her head on my knees or seated on the steps of a wooden staircase in the country, she was always ready to dive toward the woods, and holding her by the neck, I seem to be restraining her from bounding out to play, as if to keep her a little closer to me, while she dispenses to friends who admire her the sweetness of this smile that seems to pardon all and understand all, and which also expresses at the same time a straining toward the immensity of the fields, to nature's bright summer sun, showing that she is above all a free spirit whose inestimable sentiment of liberty we humans, tyrants over the weakest beasts, cannot contain. Although she had a wild streak it was vain to wish to tame, as she pawed like a colt in the snow, shaking her fur as if it were a mane, or if one played with her, running breathless for a toy, a ball, inside the house her presence was of a resounding lightness, and Scheila became a dignified and peaceful companion during the long hours I worked. Even so, I reproach myself for the little time that I devoted to Scheila during these periods of writing, in this concentration of spirit that accompanies a retreat not without egotism – doesn't the writer forget everything around her, in her struggle she loses herself in the meanderings of work, in the cave from which she attempts to extract light – it's in this way that I abandoned Scheila to herself, leaving her asleep by the work table for hours, her head suddenly morose between her white paws, not listening to her when she seemed to say to me, isn't it time to go out, to go for a walk? although she did it discreetly, with longing in her black eyes, with a rub of her muzzle against the table, egotistically didn't I know that she was always there, from one book to another, confronting with me the same secret battles in the production of a book's numerous characters, whether it was *Deaf to the City*, where the character of Florence, menaced by death, took me so far into her depths, or *David Sterne*, written in the solitude of an uncomfortable rented house in the Laurentians, where it was very cold and Scheila was such a good sport, as diligent and calm as the animals – cats or dogs, or both sometimes – asleep at the feet of hardworking angels in Dürer's paintings, in those studios where it also seemed very cold. I blame myself even more for having so often entrusted her to others, because I travelled or had to leave for work, for research, for these desertions, if I couldn't prevent their repetition, I reproach myself gravely today, now that Scheila has left us, is no longer with us – it's near her, always near her, that she loved to see her masters, not their galloping landscape of disorder in discovering the world, their taste for adventure, she only appreciated their stable presence, and nothing hurt her more than frequent departures. It was in this way, always haunted by my sins of omission, of negligence toward Scheila during these absences, that she began to haunt in her turn the books that I was later to write – was she not the perfect dog from which young Anna was separated by her wanderings in *Anna's World*, in the mesh of adolescent life where all is torn apart with the divorce of her parents, will Anna's dog not be a greater victim of the catastrophe than Anna herself, he will be alone beside Raymonde, Anna's mother, with Anna's captive doves flying about in her bedroom, a witness to the breakup of Raymonde, who lost the man she loved, a young American conscientious objector who had taken refuge with her to escape persecution, and it's in this vision, muddled by drugs, that Anna, throughout her wanderings in Mexico, sees once more her mother, the doves, the dog, the ones she ran away from, believing she has betrayed them for the adventures of the road, the ones who in the end will bring her back home, since she can't live without them. Thus, these animals that we've chosen, are they not always with us, always in our thoughts, do they not awaken everywhere our conscience before the precarious nature of animal life? Scheila was the companion of writers and painters – the great artist Mary Meigs made innumerable portraits of her, in watercolours – here she is, in front of a blue fence, stretched out before those mauve mountains that Mary went to paint in autumn, in the Eastern Townships – she was painted, drawn, in notebooks, exercise books, on bits of paper, in the kitchen, while Scheila slept in a ball on a carpet – so many sketches of these moments of her life, a life fifteen years long that would seem to us all so short. What respiratory illness carried Scheila away without our sensing her departure? Her disappearance, too soon, remains incomprehensible, shocking, painful, for who saw her weaken when she always seemed so happy to be alive, when she changed so little in her games, the gentleness of her presence hardly noticed with time. Now that she's gone, her love is irreplaceable, for she was just that, love, gentleness, and nothing in this world seems like her. Her last apparition was in a dream in which she said farewell to me, the polar cub of old had grown, and I saw her, the bear cub of the ice fields, standing upright on a mound of ice, then falling heavily and disappearing into the snow and a flow of grey, cold water as she bid me adieu. As soon as I awoke I knew that Scheila was no longer there, and that because of this loss, even if I had often loved her badly, I would be inconsolable.

STAN DRAGLAND

PENELOPE'S DOG

He might have stretched out at the foot of the bed, or at Odysseus's side, or by the cradle, but he didn't. He was Penelope's dog from the first, though their meeting was not auspicious. A sleep-cry from the child, a call of nature – it is not recorded what woke her from the dream of the stag to swing her legs out of the bed and drop her feet onto the dog, sleeping for the first time where he was to sleep each night for the rest of his life. It might have been the unexpected sensation of a warm rug in a very high relief that made her scream, or perhaps it was the convulsion of the dog heaving to its feet, out from under hers, to stand quietly in the moonless dark and await acknowledgement.

Odysseus slept like a dog himself. He was immediately wide awake and in an instant had secured his sword. The servants, raising their own cries of alarm, hurried light to the chamber where they illuminated this tableau:

The Master stands at the ready beside the bed, his sword presented diagonally in his right hand while the left reaches down and away from his side, fingers spread protectively. Behind him, the Mistress has her elbows drawn in to her sides, arms raised over her breasts, fingers pressed to her cheeks, lips parted. The dog faces them. His tail wags slightly; otherwise he is perfectly still.

Now dissolve to laughter.

Penelope crouched and extended a hand to the dog, who padded over to be patted. He was home. His fine blond fur was to greet her feet each morning thereafter in an unbroken string that lasted nearly a quarter of a century. Before the first week was out, Penelope had named the dog Argos: watcher.

There was much aimless pulling of ears and poking of eyes, at first, on the part of the child. Argos responded with good-natured mock-growls, snuffling and sneezing. There was wrestling when Telemachos became more coordinated. Out of doors Argos would fetch a stick thrown anywhere, even into the sea. He could leap three feet straight up in the air at a stick held high, when later Telemachos grew tall. But it was Penelope who knew how to speak to the dog, while he listened, rotating his head comically from time to time. And it was she who inspired the dog to play at running huge figure eights around her, while she stood at the crossing of the eight and made mock lunges at him as he passed at top speed, grinning, his ears laid back. Odysseus sometimes paused to watch them at it, but his eyes were always for Penelope. There was nothing he didn't like to watch her do. He had little time for watching a dog at play. He might so far forget his preoccupations as to pat Argos in idle greeting when he returned to the house from a long day of overseeing the labourers at his crops, or presiding over Assembly or military exercises. Or he might not.

Argos was Penelope's dog, and showed it by staying close to the young Telemachos during the day, in forays into the hills or by the sea. In later years he would sit for hours with the boy, always at the same spot on the same cliff, searching the horizon for a sail. Only when Penelope joined them would he lie down in the furze and rest his head in her lap, looking up at her with sensitive brown eyes, while she absently caressed an iris or anemone.

She knew that the recurring dream of the stag was a dream of the dog. There was nothing more staglike to her eyes than his posture in defiance of a threat to his territory, hers. The stag was there in his bounding, hackles raised like a mane from neck to tail, to drive off any four-legged intruder, though he was pure dog when he closed with any of those foolish enough to stand their ground. There were times, too, when the step of the dog rising by the fire or the loom was to Penelope the step of a man. It always called her distant thoughts home, and never with apprehension, even in the days of the suitors.

Before those days when the house was full of unwanted guests, there were many years when time simply passed too slowly, too many hours once Odysseus had left. The moment his ship was rowed from the harbour the lines of relationship on the island grew slack. Odysseus sailed with doomed companions; Penelope's companion remained. For many springs she watched the wrens and sparrows gather his shed hairs one by one, to line their nests. Soft nests, soft consoling thoughts.

Argos grew old, constantly at Penelope's side during the days and nights at her loom, alert to the new network of tensions in the air. Now he was never seen to sleep. Whenever Penelope turned from her weaving she found him watching her, head resting between his front paws. Often she spoke his name and he rose heavily to pad over and lay his head on her knee. His brown eyes were mirrors of the thoughts she confided to him, rocking gently, his head in her two hands.

In their certainty that Odysseus would never return, the suitors were breaking many rules. They immoderately consumed his provisions, laid bawdy siege to Penelope, mocked Telemachos's emotional rebuke in Council, forewent proper observances to the Gods. It was not to be expected that they would think twice about cursing and kicking the household dog, whenever they found him under foot. The folly of even inadvertently offending against the favourites of the Gods was being proven and proven to the absent Odysseus. At home the suitors were compounding offence upon offence, not the least of which may have been kicking the dog.

Was the dog's only function to occupy thirty-seven moving lines in a wonderful poem about Odysseus? It is true that Argos' only absence from Penelope's side, in those late days, was on the afternoon Odysseus returned, a day of unusually wanton riot among the impatient suitors. Penelope marked the dog's disappearance as a sign that the unravelling fabric of her life was about to rend for once and all. Telemachos was lately returned from a fruitless voyage in search of his father, during which he had so matured, so much become his father's son, that he was with more and more difficulty restrained from forcing matters to an issue. There was a bloody sword hanging over the household.

Argos made his way slowly to the margin of the sea, the days of his staglike bounding years behind him. The sea gave back a solitary man who was no stranger, though disguised. Odysseus knelt in a greeting the warmth of which Argos had never before known from him, nor solicited. So the dog was the first to acknowledge the wanderer's return, with a calm wag of the tail that recalled a lively night nearly a quarter of a century past. It was his last act, the only one for which he is remembered. But it was for the sake of Penelope he'd waited so long.

DOUGLAS GLOVER

DOG ATTEMPTS TO DROWN MAN IN SASKATOON

My wife and I decide to separate, and then suddenly we are almost happy together. The pathos of our situation, our private and unique tragedy, lends romance to each small act. We see everything in the round, the facets as opposed to the flat banality that was wedging us apart. When she asks me to go to the Mendel Art Gallery Sunday afternoon, I do not say no with the usual mounting irritation that drives me into myself. I say yes and some hardness within me seems to melt into a pleasant sadness. We look into each other's eyes and realize with a start that we are looking for the first time because it is the last. We are both thinking, Who is this person to whom I have been married? What has been the meaning of our relationship? These are questions we have never asked ourselves; we have been a blind couple groping with each other in the dark. Instead of saying to myself, Not the art gallery again! What does she care about art? She has no education. She's merely bored and on Sunday afternoon in Saskatoon the only place you can go is the old sausage-maker's mausoleum of art! Instead of putting up arguments, I think, Poor Lucy, pursued by the assassins of her past, unable to be still. Perhaps if I had her memories I also would be unable to stay in on a Sunday afternoon. Somewhere that cretin Pascal says that all our problems stem from not being able to sit quietly in a room alone. If Pascal had had Lucy's mother, he would never have written anything so foolish. Also, at the age of nine, she saw her younger brother run over and killed by a highway roller. Faced with that, would Pascal have written anything? (Now I am defending my wife against Pascal! A month ago I would have used the same passage to bludgeon her.)

Note. Already this is not the story I wanted to tell. That is buried, gone, lost – its action fragmented and distorted by inexact recollection. Directly it was completed, it had disappeared, gone with the past into that strange realm of suspended animation, that coat rack of despair, wherein all our completed acts await, gathering dust, until we come for them again. I am trying to give you the truth, though I could try harder, and only refrain because I know that that way leads to madness. So I offer an approximation, a shadow play, such as would excite children, full of blind spots and irrelevant adumbrations, too little in parts; elsewhere too much. Alternately I will frustrate you and lead you astray. I can only say that, at the outset, my intention was otherwise; I sought only clarity and simple conclusions. Now I know the worst – that reasons are out of joint with actions, that my best explanation will be obscure, subtle and unsatisfying, and that the human mind is a tangle of unexplored pathways.

"My wife and I decide to separate, and then suddenly we are almost happy together." This is a sentence full of ironies and lies. For example, I call her my wife. Technically this is true. But now that I am leaving, the thought is in both our hearts: Can a marriage of eleven months really be called a marriage? Moreover, it was only a civil ceremony, a ten-minute formality performed at City Hall by a man who, one could tell, had been drinking heavily over lunch. Perhaps if we had done it in a cathedral surrounded by robed priests intoning Latin benedictions we would not now be falling apart. As we put on our coats to go to the art gallery, I mention this idea to Lucy. "A year," she says "With Latin we might have last a year." We laugh. This is the most courageous statement she has made since we became aware of our defeat, better than all her sour tears. Usually she is too self-conscious to make jokes. Seeing me smile, she blushes and becomes confused, happy to have pleased me, happy to be happy, in the final analysis, happy to be sad because the sadness frees her to be what she could never be before. Like many people, we are both masters of beginnings and endings, but founder in the middle of things. It takes a wise and mature individual to manage that which intervenes, the duration which is a necessary part of life and marriage. So there is a sense in which we are not married, though something *is* ending. And therein lies the greater irony. For in ending, in separating, we are finally and ineluctably together, locked as it were in a ritual recantation. We are going to the art gallery (I am guilty of over-determining the symbol) together.

It is winter in Saskatoon, to my mind the best of seasons because it is the most inimical to human existence. The weather forecaster gives the temperature, the wind chill factor and the number of seconds it takes to freeze exposed skin. Driving between towns one remembers to pack a winter survival kit (matches, candle, chocolate, flares, down sleeping bag) in case of a breakdown. Earlier in the week just outside the city limits a man disappeared after setting out to walk a quarter of a mile from one farmhouse to another, swallowed up by the cold prairie night. (This is, I believe, a not unpleasant way to die once the initial period of discomfort has been passed.) Summer in Saskatoon is a collection of minor irritants: heat and dust, black flies and tent caterpillars, the nighttime electrical storms that leave the unpaved concession roads impassable troughs of gumbo mud. But winter has the beauty of a plausible finality. I drive out to the airport early in the morning to watch jets land in a pink haze of ice crystals. During the long nights the *aurora borealis* seems to touch the rooftops. But best of all is the city itself which takes on a kind of ghostliness, a dreamlike quality that combines emptiness (there seem to be so few people) and the mists rising from the heated buildings to produce a mystery. Daily I tramp the paths along the riverbank, crossing and recrossing the bridges, watching the way the city changes in the pale winter light. Beneath me the unfrozen parts of the river smoke and boil, raging to become still. Winter in Saskatoon is a time of anxious waiting and endurance; all that beauty is alien, a constant threat. Many things do not endure. Our marriage, for example, was vernal, a product of the brief, sweet prairie spring.

Neither Lucy nor I was born here; Mendel came from Russia. In fact there is a feeling of the camp about Saskatoon, the temporary abode. At the university there are photographs of the town – in 1905 there were three frame buildings and a tent. In a bar I nearly came to blows with a man campaigning to preserve a movie theatre built in 1934. In Saskatoon that is ancient history, that is the cave painting at Lascaux. Lucy hails from an even newer settlement in the wild Peace River country where her father went to raise cattle and ended up a truck mechanic. Seven years ago she came to Saskatoon to work in a garment factory (her left hand bears a burn scar from a clothes press). Next fall she begins law school. Despite this evidence of intelligence, determination and ability, Lucy has no confidence in herself. In her mother's eyes she will never measure up, and that is all that is important. I myself am a proud man and a gutter snob. I wear a ring in my left ear and my hair long. My parents migrated from a farm in Wisconsin to a farm in Saskatchewan in 1952 and still drive back every year to see the trees. I am two courses short of a degree in philosophy which I will never receive. I make my living at what comes to hand, house painting when I am wandering; since I settled with Lucy, I've worked as the lone overnight editor at the local newspaper. Against the bosses, I am a union man; against the union, I am an independent. When the publisher asked me to work days, I quit. That was a month ago. That was when Lucy knew I was leaving. Deep down she understands my nature. Mendel is another case: he was a butcher and a man who left traces. Now on the north side of the river there are giant meat-packing plants spilling forth the odours of death, guts and excrement. Across the street are the holding pens for the cattle and the rail lines that bring them to slaughter. Before building his art gallery Mendel actually kept his paintings in this sprawling complex of buildings, inside the slaughterhouse. If you went to his office, you would sit in a waiting room with a Picasso or a Rouault on the wall. Perhaps even a van Gogh. The gallery is downriver at the opposite end of the city, very clean and modern. But whenever I go there I hear the panicky bellowing of the death-driven steers and see the streams of blood and the carcasses and smell the stench and imagine the poor beasts rolling their eyes at Gauguin's green and luscious leaves as the bolt enters their brains.

We have decided to separate. It is a wintry Sunday afternoon. We are going to the Mendel Art Gallery. Watching Lucy shake her hair out and tuck it into her knitted hat, I suddenly feel close to tears. Behind her are the framed photographs of weathered prairie farmhouses, the vigorous spider plants, the scarred child's school desk where she does her studying, the brick-and-board bookshelf with her meagre library. (After eleven months there is still nothing of me that will remain.) This is an old song; there is no gesture of Lucy's that does not fill me instantly with pity, the child's hand held up to deflect the blow, her desperate attempts to conceal unworthiness. For her part she naturally sees me as the father who, in that earlier existence, proved so practiced in evasion and flight. The fact that I am now leaving her only reinforces her intuition – it is as if she has expected it all along, almost as if she has been working towards it. This goes to show the force of initial impressions. For example, I will never forget the first time I saw Lucy. She was limping across Broadway, her feet swathed in bandages and jammed into her pumps, her face alternately distorted with agony and composed in dignity. I followed her for blocks – she was beautiful and wounded, the kind of woman I am always looking for to redeem me. Similarly, what she will always remember is that first night we spent together when all I did was hold her while she slept because, taking the bus home, she had seen a naked man masturbating in a window. Thus she had arrived at my door, laughing hysterically, afraid to stay at her own place alone, completely undone. At first she had played the temptress because she thought that was what I wanted. She kissed me hungrily and unfastened my shirt buttons. Then she ran into the bathroom and came out crying because she had dropped and broken the soap dish. That was when I put my arms around her and comforted her, which was what she had wanted from the beginning.

An apology for my style, I am not so much apologizing as invoking a tradition. Heraclitus, whose philosophy may not have been written in fragments but certainly comes to us in that form; Kierkegaard, who mocked Hegel's system-building by writing everything as if it were an afterthought, *The Unscientific Post-script*; Nietzsche, who wrote in aphorisms or what he called "attempts," dry runs at the subject matter, even arguing contradictory points of view in order to see all sides; Wittgenstein's *Investigations*, his fragmentary response to the architectonic of the earlier *Tractatus*. Traditional story writers compose a beginning, a middle and an end, stringing these together in continuity as if there were some whole which they represented. Whereas I am writing fragments and discursive circumlocutions about an object that may not be complete or may be infinite. "Dog Attempts to Drown Man in Saskatoon" is my title, cribbed from a facetious newspaper headline. Lucy and I were married because of her feet and because she glimpsed a man masturbating in a window as her bus took her home from work. I feel that in discussing these occurrences, these facts (our separation, the dog, the city, the weather, a trip to the art gallery) as constitutive of a non-system, I am peeling away some of the mystery of human life. I am also of the opinion that Mendel should have left the paintings in the slaughterhouse.

The discerning reader will by now have trapped me in a number of inconsistencies and doubtful statements. For example, we are not separating – I am leaving my wife and she has accepted that fact because it reaffirms her sense of herself as a person worthy of being left. Moreover it was wrong of me to pity her. Lucy is a quietly capable woman about to embark on what will inevitably be a successful career. She is not a waif nor could she ever redeem me with her suffering. Likewise she was wrong to view me as forever gentle and forbearing in the sexual department. And finally I suspect that there was more than coincidence in the fact that she spotted the man in his window on my night off from the newspaper. I do not doubt that she saw the man; he is a recurring nightmare of Lucy's. But whether she saw him that particular night, or some night in the past, or whether she made him up out of whole cloth and came to believe in him, I cannot say. About her feet, however, I have been truthful. That day she had just come from her doctor after having the stitches removed.

Lucy's clumsiness. Her clumsiness stems from the fact that she was born with six toes on each foot. This defect, I'm sure, had something to do with the way her mother mistreated her. Among uneducated folk there is often a feeling that physical anomalies reflect mental flaws. And a kind of punishment for being born (and afterwards because her brother had died), Lucy's feet were never looked at by a competent doctor. It wasn't until she was twenty-six and beginning to enjoy a new life that she underwent a painful operation to have the vestigial digits excised. This surgery left her big toes all but powerless; now they flop like stubby, white worms at the ends of her feet. Where she had been a schoolgirl athlete with six toes, she became awkward and ungainly with five.

Her mother, Celeste, is one of those women who make feminism a *cause célèbre* – no, that is being glib. Truthfully, she was never any man's slave. I have the impression that after the first realization, the first inkling that she had married the wrong man, she entered into the role of submissive female with a strange, destructive gusto. She seems to have had an immoderate amount of hate in her, enough to spread its poison among the many people who touched her in a kind of negative of the parable of loaves and fishes. And the man, the father, was not so far as I can tell cruel, merely ineffectual, just the wrong man.

Once, years later, Lucy and Celeste were riding on a bus together when Celeste pointed to a man sitting a few seats ahead and said, "That is the one I loved." That was all she ever said on the topic and the man himself was a balding, petty functionary type, completely uninteresting except in terms of the exaggerated passion Celeste had invested in him over the years. Soon after Lucy's father married Celeste he realized he would never be able to live with her – he absconded to the army, abandoning her with the first child in a drover's shack on a cattle baron's estate. (From time to time Lucy attempts to write about her childhood – her stories always seem unbelievable – a world of infanticide, blood feuds and brutality. I can barely credit these tales, seeing her so prim and composed, not prim but you know how she sits so straight in her chair and her hair is always in place and her clothes are expensive if not quite stylish and her manners are correct without being at all natural; Lucy is composed in the sense of being made up or put together out of pieces, not in the sense of being tranquil. But nevertheless she carries these *cauchemars* in her head: the dead babies found beneath the fence row, blood on sheets, shotgun blasts in the night, her brother going under the highway roller, her mother's cruel silence.) The father fled as I say. He sent them money orders, three-quarters of his pay, to that point he was responsible. Celeste never spoke of him and his infrequent visits home were always a surprise to the children; his visits and the locked bedroom door and the hot, breathy silence of what went on behind the door; Celeste's rising vexation and hysteria; the new pregnancy; the postmarks on the money orders. Then the boy died. Perhaps he was Celeste's favourite, a perfect one to hold over the tall, already beautiful, monster with six toes and (I conjecture again) her father's look. The boy died and the house went silent – Celeste had forbidden a word to be spoken – and this was the worst for Lucy, the cold parlour circumspection of

Protestant mourning. They did not utter a redeeming sound, only replayed the image of the boy running, laughing, racing the machine, then tripping and going under, being sucked under – Lucy did not even see the body, and in an access of delayed grief almost two decades later she would tell me she had always assumed he just flattened out like a cartoon character. Celeste refused to weep; only her hatred grew like a heavy weight against her children. And in that vacuum, that terrible silence accorded all feeling and especially the mysteries of sex and death, the locked door of the bedroom and the shut coffin lid, the absent father and the absent brother, somehow became inextricably entwined in Lucy's mind; she was only nine, a most beautiful monster, surrounded by absent gods and a bitter worship. So that when she saw the naked man calmly masturbating in the upper storey window, framed as it were under the cornice of a Saskatoon rooming house, it was for her like a vision of the centre of the mystery, the scene behind the locked door, the corpse in its coffin, God, and she immediately imagined her mother waiting irritably in the shadow just out of sight with a towel to wipe the sperm from the windowpane, aroused, yet almost fainting at the grotesque denial of her female passion.

Do not, if you wish, believe any of the above. It is psychological jazz written *en marge*; I am a poet of marginalia. Some of what I write is utter crap and wishful thinking. Lucy is not "happy to be sad"; she is seething inside because I am betraying her. Her anger gives her the courage to make jokes; she blushes when I laugh because she still hopes that I will stay. Of course my willingness to accompany her to the art gallery is inspired by guilt. She is completely aware of this fact. Her invitation is premeditated, manipulative. No gesture is lost; all our acts are linked and repeated. She is, after all, Celeste's daughter. Also do not believe for a moment that I hate that woman for what she was. That instant on the bus in a distant town when she pointed out the man she truly loved, she somehow redeemed herself for Lucy and for me, showing herself receptive of forgiveness and pity. Nor do I hate Lucy though I am leaving her.

My wife and I decide to separate, and then suddenly we are almost happy together. I repeat this crucial opening sentence for the purpose of reminding myself of my general intention. In a separate notebook next to me (vodka on ice sweating onto and blurring the ruled pages) I have a list of subjects to cover: 1) blindness (the man the dog led into the river was blind); 2) a man I know who was gored by a bison (real name to the withheld); 3) Susan the weaver and her little girl and the plan for us to live in Pelican Narrows; 4) the wolves at the city zoo; 5) the battlefields of Batoche and Duck Lake; 6) bridge symbolism; 7) a fuller description of the death of Lucy's brother; 8) three photographs of Lucy in my possession; 9) my wish to have met Mendel (he is dead) and be his friend; 10) the story of the story or how the dog tried to drown the man in Saskatoon.

Call this a play. Call me Orestes. Call her mother Clytemnestra. Her father, the wandering warrior king. (When he died accidentally a year ago, they sent Lucy his diary. Every day of his life he had recorded the weather; that was all.) Like everyone else, we married because we thought we could change one another. I was the brother-friend come to slay the tyrant Celeste; Lucy was to teach me the meaning of suffering. But there is no meaning and in the labyrinth of Lucy's mind the spirit of her past eluded me. Take sex for instance. She is taller than I am; people sometimes think she must be a model. She is without a doubt the most beautiful woman I have been to bed with. Yet there is no passion, no arousal. Between the legs she is as dry as a prairie summer. I am tender, but tenderness is no substitute for biology. Penetration is always painful. She gasps, winces. She will not perform oral sex though sometimes she likes having it done to her, providing she can overcome her embarrassment. What she does love is for me to wrestle her to the living-room carpet and strip her clothes off in a mock rape. She squeals and protests and then scampers naked to the bedroom where she waits impatiently while I get undressed. Only once have I detected her orgasm – this while she sat on my lap fully clothed and I manipulated her with my fingers. It goes without saying she will not talk about these things. She protects herself from herself and there is never any feeling that we are together. When Lucy's periods began, Celeste told her she had cancer. More than once she was forced to eat garbage from a dog's dish. Sometimes her mother would simply lock her out of the house for the night. These stories are shocking: Celeste was undoubtedly mad. By hatred, mother and daughter are manacled together for eternity. "You can change," I say with all my heart. "A woman who only sees herself as a victim never gets wise to herself." "No," she says, touching my hand sadly. Ah! Ah! I think, between weeping and words. Nostalgia is form; hope is content. Lucy is an empty building, a frenzy of restlessness, a soul without a future. And I fling out in desperation, Orestes-like, seeking my own Athens and release.

More bunk! I'll let you know now that we are not going to the art gallery as I write this. Everything happened some time ago and I am living far away in another country. (Structuralists would characterize my style as "robbing the signifier of the signified." My opening sentence, my premise, is now practically destitute of meaning, or it means everything. Really, this is what happens when you try to tell the truth about something; you end up like the snake biting its own tail. There are a hundred reasons why I left Lucy. I don't want to seem shallow. I don't want to say, well, I was a meat-and-potatoes person and she was a vegetarian, or that I sometimes believe she simply orchestrated the whole fiasco, seduced me, married me, and then refused to be a wife – yes, I would prefer to think that I was guiltless, that I didn't just wander off fecklessly like her father. To explain this, or for that matter to explain why the dog led the man into the river, you have to explain the world, even God – if we accept Gödel's theorem regarding the unjustifiability of systems from within. Everything is a symbol of everything else. Or everything is a symbol of death, as Levi-Strauss says. In other words, there is no signified and life is nothing but a long haunting. Perhaps that is all that I am trying to say…) However, we *did* visit the art gallery one winter Sunday near the end of our eleven-month marriage. There were two temporary exhibitions and all of Mendel's slaughterhouse pictures had been stored in the basement. One wing was devoted to photographs of grain elevators, very phallic with their little overhanging roofs. We laughed about this together; Lucy was kittenish, pretending to be shocked. Then she walked across the hall alone to contemplate the acrylic prairiescapes by local artists. I descended the stairs to drink coffee and watch the frozen river. This was downstream from the Idylwyld Bridge where the fellow went in (there is an open stretch of two or three hundred yards where a hot-water outlet prevents the river from freezing over completely) and it occurred to me that if he had actually drowned, if the current had dragged him under the ice, they wouldn't have found his body until the spring breakup. And probably they would have discovered it hung up on the weir which I could see from the gallery window.

Forget it. A bad picture: Lucy upstairs "appreciating" art, me downstairs thinking of bodies under the ice. Any moment now she will come skipping towards me flushed with excitement after a successful cultural adventure. That is not what I meant to show you. That Lucy is not a person, she is a caricature. When legends are born, people die. Rather let us look at the place where all reasons converge. No. Let me tell you how Lucy is redeemed: preamble and anecdote. Her greatest fear is that she will turn into Celeste. Naturally, without noticing it, she is becoming more and more like her mother every day. She has the financial independence Celeste no doubt craved, and she has been disappointed in love. Three times. The first man made himself into a wandering rage with drugs. The second was an adulterer. Now me. Already she is acquiring an edge of bitterness, of why-me-ness. But, and this is an Everest of a but, the woman can dance! I don't mean at the disco or in the ballroom; I don't mean she studied ballet. We were strolling in Diefenbaker Park one summer day shortly after our wedding (this is on the bluffs overlooking Mendel's meat-packing plant) when we came upon a puppet show. It was some sort of children's fair: there were petting zoos, pony rides, candy stands, bicycles being given away as prizes, all that kind of thing in addition to the puppets. It was a famous troupe which had started in the sixties as part of the counter-culture movement – I need not mention the name. The climax of the performance was a stately dance by two giant puppets perhaps thirty feet tall, a man and a woman, backwoods types. We arrived just in time to see the woman rise from the ground, supported by three puppeteers. She rises from the grass stiffly then spreads her massive arms towards the man and an orchestra begins a reel. It is an astounding sight. I notice that the children in the audience are rapt. And suddenly I am aware of Lucy, her face aflame, this crazy grin and her eyes dazzled. She is looking straight up at the giant woman. The music, as I say, begins and the puppet sways and opens her arms towards her partner (they are both very stern, very grave) and Lucy begins to sway and spread her arms. She lifts her feet gently, one after the other, begins to turn, then swings back. She doesn't know what she is doing; this is completely unselfconscious. There is only Lucy and the puppets and the dance. She is a child again and I am in awe of her innocence. It is a scene that brings a lump to my throat: the high, hot, summer sun, the children's faces like flowers in a sea of grass, the towering, swaying puppets, and Lucy lost in herself. Lucy, dancing. Probably she no longer remembers this incident. At the time, or shortly after, she said, "Oh no! Did I really? Tell me I didn't do that!" She was laughing, not really embarrassed. "Did anyone see me?" And when the puppeteers passed the hat at the end of the show, I turned out my pockets, I gave them everything I had.

I smoke Gitanes. I like to drink in an Indian bar on 20th Street near Eaton's. My nose was broken in a car accident when I was eighteen; it grew back crooked. I speak softly; sometimes I stutter. I don't like crowds. In my spare time, I paint large pictures of the city. Photographic realism is my style. I work on a pencil grid using egg tempera because it's better for detail. I do shopping centres, old movie theatres that are about to be torn down, slaughterhouses. While everyone else is looking out at the prairie, I peer inward and record what is merely transitory, what is human. Artifice. Nature defeats me. I cannot paint ripples on a lake, or the movement of leaves, or a woman's face. Like most people, I suppose, my heart is broken because I cannot be what I wish to be. On the day in question, one of the coldest of the year, I hike down from the university along Saskatchewan Drive overlooking the old railway hotel, the modest office blocks, and the ice-shrouded gardens of the city. I carry a camera; snapping end-of-the-world photos for a future canvas. At the Third Avenue Bridge I pause to admire the lattice of I-beams, black against the frozen mist swirling up from the river and the translucent exhaust plumes of the ghostly cars shuttling to and fro. Crossing the street, I descend the wooden steps into Rotary Park, taking two more shots of the bridge at the close angle before the film breaks from the cold. I swing round, focusing on the squat ugliness of the Idylwyld Bridge with its fat concrete piers obscuring the view upriver, and then suddenly an icy finger seems to touch my heart: out on the river, on the very edge of the snowy crust where the turbid waters from the outlet pipe churn and steam, a black dog is playing. I refocus. The dog scampers in a tight circle, races towards the brink, skids to a stop, barks furiously at something in the grey water. I stumble forward a step or two. Then I see the man, swept downstream, bobbing in the current, his arms flailing stiffly. In another instant, the dog leaps after him, disappears, almost as if I had dreamed it. I don't quite know what I am doing, you understand. The river is no man's land. First I am plunging through the knee-deep snow of the park. Then I lose my footing on the bank and find myself sliding on my seat onto the river ice. Before I have time to think. There is a man in the river, I am sprinting to intercept him, struggling to untangle the camera from around my neck, stripping off my coat. I have forgotten momentarily how long it takes exposed skin to freeze and am lost in a frenzy of speculation upon the impossibility of existence in the river, the horror of the current dragging you under the ice at the end of the open water, the creeping numbness, again the impossibility, the alienness of the idea itself, the dog and the man immersed. I feel the ice rolling under me, throw myself flat, wrapped in a gentle terror, then inch forward again, spread-eagled, throwing my coat by a sleeve, screaming, "Catch it! Catch it!" to the man whirling towards me, scrabbling with bloody hands at the crumbling ledge. All this occupies less time than it takes to tell. He is a strange bearlike creature, huge in an old duffel coat with its hood up, steam rising around him, his face bloated and purple, his red hands clawing at the ice shelf, an inhuman "awing" sound emanating from his throat, his eyes rolling upwards. He makes no effort to reach the coat sleeve trailed before him as the current carries him by. Then the dog appears, paddling towards the man, straining to keep its head above the choppy surface. The dog barks, rests a paw on the man's shoulder, seems to drag him under a little, and then the man is striking out wildly, fighting the dog off, being twisted out into the open water by the eddies. I see the leather hand harness flapping from the dog's neck and suddenly the full horror of the situation assails me: the man is blind. Perhaps he understands nothing of what is happening to him, the world gone mad, this freezing hell. At the same moment, I feel strong hands grip my ankles and hear another's laboured breathing. I look over my shoulder. There is a raw-cheeked policeman with a thin yellow moustache stretched on the ice behind me. Behind him, two teenage boys are in the act of dropping to all fours, making a chain of bodies. A fifth person, a young woman, is running towards us. "He's blind," I shout. The policeman nods: he seems to comprehend everything in an instant. The man in the water has come to rest against a jutting point of ice a few yards away. The dog is much nearer, but I make for the man, crawling on my hands and knees, forgetting my coat. There seems nothing to fear now. Our little chain of life reaching towards the blind drowning man seems sufficient against the infinity of forces which have culminated in this moment. The crust is rolling and bucking beneath us as I take his wrists. His fingers, hard as talons, lock into mine. Immediately he ceases to utter that terrible, unearthly bawling sound. Inching backward, I somehow contrive to lever the dead weight of his body over the ice lip, then drag him on his belly like a sack away from the water. The policeman turns him gently on his back; he is breathing in gasps, his eyes rolling frantically. "T'ank you. T'ank you," he whispers, his strength gone. The others quickly remove their coats and tuck them around the man who now looks like some strange beached fish, puffing and muttering in the snow. Then in the eerie silence that follows, broken only by the shushing sound of traffic on the bridges, the distant whine of a siren coming nearer, the hissing river and my heart beating. I look into the smoky water once more and see that the dog is gone. I am dazed; I watch a drop of sweat freezing on the policeman's moustache. I stare into the grey flux where it slips quietly under the ice and disappears. One of the boys offers me a cigarette. The blind man moans; he says, "I go home now. Dog good. I all right. I walk home." The boys glance at each other. The woman is shivering. Everything seems empty and anticlimactic. We are shrouded in enigma. The policeman takes out a notebook, a tiny symbol of rationality, scribbled words against the void. As an ambulance crew skates a stretcher down the riverbank, he begins to ask the usual questions, the usual, unanswerable questions.

This is not the story I wanted to tell. I repeat this *caveat* as a reminder that I am wilful and wayward as a storyteller, not a good storyteller at all. The right story, the true story, had I been able to tell it, would have changed your life – but it is buried, gone, lost. The next day Lucy and I drive to the spot where I first saw the dog. The river is once more sanely empty and the water boils quietly where it has not yet frozen. Once more I tell her how it happened, but she prefers the public version, what she hears on the radio or reads in the newspaper, to my disjointed impressions. It is also true that she knows she is losing me and she is at the stage where it is necessary to deny strenuously all my values and perceptions. She wants to think that I am just like her father or that I always intended to humiliate her. The facts of the case are that the man and dog apparently set out to cross the Idylwyld Bridge but turned off along the approach and walked into the water, the man a little ahead of the dog. In the news account, the dog is accused of insanity, dereliction of duty and a strangely uncanine malevolence. "Dog Attempts to Drown Man," the headline reads. Libel law prevents speculation on the human victim's mental state, his intentions. The dog is dead, but the tone is jocular. *Dog Attempts to Drown Man*. All of which means that no one knows what happened from the time the man stumbled off the sidewalk on Idylwyld to the time he fell into the river and we are free to invent structures and symbols as we see fit. The man survives, it seems, his strange baptism, his trial by cold and water. I know in my own mind that he appeared exhausted, not merely from the experience of near-drowning, but from before, in spirit, while the dog seemed eager and alert. We know, or at least we can all agree to theorize, that a bridge is a symbol of change (one side to the other, hence death), of connection (the marriage of opposites), but also of separation from the river of life, a bridge is an object of culture. Perhaps man and dog chose together to walk through the pathless snows to the water's edge and throw themselves into uncertainty. The man was blind as are we all; perhaps he sought illumination in the frothing waste. Perhaps they went as old friends. Or perhaps the dog accompanied the man only reluctantly, the man forcing the dog to lead him across the ice. I saw the dog swim to him, saw the man fending the dog off. Perhaps the dog was trying to save its master, or perhaps it was only playing, not understanding in the least what was happening. Whatever is the case my allegiance is with the dog; the man is too human, too predictable. But man and dog together are emblematic – that is my impression at any rate – they are the mind and spirit, the one blind, the other dumb; one defeated, the other naïve and hopeful, both forever going out. And I submit that after all the simplified explanations and crude jokes about the blind man and his dog, the act is full of a strange and terrible mystery, of beauty.

My wife and I decide to separate, and then suddenly we are almost happy together. But this was long ago, as was the visit to the Mendel Art Gallery and my time in Saskatoon. And though the moment when Lucy is shaking down her hair and tucking it into her knitted cap goes on endlessly in my head as does the reverberation of that other moment when the dog disappears under the ice, there is much that I have already forgotten. I left Lucy because she was too real, too hungry for love, while I am a dreamer. There are two kinds of courage: the courage that holds things together and the courage that throws them away. The first is more common; it is the cement of civilization; it is Lucy's. The second is the courage of drunks and suicides and mystics. My sign is impurity. By leaving, you understand, I proved that I was unworthy. I have tried to write Lucy since that winter – her only response has been to return my letters unopened. This is appropriate. She means for me to read them myself, those tired, clotted apologies. I am the writer of the words; she knows well enough they are not meant for her. But my words are sad companions and sometimes I remember… well… the icy water is up to my neck and I hear the ghost dog barking, she tried to warn me; yes, yes, I say, but I was blind.

KATHERINE GOVIER

THE BEST DOG

It is cold in Ottawa, and snowing; the ploughs are out on the street below the window where Penny sits, wrapped in a faded patchwork quilt. In her hand she holds a photograph. On the floor below her is the envelope it came in; the stamps are huge, foreign. The photograph shows a man and a dog standing on a boulevard. The dog is held close to the man's knee by a short leather leash. Behind them are large walnut trees, a border of moulting rose bushes and a tall wrought-iron fence, the kind built around the closed city parks of Europe.

The dog is black and thick in the body, perhaps a little fat. The man looks boyish, but he too verges on plumpness around the middle. His lips – Penny holds the photograph up very close to her face – are pursed but open, as if he were crooning. Penny is able to tell this fact because she took the photograph, and at the moment the shutter closed the man, whose name is Mikhail, was in fact singing a love song. The song was in English, incomprehensible to passersby but not to Penny, nor to the dog, who understands in English such simple words as dogs do understand.

The dog holds in his teeth a small black leather pouch. It is a matter of pride to both dog and master that the animal can be trusted to carry this pouch when the two are abroad in the streets. In the pouch are stored the man's identity papers, his money, and also the permit which allows him to take the dog on city buses. This permit, which Mikhail would gladly draw out to show, names the dog "Mike." The fact that the man and the dog have the same name is an accident. Mikhail received Mike through a friend at the American embassy where the dog had been abandoned by his previous owner, who had been on his way to Africa and had been advised he could not take a dog with him. Mikhail and Mike have been together for five years, and are so devoted that an engagement – Mikhail's third – was broken over the issue.

All of this, and more, Penny remembers as she looks at the photograph. Penny reaches to the floor and pulls the stamps off the envelope; her nephew collects. She holds them close to her face. Detailed as engravings, in faded turquoise and orange, they look like antiquities. She can hardly believe that this picture was taken only eight months ago and by her, for she really is in the picture, just a few feet away from Mikhail, behind the camera.

In London, she had sat in the Transit Lounge on a plastic chair, congratulating herself on being sent, with her minister, to Eastern Europe. In Zurich, drinking water that cost two dollars and fifty cents a glass, she watched for travellers going her way. They were mostly men in drab suits, representatives of British firms. Their conversation was about the long waits for service in these countries, the lack of night life, the dullness of the citizens. When the aircraft was ready to board they all had to go out on the tarmac and point to their luggage, stacked under the belly of the plane, before it would be loaded. Men in blue overalls closed the airplane door. When it was opened again, they had landed. Penny stepped out into humid, close air. They had been told that someone would be waiting for them.

"How do you do, Mister Doctor Minister Kling. And Miss James. I am Oana, your translator."

The other passengers were loaded into a bus but Penny and Gerry, her boss, the translator and two men walked across the tarmac into the terminal building. The men made Penny nervous.

"You have been in our city once before," said Oana to Gerry, "but..." She turned her dark, unreflective eyes to Penny, "this is your first visit." These were not questions.

They waited in a private lounge while their visas were processed. "Exactly the same as last time," Gerry was saying in Penny's ear. "Right down to the plastic cover on the footstool." There were plum velvet sofas and padded chairs, but all were draped in dust covers. "I wonder if they take them off when the minister comes." Penny did not laugh but smiled brightly at Oana who stood a little to the side; although she did not appear to be listening she might have heard. Penny did not wish Oana to take offence.

"That's a standard sort of joke in our civil service," she thought of saying. "It says more about us than about you." But the smooth cheek, slight hollow, and severe lip line did not encourage her, and she kept silent.

Half a dozen men loaded their bags into the back of a black car. All the cars in sight were identical, small four-door sedans with tapered front and back. It was evening, and growing dark. There had been rain and now the streets were glistening; the cars darted off the arrivals ramp and into the traffic like drops of water down a window pane.

The streets were wide and the boulevards full of rose bushes. It was September; the petals were just beginning to fall. A group of women wearing wide skirts and kerchiefs, holding scythes, walked along the edge of the road. The gardening crew, going home for dinner.

The car turned into a traffic circle in front of a tall edifice with three towers.

"This is the Press Building. It is very much in the Russian style," said Oana. "Everyone knows about Russian architecture."

She smiled over her shoulder from the front seat, wrinkling her nose: it smells. Gerry elbowed Penny. "They make anti-Russian remarks to gain your confidence," he had said. "Don't follow suit."

"Your English is very good," said Penny.

Oana turned to look at the road again.

"You've come in the best month. September is always fine. And there are some very nice events planned for you."

After that, silence as they drove along. The driver held the wheel with both hands, right at the top, and took the turns suddenly, on two wheels.

Mikhail looked more like a leading man than a hired guide; he was tall, black-haired and wore an expectant expression along with a red carnation.

"I had hoped it was you I was to meet," he said, bending to kiss her hand. When he stood up a pair of moss-soft brown eyes rose to hers. "But I was afraid to approach such a beautiful lady."

It was dinner time. The small black car waited in front of the hotel: Gerry and Penny and Oana and Mikhail were going for dinner. The driver stood beside the car door, holding it open. He wore dark blue coveralls like the baggage men in the airport, and had a long, turned-down nose. He was to be with Gerry and Penny for their entire visit. As the car whirled through the traffic circles he spoke loudly in his language, pointing out the museums, the communist party headquarters, the university. Oana translated. Mikhail, Gerry and Penny were shoulder to shoulder in the back seat, leaning first one way and then the other on turns.

In front of the restaurant the driver jumped out and opened all the doors. He stood back as Penny alighted and then stood forward to shut the door. In his baggy worksuit his decorous motions looked comic. As they walked away he watched.

"What's he going to do?" said Penny to Mikhail.

"Wait until we finish and drive you home."

Mikhail led the way through a frosted door. Inside, a series of rooms opened, like something done with mirrors. Waiters with their backs against the wall bowed; the chairs were velvet; rose-coloured lamps glowed from sconces. The maitre d' led the guests past a crescent-shaped table spread with game hens and pheasants and salmon, piles of cheeses and cakes.

In the pink light, Mikhail's black hair and pallid skin looked decadent. A pearl-grey ascot stood at his neck. Penny remembered the feel of his palm when he had grasped her hand; hot, moist. Now he patted his brow with a handkerchief. For one so composed, he sweated rather a lot.

Mikhail ordered the meal; as Penny listened, the words began to have a shape to her. They were rather like jigsaw pieces, fitting together smoothly, but each having funny protuberances. "Would you like the fish or the stuffed pork?" he said to her in English. He had a cleft chin and those very frank, very brown eyes. She chose the fish.

Effortlessly, Mikhail made himself the centre of the conversation. He had three last names. Now he only used two; even that was too many for some people. It was too many for Oana, clearly, who had unfolded her napkin and was staring at it in disapproval. "I like to put the other on my card, to write it down," he said. "I wouldn't like to lose it, because it was given to my family by Napoleon."

He spoke in a matter-of-fact tone. His grandmother had been a Russian princess; his father's name was one of the oldest in the country. These things, like the black caviar which arrived in a pot with lemons on the side, were messages he seemed confident they understood; he offered it all to make a contact that went beyond the present situation. He had been seven years old, he said, when things changed. That made him forty, now, Penny calculated, ten years older than she was, ten years older than he looked.

"My first pet was a pony," he was saying. "He was so devoted, he followed me everywhere, even in the house. When we lost everything, the pony was given to a circus. And he was so sad there, he refused all food, and he died." Mikhail picked up a triangle of toast, buttered it, and used it to scoop a great hunk of caviar. He squeezed lemon on the caviar. Then he put the whole thing in his mouth.

"Mikhail writes poetry," said Oana. "We both work with special visitors, sometimes together, more often not."

Mikhail appealed to Gerry. "I believe you must do something in this life, otherwise you are like an animal. You just get up, and eat, and do some work, and wash the dishes and go to sleep. I like to make something. I even think of putting some poems in a box and burying them in the ground."

Gerry nodded, looking uncomfortable.

"And you, what do you think?" said Mikhail, turning to Penny.

At that moment, Penny was thinking about the first thing he had said to her. "...such a beautiful woman..." It was not true. She was not beautiful. She had a long, luminous freckled face and looked sad. Sometimes men became interested but soon they drifted on. Accustomed to disappointment, she was happiest when she met someone new, and could work the temporary magic. She sipped her Reisling and instantly felt giddy.

"I am so interested in your country. Here, people are very serious."

Seriousness, Oana could speak to. Everyone worked so hard. Her daughter was training to be an electrical engineer; Oana helped by watching the baby nights. There were also meetings to attend, and the shopping to do. But Mikhail! He might work for ten days as a guide and then have a week free, to stay home in the apartment he shared with his mother and enjoy the nice things they still had: a collection of porcelain, a small gem collection. He spoke five languages, had two degrees.

"I am an elitist," he said. "For me, freedom is necessary. I know what to do with it. But most people here would not know. And so I can be rather happy. My dog makes me happiest of all. He is a purebred Labrador retriever. I put him in the shows, but he can not win the medals, even though he is the best. He has no pedigree, you see. His pedigree is in the United States, where he was born."

Oana made a noise between a cough and a snarl and pointedly said nothing. Gerry dug into his stuffed pork and did not look up.

"Yes, I really love my dog," said Mikhail. The way he said love, it sounded like "laaa-ve."

Penny felt she had travelled deep into a vault of history, and was witness to old splendours, old rivalries. The play of distaste between the two guides merely made the experience richer. But as they got up to leave the restaurant, the setting began to falter. Mikhail stood back while Gerry paid for the meal; his aspect – relaxed, confident of being looked after – made the dark man seem a flatterer, a paid companion. He suggested a bar. But outside the frosted door Gerry looked pointedly at the car. It had been much more money that he expected, and there had been a fuss about travellers' cheques.

"Where can we drop you, Mikhail?" he said.

Mikhail began to give the driver directions. The driver shook his head. He would not open the door.

"Tell him we are asking him to drive you home," said Penny.

Mikhail spoke again to the driver, who this time responded with a torrent of angry syllables. Mikhail shrugged.

"It will not be possible," he said. "This man says he works for you and not for me. It is not unusual," he said, and reached for Penny's hand, kissing it. He strode away quickly. Oana had been standing in the shadow by the door. Now she stepped forward. She announced that she would go home by herself, on the bus. At that moment it occurred to Penny that the translator had not been necessary that evening, since Mikhail spoke excellent English. Penny looked at Gerry for a signal. They had been warned about the KGB. Could it be true, they were being watched?

In the back seat, Gerry settled himself angrily, bracing an arm against the door for the hairpin turns. "Some kind of nut," he said, "loves his dog."

"I think it's a cultural difference."

"You ask me, he's trouble. Something strange about his relationship to the rest of these guys."

"He speaks so well."

"He must have something. To have wangled himself the kind of freedom he's got."

Penny was watching the back of the driver's neck. The hairs were bristling.

There was a lot of this blank-faced watching. In the hotel you might walk up a staircase from the lobby and see a young man in a neat suit sitting motionless on a chair. Four hours later, you passed again and he was still there, and he had been joined by another like himself. Dull-eyed, the two would share a cigarette.

There were also the uncompromising young women at the desk making tourist arrangements. They would tell you without looking at a list or picking up a telephone that there were no tickets left, no cars left, no messages, no telex, no airflight information. "They are there to help you," said Oana. "Believe me; it would be worse, otherwise."

The meetings took place over heavy luncheons which began with plum brandy and ended with vodka. A deputy minister had been replaced since the last mission; there would be several days' wait. Penny went out in the city. Mornings were hazy, that unreal golden light coming up slowly. She visited the open air market, and it was as if she were walking in a crèche, a city of stage paste, so temporary did it feel.

Women in plastic sandals and ankle socks queued for a truck's arrival. Penny touched braids of garlic, poor apples, peppers and squash. She stopped before a gypsy woman selling bricks of something honey coloured. Was it candy? She raised some to her mouth as if to bite. *"Nu, nu."* The woman put her hand by her mouth and laughed, showing black, stumpy teeth. She picked up the brick herself and mimed smearing it over her legs. She said a word. Penny did not know what it meant. She looked at the brick again. Beeswax.

"Beeswax," she said, also laughing. "Depilation."

"Da!" said the woman.

"Ouch," said Penny. "No, thanks."

The shops held little painted wooden objects, doilies with red embroidery, thousands of peasant blouses. Penny wandered all afternoon; some of the old buildings had huge cracks down their sides from an earthquake. She returned to the hotel in the still, leafy incandescence before dark. Mikhail was waiting by the door, wearing white jeans and a green satin jacket with a felt insignia. Now Penny noticed how different his clothing was from the clothing of his countrymen.

"Nice jacket," she said.

"A gift from a tourist," he said. "It's the uniform of the Swedish soccer team." He stepped away from the wall; he was leading the black dog.

"I wanted you to meet Mike."

Mike extended a paw. He was a large, thick-necked dog with an intelligent face. His sleek fatness reminded Penny of a seal, so short-haired that he seemed more than naturally naked. He sat, and made unavoidable the sight of his upturned genitalia. He preceded the trio in the walk to the hotel, his back legs stiff and slightly bowed, his hindquarters switching slowly first one way and then the other.

They took a table in the courtyard. The dog sat at Mikhail's knee and did not move when the waiter admired him. Mikhail had come to show Penny the route of a tour he would take her on, north to the mountains. Gerry would stay for more meetings. The guide leaned against Penny's elbow as he pointed to spots on the map. When he walked out with his dog, people stared.

But the next morning, Mikhail was alone, standing stiffly beside the driver in front of the hotel. On the road, peasants soon appeared, pulling wagons and leading cows on chains. The driver settled his eyes on the highway and Mikhail slid his arm silently along the top of the back seat, behind Penny's shoulders. It was frightening, thrilling, to be sitting that way behind the hostile driver. The heat of his body reached Penny; in front of her was the thick, close-shaven neck of the driver. The subterfuge was so complicated: Mikhail was guide, and guard. That he – they – were subject, watched, at the same time, seemed to add depth, like a dark line around their images.

They entered a narrow roadway blinkered with pine. The forest had once been filled with robbers, said Mikhail, and was burned to make the country safer. More trees were planted; now it was a park where families came to picnic and paddle boats. In the parking area Mikhail spoke to the driver, looking at his watch and indicating three hours. The driver said nothing. Penny was convinced he hated them both.

That day the boat which took tourists to the island was not operating. Mikhail walked up and down the shore, gesturing to the dock on the far shore, where the ubiquitous men in coveralls sat beside barrels, but the long wooden vessel stayed tucked down at the edge of the water. He went to the kitchen door of the inn to borrow a telephone. Penny stood alongside smiling uneasily at a small woman with hands covered with warts, who was slicing bread.

"I think we will not get a boat today." Mikhail was irritated. "What do you think if we have lunch here?"

But the restaurant would not open for another hour. They walked by the edge of the lake. It was lined with reeds, and over the top of the water rode a blue mist. A boy was rowing a skiff amongst the rushes and the wisps of fog, pulling his craft back and forth crazily with just one oar.

"Here is the song I wrote for Mike. I have the words written down. He likes very much to hear me sing it."

"Sing it for me."

"No. But you can look at the words." He handed Penny a piece of onionskin, folded into a small square. She opened it.

> *Who comes to my bed each morning, eyes so bright*
> *and smiling*
> *whose tongue is warm and touches my arm,*
> *who guides the door at night? It's Mike!*

Mikhail was walking very close to her, the weight of his body occasionally swinging against hers. Suddenly he turned to face her and took her face in his hands. His lips pressed on hers. There was so much force in the kiss that her teeth were bared, her lips pressed right back. When he pulled away she stood with her mouth open, a little noise escaping her.

"Why do you not look me in the eyes? Is it so dangerous?"

She decided he was a professional seducer. She was not sure, however, whether that was going to matter.

At the inn, he insisted that they have a table far along the porch, away from all the other diners. They ate sausages made by the monks at Sibiu and the white, tart cheese which came from goats. Water lapped at the wooden posts beneath them. The retreating feet of the waiter made hollow sounds on the floor. Sometimes, when travelling, which Penny had begun to do a lot in her work, she came to a place which fit instantly into her affections as if a spot had been made ready for it. She could not believe she would never visit this lakeside again, that she would not be able, much later, to set out through trees and find it.

"Here, at last, there is no one listening," said Mikhail. "Did you know there is always someone? The driver. Even in the park, there was someone watching us."

"Does the driver speak English?"

"It is not important. He is not a nice man, some are like that. But he is insignificant. Do your friends call you Penny?"

"Yes."

"That's too bad. You should have a longer name; that is a baby name."

Penny might have thought something of the sort herself, but she did not like to hear it.

"You have no rings on your left hand? You are not engaged?"

"No."

"I would like to call you Elena. It is the name of my first fiancée, Elena. She was very like you. With blond hair."

"You only just met me."

"No, it's not true. I have met you many times before."

Penny grew stiff.

"Why do you pull away? Do not pull away from me." He put one hand out as if to stroke her cheek; then he laid it softly against her head. "Look me in the eye."

She looked, with effort. Behind him she could see that the child in the skiff had appeared below the deck. He was banging his oar against the posts sunk into the water. Bang, bang, bang.

"I am like a bird in a cage. And I have to sing that the cage is golden. We are so happy here. That is what I tell you. I tell all the tourists. I have seen people from almost every country. And I myself have never been outside. I am trapped here. Nobody can I trust. No countryman can I talk to. And so I fall in love with you, and you go away next week and I am more alone than ever."

The tears began to run down his cheeks. They were like tears running down the face on a billboard; they made no alteration in his voice or his posture.

He has said these things before to a hundred tourists with no rings on their left hand, Penny was sure. It was part of the tour, perhaps. But that did not make them any less true.

Penny and Mikhail were walking back through the replanted forest. They had gone the long way around to the parking lot, for the fun of it finding routes where it seemed no one could be watching. The spruce trees stood a hundred feet in the air on either side; the very lowest limbs swayed about their heads like dark, oiled fans; the bare earth was soft with needles. They were holding hands. Mikhail was singing the song for his dog. Penny committed to memory the exact angle of his chin as he lifted it to the sky on the refrain.

"Who guards the door at night? It's Mike!"

She joined it, it didn't matter what the words were. It was a silly song, that was all, silly for two adults in the service of their governments to be singing in the woods.

Mikhail led her to a bench by the path. He sat very close beside her and put his arms around her.

"What is it like where you live? Is there a lot of snow there? Can I see it all through your eyes – is it bright, open, and empty?" He kissed her again, hard. This time she was ready for it. She braced her neck against the pressure, kept her lips shut. In a second, he understood. She opened her eyes, but his were still closed. He was slow to let go – an idea, a possibility dropped.

Finally he sat back, away from her.

"There is something. Something that I wish to ask you."

The bench faced a straight line of trees, straight as the teeth in a comb. There was a man at the far end, walking across the clearing. When he had crossed, the vista opened, it seemed to stretch right to the airport, to the dead sleep across the Atlantic, to crisp, clean, red and white Canada.

"You are the only one who can help me."

The words fell on Penny like grace. No matter how many ladies he seduced, no matter how many men left her, she was, here, today, the only one who could help. What would be his pleasure? Her participation in a dangerous mission?

He reached into his back pocket and drew out an envelope.

"It is nothing illegal," said Mikhail carefully. "It is fine for you to do it, but not for me to do it. It is fine for you to do it for me. You must take this with you to Canada, put in the eleven dollars, and send it away for me."

She took the envelope. It was addressed to the American Kennel Club.

"When you receive the pedigree, send it to me here. You know it will mean a very great deal to both Mike and I. He can have his medals, which he deserves, to show his breeding." He said no more about love.

"By now you will have learned," Penny wrote, "that there is no possibility of getting the pedigree for Mike, without the name of his dam and sire. Since you have not given it to me I presume you do not have that information."

Beside her was a pedigree, torn to pieces. Outside, the snow was gathering more and more thickly; Ottawa winter was so long. She had written the Kennel Club and was unable to get the dog's papers. So she had gone to a friend and had a pedigree forged, easy enough to do when you know people. She had even got the thing ready to mail. It had been Gerry's idea, actually; he said it was a small thing to give the guy a charge. And it would give Mikhail a charge; Mike might officially become what his owner believed he was, the best dog in the country. Mikhail would have that to remember when faces with the likes of Oana, who had reported him for inappropriate behaviour with visitors, or the driver, who had, astonishingly, simply abandoned them that day in the park, leaving them to hitchhike.

But when she saw the photograph she knew she was wrong. She had taken the forged pedigree in her two hands and ripped it in pieces. Mikhail did not fall for false things. He knew caviar and Chinese porcelain, and he had trusted her to help him. "If there is anything else I can do, please write," she continued. She had no idea whether the letter would reach him.

CLAIRE DÉ

A DEVOURING LOVE

Translated by Sam Liebman

I loved him instantly, from the moment I began to work for him. I was still quite young, an orphan. Recently, his wife had died suddenly, he didn't have any children. He felt alone. He needed company, he needed to feel supported.

That is why I loved him: he oozed solitude, a scent of acacia honey over a base of light vinegary bitterness, and I have an exceptional sense of smell. He wasn't a bad fellow, a bit withdrawn, that's all.

I became strongly attached to him over the years. It wasn't so much a question of serving him, but mostly of having the consideration to be present. I put a sense of order back into his life. I am very strict, for example, about his timetable. There is a time for everything: a time to satisfy oneself, a time to act, and a time to refresh oneself. A certain discipline restores the serenity of the spirit.

Our life together organized itself, rapidly immutable. In the morning he would leave for his work, which consisted of filling sheets of paper with digits, from what I understood. I waited for him at home, keeping myself busy. In the evening he returned, we would eat, take a walk to help the digestion, television, then bed.

—Pierre Elliot, give me five!

It was always what he said to me when he softly squeezed my fingers, before retiring to his room. I also greatly appreciated that he allowed me to pull off his socks: it was for me a sort of intimate privilege.

I slept in an adjoining roomette. But always with one ear and eye open, ready to quickly respond to his call. Because I am from a race of grand butlers and other up-scale domestics: loyal, zealous, faithful, well-trained, conciliatory, and all that tempered with a dead-pan humour. And almost always modest to boot.

At night, I would dream of sacred cats of Egypt and of archaeological excavations where gigantic bones were discovered. At dawn, I would stretch, proceed with a meticulous grooming of my black uniform, then I would wake him with a brief hello and wash his face and his hands.

I loved him. In my own way. Never outside the bounds of propriety! I would not have allowed myself to. I know how to keep my place. I am not one of those nasty little brats bursting with noisy misplaced emotional demonstrations. He was the Master and I was Pierre Elliot, he would command and I would obey. Thanks to him, I lived in nothing less than perfect bliss for a decade. But happiness, above all perfect bliss, is the most fragile thing of all.

Right up until they forced him into retirement. He was never the same. He became malicious. He went out every day, as before, but earlier and earlier, and in order to drink.

Then he took to beating me: savage kicks in the shins, brutal slaps behind the head, vicious pokes in the ribs, and always at the most unexpected times. He didn't speak anymore, he barked his orders in an arrogant tone. Then cursed me with insults and blame.

And he locked me in. Literally caged me. I was not even able to sniff a bit of fresh air. Imprisoned, I no longer even had the right to the courtyard. Me, so proud of my appearance, so impeccable, little by little I was reduced to a shabby wretch.

Even when we were alone in the house, he took care to bolt the doors and windows, for fear that I might escape. Even so, I never tried to run away: I still loved him. I only hoped that he would get hold of himself, and get back on his feet.

My Calvary lasted years. I wasn't getting any younger, my joints were stiffening, but in spite of stingy and irregular nourishment, my devotion and a genetically resistant health always allowed me to withstand the virulent treatment he inflicted on me. Like all those abused, I was sinking with a painful delight, into guilt and masochism.

I imagined that I was going to die under the thrashing of the one whom I had served and adored all my adult life when one night, the first mild evening of an icy spring, he returned walking with a step even heavier than usual. A stride so hesitant that it terrified me and, for the first time, I hid myself inside a closet.

He became more and more agitated as he searched for me. Screeching *Pierre Elliot! Pierre Elliot!* He staggered from one room to another. I lay low. I heard him pounding the furniture, then the crash of a fall. Then nothing.

I fell asleep there, curled up in a ball. Right on the floor, among the worn-out shoes of his late wife.

The Master cooled down and hardened like a stone. Heart stoppage, probably. He was sprawled out on his stomach. I carefully turned him on his back. Despite the cruelty he had imposed on me, I was overwhelmed with grief. Such great anguish, that I forgot about hunger, thirst and sleep for over a week.

I resisted a long time before… but soon an unbearable raging hunger gnawing in my guts drove me mad. I endeavoured to proceed as neatly as possible. I started with his ears. They were very meaty. Delicious.

I had loved him alive. Dead, I loved him twice as much. I stuck to this diet for a good month. At the end, he was unrecognizable. It was a neighbour who smelled something and notified the authorities. Presently, the police don't know what to do with me, a seventeen-year-old placid Labrador retriever: after having tasted human flesh, I no longer crave kibble.

JANICE KULYK KEEFER

DREAMS: STORMS: DOGS

I

Sogno di Sant' Orsola: Vittore Carpaccio.
Venezia. Galleria dell'Accademia.

There's a strange woman in that bed, hand cupped to ear, listening hard to her dreams. My bed, I'd know it anywhere, though I've never clapped eyes on it before. The bed I was born for, no matter what my husband says. And for once he'll have plenty to say, hunting me high and low, through all the dizzy-dazzle of this gallery, gold blinds and marble stairs. Not that he'll ever find me – I've given him the slip but good. Even if he trots down a hundred corridors and opens a thousand doors, even if he runs smack into this room, no bigger than a broom closet next to all the others, he will never find my hiding place.

The bed of my dreams.

To start with, it's got a velvet canopy.

No.

To start with, it's a bed for one. Not that it's a small bed, a single bed. There's lots of room in this bed, but not for him. No husband's body beside you, hairy-chested or sleek, feet like fish on a marble slab or two warm piglets rooting up to you. None of that. It's a bed for one dreamer, and the one that dreamer dreams. It has a canopy, like I said: nothing flim-flam flighty, but dignified – ambassadorial, you might even say. Red like blood; deep, not dark.

The colour of the heart,
That pulpy bridge where all
The rivers end and start.

I'm in this city under duress, I want to make that clear. Flattened like grass under a roller. I had no part in wanting or planning this; my husband's taken me hostage here. I said that if we had to go, I wanted a bus tour, but he wasn't having any of that. A bus tour with all my girlfriends to come along: Emmie and Erna and Gert and Sal and all the others, hundreds and thousands, the whole pack of them. At least I'd have someone to talk to when he gets his brooding spells, which is all he ever does get up to nowadays. And they pick the restaurants for you, and the hotels, and every minute of your time's accounted for. You don't get a chance to feel strange, your shoes gone slippy-slidey so there's no place you can plant your feet and fold your arms and say you'll never budge. No occasion, you have no occasion at all to wonder if the person next to you, sleeping beside you and eating across the table from you all these years, is more of a stranger than the driver of the bus, who'd be friendly at least, thinking of the tip you might squeeze into his palm.

My bed has columns: sober, not spindly. Tassels hanging from each little lap of the canopy – *lap* is the only word I can find for them. Lap as in dewlap: upside-down bells; or yes, like breasts flappy as tea towels hung on the line. The woman in my bed has no breasts at all, to judge from the coverlet – you can see her feet bob up towards the end of the mattress, but nothing at all where her breasts should be. *Breasts* sounds so runaway, marshmallowy. *Bosom*'s better – except that women don't have bosoms any more. We don't even know how to pronounce the damn word.

This strange woman sleeping in my bed may have no breasts, but she makes up for it with all that hair, braided like egg challah on the top of her head. Yellow hair, like Katie Maguire's, Katie sitting beside me on the bus, grades one to six, Brookvale Consolidated. Slipping me holy pictures, swearing that if only I prayed hard enough to her Blessed Virgin my hair would jump overnight from black to gold. I prayed so hard the roof of my mouth got blisters, but my hair stayed black as coal and poker straight, even in my dreams.

This bed of mine is mounted on a platform, so it's like a stage; there's a small white dog keeping watch beside a pair of slippers, so you could hightail it out in an emergency. The pillow's big and round: not hard, but solid. Which is for the best: more headaches are caused by soppy pillows than the world gives credit for. I myself favour a pillow tough as a telephone directory, and I've never woken up with an ache in my head all my years as his wife, now officially forty-five and the achievement of a lifetime, so to speak.

We never fight at home, it's only because I know we never fight that I agreed to come here in the first place, and what should happen but we're daggers drawn? Right here in the picture gallery, him gawking in front of painting #11,001, expecting me to follow like a dog on a leash, but I said no. It was time to move on, we'd seen more than enough already, all I wanted was to sit down someplace snug and snap my eyelids shut. But he kept on staring at that picture, staring and staring, the whites of his eyes near swallowing their yolks. And the more I tugged at him to go, the tighter he held on, not a word would he say till what could I do but up and run? Find my way back here, taking the shortest cut you could imagine. Back into bed, covers pulled tight, hand cupping my chin, and my sleeve squoze-up like an accordion.

That creature coming in with a bit of greenery, snapped from the garden hedge, I'll bet – no way that's her husband. Not her twin sister, either, in spite of those skirts and all that golden hair spilling shoulderwards, like it's falling down a flight of stairs. Not her sister, not her husband, but a combination plate: that's to say, a lover. That's how I'd describe the lover I never had: close as a sister; strange as a husband in skirts.

Lover-boy – there's an expression for you. We used to talk that way, the girls and me, coming off shifts at the hospital. How's your lover-boy? Hiya, lover-boy. But this stranger here, coming in through the door to that golden dreamer on the bed – no way to tell whether it's boy or girl, what's hiding under those skirts. I haven't a clue what's going to happen when they meet, the sleeper in my bed, the stranger rushing through the door and dropping not so much as a golden hair on the carpet. Every night of my married life I've picked up his socks, his shirts, and underwear from the floor where he throws them, though the laundry hamper's not a foot away. Every night, year in, year out. That's what I'd look for in a lover: someone who needs no clothes, or never needs to take them off.

And I'm looking for a lover – why else would I have come all this way, to a place I never wanted let loose from his head? The city of love, romance thicker than the letters in alphabet soup. Thinking I just might, at the end of it all, find my lover here, boy or girl, hair like egg challah or coal dust, it doesn't matter which. Just so I find what it is I dream about and can never remember once I wake. Rolled up beside the bars of his blue-striped pyjamas. Never able to remember, though I'm whacked out with dreaming; hardly the strength to pull the curlers from my hair.

No time for dreaming when he courted me: no time for courting, either, just bim bam and next thing you know the knot's tough-tied. On account of the war, and so few of the boys coming home, you grabbed who you could get and were grateful. He kissed me some, but we never once held hands. And here we are now, in the City of Love, and what do I get but waterworks instead of fireworks. And all he can do is complain: *Everything's gone, changed, spoiled.* Nothing's what it used to be however many donkey's years ago he says he came here. Our first night, he tries to get up at two in the morning: get up and walk around to see if that's when the city combs its hair the way it used to, dresses in the old, familiar style. I say no dice, no deal, no way I'm letting you loose, no way you're lugging me out of bed – and such a pitiful excuse for a bed you never did see, more like a camp cot squared, so you toss and turn all night and all the time he's lying beside you staring at the ceiling and won't say a single word. So what have I got out of this escapade, his coming back to someplace I've never been before? What but the chance to give him the jump and land tucked up in the bed of my dreams.

Waiting for my lover, the one who's waited for me, day and night, all these mortal years. This stranger rushing in with just a few ferns, all the roses having jiggled out into this canal or that, he was running so fast to find me. When I get home and they ask me what I brought back for a souvenir from this trip of a lifetime, I'll say, A bed. The dream of a bed, and me, alone, asleep, my lover rushing in, all golden hair and shining skirts. That's what's made the whole damn fuss worthwhile. Come to this city, of all places, with a husband who turns out to be madman, or a madman who turns out to be your husband. Can't even sit down to a meal without having walked ten miles past every menu pasted to a window, never the right window, till my stomach's meaner than a snake tied up in knots.

Maybe he's noticed I'm gone; he must know something's up, even if he doesn't know enough to follow me. Maybe he's run right out, past the ticket booth, all the way to the post office we passed on our way down. Thinking I'll be lining up for stamps, sending home foggy shots of gondolas, mouldy straw hats. And just when I get to the counter, just when I'm fishing for pennies through the ticket stubs and lipstick tubes in my purse, he'll jump out of nowhere and hand some funny money to the girl behind the counter. Putting me back in my place, which is penniless and always has been.

First thing I'll do once we get home is start saving up. Every red cent I can get my fingers on. Salt them away till I can go with a whole apronful to Angelo's Carpentry and say, Make me a bed, on a platform, with a canopy and little lip-laps hanging down, a bed with room for no one but me and whatever I'm dreaming. And when it's done, I'll just lie myself down, and never get up again. Of course, I'll leave the door wide open for that stranger to slip in. Sweet and swank and quiet, so that little dog asleep beside my slippers doesn't even bat an ear.

II

Egregio Signor, Gentile Signora

I would like a room for the nights of 12-16 May, for my wife and myself. We stayed at the Albergo Marinara on our honeymoon, forty-five years ago, and it would be a great pleasure for us to return. I wonder if we might have the same room we stayed in before: number 12, overlooking the little street with the garden opposite? I realize that this may be an impossible request, and that much may have changed over the years – nearly half a century! – but your kind cooperation in this matter would be greatly appreciated.

III

La Tempesta: Giorgione. Venezia. Galleria dell'Accademia.

No matter how long you look, there's no figuring it out. Who they are, what's between them; whether they even know one another. Or notice the storm breaking over their heads: sky bruised by cloud and split by lightning; sky green as grass and deep as drowning.

The way she has to twist to hold that lump of a baby on her lap. To keep an eye on the soldier standing on the left fork of the lightning, spying on her nakedness. Her whole body gone lumped and clumsy, the way it does when you know someone's watching you and you're in no state to be seen. Naked, except for a petticoat round her shoulders: naked to the rain and cold and dark.

That soldier, onlooker, whoever he is. Why doesn't he jump across to where she's sitting, help her up off the ground? Why doesn't he get them to a place of safety, her and the baby?

Crossing the bridge, we saw a beggar, a man who looked like a soldier, though he wore no uniform. He was all alone; the cardboard square he held up said he had a wife and child in that place where all the bombs had fallen. He had no obvious disfigurement: no missing leg or arm or war wound visible. Perhaps he was mute. Perhaps, like me, he's one of those men who can never come out with a single thing to say when it matters most. But the sign didn't tell us why his wife and child were still in that terrible place and why he was here; how he would get back to them, if he intended to. Whether he was, in fact, no husband or father, but a soldier who'd picked up a gun and killed someone else's wife and child. And so I gave him nothing, and we walked on, into the picture gallery, right into the thick of this summer storm.

Stopping here, in front of this soldier, this woman nursing her baby; stopping and looking together. Under my lids I could feel her eyes; I thought she was looking through mine, until she turned to me, saying, "What are you thinking?" An impossible question; not a question at all, I can see that now. And all I had to do was open my mouth and say something, anything, just to reach across that split she'd opened in the sky. But I could only stand and stare with my mouth shut tight, as if language were a sealed room and I'd used up all the oxygen.

Always her back towards me as she slept. In the red, narrow light of the mosquito lamp her body was a cloud salted with dark stars. You can't pray to a mosquito lamp: it burns differently than the candles in churches, candles in small red jars. No matter how long we let the lamp burn, there were always mosquitoes, blurred planets circling and settling; we would awake each day with yet another stitch of poison in our skins.

We met so soon after the war that we were still in uniform: a nurse, a soldier. We met in one of those sudden, heavy rains that come from nowhere and slick even the spongiest marble. Running from two different directions towards the same shelter: a canopy of vines over a small table set outside a restaurant. Her hair thick with rain, but spilling red-gold around her face, so bright I could look at it only through her reflection. A lamp lit under her skin, burning its way right through the glass. I could tell her none of this, I made no mention of her beauty, though it lapped against everything I thought or felt, then and ever since. Night after night I've lain awake wondering what I could have done, how I could have kept her from turning away as she did; from walking into the rift opened by a storm, and vanishing. I searched for her everywhere, down every street and square, and all I found were my own footsteps. Not a lane or alleyway here that doesn't curve back on itself, and find that self changed past knowing. Five days now, walking from morning past midnight, and never taking the same route twice. Never finding the little square I'd stumbled on that night, watching her face in the window, so clear, so beautiful that face, I would know it anywhere.

The little square with a church on one side and a restaurant with tables spread under a roof of vines. The place where we met, where we'd agreed, if ever we were separated by the crowds, to come and wait for one another. Sitting up late each night, the candles dyed green by the vine leaves overhead, and then her skin, her hair, under the mosquito lamp: a cloud, a sun, red-golden. And suddenly the sky's split by lightning; the earth tears open and you fall, you keep falling farther and farther from the one person who called out the life left in you, who made the skin dance over your bones.

Coming back from the restaurant last night – the wrong restaurant, like all the others – we lost our way and stumbled into the fish market. Flakes of marble, gills, scales all licking up the light the moon was throwing down. We were alone, except for a small white dog that seemed to know exactly where it was going. It had no collar or muzzle, as most of the dogs here do, and it carried, instead of a bone or brandy cask, an empty plastic bottle, the kind you see floating where the yachts and motor launches dock.

I wanted to follow that dog, I knew he'd been sent to me. He was carrying an elixir in that bottle, something so precious it was invisible. If only I'd called out to him; if only I'd knelt down on the stones where she must, just once, have passed; if only I'd beseeched him. But again, I couldn't speak – I couldn't move, even to put my hand out, to show him I meant no harm and could be trusted. If I had, would he have given up even a few drops from his bottle so we might have found each other, come home at last, together?

Would I have returned to the hotel, carrying flowers I'd found on the way – geraniums thieved from a pot, roses sprung up from cracks in sheer marble? Pushing open the door to our room, would I have found her right there, in our bed, under the red roof of the mosquito lamp? Asleep, her hand cupping her ear, listening hard to whatever it is she dreams: lightning, silence, the opened sky.

IV

In the end they find each other: husband, wife. Somewhere outside the picture gallery; exactly where doesn't matter, since in this city every street's a hiding place and a discovery.

They are footsore and forlorn. This is their last night here, they are heading home tomorrow, everything will go back to the way it's always been. They are hungry as well as tired. This time he lets her choose a restaurant and doesn't even shake his head at what she settles on: a scattering of tables on the lip of a major canal, diesel fumes cutting whatever bouquet your wine may offer, whatever freshness still hugs the bread on your plate. Waiting for the food to come she kicks off her shoes and kneads her small, puffed feet. As always, he says nothing, pulling the bread to pieces, rolling them between his fingers, making eggs or stones, she can't tell which and it doesn't much matter.

The food is overpriced and the waiters contemptuous. She keeps her eyes fixed on her husband's shirt and tie, anticipating how, in a few hours' time, she will crouch down as she's done every night for the past forty-five years and pick them up from the floor. She sits with her elbows on the table, staring through him at the motor boats chugging down the canal, as if expecting them – only one would be enough – to dislodge a stranger, someone proffering the remains of a bouquet. She would follow that summons to the ends of the earth – she's come this far already, hasn't she?

He stares at his plate as if the smears of tomato sauce were half-digested hieroglyphics. His glasses like a slide trombone on the end of his nose, the veins at his temples a code someone's forgotten to keep tapping out. He doesn't look like a man on holiday, but like a man in mourning: not for what's been lost, but for something he's never been able to find. Someone told him, once, of an ill-matched couple who'd come to this city for their honeymoon; how the bridegroom had turned from the body waiting for him in the close, heavy bed. Turned and opened the shutters instead, falling into an endless pillow of green water.

They have eaten their appalling meal in silence. She knows as well as he how badly they've been cheated by the cook, the waiters, the city itself, which has only tantalized them, giving them nothing at all to keep for their own. She never did find a postcard of the bed of her dreams, and she is already forgetting the details of the canopy, the number of braids looped round the dreamer's head, the colour of her lover's skirts. All she remembers with any vividness is the small white dog guarding the bed – and dogs like that you can find anywhere.

He is thinking he deserved to have her turn on him and vanish. Four nights and five days of Rachel: forty-five years of Leah, lying like a bolster in his bed. Squat, stubbed Leah, her golden hair the product of a false elixir. Yet even she has tried a disappearing trick, though she hadn't the skill to carry it off.

How had he let her out of his sight, even for a moment? How had he let it happen, Rachel turning into Leah? All because he could not reach out his hand, utter a word, any word, when it most mattered?

Distress, despair, division – when all of a sudden a storm breaks out. Two couples, natives of this place, are walking their purebred dogs, and the dogs, one of them ridiculously small, the other the size of a pony, rush at each other and begin, frantically, to copulate. Their owners leap to separate them before worse comes to worst. But the harder they yank on the leashes, the faster the animals stick, their legs skewed, strained, rigid as marble. Tears and curses from the lady attached to the small dog's leash; silence from the owner of the pony as he listens, terror-struck, for snapping sounds. Until one of the superbly discourteous waiters runs to the dogs, lifts them in their agonizing pas de deux, and throws them into the canal. Whereupon a miracle occurs, as much a miracle as if the thick, filthy water had turned clear as glass. For the dogs leap apart and up onto the pavement, flapping the water from their coats. Their owners seize them and stomp off, each in a different direction, trailing dogs and abuse in their wake.

They've been staring at this piece of street theatre, the husband and wife: they are transfixed. The suddenness of this storm, the abruptness of its resolution, the possibilities opened and extinguished before their very eyes have entered them like electricity, singeing each branch of their blood. Without a word, they shoot their hands across the table, grabbing one another, holding fast. So fast they can never shake free, no matter how many mazy streets they must turn down to get to their hotel, no matter how many cues for vanishing they give to one another.

The waiter, approaching with the bill, makes no move to part them.

KENNETH J. HARVEY

MERCIFUL HOPE

The bridge was made from wood slats loosely set side by side so that they rattled beneath the wheels of the pickup trucks that drove across. Dust would rise in the wake of the vehicles, lifting in slow lingering clouds from the backwoods road just outside Cutland Junction. But rain had come the previous night and the ground was damp and packed tight; a sweet musty odour lingered in the air. Beneath the bridge, water ran high along the river's banks, the surface murky from churned-up sediment.

Muss appeared from the woods, ducking out onto the road, his young face looking like a lumpy sack of potatoes, his black hair curly and coarse and set mostly on the top of his head. The twiggy bushes rustled and Muss stopped, turning to watch, until the old half-breed beagle hobbled clear, its sad eyes staring ahead from where it stood, low to the ground, no more than five feet behind the skinny legs of its master, standing in wait.

Satisfied with sighting the dog, Muss strolled close to the bridge, glancing back to view the wasted body pushing on to follow obediently.

The mongrel came to him as he bent to tie the rope around its throat, the dog's warm eyes shining soft in the dusk, its ribs arching out from its mottled fur, its ears softly laid back as the knot was roughly tied. Muss glanced around his feet, then up the gravel road that led on into the Junction. Spotting something, he wandered back. But the dog did not follow. It sat and watched, yawned elaborately, then shook its head, its leathery ears flapping.

Muss' voice came first, returning from the distance: "Keep dem eyes ahf me."

The dog whined, a tiny squeal trapped in its throat.

"N'ver know why." He bent and coiled the other end of the coarse rope around a slab-shaped boulder that had been cracked in two. "T'ings like ya in ever'n's kitchen, ly'n 'round, do'n nut'n. Eat'n 'n' do'n nut'n. I tol' ya all dis 'fore. Dun't lees'n."

He tied a knot and then another, pulling with his hands, tugging the splintery rope to make certain it was set steady around the rock. "Dere." Standing, he blew the fibres from his hands, then shoved them into his pockets. He stared up the road, a tired glimmer in his eyes, as if hoping someone might drive along and offer casual greeting or a worthwhile piece of advice, but the road was deserted, lined with tall black evergreens and blond spotted birch and the light was wasting away, growing toward the suffocating darkness that closed in so softly.

Muss listened to the river. He heard the sound of it rising up to mingle and find itself at home with this kind of light so that it sounded clearer, forceful. He pulled a package of Export 'A' from the pocket of his blue work shirt and stuck his thumb into the bottom of the pack, pushing up. Digging down with two fingers, he lifted out a bent, black-tipped butt, and flipped the lid of his father's old Zippo, the smell of it never failing to please him.

"Sit'n' dere like dat," he said, puffing with the flame rising so close to his lips he had to work fast, the heat full against him. He leaned back and snapped the lighter shut, a lingering orange wash in his eyes. He shoved the package into his front pocket. "May'b' dis'll help ya run." Squatting down, he cuddled the dog and the boulder in both his arms and stood, holding the weight only long enough to receive its impression before tossing it forward.

He had expected the sound of a large splash and a smaller muddled plunk, but there was only one sound of water rushing up. Not a sound from the dog. Not a yelp or a moan, only the dim sight of it dropping through the air with its eyes opened and its legs not even kicking, its paws bent and tucked in close to its white and brown chest.

The sound of the river was turning louder as darkness steadily sealed itself. Muss stood on the bridge with no railings, then inched close to the edge to watch the deep water. It was only water, he told himself. Nothing moving down there. There were rumours that at night, as the river blackened, the bottom slowly fell out and what was thrown in there would find its way down into the blind rush that led away, carrying things to a place of calm and contentment.

Flicking his cigarette into the flow, he imagined the whispering sizzle it would make when it hit. But even the sound of this was denied him. He glanced around and decided that the night was turning its back on all his intentions. It would never forgive him, nor welcome the convictions he had settled on. He heard his stomach grumble, but did not feel the movement in his gut. It was merely a murmur coming from a remote place in the dark that he had learned to hold away from himself. Leaning as he was, staring down into the wet rushing shadows, he backed away for fear he would fall into the water. It drew him sometimes, knowing what it was there for, what it was meant to take away.

The kitchen was hot where he sat at the table, moving a tin ashtray in slow circles with his fingers. If there was one thing Muss

Drover could claim as practically guaranteed, it was wood for the stove. The certainty of heat. He would cut the trees in the thick forest behind his house and haul the stripped limbs out into the yard where he sawed into them. He kept the stove raging. The kitchen was stifling with heat, so that he sweated continuously. But he insisted that the heat was not for himself. It was for his frail mother, even though it never seemed to reach her room, leaking out through the gapped matchboard walls beyond the kitchen on the bottom floor.

Mother Drover was sleeping in the upstairs bedroom. Muss had brought her a biscuit and a cup of tea after arriving home. He had carried it up the stairs and, reaching the top landing, carefully turned for her room. She was cold where she lay back in the bed, staring at Muss, her sappy eyes casually shifting down to watch the space beside him, her thin-fingered left hand dangling where it always was, over the edge of the bed, waiting for the touch of the mongrel's wet nose and quick insistent head.

Mother Drover did not say a word; the silence of the last few weeks, only biscuits and tea finding their way to her. And occasionally the cured fish that stung her mouth with its intensity of salt burning her cool lips. The old dry potatoes and no table butter. She sighed her usual rising sound as Muss helped her to sit up and back against the two pillows. A droplet of sweat dripped from his narrow nose as he looked closely at his mother with no words in him, before stepping away, moving from the room, but leaving the door open and briefly smiling back, wanting the heat to find its way into her room, frustrated by how the air here was always cool to the nose and the fingers.

Mother Drover raised the biscuit, holding the edge between her gums, and snapped off a piece. She quietly sucked it in her mouth until it turned to paste. Everything was mixed together now, what she remembered and the feeling of it turning soft in her mind, the spark and purpose of timely thought abandoning her. Raising the tea, she took a wet sip. It was hot and – when she swallowed – harsh, leaving a scalding trail. Moaning and stretching her neck for an instant, she laid the cup on the wooden tray across her lap and cracked loose another piece of biscuit. Her eyes studied the room and she grunted lowly and gently nodded to herself as if confirming suspicions she had held for decades. The house was growing old around her. Her son seldom spoke with her. He seemed afraid to talk. It was fear or shame. She could not strike a wedge between the two. She wondered about the tea, when it would turn watery, the same bag used for the third time. She sniffed the second biscuit, then placed it back on the tray with dislike. Slowly brushing the crumbs from the bosom of her nightdress, she stared at the off-white wallpaper with the tiny red roses and faded green stems; it was peeling away from the moulding at the ceiling, widening brown outlines of water stains flawing the surface. The flickering dimness of it witnessed by the light of three candles, one on her night table, one on the tin circle set atop her washstand, and the other – the third that was usually positioned on a small shelf beside the chest of drawers… the third – gone. It had burnt itself out and, with a brisk sudden shiver, Mother Drover sensed the darkness that was over her shoulders, out the window where the night sky hung low. It was brewing there, casually slipping in closer when the third flame had hissed out. Deceitful. It was always present. The darkness was always present, she informed herself. It was only the light that made it appear to be gone. But it was always present. Take away the light and what did you have? Close your eyes and where were you?

She stared at her husband Hoddy's washstand and dresser. One night she had woken to see Muss carrying the tilted washstand to the door, but lingering at the threshold, with the piece of furniture in his hands, looking off through the window as if paused by the clearing sight of the sky lightening or darkening – it was dusk, maybe dawn, and Mother Drover was sleeping across these borders, confusing them. Muss looked at her, but her lids were only open a crack and he was blind to the knowledge of what she saw, what she remembered. She wanted to tell him. The need was there, but it was quashed by a sense of finality, of things moving away from her, as if to utter such certainties would mean the absolute end of her. She could not help but sigh, and Muss returned the washstand to its place. What would he get for it, anyway? The merchant – Wil Normore – was a thief, though a kind thief, all the same, from what Mother Drover remembered. He would lend with one hand and steal with the other. This duplicity reminded her of the disparate exploits she had been through. She sighed again with the burden of such complete thoughts pressing down on her as if to drive her from her own body. She had watched her son open the drawers of the washstand, feeling the worn wood, the smoothness of the joints. Muss was thinking of his father, of the dovetailing and how the trees had been planed and cut to fit together as if they had been one artful thing all along, needing only the instruction of the old man's craft to embellish the almost obvious.

Mother Drover had nodded to herself in silence, knowing this for a fact. She lay quite still with her thin soft arms beneath the heavy quilts, and watched Muss brush his fingers over the wood. The sound of the stroking motion had made her blush, and she had felt the heat rising in her cheeks and the soft stirring in her thighs that came to her as if she were a young growing girl finding pleasure in the sight of something that crossed over the line from startling into thrilling. She knew there was something there, how her own son reminded her of her husband, how this act of intimacy was bearing them closer, and there was nothing she could do to cleave the unity.

Remembering like this, she let her left hand hang over the side of the bed. The distance to the floor seemed well beyond her reach with the open air against her skin. She weakly bent her fingers back and forth.

"'ere mongr'l," she said to herself, speaking in a slow and distant manner, as if the dog were elsewhere now, curled and sleeping in a place where only mournful voices could find their way. Quietly moving her hand back and forth, "You 'member 'oddy, mongr'l. Me 'usband 'oddy. When I'd wipe the sawdust from y'r belly..." Mother Drover grunted, agreeing with herself. "You be sleep'n' in 'is shop. Sad-eyed dog." Raising her hand and sloppily wiping at her big nose, she pressed her lips together in grim appreciation of the thought. "All ya be want'n' was fur yer head ta be rub'd. Dat's all, me love. Dat's all ye be affer."

Muss opened the back door shortly after hearing the shotgun blasts, the sounds so close he could discern the vibrations against his fingers and against the bottoms of his feet. He drew a damp sleeve full across his face. Someone was hunting in the night, moving through the still black-snapping woods with a flashlight taped to the barrel of a shotgun, and firing at what moved through the bold beam of light. He could smell the gun powder, the quick burn of it in his nostrils, but then he caught a whiff of whatever had been shot cooking in a pot and realized that it was merely his imagination attempting to make a fool of him. He blew some air from his lips, driving away a droplet of sweat that hung there. Then he turned and lifted his own shotgun from the corner.

Pulling on his green wading rubbers, he trod off, through the field, to the edge of the woods. Turning back once, he surveyed the big square house and the impassive light that spilled through the back screen door, making him feel as if he was a stranger, disconnected from what he was inside himself, far away and plainly watching. The windows were black. He glanced up at his mother's room, wondering about her position in the bed, aware of her indifferent look and the heavy sense of resignation she nurtured for everything that had been taken away from her. It was a longing for such things, or for the death that would take what little remained, relieving her. He wondered if she had understood about the dog, always believing that if he kept things from her, then she would be saved from the stark inner thrust that struck out from such calamities. But he felt foolish thinking this way, realizing where he had come from and how his mother could see things by the way he moved and by the words he tried not to say, the silence sure to fill in the bearing of any unspeakable truth.

The woods were black when he faced them. He slid the flashlight button forward and the beam brightened the grass and brittle blueberry brush at his feet. He thought of hunting in daylight, but so many people shooting had become a dangerous proposition. Fewer hunters were out in the dark, and what animals remained were better found at night. Traps were useless; the animals caught there were snatched away by the hunters who roamed in sunlight, making money from the pelts that were whole and not sprayed with shotgun blast.

The branches ahead of him were white and grey and seemingly hard and delicate the way they climbed away from themselves, narrower and greyer at the tips in the fullness of the beam, the tips stirring against the low black sky, reaching and almost touching. The sky's blackness beyond the light seemed to sway as Muss walked, the blackness shifting with his steps so that he stopped, steadying himself against this impression of misplacement. He waited, then moved, but paused again, listening.

Another shotgun blast echoed above the trees, crackling out over the distant water. There was no way of telling which direction it was coming from; the sound rose and flooded above the vast wilderness as he pictured his stunted body between the dense trees as if he were gazing down from the sky. Muss first believed that the sound was arriving from his left side, toward Blind Island, but when the next blast rushed down at him, he stared up, aiming his light at the sky. He thought of shooting to bring down the abiding presence, but what would flap screaming, tumbling, from above would certainly crush him and pin him beneath its dead weight.

Muss slowly levelled his head, guided the light down against the woods, the beam threading through the lattice of branches and dark brown tree trunks. The light scoped ahead, conveying his sight beyond himself. A rustling in the bushes to his left snagged his breath and he spun and tugged away the tightness of the trigger, the orange flame staining the air for an instant as the stock punched against his shoulder. The rush of smoke and the smell. The frenzied rustling on the ground; a sideways kicking of limbs through the dry grass and brush.

Hesitantly stepping nearer, Muss could see where the lead pellets had spread and lodged along the bottom of a tree, and further to the right, thrown beyond where the other lead had found its place, the limp carcass of what he believed to be a lynx. The shadowy darkness bewildered him, imposing a fear that the lynx might be something else, something unheard of and unstoppable lying there waiting to leap to its feet and swallow him as he took two steps and shot again, the bulk of the animal unmoving, only the slight meaty jolt of the lead scattering in its hide.

Muss kept the light targeted on the lynx's face, finding the tip of its tongue slightly out, its eyes open and staring on the sideways angle of where it had dropped. Touching the hide, he felt it was warm and thick and squeezed it between his fingers to appreciate the enduring heat. Then he pressed against the small wet holes he had made, wiping his fingers into the fur, then in the grass, sensing the coolness, the seemingly hollow impression of the earth.

Shots reverberated and held in the air. He flinched and ducked, holding himself and looking back. They were behind him now.

Untying the rope from where it was wrapped around his waist, he carefully pulled the length of it through his hands to hold it straight. He slipped one end beneath the lynx's wide furry throat, prodding it along the grass until he could feel its frayed tip coming out the other side, then tightly tied it around the lynx's neck. Tugging, he saw that the carcass would move without trouble, the head rising slightly, the weight of the body slipping forward. He dragged it behind him through the woods and out into the tall grassy clearing where he could hear himself breathing under the open night sky, then back into the sheltering woods that led to a narrow grove of trees. He forcefully shouldered through, snapping branches toward his house on the other side.

The black light was still on and dully brushing the grass. He dragged the lynx with both hands, his arms tiring, the shotgun shoved down one of his long green rubbers, the brutally hard tip of the barrel scraping the skin from his ankle. He had to keep pausing to straighten the shotgun. It was awkward, and when he arrived at the point behind the house, he pulled it out of his boot and let it fall to the grass, the cold thud of it sounding in his feet as he hauled with his shoulders and with the full length of his arms, until the lynx's head was resting on the back bottom stair. He tugged harder, the carcass sliding up one step, then another, and into the kitchen where Muss let it head drop onto the wooden floor, its eyes still open in the keen silence that followed, staring at the legs of the kitchen table. The tip of its tongue was pink and its ears were pointed and black at the peaks. Muss thought of its head as he stood there, folding open his hunting knife. He considered the weight of it and then he studied the paws. They reminded him of the furry hooves of the work horses he had seen coming up from the iron-ore mines on Blind Island when he was a boy, his father down in the big hole, red dust everywhere, on the people and on the horses and in the streets, the gritty abrasive taste of it in his mouth, making him think of spitting it away like the taste of fear that he recalled experiencing as a teenager when it was announced that the mines would be closed. It had been his family's only way of life and they had been cast away from it, their bodies like the literal roots of their generations torn from deep in the red earth where his father had been a mucker.

Those years ago, when he had heard the news, he had gone off at night, down to the stables where they sheltered the horses, deep in the mines. And in the dim light of the lamps with the dank animal smells trapped around him, he had killed one of the horses by thrusting a knife into the big vein in its throat. He had watched it die under the brighter light of his flashlight, its eyes shifting big and frightened as it dropped heavily to its knees and then struck the ground with its head as it went down with a blast of air from its huge nostrils. Muss had found a bucksaw and sawed through the front hooves of that horse and held them in his hands. The severing had felt insufferable, but lent him such strength through release. He was driven by a force working exclusively outside of his own body, having no relation to his person, a force that invented itself through the twisting of him and all of his family out of shape. It did not wait for reaction. It had no regard for petty physical or emotional replies. So he had taken one of the heavy hammers and spikes used to lay the track for the ore cars and nailed the horse's hooves to the front of the shaft entranceway. That would show them the ugliness of what they had done. And it would show them the strength and courage of his people.

Months later, Muss' family had moved across the water and settled, doing nothing, only lingering, cast out, his father's new bitter heritage: disheartened until death.

Muss kneeled before the lynx, took hold of its front paw. Tightening his grip on the knife handle, he vigorously worked his wrist to cut into the fur and through that paw, but the paw was too thick. He collected the short-handled axe from the back porch and whacked through the tendon and bone. Then – shifting in a duck-walk – he whacked through the other three – front and back. The lynx lay there, crippled, blood seeping in four black-red puddles that only went so far and then congealed. Muss lifted the two front paws, one in each hand, receiving the impression of their weight, pressing them together and in against his chest to fix them in place as he stepped out into the yard.

Remembering what he had forgotten, he laid the paws on the step and stomped back in for his hammer and four galvanized nails. He returned to the night air and drove a nail through each paw, two rows of two – one above the other – on the planking of the house. He considered it a sign for the hunters, notice that he was still alive and built of the steadfast daring required to cut down an animal of this calibre, carve it up and set the head on the stick that held the clothesline off the ground. Four-inch nails and blood trickling from the open ends of the paws to suggest that the house itself was somehow wounded, following the slow trails with his eyes. Following and following until they touched and sank into the ground, moving deeper, moving down, replenishing.

Turning and standing steady to face whatever presence was studying him from the forest, he needn't even say the punishing words that clung to him, hung around him in the cooling night air, like the heat misting from his unbearably hot kitchen.

The meal was more than he could eat. He saved what was left of the flank roast, storing it in the short round-edged refrigerator. He sat at the kitchen table, cutting up the last of the soft shrivelled turnip and carrots, glancing out the window as the sun came warm and orange-red through the evergreens. The colour never ceased to please him; the feel of it and the claim it made that the night had been driven back. The stew that he was making was mostly for his mother. She was fond of stew and he cut the meat into fine, small strands, so she could chew them with little effort.

It would be ready for breakfast when she woke from her sleep. He would let the meal simmer and wash the blood from the floor, wondering why he had not skinned and cut up the animal on the back lawn, wondering why he had needed to drag the carcass into his house. But knowing in himself why, being this close to such fierce and terrifying hunger, he understood it was a private act of testimony – the slicing open and tearing out of the thrust that had made this creature move. His hunger was like a lazy thing now, dulled for the time being by how he had filled himself with the complete taking of another.

Muss Drover had dropped the last of the vegetables into the pot and stoked the fire within the stove's iron belly before he sat back at the table, waiting to hear his mother knock the chunk of iron ore rock from her night table onto the floor above, the signal that she needed him.

Muss was sitting, waiting for the sound. Stirred so by anticipation, he was not startled by the sight of the dog, especially now, after the death of the lynx.

He tried to watch above the scorching rush of flame as he lit a cigarette stub, but he had to close his eyes against the heat, the intense light giving depth to the rutty unevenness of his face.

Snapping shut the Zippo casing, he stared through the window, saw the old beagle dragging slow along the path down the centre of the field, pausing on its shaky legs before coming slow again, its head bent down and to the side, its tongue hanging out, gasping, coughing dryly.

Muss stood from the table, smeared a palm across his face, over his brow, then wiped the sweat on his pants. He took a piece of raw meat from the refrigerator, and it was still warm in his hand, only chilly around the edges. He opened the back door, stepped down the stairs, taking his time to walk across the open field, along the rough overgrown path, until he was close to the dog and saw what it was dragging: the boulder at the end of the rope, the fur worn from the mongrel's bleeding throat, its tongue hanging out so that it lapped at the meat, lapping only for the wetness of it, not knowing hunger any more, only thirst. The strange smiling snout and the weakness and pain in its jaws, as if it had been laughing too much.

Muss lifted the rock, then scooped up the dog in his skinny arms. He carried the mongrel through the house, climbing the stairs and carefully treading into his mother's room. He waited there, holding the dog with its sad eyes staring up, watching Muss's face, appreciatively lifting its head to lick Muss full on the mouth with its tickling sandpapery tongue. Mother Drover was sleeping, her short grey hair thin and loose over the pillow, but her skin seeming fine and smooth despite her age.

Muss stood there breathing, the chill making the inside of his clothes extra cold. He set the dog down beside the bed but did not bother to untie the rock. He left the bloodied rope where it was around the mongrel's throat. Then he went out of the room, leaving the dog nervously sniffing at Mother Drover's hand.

Muss took his time treading down the stairs. He was thinking of the lynx's paws, saw them slashed loose and bounding minus body through the air. He caught a healthy whiff of the stew while watching his feet take the final stair. The smell itself invigorated him and he hurried along the wooden plank floor, then out the back door, moving without thought or effort to the place where he raised the hammer and worked to draw the four-inch nails from the lynx's paws, yanking on the hammer handle, pulling and jerking, until the galvanized points were plucked loose and – one by one – the furry clumps dropped onto the ground.

A soiled roll of string was collected from the kitchen drawer and he unwound a piece, used his unclean knife to cut through. Bending to retrieve one paw, he wrapped the string around it and then tied a tight knot. He took the other end and secured it to the second paw. Dividing another length, he tied the third and fourth paws to either end, then raised their weight and swung them around his head, spinning the paws tentatively at first, then faster, hearing the swooshing sound breaking up the air, faster, he worked his arm and shoulder, investing great effort into making them bound at unbelievable speed, the swooshing sound almost a steady whir, he heard the stride and crashing of the paws through the forest brush as it bolted for its prey, seeing the lynx coming for him, its head down and watching, its mouth ripping open with a vicious feline cry. He spun the paws at resounding speed, his eyes squinting beneath the blur of fur that circled his head, the need to shout rising as the rush of attack and escape welled up inside him. He would make that animal cry. He opened his mouth to match the discord, but found only running, pouncing laughter galloping up. Despite himself, he yipped and shouted at once, the laughter like the striking of teeth.

Muss's mother heard the sound as she slowly woke, knowing by the laughter beyond her room that she should be smiling even before she felt the moist nose against her hand. She smelled something cooking and moved her fingers back and forth until the mongrel edged its head closer, pushing against her fingers, wanting the scratching of her fingernails, pleading with a nudge, then weakly dipping its muzzle to paw at its open mouth, and hack with one retching cough shivering through its body.

"Wha' dey done t'ya, mongrel?" asked Mother Drover, feebly lifting her grey head and edging toward the side of the mattress to peek a look. The sad eyes stared up to meet her gaze, urging her to lean out further and use both nimble hands to carefully undo the knot.

TIMOTHY TAYLOR

Smoke's Fortune

After some talking, Fergie offered us forty dollars to shoot the dog. Smoke haggled with him, standing in that little screened porch tacked onto the front of Fergie's house, but he just said the dog was dying anyhow and swatted at a fly. Smoke said we wanted forty dollars each, and that we knew the dog had bitten a kid, and that the RCMP said kill it. But Fergie didn't budge even though we said we'd bury it and all. He said, "I know I can't kill the bastard anyway. Here's your forty dollars. You boys take it."

So we took it, Smoke and I. Then we got my Ruger .30-06 out of Smoke's truck and went to the shack by the yard where Fergie kept all his wrecks and parts of cars. He kept two dogs in there. They were fenced, but I guess there was one kind smarter than that fence. When Fergie found the kid, and then the dog with blood in her mouth even he knew what had to happen. And Fergie was a guy crazy for his dogs.

Frank Hall was in the shack propping up the desk with his feet, and he laughed when we came in.

"Here come the hunters," he said, and came over to the counter. "Don't get bit now, you hear?"

That was Frank, always winking and ribbing, but Smoke flipped a bit. He grabbed Frank's jacket and pulled him hard up into the counter so some coffee spilled. I was glad I was carrying the rifle so nothing went off or anything. Frank just laughed again like he couldn't care, and got a fresh toothpick out.

The yard was set out like a football field. Blocks on the fifteen-yard line, exhaust units on the forty, stacks of bodies on the forty-five. All with some roads for the trucks running out into the junk and then back into the corner by the Haffreys' land.

The dogs knew Smoke, but since I'd only started with Fergie in July, I carried a deer steak. This was Smoke's idea. I wasn't too sure really. If they didn't recognize me I figured the steak might give them the wrong idea. So I hung back a bit while Smoke went ahead looking for the dog.

"This fucking heat," I heard him say.

"What," I said.

"I can't see through this heat," he said.

"It's hot, all right," I said swinging the steak.

We kept on walking through the blocks. There was about a half acre of them I guessed. Up ahead I could see the stacks of pipes, then the rads, bodies and smaller parts all grown up with weeds and grass. Fergie kept a yard for certain, everything neat and separated and lined with rosehips.

"Smoke," I said.

"What."

"Listen, I shouldn't be carrying the steak and the rifle. I mean, I can't shoot her one-handed. I figured maybe..."

But Smoke came back to where I stood and said to me slowly, like it didn't need saying, "We find her, you throw the steak, then you shoot her. It's easy."

I looked at him.

"I'm here to do the finding," he said. "They like me."

This was how Smoke got you to do things. He made it real obvious, and then kept on telling you anyway. So by the end of his telling, you were wishing he'd be quiet and let you do it.

We went on walking, through some trucks and into more blocks. I guess there might have been a thousand old engines there, all black and rust-coloured. Right where we were, the grass grew up through some of the cylinders. They looked pretty in all that junk, which was mostly just oily.

Smoke was poking on ahead, into the big stacks of bodies. It was well-known junkyard knowledge that you watched yourself in the stacks. Frank always told about Marcel, who came out from Quebec and was rushed under a stack. He was tugging at some piece of dirty junk and pulled about three trucks down on himself. Right out from Quebec, had a job for maybe three weeks, and pulling on something he was probably barely curious about and *boom*. So I was watching Smoke a bit because he would tug on stuff even though he'd probably been in a junkyard as long as Frank, or even Fergie. That was Smoke's way, tugging on things even when he was in the stacks.

"Here, here, here," I heard him say, like he was coaxing something, and then I saw him back out from under a big cab-over with his hand out. I stayed back near the blocks, holding the steak, ready to throw.

Smoke came back further and a dog came out of the grass. I could hear it panting and breathing all hanging with saliva the way they do when it's hot. This was all the sound, next to Smoke saying, "Here, here, here. Yes, yes. Easy boy."

When they were right in front of me Smoke just held his hand out, dangled it in the dog's face and waited. Then I'll be damned if the dog didn't start smiling, only all I saw was that whole face change, and the eyes squint back and tight, and the teeth drop out of the black lips, and the mouth crease back along the sides. I have to admit I dropped the steak and brought the Ruger right up fast thinking about squeezing not jerking the trigger, and letting the bastard move at you before you fire.

Smoke turned his hand over and cupped the dog under the muzzle and said, "Just show them slow, like that, see?"

Jesus, I was like a stone. I think I even turned grey-coloured.

"Hey, that's great, Smoke," I said.

"What are you going to do? Shoot me or what?"

"No, hey," I said, lowering the rifle and stooping to pick up the steak. "No."

"This here's the one that likes me," Smoke said, all grins.

"Yeah, well, I guess I can see you've met."

"Here, I'll go put this one in the pen so's we don't have to catch him another four times. Give me some steak."

I propped the rifle between my knees and managed to get my knife out. I hacked off a bit and tossed it.

"OK, I'll be back. Have a smoke or something. Don't wander around and get lost."

"Right," I said. And I sat down on the nearest block and smoked. It was too hot to smoke actually, but I was feeling like having one. Sometimes when I want a smoke the worst, I don't even like it when I light up. It'll even make me feel sick sometimes. I figure that's just like me to feel sick about something when you want it the most.

Smoke came back patting dust out of his pants, looking all keyed up again. He was glad to find the one dog. Now he was thinking about finding the bitch, and it wasn't getting any cooler.

"OK, OK, OK, huphuphup. Move it out!" he started shouting like a crazy person. "Here pup, here pup!"

"Jesus, Smoke, you'll get her all riled."

"Relax on the trigger, old son. I'm finding dogs. Come here, dog!"

So we went off farther, looking. Right into the back parts of the yard where the real junk was. Some of Fergie's stuff back here didn't move too often, I figured. The back of some old Seville was rusting off to one side, fins slanting up through the weeds.

Smoke was poking, pulling on things like nothing could ever hurt him. Under a pile of fenders twenty, thirty feet high, he pulls up a piece of a radio or something and says, "Well, shit, look at this." I think a fender even fell off about a foot away and he just shuffled over and said, "Hey, easy now."

"Smoke."

"Yeah."

We had stopped again. I was getting dust down my shirt.

"Smoke, we're getting way the hell back here."

Smoke came over and took a drag off my cigarette and then took one out of the package in my shirt pocket, and lit it off an old Zippo he carried around. I've seen Smoke use about three of his own cigarettes over the years and that includes the one he keeps behind his ear. He's never without the Zippo though, he loves that old thing.

"Well, she's out there, son," he said.

Then, as he dragged on the cigarette, Smoke got to thinking and he sat down on the grass, quiet, and I slid down so my neck could crook between the manifold and the block on this old motor. There were clouds floating by really peacefully. Maybe forty clouds across the whole sky.

"Smoke, you figure that cloud's a hundred miles across?"

"Where?"

"There. That's one that looks like a couch or something."

Smoke started craning his neck all around, trying to think of an answer.

"Well," he said finally, "you know, I think they're actually a whole lot smaller than people think. The sky's actually smaller than people think, too. You take Fergie, say, thinks he's a smart guy. Now he'll tell you that this sky's so big you can't even start to understand it. But it isn't. It's really quite small to some scientists. And getting smaller every year."

Smoke kept on talking. I was remembering about last Saturday at the Tudor. There was a lady there I'd never seen before. Really pretty, in a skirt, looking around her like she was a little scared or something. Like maybe she got a flat going through town on her way to Red Deer and ended up here. Sitting at this bar, sipping a Coors, waiting for someone from the garage.

Well, Smoke caught one sight of her and went right up to her like she was waiting for him in particular. "Are you the lady with the flat?" he said, like Magnum P.I. or something. You know, here's a time when I'm thinking, Maybe this lady had a flat. Smoke, he's thinking, Maybe, maybe not, no difference. And I get to wondering sometimes why it is that Smoke thinks he can ask people right on if they have a flat just because they're pretty.

Then Smoke shifted over in the weeds and looked down at me. I noticed he had stopped talking.

"You entirely comfortable, son?" he said.

"Why yes, Smoke," I said. The exhaust manifold felt smooth and cool on my neck.

"Well, don't you wake up if you can kill that bitch sleeping."

"Oh, I'm not sleeping."

"Well, what do you think?"

I stalled a bit, wondering what I might have missed. I pulled myself up a bit, looking around for the steak. It was all ground with dirt and I wondered if a rabid dog would still like it.

"What about this steak?" I asked Smoke finally.

Smoke looked at it.

"Doesn't look too good, does it?"

"Not to me," I said.

Smoke shrugged and looked around.

"Say, I'm going to beat the brush around here a bit, maybe drive her back toward you so you can get a shot at her." He squinted a bit into the weeds.

"Uh, well, Smoke, I'm not too sure here..."

He was on his feet, gliding into the grass.

"Smoke, Jesus!" I jumped up. Smoke stopped and turned slowly, following his nose around like he was finding me by smell.

"Listen, I mean, why don't we fan out together?" The idea of wandering around these stacks with both Smoke and a rabid dog cut loose seemed like craziness.

Smoke looked disgusted for a second, like I was about twelve years old for being spooked by a dog. "You got the fucking gun," he said. "You just use it when the time seems right."

I stood there for about a minute after he left. Not moving. Swearing quietly and keeping my breathing even and shallow. The grass stretched out around me, yellow and burnt, stained with oil so the heat made your head swim with fumes. The sun kept rising higher overhead like it wasn't planning to set that day.

I backed up, holding the Ruger against my thigh, feeling the rough patterned grip on the stock grab little tufts of my jeans. I was feeling backward with my left hand, until I felt the big stack of radiators behind me. I crouched down, watching the dry weeds and thinking.

The rads had a lot of sharp edges so I stopped and pulled on my hunting gloves, which let your trigger finger hang out. Then I slung the rifle flat across my shoulders and began looking for a place to start climbing. The rads were stacked in a huge pyramid, maybe forty feet high. I put my boot up on one and pushed, knocking one off higher up. It came sliding down the stack, and I rolled to one side. It hit my shoulder and then the ground.

I started again. Trying to stay on top of the metal pieces as I climbed. My boots gripped on the rough edges all right, but as I got higher I was knocking them off left and right, kicking twisted chunks of metal down into the lane. I kept thinking, Fergie will kill us if we don't clean this up.

When I got to the top, I was afraid to look down for a while. I pinched my eyes almost shut and wormed my way onto a flat area at the top of the stack. Here I shifted around and got myself cross-legged. Then I slung the Ruger off my back carefully, trying not to shake too much. I sat like that, with the rifle up, stock up against my cheek, elbows on my knees. Then I opened my eyes wider and started looking around the yard.

Smoke was pretty small from up here. He was moving up and down the lanes, cutting across the grassy bits between the bodies and the blocks, trying to sweep through the yard toward me, and flush her out. It was kind of hypnotic, like watching a spider wait out a fly. Only now I wondered whether Smoke was the spider or the fly or what.

He was right up to the exhaust pipes, all jumbled with the weeds. He was bobbing his head again like he was smelling something, taking a quiet step or two every so often. I nestled the rifle into my cheek. The wood was oily and hot from the sun. Through the scope I could see Smoke and about two feet all around him. With my other eye open, though, I could still see the rest of the yard. My dad taught me that. A lot of people think your scope eye stops working if you do that, but it doesn't. You start seeing better. As you stare and you don't blink, you suddenly start getting every little movement all over the yard. And in the middle, this circle of larger detail.

I could see Smoke breathing slowly, his cheek sucking in and out. I could see the brick-red sunburn across his neck and the line of dirt around his collar. Across the top of my sight, I could see a truck on the highway, maybe a mile away. You could barely hear it growling, but I could see it moving and see the black exhaust jump out the pipe every time he took another gear. I could see them both, Smoke and the truck.

Smoke kept on crawling through those pipes. Near the far side of the pile he slowed right down and froze. His one hand was up hanging over a tailpipe, the other behind his back, his nose pointing. I tracked the crosshairs of the scope over his shoulders into the grass, then back into his open hand. His hand went into a fist, my left eye was shaking, trying to see all over the yard and concentrate on Smoke at the same time.

Suddenly he jumped to the left, swinging his hand down and pulling the pipe with it. They crashed and rolled across the dirt and he leaped backwards and rolled on one shoulder, coming up in a squat with his hunting knife hovering in front of him, blade up. The crosshairs hung in open air for a moment, a foot in front of his face.

In that second when Smoke was still, I saw her. In my left eye, in the big picture. She was there, where we'd dropped the steak, maybe twenty yards from Smoke. She was muzzling the meat, pawing it. Trying to figure out why it smelled so good and looked so bad, I guess.

She wasn't looking too good herself. All matted and caked around the mouth, dripping drool on herself when she shook her black head. Her sharp snout had flecks of grey, her chest was muddy and her legs shook badly. Her hair was dull, and she panted as she pawed the meat, then jumped back and shook her head from side to side. Just a half-crazy old Doberman, mad at the world and hungry.

When she heard Smoke dump the exhaust pipes, she stopped and listened. She turned and thrashed on her back in the dust then stood up again. I didn't move the rifle too much, just let it coast over as Smoke started out down the lane again and cut into the weeds towards her. I was dead still except for that, that tiny movement of the barrel; Smoke walked along slowly, whistling softly, wondering where I was, maybe, crosshairs on his shoulder. When he crouched down, I'd freeze entirely. No breathing, both eyes locked open, I think my heart stopped even.

I guess I kept meaning to do something, but I didn't want to. I felt almost sleepy except for my face smeared into the Ruger. Pretty soon they were both moving again. Smoke in the scope. The bitch in the yard. I was seeing them both, eyes running with tears. When she saw Smoke through the weeds she went still and tight, low to the ground, like a piece of steel sitting with the others. I was thinking about shooting her then, but I was afraid the bullet would skip right off her, ricochet around, maybe hurt someone. Her lips went back into a grin; her teeth hung with dirt and saliva.

Smoke was batting at some weeds with an old antenna. I was looking at his scalp with my right eye, thinking I could feel the itch of the dirt and grass in it. I scratched it lightly with the crosshairs. From the back up across the top where it was tangled, down into the slick sideburns and the tuft in the ear.

And I was watching these two tangled bits of hair and dirt and saliva get closer together and thinking about how my finger, soft on the trigger, was going to do something soon, very small, and stop them from hurting each other, which seemed a shame, although also very natural.

And then she moved up fast, coming off the ground like a jet, real low at first and then wide and high. Her front legs in and close to her chest, her head forward, brows over and down to protect her eyes, her mouth lipless, showing every tooth and every rib on her black gums. Streaming saliva. And I just sat there until I saw her pass from my left eye into the right, and when she burst into my scope I shot her.

And then she seemed to vanish, and I lowered the Ruger, and Smoke had spun around like a drunken wrestler and was sitting in the grass, his knife still in his belt, his face blank, his mouth open a bit.

I climbed down and walked into the lane past the broken dog. Smoke was on his feet again, grinning. As we stood there he took a cigarette out of my pocket, lit it off the Zippo, and said, "Nice piece of shooting, son." And I guess I knew he'd say something like that.

LYNN COADY

BIG DOG RAGE

Even though I was only five or something, I can remember the first time I met him because I was brimming with hatred and rage and despair. Being a child, I'd never felt such things before, not all at once. His dog had killed my dog in front of me, picked her up in his teeth, shook her once, and broke her neck. We'd collided in the woods behind my house and had been having a pretty amiable chat for a couple of kids when his Lab went crazy. It was on a leash – he'd been taking it for a walk. Mine wasn't, because I had just wandered down into the woods to play and she followed me like she always did. I don't remember much about it. I just remember being in the vet's with my mother and his parents and my dead dog having been carted off somewhere and his about to be put to sleep, and he was crying and hating me as much as I was hating him and his dog was wagging its tail and trying to put its nose up my crotch.

We got to be friends after a while because my mother was after his parents for compensation or something and would drag me over to his house and we'd go off and play spaceman while they had it out. Spaceman was his own game and entirely original. He would pull all the pillows off the chesterfield and chairs and we would bounce around on them pretending to be on Mars or somewhere. If a monster came, we would both jump in his father's recliner chair and recline rapidly, launching ourselves out into space. He vowed he would never get another dog, and so did I.

We whined to go over to one another's houses every single day for the next five years. My mother thought I was crazy because she was the kind of person who identified people immediately as being either good people or bad people, no one was in between, and it was always based on how other people's actions affected her. She thought Germans were bad, for example, not because of anything they had done historically, but because some Germans had bought up all the property in Dunvegan that used to belong to her family. The Newbooks had killed our dog, so they were bad also. That was how we met them. It made them our natural enemies, she thought.

And then she would talk about him like he was my boyfriend. He's going to break your heart, she would tell me. He broke your heart once, he'll do it again. She meant because of the dog, but I had gotten over it, and it irritated me that she never would let me forget.

Gerald and I made a game of it. The vet had said *Big dog rage*, and it was three words we never forgot. Big dogs see small dogs and become infuriated by their very presence, the vet told us, their very *being*. Big, friendly dogs, like yellow Labs – a breed I can't see to this day without hyperventilating – dogs who would normally never hurt a fly. Out of the blue they will jump on a little dog and kill them.

Big dog rage! he would suddenly shout in the middle of a cartoon, and lunge at me, teeth and claws.

His mother told me years later that when Gerald was a baby, she had left him with that same Lab, the Yellow Labrador of Death, in the living room while she went to the kitchen for something. She heard the Lab make this gurgly, pleading sort of noise that he'd never made before. She glanced back into the living room and saw that Gerald had stretched out his chubby hand and grabbed hold of the yellow Lab's scrotum, and the Lab was just sitting there, waiting for Gerald's mother to do something about it.

He could stop himself from biting the kid's arm off, she said to me, *but he wouldn't stop big dog rage.* Gerald's mother always got weepy when she talked about that dog. I think she actually loved him more than Gerald ever did, more than any of my family ever loved the black poodle. My mother always said it was the *principle* of the thing, referring to all the grief she put Gerald's parents through afterwards, insisting the Lab be put to sleep or else she would call the police and get them to do it. *Imagine what could have happened to the little girl,* she said, meaning to me. That's what she told them she was going to say to the police. So in the end Gerald's parents gave in and put the dog to sleep. His name had been Harvey, after the imaginary rabbit. It was Gerald's mother's all-time favourite film.

We played spaceman and big dog rage. We dressed up as Siamese twins at Hallowe'en. We decided we were going to be exactly the same person when we grew up. We would dress alike and have the same haircuts. We would talk at the same time when people asked us questions, and say precisely the same thing. We would be the same person, so we would just be able to talk like that. We would have the same job and live in the same house. Many of our days were spent practising for it, trying to find clothes that looked exactly alike, trying to talk simultaneously to his mother. We played on the same teams, and even though I was better than him at sports, I made it so that I wasn't. He quit Scouts because they wouldn't let me join.

His father made Gerald become an altar boy, however, because Gerald's father had been an altar boy when he was a kid, and my mother would not let me be an altar girl because she thought it was against the Pope. That's how it started. So he was up there serving mass on Saturday evenings and Sunday mornings, and I would watch him, agonized and inwardly raging against the Pope, while Gerald puttered around the altar, ringing the bell and carrying around the host.

"It's stupid," he said.

"But I want to do it because you're doing it."

"I know, but it's better if we figure out a way for me to get out of it, because it's stupid."

"I can write to the Pope." My mother had me believing that writing letters was the best and only way to change anything. I believed I could just write to anyone I wanted and they would read it, because that's what she believed. Even if they never responded, even if nothing ever changed, deep in my mother's heart she trusted that every recipient would be deeply shamed and chastened by her words. She wrote to newspapers, MLAs, businesses, lawyers, all the people who had wronged her over the years, on a regular basis.

"No," he said. "The Pope will never change his mind. I have to get out. I have to show I'm not worthy to serve the mass."

"How?"

"I can sin." His face lit up, epiphanic. "I'll become a sinner."

"No! Just pretend to be a sinner."

"If I pretend to be a sinner, then I'm still sinning because I'm lying," he insisted.

"But you won't have sinned in your heart."

"But I will have if I lie! There's no escape. I've got to sin."

I floundered. It was a theological quagmire, but Gerald wasn't interested in negotiating it with me. I could tell he was excited about it, about having no choice, about circumstances conspiring against him like this. He had decided on his course of action.

Mass became suspended, torturously so. Gerald kept testing his boundaries, and I never knew how far he was willing to push it. He started digging at the interior of his left nostril one day while the priest gave the homily, but this was commonplace boy-behaviour as far as the congregation was concerned, even if it did occur on the holy altar. His father merely smacked him one on the back of the head and told Gerald not to let him catch him at it again. And the priest had had his back turned the entire time anyway.

"It's gotta be the priest," Gerald reflected. "He's the only one who can kick me off the altar. The priest has gotta catch me at something."

The whole thing made me uncomfortable because it looked to me as if Gerald was getting ready to do to the world one of his favourite things to do to everything else: take it all apart. Unscrew all the teensy imperceptible screws, and start tinkering around inside.

Gerald held the round, golden tray underneath the priest's hands as the latter fumbled the host towards the waiting tongues and hands of the congregation. He waited for it to be my turn to receive so that I could get an up-close view of what he was going to do. He simply dropped the tray onto my foot and then picked it up again.

"You old slut," he said to the tray. He breathed on it and then polished it with his sleeve.

If the host had not melted onto the roof of my mouth I would have choked on it. I thought the priest would reach out and knock our heads together – I was certain he would have assumed that I was involved in Gerald's blasphemy somehow, that the word *guilty* would have appeared on my forehead in blistered, red script.

But the priest was cool. He knew it was important to correct Gerald, but more important was the necessity not to make a scene. So he glowered for only a split second, and waited until after mass to give Gerald a brief, kindly-but-stern talking-to. He told Gerald that God didn't appreciate that kind of language, and that was that. Say an act of contrition and try to be good. Gerald was disguised.

"It's no use," I told him, hopeful.

"It didn't work because the only people who saw and heard it was you and the priest," said Gerald.

The next Sunday when it was time to ring the bell before communion, Gerald just kept ringing and ringing it until he was sure the priest and everyone else was looking at him and then he did this little dance to the bell-music that he used to do for me which he called the Dirty Boogie, and which basically involved just waving his pelvis around. He made a face at the two other altar boys, and they cracked up, and so did all of the less pious parishioners, of whom there seemed to be quite a few. But I was frozen in my seat. My mother punched me hard in the arm because she was wiser than the priest – she knew I was, at the very least, guilty by association.

When Gerald was allowed to appear in public again, he was as giddy from the crime as if it had occurred moments ago. He would climb up to the top of the monkey bars and perform the Dirty Boogie for everyone, and everyone on the ground would cheer and do it with him. Then he would leap onto the ground and lead everyone in a Dirty Boogie danceline. He was the most popular boy in town. Meanwhile, everybody's parents had started making dire predictions about Gerald. To be kicked out of the altar boys apparently did not bode well for a young man's future. It was taken as the worst sort of omen.

I was disturbed for all the obvious reasons. To serve the mass was sacred, but Gerald had acted like it was any other foolish thing your parents would force you to do, like violin lessons. Something to be weaselled out of at all costs. When I was very young, I always thought it was God. I'd hear the sound of bells suddenly echoing throughout the church and would look around wildly, in a panic. I started to get nervous and fidgety every Sunday before communion, waiting for the disembodied bells to sound, until finally my mother grabbed my swivelling head and forced me to watch the altar boy reach unobtrusively down beside his chair to give the bells a shake. It was one of the first religious anticlimaxes of my life, but I still thought ringing the bells at Mass had to be one of the holiest things a kid could ever hope to do, and Gerald treated it like doing the dishes.

And Gerald had committed all these sins to be with me, but now that he was such a big shot he wasn't with me as much any more. Other boys began to take an interest in him because he was bad. Gerald loved it. He waved his pelvis around every chance he got, at teachers, girls, and parents. Boys followed, and imitated him like monkeys. When people got tired of that he had to think of something else to do.

He clamoured to be in the Christmas play. And not just as a haystack or donkey, he wanted to be something right up front, a wise man or an angel, if he couldn't be Joseph. He wanted to be Joseph, but at this point, with his reputation, it was laughable. He managed to get himself positioned as Balthazar, all decked out in a bathrobe and a big bedsheet-turban, and when it came time for him to present the frankincense to the Baby Brenda doll they had sat in a pile of straw, instead he opted to shout, "Go long!" and punt the doll across the stage with his foot, in front of all the parents. One of the shepherds in back instinctively raised his tinfoil-wrapped hockey stick to keep the baby from flying off into the wings, and the effect was as if some kind of spontaneous sporting event had broken out. I was an angel, told to stand at precisely the opposite position on the stage from where Gerald was supposed to present his offering. I'll never forget the floppy, swaddled body of Christ shuttling towards me like that.

So practically overnight Gerald had turned himself into the kind of boy who doesn't get chosen to be in Christmas pageants any more, or any pageants. Who isn't trusted to carry the milk money up to the office and is followed around the schoolyard relentlessly by the recess monitor. My mother was filled with satisfaction. In the later, wet winter months, somebody left a naked Baby Brenda doll with tits drawn on it on my doorstep, like an orphan. I took it in and washed it and dressed it up in clothes and put it to bed, but after a while it started giving me nightmares, so I threw it in the closet. Then all I could think about at night was the doll lying in my closet, so one morning I got up and put it in my mother's closet.

In the wintertime, the backyard of my house, sloping down into the woods, got turned by local kids into the beginning of a long, meandering sled-hill. They would pour buckets and buckets of water all along the whole thing until it was so unbearably slick that the moment you set foot on it, you would find yourself propelled into the woods at breakneck speed and there would be no way on earth you could slow yourself down. You would shoot past trees and bushes and screaming kids until finally you would find yourself rapidly approaching "the hill" – the steepest part of the whole ride, full of bumps and kid-made ramps. This was the climax of the ride, the only problem being that the bottom of the hill gave way to the Trans-Canada Highway, where pulp trucks went barrelling past on their way to and from the mill, making their loud and angry farting noises. There was a pretty deep gully which kept most of the sliders from shooting right out into the highway, but I had seen a couple of the speedier ones come so close my heart jumped. Even so, it didn't stop me, or anyone else, from spending entire twelve-hour days repeatedly hurtling ourselves towards the speeding traffic.

I remember the queer frenzy of those times, the bright snow against the grey sky, how the snow seemed like this cushion that would come between you and any harm, even though we were constantly almost breaking our necks and braining each other with snowballs, and kids would leave crying and dripping and come back in different snowsuits half an hour later, all memory of past offences having dried up as well. Nothing could keep us from the speed.

The only place I saw Gerald on a fairly regular basis then was the hill, shooting past me, loaded up on a sled with five or six other screaming boys. In the summer we used to sit on the top of the hill and watch for a pulp truck to go by and as soon as it made its noise, Gerald would jump up, make a face, and wave his hand in the air – "Oh my God! Hold your breath!" – and I would pretend that it was too late and I was already dead.

I had seen his mother around town and her face would melt like it always did when she saw me, because she associated me with the tragedy of dead dogs and childhood. She would hold my face in her hands, with her eyes all dewy, and ask why I never came to visit, and I would curse Gerald for having the sweet, soft mother that I wanted, and for cutting me off from her. I missed the whole decent normalcy of his entire family – the sweet, soft mother, the remote, joking father, and Gerald completing the triangle. They struck me as being wholesome and complete in a way that me and my suspicious, letter-writing mother could never aspire to. No matter what my mother said about the Newbooks, I always understood that they were better than us in a very fundamental way, and later I grew to understand that this was the reason my mother hated practically everyone.

But I wanted to be with people like that, those my mother said would break my heart. I wanted to be friends with my mother's enemies and prove that I was not like her, but like them.

On the top of the melting hill, I saw Gerald was scarcely two feet away from me, hands on his hips, yelling orders at a bunch of boys sprawled down at the bottom. He was screaming his head off so that they could hear him and his face was red under his blond hair, and I thought he looked like a Viking and

I wanted him to belong to me again. I lobbed a lightly packed snowball at him and he spun around as if to say: *Who dares!*

"Nice doll," I told him.

"What?"

"Nice doll."

He cocked his head. "Nice dog?"

"Nice *doll*," I said.

"Nice doggie," Gerald said. "Good doggie." He panted at me and threw himself, stomach first, down the hill. I sat down.

He returned, pulling behind him a very lovely new sled I had seen before in the Christmas Wish-book, black, like his snowsuit, and sort of designed to look like a cross between a speedboat and a motorcycle. He was excited.

"Did you see that?" he said. "I came *this close* to the highway and I was only sliding *on my stomach!*"

"Where'd you get that?"

"Someone gave it to me." He glanced down at the sled. "On this thing I'll overshoot the gully, no problem. I'll be completely killed."

"Let me go on with you," I said like nothing had ever happened. "More weight will make you go faster."

He looked sceptical.

"We'll end up right in the middle of the highway!" I enthused. "Death will be instantaneous! We'll just be one big blot on the road."

"When I come back," he promised, flinging himself down onto it and flying away.

MATT SHAW

Tendle & Oslo

Tendle did not bring home the dog because she had a vision of the perfect family, as was her husband's thought. The dog was very tall with thin, grey legs. He had the body of a Great Dane, but his snout was speckled and sharp. He was a very ugly dog, her husband said, and Tendle agreed with him on that count. At the shelter he was the most forlorn, his big head tucked between his paws, his body a hopeless sprawl on the concrete. Sophocles, the dog, was nine years old and very quiet. The first night was solemn. Oslo had no questions about the animal, no admonitions or grievances or questions. He believed he knew everything, and Tendle gave the dog his privacy so he might become acclimated to the imperfect family.

Oslo had for many years in bed laid his arm across Tendle's back as though to keep her in place. But tonight she rested at the bed's edge, her arm resting on the belly of the dog on the floor beside her. Her husband's arm lay in the emptiness between the two bodies upon the sheets. Oslo could wake without disturbing his wife, and the thought of such morning peace lulled him. The dog woke with Oslo, but never left the embrace of Tendle's arm. Oslo drank long cups of coffee at the table alone, with the newspaper underneath his feet and stared out the window before he drove to work.

Oslo was of retirement age but he stayed at the pressing plant because it was a good wage and somewhere to go. *Why do you need to go anywhere*, Tendle wanted to ask her husband, *what is wrong with right here in this house?* She asked instead the wise Sophocles, who made her mornings much less lonely. The dog never answered but grew livelier in the house with each day, and the horrible questions Tendle wanted to ask were lost in the joy of her new friendship. He fetched balls and sat at her feet and moaned to be let out the door to pee. With her husband gone, the oppressive weight of the kitchen vanished. The house grew warm.

Oslo had made it clear there was little he wished to share with her, although she had many fears herself and no one in whom to confide. Her hair, which fell across her eyes in a boyish brown mop like a young Beatle, failed to age alongside her face. In the mirror she looked neither old nor young. What was she then? The common denominator of her assessment was *not:* she was *not* Tendle. The dog thought the logic was sound. Whenever she thought these sad thoughts he sat beside her, staring into her face. What was this dog, neither a Great Dane nor a cattle hound?

Tendle's eyes were crumbling into caves, and the tip of her nose had grown into a bulb, seemingly without cartilage to hold it in place. Her teeth loosened from general neglect. She brushed, but not nearly enough. She could wiggle them with her tongue. She could fold her ears against the sides of her head, or pull down the loose jowls around her thin mouth. She proved to herself she could look the part of *not* Tendle, too. With Sophocles at her side she felt comfortable exploring the dark recesses of her face, exposing the wrinkles and crevices beneath the hundred-watt bulb.

Oslo never tolerated such narcissistic preening. He had once asked Tendle, shortly after they were married, to remove all the mirrors in the house. Tendle knew then how to handle Oslo, who was already mildly perturbed. It was silly and she told him why. The mirrors in the house stayed, but Oslo grumbled. When she looked in the mirror these mornings, Tendle couldn't help but wonder whether such was the event setting all of Oslo's future cantankerousness. When Oslo saw Tendle exploring herself, pushing her teeth with her tongue, he reproached his wife as an owner does a puppy.

Brush them, Tendle, damn it, he said. *Don't wiggle them, you'll make them come out sooner.*

Of course, I brush, she said. *Don't be ridiculous and hurtful.*

I haven't seen you brush in fifteen years, he said.

You haven't barged uninvited into the bathroom in fifteen years.

I have so!

You have not and you know it, your common decency – your manners, although such a word seems archaic with you – have given you that one tie of gentlemanliness. And, she added, *that is ridiculous, that wiggling them will make them come out sooner. They will come when they do; that they are is no secret. And the sooner you see it, Oslo, the better for us both.*

But to Oslo the situation was not worth discussing, and so Tendle learned to walk back through the bedroom in the dark, stepping over the sleeping mass of Sophocles, who always lay in the same place. When she slept she kept her hand on his belly, and her husband's arm fell in the space between their bodies.

Because Oslo began to rise earlier than his wife, the number of such arguments that occurred in the morning disappeared. He would finish his bathroom business before the sun had even begun to rise, heaving itself from the earth and ascending through its daily morning ritual. He thought the morning sun was as ugly as his wife's loose teeth. He drank his coffee and read the paper, but reading so early in the morning, when the sunlight was still depressingly grey upon the newsprint, gave him headaches. He turned to the TV news but it was ostentatious; the morning talk shows banal; the weather network predictable; the sports scores empty numbers; the DOW Jones stock a pendulum, predictably *pendumulous*.

These early mornings, on days off from the press, Oslo put his hands to work, however little he knew about building things. He constructed lopsided eavestroughs that formed a craggy, rough-hewn perimeter around the house. He planted a garden of green peppers and tomato plants in cones. (Only half the garden ever bloomed, being the only half he got around to planting.) He built a doghouse of cheap pine. It seemed ridiculous to him at that time, but what an omen it would become later, with the necessity of many more doghouses. He renovated the porch, he worked the yard and pulled weeds, he insulated the attic. He did these things as long as he could bear and then he left them. He cared little if he finished or was successful.

Tendle thought her husband was improving himself. With Oslo in the garage or the yard, her own morning ritual was unimpeded. The sun rose vigorously. She wiggled her teeth joyously in the mirror. How malleable! How playful! How unutterably *young* wiggling her teeth made her feel! She felt like a twelve-year-old girl who dreamed of marriage and play ovens and first dances with boys doused in their fathers' cologne. She imagined her hymen was intact again. How like the sun it would burn! She blushed. She wiggled her teeth.

Such youth was not what her husband noticed. It wasn't about the brushing of course, but the widening gap between himself and his wife that he saw that morning when she wiggled her teeth in the mirror: her receding beauty, the apnea that blocked her sinuses and lungs, the tiny pain he felt between his testicles when he awoke from sleep. The chores weren't done out of thoroughness but fear, which was that everything he loved (which was only Tendle) was leaving him, like a bottle pulled by the tide into the ocean.

What Oslo was learning in the yard was how to build quietly. Hammers didn't ring, and cords of wood never hit the ground with heavy thuds. The saws were muffled. Tendle, upon discovering the doghouse (and wondering whether its intent was a gift or banishment for Sophocles) was aghast that her husband had completed the task under her nose without discovery. Oslo said, with a smile, that the first doghouse had been built without once waking the dog. Oslo was right: Tendle had never taken her hand off the old boy's belly before she rose in the morning. The doghouse was a single completed project among dozens, and the house looked like gothic architecture without the beauty. Scaffolding lined the house and mounds of dirt for the garden sat at the end of the driveway.

Convinced that the changes were something like progress (stiff old Oslo manoeuvring those boards like a young carpenter!), Tendle brought home one dog and then another. At the end, Tendle had fourteen dogs. All were a mottled blending of two entirely unique dogs (in the best cases, mutts themselves) into one unidentifiable mongrel. What was said in the silence of that first night that had led them here?

With so many dogs Tendle could no longer keep her eyes or hands on them, and the animals varied wildly in ages and dispositions. When she woke and saw the newest mess in the garage or yard, she surveyed the evidence to surmise exactly *who*, dog or man, had caused the scene. Yet, despite the chaos, Oslo was calm and made little insult about the dogs. He was calm and at peace. Tendle thought it best not to question him.

She lost her teeth one by one. If they fell into her mouth she was careful not to swallow, and placed them in her night side table in an old ring box. Sometimes she woke to feel a new space between her teeth. Where had the tooth gone? It was very important to her that Oslo never saw a thing, perhaps causing the temporal peace to implode. And if she could not find the tooth between the sheets she looked down at Sophocles (despite all the new companions, he slept in the same spot he always had), who stared at her as if to say, *What tooth, Tendle? It is all taken care of.* Oslo, now masterfully silent and phantasmagorical, might burst in the room at any moment, and Tendle always felt relief at a prompt discovery or Sophocles' assurances. She was learning to be discreet herself, making tiny spitballs out of paper, sticking them between the gaps, and taking supreme effort not to smile too widely during emergencies, a fairly easy task with solemn Oslo. When Oslo was at work she visited the orthodontist and had dentures fixed, and paid with money she had stashed in the nightstand drawer beside the ring box. She was careful to make sure the dentures were white, but not too white, straight but not too much so.

Oslo worked diligently at the doghouses. Perhaps the completion of the first spurred him on, or perhaps he saw some improvement in his workmanship that helped his self-esteem. None of the following doghouses were an obvious improvement on the ones that came before. Some were taller, or wider, depending on the dog, and the colours or grains of the planks rarely matched. When he finished the latest doghouse, he carried it out back and set it next to the previous in a long row across the backyard. With every doghouse he placed beside another, Oslo had to admit, sadly, that each doghouse in the row made the others look less natural and at ease, a contradiction. *Who had ever seen six, seven, twelve doghouses in a single small backyard?* But there were two more to finish. And there was the siding, and the eavestroughs, planting the other half of the garden, clearing out the garage, the necessary yard sales: there was a life's work and less than a life to do it in.

Some of the dogs slept in the yard. They were free to go where they pleased through a pet door, and in the mornings Oslo always saw snouts poking out from the doorways.

Inevitably there were far fewer snouts than doghouses, most of the dogs preferring the warm carpet of the main house. But there were some who desired solitude and independence, and these Oslo liked best. They enjoyed his work, and he them: when he built the doghouses he tried to keep watch and avoided waking these companions. However, Sophocles never left Tendle's side, and his doghouse (one of the smallest and most askew) was never inhabited by a dog. Its roof was, at the front, flat and wide, and Oslo used it as a bench when he tired in the morning, sipping a cup of coffee.

Who is Oslo now, Tendle thought one night as she went to sleep, Oslo's space beside her vacant. *At work is he the same old Oslo? What pleasure does he derive from the doghouses, or the dogs?* She tucked the blankets tight around her; Oslo's side of the bed was perfect. He might never have been there. Yet, inside, Tendle still felt like a perpetual housewife. Her desire for perfection still ached. *And when will Oslo come to bed?* But she did not know. She fell asleep.

When she woke she lay not on her side of the bed but Oslo's. To her dismay, her arm was not on the belly of Sophocles. He was not in his space. There was only a collection of mottled hairs on the throw rug. She threw herself off the bed and the comforter dropped to the floor. He was not in the washroom and she paid scant attention to the mirror. The dentures were tucked in their solution in the bedside table. In her anxiety she nearly forgot to wrap a robe around her waist.

She stumbled down the steps. There were some dogs in the kitchen, and two in the living room, their varying shades of grey and brown and black spotted across the purple couches. But none was the large and beautiful Sophocles. She ran into the yard. Snouts peered at her from doghouses, but none raised at the smell of the unusual morning visitor. Which house had Oslo built for Sophocles? *That must be it.* She ran down the row, peering into the round and square and oblong doorway of each house. She saw blue and green eyes, long and short snouts; some animals thumped their tails against the walls.

She peeked into the farthest doghouse, which looked as though it must have been the first. The roof did not fit properly and in between the seams and joints were gaps and cracks. She put her hand on the roof to steady herself as she knelt. She felt a sliver pierce her skin and the house rocked loosely under her weight. There was no dog inside and it smelled as though there had never been.

Tendle! Tendle! Good morning!

She heard Oslo's shouts behind her and rose. How quiet he was! He was dressed in a white, buttoned shirt, his hair slicked against his head with thick pomade. He wore black shoes and black socks, and he had Sophocles by the collar. The great dog pulled hard toward Tendle and dragged Oslo with him. Tendle saw sweat stains forming under his white shirt. It was such an unusual sight, Oslo dressed so well, and an unusual sound, Oslo moving so ghostly, that she gaped her gummy mouth at him. Stunned, Oslo released the collar and began to shriek as the dog lavished Tendle with kisses.

NOTES ON THE AUTHORS

BLAIS, MARIE-CLAIRE (b. 1939). Born in Quebec City, Blais has lived in Montreal, France and the United States, where she now resides, in Key West. Her novels in English translation include *Mad Shadows* (1960), *A Season in the Life of Emmanuel* (1966), *The Manuscripts of Pauline Archange* (1969), *The Wolf* (1974), *Deaf to the City* (1980), *Pierre* (1991), *These Festive Nights* (1997), and *Augustino and the Choir of Destruction* (2007). Her collections of poetry were published in English as *Veiled Countries/Lives* (1994), her plays in *Wintersleep* (1999), and her articles for *Le Devoir* in *American Notebooks: A Writer's Journey* (1996).

CALLAGHAN, BARRY (b. 1937). Born in Toronto, the son of Morley Callaghan, he became an English professor at York University and also founded the journal *Exile* and the publishing house Exile Editions. Callaghan is a poet, novelist, journalist and translator; his books include *The Hogg Poems and Drawings* (1978), *The Black Queen Stories* (1983), the memoir *Barrelhouse Kings* (1998), two volumes of collected non-fiction, *Raise You Five* (2005) and *Raise You Ten* (2006), and the short-story collection *Between Trains* (2007).

CALLAGHAN, MORLEY (1903-1990). Born in Toronto, he studied law at Osgoode Hall and was called to the bar, but never practised law. His novels include *Such Is My Beloved* (1934), *More Joy in Heaven* (1937), and *The Loved and the Lost* (1951), among others. A well-known short-story writer, with numerous collections such as *Now that April's Here* (1936) and *Morley Callaghan's Stories* (1959), he was also the author of a memoir about his youthful literary adventures abroad, *That Summer in Paris* (1963).

COADY, LYNN (b. 1970). Raised in Port Hawkesbury, Nova Scotia, she lived in Vancouver before settling in Toronto. She is a novelist, short-story writer and playwright, whose books include *Strange Heaven* (1998), *Play the Monster Blind* (2000), *Saints of Big Harbour*

(2002), and *Mean Boy* (2006). She also edited *Victory Meat: New Fiction from Atlantic Canada* (2003).

DÉ, CLAIRE (b. 1953). Born in Montreal, where she still resides, Dé is a fiction writer, actress and playwright. Her books, translated into English, include *Desire as a Natural Disaster: Short Stories* (1995), *Soundless Loves* (1996), and *The Sparrow Has Cut the Day in Half: A Pointillist Novel* (1998).

DE LA ROCHE, MAZO (1879-1961). Born in Newmarket, Ontario, de la Roche is remembered for her *Jalna* novels – which became international bestsellers in the 1930s – about a grand house in a fictional town based on Clarkson, Ontario. Among her books in the series are *Jalna* (1927), *Whiteoaks of Jalna* (1929), *The Master of Jalna* (1933), *Young Renny* (1935), *Return to Jalna* (1946), and *Morning at Jalna* (1960). She was also the author of short stories and a memoir, *Ringing the Changes* (1957).

DRAGLAND, STAN (b. 1942). Born in Calgary, Alberta, he was founding editor of Brick Books and *Brick* magazine; he also taught at the University of Western Ontario before retiring to St. John's, Newfoundland. A fiction writer, poet and literary critic, he is the author of numerous books, including *Floating Voice* (1994), *Peckertracks: A Chronicle* (1978), a literary memoir, *Apocrypha: Further Journeys* (2002), and *Stormy Weather: Foursomes* (2005).

FERRON, JACQUES (1921-1985). Born in Louiseville, Quebec, he graduated in medicine from Laval University, and practised medicine first on the Gaspé Peninsula and later in Montreal and Longueuil. Active in politics, he founded the Rhinoceros Party in 1963. His books of stories, in English translation, include *Tales from the Uncertain Country* (1972) and *Selected Tales of Jacques Ferron* (1984); his novels include *Wild Roses* (1971), *Doctor Cotnoir* (1973), *Quince Jam* (1977), and *The Cart* (1981).

GALLANT, MAVIS (b. 1922). Born in Montreal, Gallant has lived in Paris since 1950. She is the author of two novels, *Green Water, Green Sky* (1959) and *A Fairly Good Time* (1970); a collection of non-fiction, *Paris Notebooks: Essays & Reviews* (1986); and several collections of short stories, including: *The Other Paris* (1956), *My Heart Is Broken* (1964), *The Pegnitz Junction* (1973), *The End of the World* (1973), *From the Fifteenth District* (1979), *Home Truths* (1981), *Overhead in a Balloon* (1985), and *In Transit* (1988). *The Selected Stories of Mavis Gallant* was published in 1996.

GLOVER, DOUGLAS (b. 1948). Born near Waterford, Ontario, he has taught in several American universities and now lives on his family's Ontario farm. His short-story collections include *Dog Attempts to Drown Man in Saskatchewan* (1985), *A Guide to Animal Behaviour* (1991), and *16 Categories of Desire* (2000); his novels, often with historical settings, include *The South Will Rise at Noon* (1988), *The Life and Times of Captain N.* (1993), and *Elle* (2003). *Notes Home from a Prodigal Son* (1999) is a memoir that includes essays and interviews.

GOVIER, KATHERINE (b. 1948). Born in Edmonton, Govier writes fiction and non-fiction; she has been a visiting lecturer in Canadian and British universities, and now lives in Toronto. She has published eight novels and three collections of short fiction, including *Random Descent* (1979), *Going Through the Motions* (1982), *Fables of Brunswick Avenue* (1985), *Angel Walk* (1996), *The Truth Teller* (2000), *Creation* (2002), and *Three Views of Crystal Water* (2005).

HARVEY, KENNETH J. (b. 1962). Born in St. John's, Newfoundland, Harvey now lives in an outport on the island. Founder of the ReLit Awards, he is the author of more than a dozen books, including novels, short stories, and non-fiction: *Directions for an Opened Body* (1990), *Brud* (1992), *The Flesh So Close* (1998), *Skin Hound* (2000), *The Town that Forgot How to Breathe* (2003), *Inside* (2006), and *Blackstrap Hawco* (2008).

JOHNSON, E. PAULINE (1861-1913). Born on the Six Nations Reserve near Brantford, Ontario, the daughter of a Mohawk father and an English mother, she was primarily a poet who gave dramatic readings, in Native dress, of her work – a precursor of contemporary performance artists. Her books include *The White Wampum* (1895), *Canadian Born* (1903), *Flint and Feather* (1912) and, published posthumously, *Moccasin Maker* (1913).

KULYK KEEFER, JANICE (b. 1953). Born in Toronto, where she now resides, Kulyk Keefer is a professor of English at the University of Guelph. Her books include poetry: *White of the Lesser Angels* (1986) and *Marrying the Sea* (1998); non-fiction: *Reading Mavis Gallant* (1989) and *Honey and Ashes: A Story of Family* (1999); and short stories and novels: *The Paris-Napoli Express* (1986), *Transfigurations* (1987), *Travelling Ladies* (1990), *The Ladies' Lending Library* (2002), and *Thieves: A Novel of Katherine Mansfield* (2004).

LEACOCK, STEPHEN (1869-1944). Born in Swanmore, England, Leacock settled in Ontario in 1876 with his family, and later taught in the Department of Economics and Political Science at McGill University in Montreal. His collections of humorous stories, in over thirty volumes, include *Literary Lapses* (1910), *Nonsense Novels* (1911), *Sunshine Sketches of a Little Town* (1912), *Arcadian Adventures of the Idle Rich* (1914), *Frenzied Fiction* (1918), and *Winsome Winnie* (1920).

MACLEOD, ALISTAIR (b. 1936). Born in North Battleford, Saskatchewan, and raised in Cape Breton, MacLeod has been a professor of English and Creative Writing at the University of Windsor, Ontario. His books include several collections of short fiction – *The Lost Salt Gift of Blood* (1976), *As Birds Bring Forth the Sun and Other Stories* (1986), and *Island: The Collected Stories* (2000) – and the novel *No Great Mischief* (1999).

MONTGOMERY, L.M. (1874-1942). Born in Clifton (now New London), Prince Edward Island, she moved to Ontario after her marriage. Her numerous books, which became popular internationally, include *Anne of Green Gables* (1908), *Anne of Avonlea* (1909), *Anne of the Island* (1915), and *Anne of Windy Poplars* (1936), as well as several collections of short stories and novels that did not relate the continuing adventures of her orphan-character, Anne Shirley.

PAGE, P.K. (b. 1916). Born in Swanage, England, Page and her family came to Alberta in 1919. She later lived in Montreal and, after her marriage, in Brazil and Australia, before settling in Victoria. Her poetry collections include *Cry Ararat!* (1967), *Poems Selected and New* (1974), *The Evening Dance of the Grey Flies* (1981), *The Glass Air: Selected Poems* (1985), and *Hologram: A Book of Glosas* (1994). She is also the author of books for children, collections of short fiction, and *Brazilian Journal* (1987).

ROBERTS, CHARLES G.D. (1860-1943). Born in Douglas, New Brunswick, he taught English literature at King's College, Windsor, Nova Scotia, and later lived in New York and London, returning to Canada to reside in Toronto. As a poet he is known for *Orion* (1883), *In Divers Tones* (1886), and *Songs of the Common Day* (1893), among other collections; his novels and books of short fiction include *Earth's Enigmas: A Book of Animal and Nature Life* (1896), *The Watchers of the Trails* (1904), and *The Haunters of the Silences* (1907).

ROOKE, LEON (b. 1934). Born in Roanoke Rapids, North Carolina, he lived in Victoria before moving to Ontario, where he now resides, in Toronto. His numerous novels and short-story collections include *Last One Home Sleeps in the Yellow Bed* (1968), *Cry Evil* (1980), *A Bolt of White Cloth* (1984), *Who Do You Love?* (1992), *The Fall of Gravity* (2000), *Painting the Dog: The Best Stories of Leon Rooke* (2001), and *The Beautiful Wife* (2005).

RULE, JANE (1931-2007). Born in Plainfield, Pennsylvania, Rule settled in Vancouver in 1956 and moved to Galiano Island in 1976. She was the author of several collections of short stories – *Themes for*

Diverse Instruments (1975), *Outlander* (1981), and *Inward Passage* (1985) – and her novels include *Desert of the Heart* (1964), *Contract with the World* (1980), and *After the Fire* (1989). She was also the author of several works of non-fiction, including *Lesbian Images* (1975) and *Loving the Difficult* (2008), a collection of essays published posthumously.

SCOTT, DUNCAN CAMPBELL (1862-1947). Born in Ottawa, Scott served as Canada's Deputy Superintendent of Indian Affairs. He was a poet and non-fiction writer – the poems in several of his early collections, such as *New World Lyrics and Ballads* (1905), concern his experiences with Canada's Native population – as well as the author of two influential short-story collections: *In the Village of Viger* (1896) and *The Witching of Elspie* (1923).

SETON, ERNEST THOMPSON (1860-1946). Born in South Shields, England, he immigrated to Canada with his family in 1866. Raised in Toronto, Seton became a naturalist and nature artist, moving to a homestead near Carberry, Manitoba, in 1881. His first books were *The Birds of Manitoba* (1891) and *Studies in the Anatomy of Animals* (1896). He is best remembered for his collections of animal stories, including *Wild Animals I Have Known* (1898), *Animals Heroes* (1905), and the four-volume *Lives of Game Animals* (1925-27). His work was the basis for the *Boys Scouts of America Official Manual* of 1910.

SHAW, MATT (b. 1982). Born in London, Ontario, he now lives in Toronto. Shaw is the winner of the $10,0000 Journey Prize, and is the author of the collection of short stories, *The Obvious Child* (2007).

STRAND, MARK (b. 1934). Born in Prince Edward Island, he is a poet, essayist and translator. Strand has served as Poet Laureate of the United States, and lives in New York City, where he teaches English and Comparative Literature at Columbia University. His many books include *Reasons for Moving* (1968), *The Story of Our Lives* (1973), *Selected Poems* (1980), *Mr. and Mrs. Baby and Other Stories* (1984), *The*

Continuous Life (1990), *Dark Harbor* (1993), *Blizzard of One* (1998), and *Man and Camel* (2006).

TAYLOR, TIMOTHY (b. 1963). Born in Venezuela, Taylor is a short-story writer and journalist who now lives in Vancouver. His books include *Stanley Park* (2001), *Silent Cruise* (2002), and *Story House* (2006).

WATSON, SHEILA (1909-1998). Born in New Westminster, British Columbia, she was an elementary and high-school teacher before earning her doctorate and becoming a professor at the University of Alberta. Her books include *Four Stories* (1979), *Five Stories* (1984), and several novels – *The Double Hook* (1959) and *Deep Hollow Creek* (1992) among them.

WILSON, ETHEL (1888-1980). Born in Port Elizabeth, South Africa, she immigrated to Vancouver in 1898. She taught elementary school until her marriage in 1921. Her novels include *Hetty Dorval* (1947), *The Innocent Traveller* (1949), *Swamp Angel* (1954), and *Love and Salt Water* (1956). *The Equations of Love* (1954) includes two novellas, and her stories were published in *Mrs. Golightly and Other Stories* (1961).

Permissions

MARIE-CLAIRE BLAIS, printed by permission of the author. BARRY CALLAGHAN, reprinted by permission of the author. MORLEY CALLAGHAN, reprinted by permission of Barry Callaghan, for the author's estate. LYNN COADY, reprinted by permission of the author. CLAIRE DÉ, reprinted by permission of the author. MAZO DE LA ROCHE, reprinted by permission of Lang Michener/Intellectual Property Law Group, for the author's estate. STAN DRAGLAND, reprinted by permission of the author. JACQUES FERRON, reprinted by permission of Hurtubise, for the author's estate. MAVIS GALLANT, reprinted by permission of the author and Georges Borchardt, Inc. DOUGLAS GLOVER, reprinted by permission of the author. KATHERINE GOVIER, reprinted by permission of the author. KENNETH J. HARVEY, reprinted by permission of the author. JANICE KULYK KEEFER, reprinted by permission of the author. ALISTAIR MACLEOD, reprinted by permission of the author. P.K. PAGE, reprinted by permission of the author and The Porcupine's Quill. LEON ROOKE, reprinted by permission of the author. JANE RULE, reprinted by permission of Georges Borchardt, Inc., for the author's estate. MATT SHAW, reprinted by permission of the author. TIMOTHY TAYLOR, reprinted by permission of the author. SHEILA WATSON, reprinted by permission of F. Flahiff, for the author's estate. ETHEL WILSON, reprinted by permission of the University of British Columbia, for the author's estate.

A Note About Diana Thorne

The cover illustration of "Peppy," a pastel drawing by Diana Thorne, comes from *Puppy Stories* by Evien G. Beaudry, published by Saalfield Publishing Company of Akron, Ohio, in 1934. Considered to be one of the leading dog illustrators and painters during the height of her career from the late 1920s through the '40s, Thorne is now somewhat of a mystery figure. Most sources cite her birthplace as Winnipeg, Manitoba, in 1895. Throughout her life Thorne claimed to have been born there, but she was in fact born in Odessa, Russia, as Anna Woursell, in 1894, and immigrated to Canada with her family (her father was a wealthy cattle shipper). She spent her childhood first in Winnipeg and then in Calgary. In 1912 her family moved to Germany, where Thorne began her art studies. Because of the First World War, her Russian-Jewish/Canadian family was closely observed by the German government, their money confiscated and Thorne's brother, of military age, interned. Thorne next moved to England, later settling in the United States, around 1920. Based in New York City, she often had to move her studio to Boston, Chicago and Detroit, where she painted commissions. With more than thirty books to her credit as author and/or illustrator, Thorne had a long association with Saalfield, a prominent publisher of children's books (the press closed in 1977, and its papers are housed in the Archives of the Kent State University Libraries). She was also the author of *Drawing Dogs* (Studio Publications, 1940), a popular primer that went through several editions in the U.S. and Britain. Thorne's work appeared in prominent exhibitions across the United States and was often printed in *The New York Times* and *The Christian Science Monitor*. Though less well-known in Canada, she was the subject of a 1929 profile in *Saturday Night*. Admired for her ability to catch dogs in action, she painted a portrait of Franklin Delano Roosevelt's beloved Scottish terrier, Fala, and also the dogs of many celebrities of her day, including those of Gary Cooper and Katharine Cornell. Her last years were plagued by financial problems and health concerns. She died in one of New York City's public hospitals, on Welfare Island, in July, 1963. – RT

FSC
Mixed Sources
Product group from well-managed
forests and other controlled sources
www.fsc.org Cert no. SGS-COC-2624
© 1996 Forest Stewardship Council